Adam Westlin and the Siege of the Vampire City

by

A. J. Nance

RoseDog Books

PITTSBURGH, PENNSYLVANIA 15222

RoseDog Books
701 Smithfield Street
Pittsburgh, PA 15222
Visit our website at *www.rosedogbookstore.com*

ISBN: 978-1-4349-8836-2
eISBN: 978-1-4349-7830-1

I dedicate this book to my loving family. Grandmother you were my light when I had lost hope. I'll always love you.

Chapter One

Human girls were never this much trouble!

Hello, my name is Adam Westlin and today may be either the worst, or possibly the best time of my life. I'm just a seventeen-year-old guy with fairly strong Latin features. I'm 5"10 with black hair and light bronze skin. I really haven't had the best of track records with girls. My last girlfriend, the blue-eyed blond who shall remain nameless, pretty much ripped my still beating heart right out of my chest.

But I digress; it is getting better…the bitch! I moved back to a little town in the middle of nowhere called Tinsdale, with my family and little brother Tannon. Well, actually, we live just five miles outside of Tinsdale Grandma, Grandpa, Tannon, and myself. My grandparents have been taking care of my little brother and me pretty much all our lives—ever since our mom, the massively flawed person that she is, proved she was too young and immature to raise us properly. I'm not complaining, though. I love Grandma and Grandpa with all my heart. I do not believe that anyone could have done a better job raising us. My little brother, Tannon, is, by the way, the most evil little kid anyone has ever seen. Okay I kid a little; I do love him. But come on, I mean ten years old and the kid runs through the woods at all hours of the night. He goes eating worms, dirt, and whatever else he can find; sometimes, he is howling like mad. Oh, God, I really hope that's only dirt he's been putting in his mouth. But it's not all bad, as there's Grandma Westin here to keep the peace, like she always does.

Without her, sometimes I think that Tannon and I would just self-destruct. Grandma has mid length brown, lightly graying hair done up in a bun. Her oval shaped face is oddly young looking for her age. She also has the most strangely beautiful blue eyes, I've ever seen on a fifty-five year old woman. I swear there are times I think she can really read my mind, with those confounding eyes of hers peering into my very soul. Grandpa, on the other hand, seems like he can barely see anything at times. He is fifty-eight years old and a few inches taller than Grandma, who is, by the way, 5'7, making Grandpa actually about my height. He has gray hair and matching stubble. He's every energetic for his age and enjoys working on the house. He also keeps busy out in the yard whenever possible; that is, when he is not making me do it—. And, of course, when he's not searching for his lost set of gold framed reading glasses. The man loses them nearly every other day. Back in his prime, I hear he was a pretty good army guy—not that I am interested in that sort of thing. Mostly, it's because he tells me so, just about every time I turn around. We live in a two-story house with white siding, sitting on three acres of open fields, woods, and creeks. It really has its own kind of beauty out here, especially in the summer, when you can just seem to get lost in your very own perfect world... Man, I really hate it here. I'm restless, I have to get out. But I can somehow sense that my family needs me. Or at least, they will, some time in the very near future. Still, it just feels like there's something more, something that I'm meant to be doing. Like, somehow, there is a destiny out there calling to me. Even in my dreams, there's a girl—there's always this girl. She has pale white skin, and red silky hair done up off of her shoulders. She possesses ample breasts with a pleasing form, and she wears a golden tiara with all these incredible tiny designs all over it, jeweled and sparkling. Groomed upwards at the back, her hairstyle created two points at the top left and right, in direct contrast to the cute, little bangs she wore in front. Her clothes were a form-fitting silk purple suit and red v-shaped belt. Strange runes went up each sleeve in a lighter purple color. And she wore a gold necklace, with a haunting red stone at its center around her neck. I stared at her as my mind flashed on sights, sounds, and horrible, impossible things.

I saw what looked like dragons, beasts, and monsters; even death himself was coming for us, in a heavy black robe cut off a few inches above his knees. He also wore black pants and brown leather boots. Sharp blades of gleaming silver materialized from open wounds in his wrists, as liquid silver blood dripped down to create scythe and sickle weapon forms.

The girl called to me.

"Wind, Vale Shadowwind!" she says over and over again, breaking my heart. She was pleading like I was the only one who could save her. Meanwhile, the frightening black robed figure with light blue, windswept hair reaching an angled point in back loomed over her. I started to feel myself wanting to help her, needing to help her. Shadows moved quickly around us, taking terrifying, frightening form. Seeming to close in on every side, they tore, grasped, and reached as I threw myself after her. Suddenly, the shadows disappeared as eerily as they came, when our hands finally touched in a dim burst of light. That's when I woke up in a cold sweat, stomach twisting, ready to ralph. Tap, tap, tap—what the...? I sat up in bed rubbing my eyes, and telling myself "I'm never going to eat nachos and ice cream after twelve o'clock at night again." Tap, tap, tap—"Man, I feel lousy!" I stumbled to my feet opening my room door—when…holy crap! Tannon Oswald Westin jumped out at me, wearing a ridiculous wolf-eared hood and plastic fangs. His brown eyes looked innocent; his likewise brown hair was wild and unkept, much like the rest of the boy.

"Today is Fun Friday and you better be ready, Adam! Because…," he hesitated. "You'll never catch me!" Tannon blurted with a tiny, mischievous sneer. He then socked me right in the face with a flyswatter. I fell back a couple of steps catching my balance.

Looking around angry as all hell, I yelled. "I'll get you, you little snot!" I shot out of my room around the corner, and down the stairs after the giggling little imp.

Soon I was stopped cold by Grandma's otherworldly gaze.

"When are you boys going to learn to get along?" she asked sternly.

"When he stops swatting me like I'm a giant horsefly every morning!" I replied.

Tannon laughed so hard I could have exploded—I mean, boom! Blood and guts everywhere. But seeing as how this is reality and not a fantasy, I settled for just calming down and taking a deep breath. I turned to meet Grandma's piercing stare.

"Good morning, Grandma," I said as I put on a quick, fake smile. "I was about to go out into the yard to work on a few things," I lied.

Grandma stood there for a minute, looking off into space. Slowly, she turned back to the oven of lightly frying breakfast, while I prepared to finish what Tannon had started.

Her voice then shot back to me, "In your underwear?"

I felt numb all over as I looked down at myself. I think I turned three different shades of red. Then I bolted back upstairs, closing my room door behind me with a thump. *That tiny little monster*, I said in my thoughts. *How does he keep doing this to me? Oh, he will pay!* Thirty minutes later, I arrived downstairs fully dressed in a white t-shirt and blue jeans, to a well-prepared breakfast. Grandma calmly sat at the six-seated kitchen table, while she sipped hot steaming coffee. A truly countrified sounding Grandpa sat across from her, talking about the merits of four-wheel drive pickup trucks, which I didn't fully understand—, his accent, I mean, because he's from the city, where he was born and raised as far as I knew. Next to him was perched an overly happy Tam Tam, the nickname for Tannon, the thing slash creature I call my little brother.

I sat at the table next to Grandma just in time to hear Grandpa say, "In a powerful hurry to get to work this morning weren't cha, Son?"

He and Grandma always called both my brother and me "son." I guess when you live with someone all your life, you really can't help it. I blushed a little thinking of my earlier unfortunate nakedness, which I knew was what he was getting at.

"I'm going to need you to work on that there car of yours today," he said. "You keep her up and running, and she'll treat you right, Boy."

Hesitantly, I replied, "I'll be all over it today, Grandpa." I then clumsily pushed on to add. "Nothing like getting an early start!" Tam Tam laughed. I bet I could sell him as a science experiment up town, and no one would know he wasn't a monkey.

"Well, being that y'all got so much OOTH today, I'll be needin' ya ta take care a them there damn rose bushes," Grandpa said.

Grandma's eyebrow rose, shooting the elderly man a poisonous look. I swear Grandpa sank behind a swiftly lifted newspaper, like he was one of Grandma's old grade school students. Clearly, the lady didn't tolerate cursing.

Deciding to think positively and not giggle, I looked around at my dear family.

"Good morning, everyone!" I said brightly." Then I gave a speedy prayer of thanks, before I started to eat. Lifting my head from the breakfast plate, I homed in on Tannon. "Did you finish all your school work yesterday, Tannon?" I asked politely with a wicked smile.

He fidgeted in his chair slightly. Grandma stopped trying to eyeball Grandpa through his lifted newspaper. Focused on Tannon like a laser, she had a serious look in her beautiful eyes. Grandma asked, "Tam Tam, have you finished your work packs from yesterday?"

You see, Grandma is a retired schoolteacher, with more than thirty years of teaching experience. She's been home schooling Tannon, ever since she had him read a fourth grade level text book, and found out he was way behind where his reading level should be. The public schools weren't helping the matter, either. So she simply pulled Tannon out. That was about a year ago, and he has really improved now. Where he could hardly read at a second grade level, he's now reading novels at a fairly fast pace, and is flying through his studies. Grandma hasn't lost a step these past couple of years of retirement. She immediately started asking questions about Tam Tam's schoolwork, adding something about extra assignments, to teach him to take his responsibilities more seriously.

Ha, ha! I silently thought. I reassured Grandpa that I'd take care of the car and yard work again.

I then finished my breakfast and stepped outside, to let my family clear the table. It was an exceptionally hot day today. Upon finally finishing my chores, the late evening breeze was cooling and welcomed.

I decided to explore the grounds a little. I had been getting odd feelings lately, they almost seem like warnings. Like something was trying to keep me away, from the path on the western end of the property. Now that I think about it, perhaps it was actually calling to me instead. I had never followed the path all the way through, being too busy, too lazy, or maybe just too damn scared. I walked briskly, thinking as I often do about how nice it would be, to get out and leave this place, maybe see the world and what it has to offer in all its glory.

Making my way through the semi tall yellow grass as I daydreamed, I tripped on something. Before I could blink, I was hit with a flying cup of what looked like red paint. Obviously, it was one of Tannon's pranks. "Oooh, that miserable, shrunken little troll!" I whirled around ready to choke some troll. Just then, I heard it, a kind of rippling noise, like nothing I'd ever heard before. Slowly, I edged up the oddly well-beaten path, much farther than I had ever gone before. Gradually, I laid eyes on a very well put together red-haired young lady. She had very sizably developed breasts and shapely hips. She stood a couple of inches or so shorter than I was, about 5'8. Bewildered, the girl peered into another direction, standing in a strange, circular clearing. Where her eyes rested, nothing seemed to grow—at least not very much. There were two twisted, stunted looking trees and in front of them, two old four and a half feet stone columns sat. Each one had weird runes carved at the top of it.

"Hey there, you need any help?" I offered.

She stiffened, slowly taking her gaze from the space between the two pillars. Our eyes met and, holy crap! It was the same girl from my dreams, or nightmares—only, without the monsters and weirdness! She questioningly looked me deep in the eyes for a moment. I totally didn't mind: She was hot, and I mean perfect ten hot! Her legs were long and sexy, her arms and waist slender and attractive. I must have looked like a fool, standing there with red paint all over my neck, white t-shirt, and blue jeans. She approached me with an otherworldly speed, stopping only inches from me. Her body smelled of sweet, exotic flowers—exactly what kind, I simply couldn't tell. The girl stared intensely at my neck, even sniffing it a little.

Her eyes roved over the paint stains so hard, I thought she'd bore a hole straight through me. Man, what was her problem?

"Hey there, Sugar, my name's Adam Westlin. Is there anything I can do for you?" I asked gingerly, taking a step to the side.

Finally, her eyes rose to mine. Her skin seemed really pale and white. The light seemed to reflect off of it somehow. She opened her full, seductive red lips.

"Where is this?" she asked.

I stared at her. "You're in the hay fields just west of my home. A few blocks from highway 300."

The redhead gazed off in the direction I pointed. Then she turned to me and asked, "What world is this?"

I choked slightly, quickly replying, "Earth!" *Okay, so clearly looks aren't everything* I thought.

She paused, beautiful green eyes wide as saucers.

"No!" she whispered to herself, turning back in the direction of the stunted trees and stone columns.

Suddenly, the girl looked about nearly every horizon. It was then that I noticed her stumbling as she walked, limping slightly. She looked lost, like she hadn't a friend in the world. Seeing her pain, I walked up behind her, taking the redhead's elbows to calm and steady her. I could sense the agitation in her tense body.

"You're hurt," I said softly, holding her close to me. She seemed to weaken at my very touch.

Slipping in slow motion to the ground, while I tried to support her, the radiant young lady sat in the yellow, stunted grass of the clearing, taking rapid breaths.

"Are you all right?" I asked.

As I got a closer look at her, I realized she was bleeding. I took a clean cloth from my back pocket, pressing it to the nasty wound in her side, to slow the blood. My touch appeared to spark or flash for a split second, which I quickly dismissed. Meanwhile, she relaxed and breathed deeply of my scent. Oh, man, she was so freaking hot!

"I'm going to have to get help!" I said, overly excited. I was about to bolt for the two-story house with white siding, when her soft hand caught my wrist. Without thinking, I gently caressed her pale cheek, calming her once more. Lightly cupping her lower face in my hand, I spoke kindly.

"It's okay. I won't let anything happen to you."

She reluctantly let go. I seemed to feel a connection of some kind with the beautiful girl. I did all I could to make her feel safe. We simply waited a moment or two, and she began to think. Then she came closer peering at me with seductive, sparkling, green eyes. She started rubbing her hands against her body wantonly, needing me like I was suddenly the only man on earth, and she was the only woman. Being a seventeen-year-old teenager bursting with pent-up hormones and desires, I immediately stopped all thoughts dead in their tracks, possessing her in my arms and kissing her beautiful, soft lips. I pressed my body forcefully against hers, lovingly touching her radiant skin. My hands began to explore every part of her perfect form. She held me closer and closer with such passion, I thought I'd faint. Suddenly, the girl pushed me away with a surprising amount of strength. Alongside heavy gasps, she called out to me.

"Wait, wait, please!" she said with tears in her eyes. "This isn't right, you don't even know my name!"

"Wind Vale Shadowwind," I said breathlessly as I pulled my head up, to peer deep into her green eyes, which turned shining red. Her full, red lips parted to reveal small, white, pointed fangs, which I hadn't noticed before. I was sure they hadn't been there earlier. She clutched me tightly to herself in an embrace, that I had never felt before—not from any other living thing, much less a gorgeous redheaded girl. My God, she couldn't have been any older than I was. Why the hell was she so damn strong?

The girl slowly inhaled, savoring my scent again. Her eyes met mine, and I must have looked like a deer caught in someone's headlights. Instantly, she bit powerfully down into my flesh.

I gasped, totally surprised and unable to cry out in pain, as she sucked seductively and hungrily at my neck. All I could hear was gulp, gulp, gulp, as my life's blood slid hot and sticky down her beautiful throat. Sensations tingled all over my body, almost like an electric fire, when she sucked away fulfilling her desires. Soon, I couldn't even feel the pain anymore, only the awesome, shocking pleasure of her penetrating bite flowing through me.

Fearlessly, I embraced her, even as she was squeezing me possessively. I ran my left hand over her firm, yet soft, circular buttocks, rubbing gently around and around, while my right hand held her hot against my light bronze complexioned, lightly muscled body. I could feel her heaving breasts and hard nipples pressed against me. I lifted my head to gently nuzzle against her sweet smelling ear and hair. Her body relaxed, taking slower, more relishing gulps of my warm blood. The girl groaned sexually, feeling my manhood hard against her, longing for release. Reluctantly, she brought her face to mine, looking me in my brown eyes.

Suddenly, the girl started to cry.

"It's okay. I will help you in any way I can," I told her. Once again, I could feel the strong connection that I couldn't explain. I knew somehow that this was important.

Gazing at me, her magical red eyes almost glowed, then quickly grew worried. I could sense fear coming from her for some reason, even see it in her flawless face. A little worried, I pulled myself from underneath her curvy body. She warily backed away. That's when I heard it again—that kind of rippling noise. Only, this time, it seemed louder and stronger. It came from my right. I gave a quick glance in that direction, seeing the two old stone columns, with runes at the top of each one. They had weirdly twisted, stunted trees growing behind them. But this time, a freakish sort of vibration was taking place, violently rippling between the two columns, like some kind of shadowy opening in the fabric of reality itself. As I lay upon the strangely hard earth, I realized the vibration seemed to beat in time with my heart. Reaching up to wipe my forehead, I soon saw that my hand was covered in blood. I looked down at the pool of scarlet welling beneath me. Then I peered back to the redhead, who was slowly circling me cautiously. Watching her closely, I noticed that the wound in her side had healed. She wasn't limping anymore. I smiled at that realization, then blacked out.

Chapter Two

Boom, thump, crash, boom, thump, crash! I slowly opened my weary eyes. Quickly, I realized I was on the back of a noisy, straw-filled, horse drawn, wooden cart with side rails. Looking to its shaky front, I caught a glimpse of the beautiful girl, whom I had met earlier. She encouraged a wild maned, fire red stallion with great vigor, whipping its leather reins forth.

"What are you doing?" I asked.

She gave a quick glance at me and turned back to the stony dirt road.

"Good, you are awake!" the girl exclaimed, veering off the route into a well-hidden red grove. Yes, the leaves and grass were strangely blood red. When the cart came to a stop, many little fireflies zipped from the surrounding bushes and trees. Thinking fast, I caught one, opening my palms to reveal not a firefly, but a tiny, glowing baby-like creature with wild, crazy hair that sort of reminded me of a lion's mane.

"They're sprites," the girl said absentmindedly. "You'd better not hold it long or its brothers and sisters will…"

Suddenly, four devious sprites, two on each side of me, flew quickly, blowing my hair upwards. They shocked me with a jolt, when they freaked me out.

"Never mind," the beautiful girl said, smiling.

The devilish sprites zipped away, squeaking in laughter. Embarrassed and brushing my black hair down with my hands, I focused on the shapely girl, walking to face her at the center of the bizarre, scarlet grove in the late evening.

"Sprites?" I asked her, looking baffled.

"Yes," she replied. "You have crossed into the lands of Phantasma."

I laughed, which I quickly ended after the attractive female's angry glare. She lifted one dainty hand towards me. I was blown backwards against a thick, leafy tree with a thud, by a powerful gust of wind from nowhere. Her eyes started to shine red once again. As they narrowed, she told me, "This is no laughing matter."

"What are you?" I asked weakly, still wondering how I got from there, to here so fast.

"I am Vale Shadowwind. I was named after the great vampire goddess of true, and I am a vampire junior high priestess in training. I was drawn to this area by strange occurrences. I have done all I can to reach and investigate irregular events in the Crimson Plains. By fighting when called for and being discrete when able, I have escaped many wicked pursuers. Yet, while trying to reach a small body of water, to drink and clean my wound, I somehow ended up in your world."

My mind reeled.

"You're a vampire?"

"Yes," she said flatly. "Or would you like another dinner date with me? I think I may still be a little hungry," she told me, giving her flat tummy a little pat.

I took a shaky step back. "You brought me to another world?" I accused.

She looked away to the powerful, well-muscled red horse. It blew air through its nostrils, and shuffled its hoofs a bit. "No, actually you brought me to your world," she replied.

"That's impossible."

"No, I saw you on the ground in that clearing. Your eyes glowed with an incredible power I've never seen before. I even felt it when you touched me, Adam. Your blood tasted like caged lightning itself," she blushed a little. "It healed me faster than anything I've ever known. Don't you remember? You opened the rift."

I flashed on the pulsing blackness I'd seen between the two old columns. "Yes, I remember, that you tried to kill me!" I accused her for the second time.

Sprites flew about making tiny gasps, as they watched us childishly. This time, Vale laughed at me. "No, you saw your own blood and fainted," she said. I turned bright red, realizing that it was true. In that moment, I secretly wished that I too had wind powers. That way, I could throw her up against a tree... Nah, better not think that way, I might end up on the menu again. She smirked and a few sprites burst into squeaky laughter.

"Strange occurrences have been happening in the Crimson Plains, for at least a couple of months now," Vale told me. I nearly choked. Seeing my reaction she inquired, "What's wrong?"

"That's how long I have been having visions of you," I answered. Vale turned a ghostly white, which was a good trick for someone so pale to begin with.

"Visions?" She said. "Tell me of these, visions." So, after letting the cat out of the bag on the whole you're-in-my-dreams-I'm-here-to-save-you-thing, I waited for a reaction and she did not disappoint.

The redhead looked at me saying, "These things cannot be a coincidence. My people's need for hope, the black robed, blue haired figure you speak of." She turned away, "The fact that you knew my name."

"But I didn't..."

"Vale Shadowwind is my name, and wind is the element to which I am most attuned... I think I need to get you to Greyveil as fast as possible."

"Greyveil?" I asked.

"Also made the namesake of the vampire goddess of true, some 600 years ago. It is the vampire city, the Capital of the Vampire Territories," she revealed. Fear coursed through me.

"Now, wait one minute, I have a few questions! If memory serves me, and it usually does, you're a vampire and you bit me. Does that mean that I'm turning into a vampire? Or that I am going to be your minion or something?"

Vale took a deep breath, "Humans are rare in Phantasma," she said. "Some even believe you're extinct. And you are not a normal human, Adam. I don't know the affect, if any, it will have on you. A vampire's true bite has always created a bond between two people. As to what that bond is, depends on who those people are, and how strong they each are. Evil people have evil relationships; likewise, the good have honorable relationships. As for turning into a vampire, like many other species in Phantasma, someone not born to a certain species, can only be changed on the night of alignment, when the twin ruby moons touch and offer their blessing. That is the only time anyone may change."

At that moment, I peered into the dark evening sky, to behold two huge spheres hanging majestically in the lightly clouded sky. There were indeed two moons, though not ruby or even red. *Oh God, I really am on another world*, I thought.

"I must take you to see Jaru. He is my teacher and is knowledgeable of a great many things. He will certainly know what to do... What's that?" Vale suddenly stiffened.

I heard nothing. She walked towards the road as though listening intensely for something. "What is it?" I asked in a low voice.

"We must leave this place now!" Vale yelled.

Both of us hurried back onto the horse-drawn cart. Vale was in front and I was in the back, shooting from the scarlet grove, back onto the stony dirt road. Sprites flew about crazily, disturbed by our quick movements. I could soon hear hoof steps galloping. Peering behind us, I saw two misshapen, dark warriors riding shadowy steeds. They closed in on us fast as the road began climbing a small, steep mountainside. The warriors drew their filthy swords, hissing, ready to attack.

"There are weapons under the hay!" Vale shouted while she whipped the reins feverishly, to keep tight command of the red stallion.

I quickly felt around under the dry straw, pulling up a shiny spear and sword. I thrust the silver tipped spear into the first twisted rider, when he tried to grab onto the cart. He made an ungodly sound, as he fell to the ground unnaturally. The second warrior quickly took his place. Hissing more fiercely, he took a wild swing at me with his sword. His face seemed little more than old bandage-wrapped bones, crawling with foul, black insects. As he missed me by mere centimeters, I smelled death and rot on him. Knowing then that whatever they were, they were long dead. Swiftly, I dodged his sword swipe again. Then I saw a heavy, black, mechanized, horseless carriage thundering up behind us. It was driven by a foul, helmeted, one-eyed undead warrior. A door in its roof opened up, and four horrible things shot from it. They flew in erratic patterns swirling around us. Seeing them clearly, I glimpsed that they were drawn up flying, disembodied heads. Dear God, what a nightmare! Some had rotting flesh and sewn shut eyes, yet they could somehow still see. They screamed terribly, biting and snapping viciously at us. Vale threw a hand back, unleashing a visible ball of compressed air. It hit, striking one of them to the ground lifeless, leaving three more. I slashed wildly through the night air taking down another two. The remaining dead warrior grabbed onto the cart's side rail. Hanging from it, he slashed at me with total abandon. I blocked his unkept, dirty blade with a clang when it hit my own. A dark figure emerged from the open door in the top of the enemy carriage. He had light blue windswept hair, black fingernails and a heavy, black robe. He also possessed long sleeves each one stretched wide at his wrists. The heavy robe was folded over his chest, pinned shut at his heart, and cut off above the knees. Oh crap, it was the death figure from my dreams, and man, did he look pissed. A hooked sickle with a shimmer of liquid silver, materialized in his black-fingernailed hand. He jumped impossibly high to the top of the dark carriage, then to our speeding, red stallion drawn cart. Standing at least six feet one, his gaze was a soulless silver against the whites of his eyes. He had no emotion at all in his face, radiating total terror. Then the wicked death figure bursted into a fury, of sickle swings and powerful kicks. Who was this guy, the big brother of all psychopaths? I dodged, barely plugging the last dead, bandaged warrior with the spear, losing the weapon as the corpse held on to it, contorting to the ground. Vale swerved the cart recklessly, causing the pursuing enemy carriage to hit the jagged mountain wall. It broke two of its wheels, shattering them instantly. And Vale hit the undead driver with another ball of magical wind. In seconds, he crumpled to the ground. On the still speeding cart, the clearly powerful black robed being was standing before me. He swatted my sword swings away like they were nothing with his hooked blade, no matter how much strength I put into them. Suddenly ammoniating a darker awesome presence, the wicked figure glared fiercely and spoke, "The girl is to come with me!" he commanded in a deep and terrifying voice.

I swung mightily for his neck, but he caught it with one bare hand. The last horrible flying head careened, screaming for me. I seized the repulsive thing with a dim flash of light from my hands. The robed figure's face grew surprised. I pitched the somewhat shrunken head at him, striking his upper chest. It went flashing with the same dim light. Amazed, he looked at me as though his very gaze could hurt me.

"I am a deathreaper of the House of Ravenos, from the dark mountain lands of Yarra Sett. Do you really think you can stand against me?" He asked with a truly frightening sneer. I slumped to my knees. Vale peered back to us, seeming to lose hope. The cart began to reduce its speed, with the reaper relaxing a bit, letting down his guard.

"I can try!" I yelled. Then instantly, I jumped into a flying sidekick, tagging him in the dead center of his chest, which felt as hard as stone. The impact exploded in a blinding white flash. The frightening deathreaper was sent straight through the side of the wooden cart, then over the edge of the jagged mountain. We picked up speed and rode away, with Vale whipping the red stallion's reins.

"Who was that?" I asked.

"The figure from your dreams! He is the deathreaper, Reev, a very strong enemy to my people. That won't stop him long," she said, having an amazed expression on her face.

Vale turned her attention back to the road… My stomach clinched at her words, "won't stop him long?" What the hell is he, a Greek god? "Let's make some fast distance between us and him!" I suggested.

"Good idea!" Vale replied over the rumble of the speeding wooden cart.

I then collapsed, only just catching myself. Vale looked at me, her eyes immediately going to a small cut. It must have happened in my fight with Reev.

"Hold on, you've been injured! We have to go for medicine. I know someone nearby," she revealed. Over the long ride, I felt worse and worse. I didn't even notice the beauty of the new, enchanting land, or that the trees and grass around us had gone from blood red, to a more sensible natural green. We eventually came to an odd little cottage. It had a lovely pond and a crude wooden log fence around it. As we went up the gray stone path to the round topped, wooden door knocking, Vale supported my weight. I saw huge, devil horned bullfrogs the size of small dogs, throwing their tongues at what looked like, the biggest alien mosquitos I have ever seen—well, the *only* alien mosquitos I had ever seen.

The door opened and Vale swiftly spoke.

"Greetings, Sister Nemm."

A little, three-feet spritely girl shot out, hovering around us in quick circles. Clearly, she was not really related to the hot vampire priestess in any way. She had three yellow (not blond) ruff looking hair puffs, though I bet they were all as soft as clouds. The two on the sides were the same size and length. The one in the back was like the others, only longer and they all reached skywards at an angle. Nemm wore a green one-piece dress that had loincloth-like flaps. The flap in the front reached mid thigh, with two long dress tales hanging in the back, above ankle length. The dress also had jaggedly cut cloth designs sticking up on each shoulder. It all looked just darling with matching little green gloves and shoes.

"Quick, quick, quick! Come inside, Miss Silvia has been very worried, Priestess!" she squeaked in a cute voice. We entered a quaint medium-sized living room. It had many curved archways and expensive furnishings. Well-kept chairs and stools were everywhere. They possessed thick, comfortable looking square and round, red cushions. Odd otherworldly objects of every type lay around as if on display.

"You've finally made it back. I see my red stallion was reliable," came Silvia's voice. "I thought he might throw your cart for sure. You're not well trained with my horses after all, Vale." I felt somehow worse at that small bit of information. I supported myself by grasping my knees, and Vale turned a slightly off shade of pink. "Please take a seat, I'll be with you in a moment," said Silvia's voice from the neighboring room.

Vale simply told her, "You have fine horses, Silvia. We wouldn't have escaped Reev and his escort without him."

The spritely girl flew to the ceiling, mouth agape, and tiny hands on her cheeks.

"No, no, no, deathreaper not good!" she said, shaking in fear. In a clatter of pots and pans, Silvia quickly entered the room. She was very worried and her green eyes were wide. "He will be coming…Reev is relentless! We have to get out of here, NOW, girl!" she declared. Then her eyes finally fell upon me, growing even larger. When we saw one another Silvia hissed, and her small lips parted, expanding to gargantuan size. Her jaw and lower face stretched impossibly paper thin and wide, revealing that nearly every tooth in her mouth, and I could see them all, was sharp and pointy like little fangs, with gaps expanding between them. I'm guessing Silvia wasn't real big on chewing her food. Her mouth widened into a deep, seething maw, well wider than the width of my shoulders. I saw that her throat possessed a semi long, forked tongue. The serpent-like organ whipped about, quickly tasting the air. It was then that I noticed her body. Five feet ten inches upright, she wore a red skirt, which also covered the top half of her body in a cute blouse. Below the waist, Silvia was a huge, shiny, diamond backed rattler. She stretched another five-and-a-half feet across the wooden floorboards. Oh, wow! Silvia was half snake—okay, maybe a little more than half!

"You are a naga, aren't you?" I asked. I had seen a little something about them on the internet. She gave a little nod, yes, then bore her well polished nails at me. They appeared to lengthen as Silvia started towards me, hissing loudly.

"Silvia wait!" Vale shouted, coming between us, arms spread wide. A mighty wind blew, somehow created by the redheaded vampire, in the naga's sealed cottage. Nemm zipped to another room, frightened.

"Reev isn't following us! This is Adam Westlin," the young priestess motioned to me cautiously, still holding Silvia at bay, while I winced grasping my now inflamed wound. Crap, today really was not my day! "He is much of the reason I was able to escape" Vale told her.

Silvia's face slowly began to take its original shape. Her well-polished claws retracted and lowered. Vale continued, "It was he who knocked the reaper from the mountain."

Instantly, Nemm flew back into the living room, now fearlessly looking me up and down. "What!" she squeaked. Silvia asked, "But how? Reapers are not known to be easily defeated."

"Adam is very brave," Vale hesitated a moment...then told her, "He has a power that hurt the reaper."

"But deathreapers have a high resistance against physical harm, as well as magic. That seems highly suspect, Priestess," the snake lady replied.

"I know that but this human..."

The naga hissed in disbelief, "HUMAN!" Nemm laughed childishly, enjoying the commotion.

Then the small, magical girl hung on every word. "Yes, human!" Vale continued. "He has powerful magic that may give Phantasma a fighting chance."

Silvia nearly hit the floor, when she peered at my bitten neck. "I see. Is that why your priestess wind powers have suddenly gotten so strong?"

Vale looked uncomfortable. "I have studied and focused my wind spells for many months now, Silvia. I just may have improved a little bit," she said, almost angry. "But now, we must see to the deathreaper's mortal cut in Adam's side," Vale concluded.

Silvia suddenly spoke. "Have you...?"

Vale gave the snake lady a terrible look, and she reluctantly redirected her efforts. Silvia slithered to me in her red mini skirt, slash blouse. Gold bracelets adorned her wrists and she had brown hair. It was done up tight and tied together with a pink ribbon. Gently, she placed me on a super comfy couch.

Silvia then slowly lifted my red paint stained white t-shirt, examining the raw, blackened wound closely. I was really surprised when she spit her semi long, forked tongue out, instantly exploring deep inside the painful cut. Seeing my more than a little worried reaction, Nemm hovered above me, saying, "Miss Silvia is a naga and as such, her saliva has cleansing and healing properties." The snake lady's tongue retreated back into her small, red-lipped mouth. Silvia puzzled for a few seconds then revealed, "Adam is in no danger. The wound is infected but not life threatening."

Vale asked "how?" then stopped, saying instead, "When I drank his blood in the other world, it healed me...almost instantly. The wound was only from an undead soldier, but still..." Silvia glared at her and Nemm's mouth nearly hit me, as it gaped open above.

"What do you mean other world?" Silvia inquired. "I have found that the hauntings of the Red Plains were not connected to the great beast, but were actually Adam's power somehow punching a hole through the veil, into our world. I saw him do it myself," Vale added.

Nemm hit the floor breathless this time, and Silvia studied me intensely. "You are full of surprises Master Adam," she said. "But while you may be resistant against the reaper's poisons, I am afraid we must still suck it from your body. House sprite specimen one-forty-two!" commanded the naga. Nemm streaked out, then back into the room, carrying a large jar almost as big as she was. She sat it on a wonderfully crafted wooden stand, next to the couch where I lay. I looked at the jar and I was instantly reviled, at the sight of an awful, newborn sized slug, which thrashed round inside of it. The thing had tiny wiggling tentacles on its head, and a horrifying toothy mouth. It fidgeted around in a thick blue liquid. Vale cringed, turning away at the sight of it.

Oh, hell no, I thought as I struggled to get up. Nemm quickly hit me with a small flash of light. I stared for a moment looking at the surrounding ladies. They glared back in return, flabbergasted.

"Why did it not work?" The little house sprite asked no one in particular. I again made an effort to stand—and was quickly stopped by the vampire's soft hands on my chest.

"The poison may still cripple or harm you, Adam. I'm sorry, but I have to do this," said Vale. Before I could react, she quickly punched me out.

Chapter Three

The next morning, I woke up in a large, fluffy bed with a strange pressure on my chest. I looked down finding Nemm, curled up sleeping away, thumb in mouth. I jumped a little in surprise, and her head sprung up instantly. Awake and alert, she shot from the room. Then I felt something moving next to me rassling the covers. I looked over to see a half awake, half-dressed Vale. She was trying to get more comfortable, on the extremely fluffy mattress.

"Ooooo!" she stretched, "it's only Nemm, this is her room after all, Adam."

I lamely pulled up the covers, realizing I was totally naked. Vale lazily turned to me, seeing my baffled expression through heavy eyelids.

"After our first meeting, I'd think you would be a little more comfortable around me." She smiled as her fangs seemed to unconsciously extend. My mind flashed back to the clearing, and the two weird columns that had those runes carved at the top of them, when we were impassioned, and our bodies were desperately trying to become one, with Vale satisfying her dire blood need. She reached for me absentmindedly—and seductively. I quickly retreated, wrapping a loose cloth from a nearby stand around myself.

"You are well-gifted indeed, Master Adam," the vampire said, peering at the cloth as though she could see right through it. I swiftly exited the room. Vale seemed content to curl up and continue sleeping.

Entering the living room just outside the door, I heard a voice.

"Don't mind her. Vampires, even vampire priestesses are pretty much useless, until at least twelve o'clock, late risers."

I spun around, finding Silvia sitting in a nice, clean dining area, next to an odd little oven, not far away in its own little corner, with many wooden cabinets. The small area was complete with a medium-sized café table, and four chairs at the far end of the living room.

"I have prepared you an attire that is less likely to attract unwanted attention," she said. Silvia continued: "I expected you awake around the same time as Vale. Usually, those first bitten sort of synchronize with the vampire who bit them, at least for the first few days. I was certain I would be washing your bloodstains from my sheets today, Adam." My face warmed as I stared at her. "Then again, nothing about you is typical," she added.

After dressing myself in Silvia's very normal-looking restroom, in a semi shiny blue shirt and slacks, complete with brown leather belt and boots, I equipped a brown side pouch, and what looked like a tailored, likewise brown, waist-length cape. Going back to the dining area to sit with the snake woman, she touched a small crystal built into a little copper disk. Beautiful music poured from it, more clearly than I had ever heard. I realized I had seen similar crystals all over Miss Silvia's restroom.

"What is that?" I queried.

"Only one of my favorite music crystals," she said. I viewed the little copper disk, completely transfixed. Silvia stated, "You should probably know that the life's blood of Phantasma is magic. We store it, channel it, and use it in everyday life. Some of the more gifted of us, directly using spells, though we have learned to create and use crystals, like the one in my music player, as well as in many other things around my home, to harness its gifts for the use of the less inclined. It is these rechargeable crystals that power most things in our world, from lights and stoves to our very cities."

"That is fascinating Miss Silvia," I stated with genuine wonder. "Sort of like electricity in my world."

"Electricity?" she asked.

"It's kinda like harnessing lightning for power."

She seemed very interested, saying, "Really. You know, Master Adam..."

"Just Adam is fine," I said.

She continued, "I am a bit of a seeker of knowledge, hunting down new truths, and ways to improve the quality of life in Phantasma."

"Like a scientist," I said.

Silvia paused for a moment repeating, "Scientist? Yes, I think I like that. My home is a kind of supply station for travelers, like the young priestess. They come here and I supply their needs, usually knowing that I am helping to improve things for our world," she told me very seriously.

I couldn't help but wonder what she was not telling me. Then I saw Nemm peeking from behind one of the hall archways shyly, showing her pretty brown eyes. I felt bad, that I had frightened her from her own room, previously.

"Good morning, beautiful Nemm. I'm sorry I scared you earlier."

She flew to me still looking shy.

"I'm just not used to waking up to such a pretty, young lady."

Nemm seemed to blush and relax hearing my words.

Silvia gave a little half smile saying, "Why don't you take Nemm for a little exercise outside? House sprites are a bit more tolerable, after they've played awhile. I'll have breakfast ready upon your return."

Outside in the fresh air, Nemm darted about like an oversized bumblebee, while I ran out into the tall, tree-filled open spaces around Silvia's cottage. Nemm giggled happily, and we tossed a leather ball back and forth. She flew to and fro catching it, and throwing the ball back to me. I felt great, like I was drawing energy from some unknown reserve.

Getting stronger and more focused, I lost track of time. Somehow, I didn't seem to get tired, at least not noticeably so. I could jump farther, move faster, and think more clearly than ever before, which was great for Nemm, because a simple game of catch took on a whole new meaning. We darted from tree to tree, scaring the local wild life, mostly two-tailed foxes and more of those dog-sized, devil-horned bullfrogs. Even in the treetops, I nearly flew with us pitching the leather ball back and forth. Gleefully, we both jumped and flipped through the air. As wonderful a time as we were having, eventually, we stopped briefly, settling on a nearby gray boulder.

I asked, "Why are there so many of those frog things, and two-tailed foxes out here?"

Nemm replied, "They're Miss Silvia's favorite snacks."

"That's not what she's making for breakfast is it?"

"No silly, she doesn't cook them for others; well, not usually. She just gulps them down. It's quite a show to see," Nemm said, giving a giggle then flipping in midair, while adding, "Silvia likes it when someone watches."

My mind thought back to last night, at the sight of her deep heaving throat and gaping huge mouth. I couldn't stop myself from my next few words.

"Has Silvia ever eaten…"

"People…?" Nemm finished for me. "Only thieves and bandits. If she hadn't, Silvia and Nemm would be dead, dead, dead," the sprite girl answered in a serious, but cute voice. (Mental note: Don't ever steal from the naga lady.)

Back at Silvia's, after Nemm and I had eaten a delicious breakfast of Gore Soup, Eyeball-jelly, Dragon-lard and toast. Don't ask. Vale continued to sleep undisturbed. The snake lady then invited me into her cellar, through a trapdoor in the floor, near the dining area. I of course had I bad feeling, but didn't want to be rude.

She told me, "There's something you must see, Adam Westlin."

In the dimly lit, but spacious cellar, there were maybe hundreds of sealed jars, all with different contents, ranging from alien-looking worms, to dried-up old turtleheads. (Wonder what they're used for?) Silvia slithered to a long glass holding tank. It was half filled with dark blue fluid, in the center of the room. As I struggled to see inside… Thump! Splash! I jumped back, viewing the horrible slug from last night. Only, it was four times larger, with two new, big, arm-like tentacles, flailing about madly.

"It drew the poison from you last night," Silvia told me. "But your blood seems to have affected it. For some reason, your blood appears to have empowering properties, in our world, Adam." Staring hard into my face, the naga continued, "Also in the young priestess upstairs." Her eyes fell upon my now fully healed neck. The room felt a bit more unsettling, as Silvia moved closer to me. "I suspect you may be more important than we know" she said. Slowly, the naga wrapped around me. I could feel the warmth of her thick coils.

"I'm only trying to help and find out how to get home," I revealed.

Her face was now inches from mine, peering into my eyes with her forked tongue, beginning to taste the air feverishly.

"If I can help you, you have only to ask Miss Silvia," I offered.

Her coils tightened a little. I saw Silvia's mouth smile and start to stretch open slowly. Thinking fast, I reached into an open, nearby specimen jar, grabbing behind the head a plump devil-horned bullfrog, about the size of a small, fat dog. I waved it like a wounded animal in front of her predatory eyes. She seemed surprised for a moment, then, slowly and seductively, she moved her mouth to the waiting round frog. She kissed it wetly. Hesitantly opening her mouth, Silvia took in its thick, somewhat short hind legs, with a very active forked tongue. Her mouth seamlessly slid over its basketball-like body, and her eyes never left my own. Very slowly, the bullfrog sank into her well-stretched, lipsticked mouth. Silvia's lips slid over it, like an otherworldly gorgeous woman-shaped cotton sock, taking in a round froggy foot. As her lips neared my hand, her tongue reached forth, caressing and tasting the flesh of it. I released the frog from behind the head. Quickly, Silvia took me by the shoulders, her lips shrinking to their normal, perfectly red size. The huge basketball-shaped lump slowly descended down her throat, going through her heaving breasts, then to her waiting stomach, where it rested. The female naga gently laid a hand on the round mound in her belly. She gasped, and it disappeared into her muscular coils below. Silvia no longer seemed to want me for a snack. Her hands started to rove all over my body, and her breathing grew hot and heavy. I realized Silvia wanted something um…else, when she placed my hands under her red mini skirt, onto two very warm, full and firm buttocks. The naga lady's body seemed to envelop me, as she slowly lost control.

In that moment, the trapdoor flipped up. A red shining-eyed Vale hurried into the cellar. Silvia retreated, her coils loosening and falling to the floor. Vale stood stiffly on the stairs only saying, "Silvia, prepare our things for departure. We're leaving. Adam, come with me now!"

A short while later to the right of the house, down a well-worn dirt path, there were stables and an unpainted wooden barn. I hadn't noticed them before. Nemm was busy in the barn, at the very last stall on the far end, loading supplies onto what I assumed to be, another red stallion or mare. We hurried on soft, Sweet-smelling hay, passed the other well-kept stalls, that held the most impressively muscled, majestic horses I have ever seen.

The vampire was focused on eating some sort of red fruit, while she walked. Some of the horses snorted and reared at us as we hasted. I swear, a particularly large red stallion blew flames from its nostrils, when he too snorted at us. Silvia said nothing, only slithering along. She carried a satchel of supplies behind Vale, eyeing me all the while. *Goodness, what is that about?* I wondered. We reached the last stall and to my amazement, I saw the spritely Nemm finish saddling a huge, white bat. I jumped, taken aback at the sight, while the thirteen-feet long beast busily ate away, finishing a big bowl of those red mango-like fruit, that Vale was obviously enjoying. Nemm finally took notice of our arrival, opening the stall gate.

"Wingrider is prepped and ready, Priestess," she said, zipping to the side, allowing us through. As we approached, the mighty bat grew agitated. Vale swiftly calmed the beast, by gently speaking these words into his ear: "*Sen nuw sa la wen,*" to which he instantly relaxed.

Vale mounted first then pulled me up behind her. On the back of the furry white bat beast, she made certain to strap me tightly into the saddle. Wingrider grunted and screeched, protesting a bit. Silvia passed the satchel to me, and the beast started forward through the opened stall gate. He crawled on his front wings and hind legs. After coming through the barn doors, the huge bat took flight. Leaping unevenly, it spread its white wings with tremendous force, spearing itself into the waiting noon sky. Higher and higher we climbed, soaring. As we elevated, I lost all feeling in my body. The strange sensation caused me to hold myself tightly to Vale's body. Her reaction was to go even faster and higher. I was never so thankful, to be strapped to the back of a giant flying bat in my life. Peering out into the new, alien world all around me, I was astounded at its awesome, grand beauty. I could see tall, fearsome mountains and a winding road. It continued all the way through lightly forested hills, to the fenced-in-by-trees open area, where Silvia's home sat in the distance. *That must have been* the *route we took last night, escaping the deathreaper Reev of the House of Ravenos,* I thought to myself. Not far from Silvia's were sparkling freshwater lakes. Geez, I wish I had known that. I could have really used a swim and maybe a bath, coulda, woulda, shoulda. Later, I was getting better at handling the G-forces. My spirit no longer felt like it was going to detach from my body. I looked to the far horizon, seeing a black land dotted with spooky structures and scary towers.

"What is that?" I inquired as we streaked though the early evening blue sky. Vale turned her head only a second then faced forward, hesitating. I was about to ask again when she answered.

"It's the Demon Zone, the Soulless Lands ruled by the spirit beast, Drexelon."

My eyes grew large and fear took hold of me. Instantly, a swirling ball of orange light shot passed our right flank. Vale cast her eyes downwards, yelling against the wind.

"Serpent Riders! Hold on, Adam!"

She dived to make us leveled with our pursuers. When I looked back, I could see three large, green-scaled, terrible, purple-winged serpents. They had four yellow, black-slitted eyes, two on each side of their huge heads. The beasts also possessed dagger-like teeth. What looked like warrior elf women rode saddles on their backs. The one to the left had semi short green spiked hair.

It appeared a little like fire, but not real flames, of course. Actually, they all had a flame-like quality to their hair, with the woman in the middle's hair being long and red. It showed fluffy bangs in its front. The last one to the right wore a long, narrow, purple ponytail. She displayed a bang as well, though it was generous and pointed, covering nearly half her face. They all had lengthy slender pointed ears, reaching to the sides sort of like airplane wings. But the one with purple hair's ears slanted downwards. All possessed thin supermodel bodies. They wore strange-looking leather tank top suits, each colored slightly different, matching the shade of each women's hair. The elves also each sported thigh-high black leather boots.

Steering the huge white bat, Vale tossed a wind spell at the middle redhead, which the she-elf dodged, sending a glowing spark of a spell in return. It barely missed us. Concentrating in the strong wind, I could somehow sense Vale drawing and storing energy, seemingly from the great bat we rode atop. She turned and released it in a bright flash of three blue, glowing wind spells. Two pursuers veered out of the way, but the green-haired third was hit, though her serpent quickly recovered from the blast. The female elves immediately seemed really upset. All three warriors attacked at the same time, in a flurry of flying spells. We dipped, swerved, and loop de looped to avoid them. I couldn't tell which way was up. The land was suddenly above me, instead of below. I lost all sense of direction riding the mighty bat. When we executed the final loop de loop, soaring upside down over the serpent-riding elf women, I held very tightly to Vale, beginning to feel her now in some manner, draw power from my grip around her waist, instead of from the huge bat, Wingrider, that we rode. She instantly sent a free hand forth, firing off a huge wind spell which to my surprise exploded, knocking the redhead and her winged serpent from the sky.

"Whatever you're doing, keep doing it!" the princess yelled against the fierce wind. I gladly held her even tighter. The remaining two elf women regrouped in front of us, continuing their barrage of deadly spells. Vale tensed hard, saying, "*Ku tarra vin!*" to the powerful bat. In a single piercing scream, it unleashed a beam of pure, deadly sound, knocking the head from the green spike-haired elf's serpent. The final purple ponytailed elf woman fearlessly stood, on the back of her undulating green serpent, as her comrade fell from the sky. She chanted unheard words and gestured with her hands.

Vale held close to Wingrider and I clung tightly to her. We tried to close the distance between us and the enemy. A magical sort of purple electricity built up around the elf, and her serpent. Closing in, Vale sent forth her free hand saying, "Don't let go, Adam!" Then, she fired another huge wind spell.

The purple-haired elf woman launched her purple lightning attack. It exploded, when the two spells collided in a gigantic fireball of multiple colors, sending us all spiraling to the breathtaking landscape below.

"We have to do something!" I yelled in a panic. Then, seeing that both Vale and Wingrider were unconscious, I instantly reached for the reins. I tried to awaken the beast and break our swift descent, to no avail. As we careened to impact, I threw my hands forth, out of sheer instinct and desperation. Reaching deep inside myself, I somehow materialized a blanket of ghostly white energy, that cushioned our fall. Quickly, I dragged the priestess away from the motionless giant white-furred bat, afraid it may wake and try to eat her or something. After pulling Vale to safety, she rested under a large, nearby oak…

Ring, ring, ring!

What the hell, ring, ring, ring? I feverishly searched through my leather side pouch. Surprisingly, I came up with my cell phone. Silvia must have packed it for me. Bless her snakebutted, slithering little heart. I flipped it open to a very fired up, countryfied sounding Grandpa, saying, "Boy where the hell you done got off ta?"

I sure was glad to hear his voice, and I was getting really good reception in another world! Weird…

"Grandpa, I'm so sorry that I'm not home right now."

"If you so sorry Boy, then bring your narrow bee-hind home, and get to work on ma tractor."

"I'm sorry, I'm trying to find a way home. But I'm not even sure where I really am!"

"Gal dang it Boy, you better not be pulling the wool over ma eyes, and if in you ain't. Is there anything we can do for ya Son?"

God, I love that man.

"Let me speak to Grandma."

She was instantly on the phone.

"Ooh, son, is everything okay? You can tell me anything, you know that."

"I didn't mean to worry you, Grandma. And I understand if you don't believe me. But I just need to say this. I am somewhere in another world. But I think I have the power to get back home. I just don't know how to use it yet."

"Oooh Son," she started. I cut her off adding, "Don't worry, I'll be back as soon as I can. Tell Tannon he's the man of the house, till I get back!" (Translation: Man of the house equals more chores.) He's going to love it! (Translation: No, he won't!) "I love you all and I'll be home soon, take care of yourselves." I flipped the cell phone closed, thinking what a weight it was off my chest, just to speak with my family.

I turned around to a tall, barrel-chested, well-muscled, brown-slick-haired vampire. He wore a shoulder padded, black, sparkly two-piece suit. It had a red diamond shape on its center chest. Leather brown boots with two straps around the calves adored his feet. And he had on regal black gloves, complete with a sword and flowing black matching cape, which bolstered a red inside lining, finishing the outfit. One well placed punch from him and I was out. Is it just me, or is this starting to happen way too much?

Chapter Four

I came to tied up in a well-lit, large tent—a very nice–looking, well-lit, large tent. It was made of a black material cloth, and its inside was filled with a spacious bed. Silk covers and animal skins lay on top of it, while odd G.V.-covered war banners hung everywhere. Straight forward from the entrance, a desk full of charts and many quills was stationed. There were also a lot of weapons set up, in the far corner next to it. I could not see what was written on the charts. I can only assume, they were some sort of battle plans.

My hands were bound and my face hurt. *That bastard punched me*, I thought to myself, as I tried to wiggle free. In the middle of my efforts, a tall vampire entered the regal tent. Lightly armored, he wore a black-hooded cloak. His blue eyes met mine, and I realized he actually had big grey bat wings, coming out of his back. (What the?...) He gave a small grunt of annoyance, and retreated back through the tent's entrance flap. Moments later, the barrel-chested, sparkly, black suit-clad vamp, who forced me into naptime earlier entered. Taking an animal-skinned chair, he sat before me. I looked at him uncomfortably tied up against the tent's center support. He gazed back at me like I was nothing.

"Where is Vale?" I snarled at him. "What have you done with her?"

Completely cold, he finally opened his mouth to say, "I am Greyveil Commander Aldett. Who are you, stranger? Where are you from, and why are you traveling with our princess?"

"Princess!" I blurted. My expression was completely of surprise, and my mind struggled to make sense of his words.

"Yes, Vale Shadowwind is the second princess in line, to the vampire throne of Greyveil."

"But she told me she was a priestess in training."

"She is," the tall, muscular vampire stated. "Princess Vale is making great efforts, to become a strong spiritual leader to her people. Now, I need for you to answer my questions. Make no mistake traveler, the only reason you are alive now, is that I saw you save the princess's life, with your powerful magic, though I haven't determined if you are friend or enemy yet."

I took a breath. *This feels like getting caught with a vampire president's daughter*, I thought as I began.

"My name is Adam Westlin. I am from a place called Earth. I'm traveling with the princess to see her teacher, a man called Jaru." The expression on Aldett's face intensified. I continued, "Because I may have the power to get home. But I don't think I know how to use it correctly."

Aldett sat gazing at me, looking me over. Then he simply said, "Bring him to the testing ring."

The testing ring, what the f—is that, I quietly pondered to myself. I soon found that I was pushed and prodded roughly, by two grey-winged vampire soldiers, to a circular ring area. It was surrounded by a thick brown rope. As we walked, irregular little alien bugs scurried across the ground. Well, I suppose you really couldn't call them bugs. They had a lot more than six legs. Waiting for us at our destination were two more big, grey-winged vampires standing guard, at what I could only assume was a mob of more, smaller vampires, though they looked more like armed unwashed humans. They gathered all around the ring, being rowdy, in the middle of what was obviously a vampire war camp. It was full of small brown tents, wooden benches, well-beaten paths, and barrels. The place was well hidden in the thick forest trees. I was thrown down into the center of the testing ring's dirt floor.

Aldett stood just outside of it, saying in a mighty voice, "This traveler claims to be from another world!"

The onlookers started to whisper.

"He has saved the life of our princess, Vale! I have witnessed this with my own eyes!"

The crowding vampires cheered aloud looking a little rabid.

"I believe this Adam Westlin to be a great warrior, sent to us in our time of greatest need! If his words are true," Aldett said gesturing to me, "he may be a powerful help to us!"

The warrior vampire hesitated for about five seconds, then loudly blurted, "The time has come for him to prove it!"

What the hell is he talking about? I wondered, staring at him and the excited vampire crowd. Then he said it and I wished he hadn't.

"Three rounds! The first vampire to win tastes the prize of Adam's blood!"

Oh hell, no! I shot to my feet with my heart pounding.

Two filthy vampires entered the ring, wearing what were clearly vampire soldier uniforms. They were little more than dark grey shirts, slacks, and brown boots. The vampires rushed me; one was bald, the other blond. Baring their fangs, they hissed. I ducked down as they approached, punching them both squarely in the stomach. Seeing them stunned, I quickly reacted, catching the bald vamp in head scissors (I love Saturday night wrestling on TV. I even tried out a few moves on a very unwilling, unruly little brother—whenever possible, he, he.) I then tossed him on his shiny head. He was out cold.

The blond found his footing. He started to kick and punch furiously. It was very similar to the martial arts. But this guy was leaving himself way, way open. So I stepped into one of the huge gaps in his defense, unleashing a swift uppercut, hitting him solidly on the chin. I was surprised when he did a backwards flip, from the force of my punch. The defeated vamps were taken away, while their comrades had a small taste of the blood, that came from the blond's bleeding mouth.

Laughing with excitement, Aldett spoke mightily.

"Round two! Let us show this traveler the pride of Greyveil's vampire sons."

The surrounding mob cheered in ecstatic agreement. Many vampires spilled the few drinks passed out to them, in their excitement. Aldett pointed to one of the built-like-a-brick-sh—house, winged vampire warriors. He gave a little nod. (Damn, am I some kind of trouble magnet or something?) The tall vampire entered the ring as the mob roared. He spread his wings to appear even larger and more menacing. With brown wavy hair and strange symbols tattooed down his right eye, he sneered at me.

"Your sweet blood is mine!" the vampire said, with a fanged smile. Offensively and without fear (Okay, maybe a little fear.), I ran up to him—and was quickly swatted away, by his huge bat wings. Catching myself on the thick, brown ropes, I swiftly spun to strike the vampire warrior, with a flurry of punches and kicks. All of them he blocked and parried away, giving me a little shove for good measure. The warrior smiled at me again. Remembering my little session with Nemm, and our time playing catch, I flipped backwards, catching his chin with my boot, and sending one broken fang flying, to the excitement of the crowd. The vampire was thrown back, and I tried a few quick jabs, finding it like hitting a cinder block. He swung for me wildly. I ducked and came up to his groan with a stiff kick.

Aldett looked on saying, "Most effective," with a hand clasping his chin. The crowd roared on and the warrior took tiny steps, making little squeak-like noises, while trying to stand up straight. I quickly jumped on his back, grabbing his neck in an iron gripped sleeper hold, (Like I said, I really like wrestling.) through the opening between his grey wings. With all my might, I squeezed. The vamp warrior with the wavy hair and tattoo down his right eye, slowly slid to the ground unconscious. Aldett looked absolutely displeased. He held up his hands, and there was instant and total silence.

"Truly the traveler, Sir Adam Westlin (Oh, I'm a "Sir" now, cool!) of Earth is every bit the warrior, I believed him to be! Therefore, in this final contest, I will be his opponent! For he has proven himself worthy." This just gets better and better.

Oh, well, they may be vampires, but they're only men—really strong, freakishly tough, bloodthirsty men. Aldett jumped ten feet up and landed in the center ring. He faced me with tremendous force of will, and a steel gaze.

I wiped some dirt off my mouth. Okay, so maybe they're not really men at all. The way my day is going, his real name is probably Clark Kent. Better watch out for heat vision. I punched, he caught it. I tried again. He swatted it away with amazing speed, kicking me in the stomach. I staggered a bit. The commander tried to connect with a left hook, but I quickly swept his legs from under him. Aldett plummeted to the dirt floor of the ring. Smiling as he rose up slowly, he brushed the filth from his regal black suit. Swiftly, the mighty vampire caught me with a punch to the gut, that turned into a bruising grab. When he clutched my mid-section, Aldett lifted me high into the air on one large arm, tossing me to the ground effortlessly. I attempted to rise. But the powerful vampire launched into a rage, I really hadn't expected. Bang, bang, boom! his blows hit me like bricks, sending me to the waiting dirt floor below. The crowd exploded in crazy cheers for the vampire commander, which quickly died, when I got to my feet panting. Aldett turned to face me.

Without warning, I ran with a speed I didn't even know I had. I tackled the sparkly, black-clad vampire, hitting him with such force, that we flew ten feet outside of the ring, landing with a loud thump. I stood there staring into the mob of dirty vampires. They all gasped, gingerly backing away. Aldett simply looked up at me with huge eyes, speechless from the ground. A rustle of leaves caught my attention. Looking up and nearby, I saw Vale hurrying to the ring area.

When our eyes finally met, she too gasped, saying, "Adam quickly come with me!"

The princess threw some vamp's nearby small, green blanket over my head, and we quickly walked away. Back at Aldett's rich-guy tent, Vale pushed me inside, giving scary, threatening looks to anyone, who even looked in our direction. She sat me on the animal skin covered bed, which was amazingly soft. You know, for a camping bed. Vale took the blanket off me, tossing it aside. She scanned my face intensely.

"What is going on?" I asked while she held my face. "Why are you treating me like some little kid?"

I glared at the priestess angrily. She slowed down, but she remained close still staring at every inch of my face. Immediately, Vale apologized.

"I'm sorry, this should not have happened. I only regained consciousness just now." She shuttered a little. "They should not have treated you that way."

I put my arms around her. "It's okay," I said. "I'm fine. They only gave me a few bruises."

"You could have been a lot less than fine, Adam. If I hadn't..." I gently touched her soft face, kissing her as if trying to take away her pain.

"It will all work out," I told Vale, hoping deep inside myself that I was right. I embraced her, rubbing her back to soothe her.

"You saved me, didn't you? When the elven sister's spell collided with ours."

"You mean when your spell collided," I said kindly.

"No," Vale answered, "my powers…," she stopped for three quick breaths, then continued in a lower voice, "have never been that strong. The only reason that has changed is your blood." Her sparkling, green eyes looked away. "When I drank from you, it did something to me, changed me deep inside. It is still changing me. I can feel it, Adam." Vale was looking intently at my lap, refusing to look me in the face.

"I won't let anything happen to you," I breathed.

"It made me stronger," she continued.

"You're a vampire," I stated. "You're supposed to be really strong."

She quickly replied, "You don't understand, in a bloodbond." *Bloodbond?* I thought. "The person a vampire bites draws strength from them, in an equitable and acceptable relationship. The one bitten is able to draw on the power of the vampire, to gain a special advantage from the bond, also gaining the vampire's watchful protection. Then maybe on the night of the ruby moons…" She looked at me soulfully deep with her beautiful green eyes. "They will accept the change." *God, I really don't want to be a vampire. I've always accepted myself the way I am.* "The vampire gets the blood; the person bitten gets protection and a new life.

"Everybody gets great sex," she blushed, "win, win. But for some unknown reason, that is not the way our bloodbond is working. You're not attracted to me properly, and you're not drawing power from me. In fact, I think I am the one getting strength from you. When you touched me, while we fought against the winged Serpent Riders, I tapped into your power, through the bloodbond. You are also supposed to be magically drawn to me. I don't…think that's happening, though I can sense your whereabouts, even your mood if I concentrate."

I stiffened, thinking that's kind of weird, sensing it as if it were some sort of cue to be taken. The princess began nuzzling me. Wow, it felt good! Then Vale slowly started kissing me. I could soon feel sharp fangs, brushing against my skin in her kisses. She smoothly worked her way to the place on my neck, where she had originally bitten me. A small shiver arose through me. *Oh God, I believe I know what's next.*

Aldett burst through the regal tent's entrance flap. Vale sighed, her lips retreating, though she was sitting so close, I could still smell her exotic flower scent. The sparkly, black-suit-wearing vampire immediately bowed to the princess, saying, "Mistress Shadowwind, is all well with you this day?"

I couldn't help but quickly stifle a giggle. Aldett's attention swiftly went to me, and I stiffened. He placed an animal-skinned chair, and sat looking like a stone statue.

"Is this traveler a friend of yours, Princess?" he asked without even looking at me.

"Yes, he and I are going to see my mentor on important business, Commander Aldett. Lord Jaru has vital information that may allow Greyveil, to stand against the spirit demon beast, Drexelon."

As Vale spoke, I could see in my mind the image of a terrible horned beast. Shadows clung to his skin like he was made of them. When he moved his super muscular body, his spirit appeared to follow two steps behind. The shadow he cast was alive and menacing. It moved freely on its own in a haunting, shattered world. The horrible being looked at me. Terrified, fear materialized from nowhere, and my mind flashed back to reality. Aldett and Vale were both staring at me with wide eyes.

"Is something wrong?" I queried.

Aldett angrily stated, "Your eyes were glowing. Just like out in the ring, traveler!"

What! I thought, but I remained silent. He put a hand on his sheathed sword.

"I had a vision of a huge horned beast cloaked in darkness. He had a free moving spirit, and a living shadow existing in a broken world."

They both looked amazed.

"You've had a vision of the demon king?" The male vampire spoke, nearly floored, slumping back in his seat.

"That is impossible! No seer can gaze beyond his cloak of shadows. No one can..."

"He also threw the deathreaper Reev off the mountain pass, after fighting him," Vale revealed absentmindedly.

Aldett looked like he was having cold chills. He stared off into space.

"The king must hear of this, Princess." He turned to her saying, "Now!"

Vale stood up guarded, with anger starting to show on her perfect face.

"I will tell him, but first, I must speak with Master High Priest Jaru. Our very future may depend on it. I command you not to talk of this with anyone, until I have!"

Aldett stared quietly, then bowed saying, "Princess Dailania has returned from her travels abroad. Being aware of your relationship in the past, I thought it best you should know."

Vale's expression was first surprised, then a little worried, which she quickly hid.

Aldett stood up, wasting no time. "I shall have my Honor Guard escort you. The carriage will be ready within the hour. Of course, you're flying steed Wingrider will be attended to, then returned to the palace, as soon as my men are able. But we must move quickly, Princess, lest your enemies have unintended opportunity."

Enemies? I wondered just how many does she have? I walked through the weapon, and wooden bench-filled vampire war camp with Vale, towards the near fully readied unpainted horseless carriage. It reminded me an awful lot of the deathreaper's iron clad, black ride. Then I heard something. It seemed muffled and I barely caught sound of it. Turning as I walked, I followed the odd noises with Vale in tow, watching me closely. Eventually, it led us to the far corner of the camp. As the noises grew louder, I saw that it was the tall, winged vampire with the wavy brown hair, and tattoo down his right eye, the one I had fought earlier. He was hurt, trying to hold back his groans of pain, while clutching the left side of his mouth, the side his fang was now missing from. A few of his fellow vamp soldiers were ridiculing and teasing him, even going so far as to sneak little hits, when his attention was diverted by his intense pain.

The three filthy vampires laughed merrily, saying. "What kind of Honor Guard are you? You were beaten by a kid half your size." One of them really got bold adding, "After months of being afraid of you, now that I look at you, and I mean reeeally see you, you don't seem so tough to me anymore. I don't think you ever were." He slowly started for the club at his side. Ooh hell, seeing his intent, I rushed retrieving an empty cup from a nearby wooden bench. I dug around in my newly returned side pouch, finding my pocketknife. Flipping it out, I sliced the inside flesh of my hand, quickly letting some blood drain into the wooden cup. I then wrapped my hand tightly, with a clean cloth from my pouch—no need to advertise to a bunch of hunger vampires.

Running quickly, I gave the cup to the big guy with wings. He appeared stunned seeing it in his hand. With a couple of quick sniffs, he instantly knew what it was. Drinking my blood swiftly, he stood, dropping the empty cup to the ground beside him. When his lips parted, I could see his lost fang restoring itself. Which is what I had hoped would happen. I didn't mean to hurt him so badly. And I couldn't stand the way the other soldiers were treating him. The winged vampire watched his would-be attackers, slowly motioning their retreat. Instantly, his huge hand grabbed one of them, lifting him seven inches off the ground, as his friends cowered, frozen by fear, unable to move. The filthy vamp solider leader now saw eye to eye, with the sizable-winged vampire. I simply turned around and began walking back, towards the nearly prepped carriage. Vale smiled to the background noise of big pounding fists, and well-deserved screams of pain. We soon entered the unpainted wooden carriage, sitting on fine satin red seats. A platter of delicious food waited inside, of which I took a few bites. Vale was eyeing me with a cute smirk on her face, while she sat on the opposite side of the attractive carriage.

"What?" I asked.

"That was very noble, Adam. You helped an enemy, though you didn't have to."

"I didn't like the way they were treating him, taking advantage like that. And my blood healed you really fast. I was hoping it would do the same for him."

"It seemed to work faster, actually," she said, as her smirk widened to a full smile. "I think you're getting stronger, Adam."

A little swell of pride took root deep inside of me. It was then that I noticed the winged vampire with the tattoo, was standing at the opened door of the carriage. I wonder how long he had been there?

The big vampire bowed his head, saying, "Adam Westlin, your kindness will not soon be forgotten. I pledge my services to you now. Know that if you should ever have need of me for anything, I will be there."

"Thank you Swicer," the princess said. The tall vampire took his position on a nearby horse, guarding the carriage. Vale was beaming so hard at me I thought I'd go blind from the rays of pride, that shined from her. She shut the door and we were alone.

Chapter Five

"So you are a princess, too?" I asked. I guess no separation of church and state ever happened here.

"In the Kingdom of the Vampire Territories, the royal family members are also spiritual leaders to our people. So in addition to my being a high priestess in training, I am also the land's second princess, to the winged King Sevorift Shadowwind, my father."

"About that, I meant to ask, why is it that some vampires have wings and others don't?"

Vale began, "Certain vampires are blessed with either great strength or magic. Sometimes, but very rarely, they are blessed with both. My father is such a vampire. They are the elite warriors of my people, and are called the Honor Guard. They are our protectors, and yes, I am second in line for my father's throne, after my older sister, Dailania."

"Exactly how old are you and your sister?"

"I am seventeen and my sister is nineteen." I heard the driver taking his place at the front of the horseless carriage, with a series of small thumps. Then I saw the three other winged vampire soldiers gallop up on horseback. As I watched through the carriage window, they took their guard positions at the remaining three corners of the carriage, Swicer didn't occupy. The carriage started silently forward, which was strange, because I was sure it didn't have an engine. As it began its long journey, I continued my conversation with Vale.

"The second in line?" I asked Vale.

"Yes," she replied. "Again, I have an older sister, Dailania Shadowwind, the dark dancer."

"Why is she called 'dark dancer'?" I asked.

"Often, the members of the Vampire Territories' Royal Family are gifted, even above the elite vampires, with truly incredible powers. My gift is Elemental Wind, as you already know. My sister's gift is the gift of Magical

Motion. When she moves her body and dances, she is able to call upon mystical forces." Vale stopped for only a breath, saying, "Dailania has always been stronger than me. Perhaps, because she is the older sister. When she dances losing herself in a song, I have witnessed small armies falling before her destructive might. Now, Darkdancer has returned, after two long months of peace at the palace. Adam, you should know that I and my sister, do not see eye to eye.

"Dailania is manipulative, cruel, and has always..." Vale hesitated, meeting my gaze. "Tried to take what is mine." (Okaaay, Vale was starting to appear a little creepily possessive.) "When we go to the palace, you must not wander, and stay close to me at all times."

Well, I am a stranger, in a strange land, so I told her, "I'll do my best."

Hearing my answer, Vale relaxed.

"Tell me more about your father," I said.

She stiffened right up again. "My father, King Sevorift Shadowwind, is currently fighting a war, along with the rest of Phantasma, trying to keep the demon, Drexelon, at bay by diplomacy with other kingdoms and covert action. The beast is far too powerful to face head on or alone." Vale began to cry. "Oh, Adam, that is why we need you so desperately. With your help, we will at least have a chance. I know it deep in my heart. That is what your blood is telling me."

I was a bit surprised. My blood talks to her? She moved from the cushioned, red, satin seat across the carriage to sit beside me, with tears running down her pale face.

"You know that the bite I gave you back in your world, is my claim on you as my own, right?" What! my mind screamed, but I said nothing. "As long as we are near, I will be able to find you and the other vampires, will know you are mine. They will not seek your blood."

"If that is true, why did Aldett have me fighting to stop him and his men, from sucking me dry?" I asked.

The princess looked down at her hands, appearing uncomfortable.

"Because the commander is very protective of me. The story you gave him, though true, was so fantastical, he could only have you prove it, being that I was unable to speak in your defense." She seemed to slump just a little. "The commander has a way of using everything, at his disposal to motivate his men. He works diligently to keep their spirits high. As a priestess in training, I try to help. But Commander Aldett has little choice against the unstoppable beast and his allies, the deathreaper, Reev, being one of them."

Instantly I remembered the utterly frightening black robed warrior. I tore my mind away from the terrible thought. "Can you tell me more about this Drexelon? Where did he come from and what has he done?"

"That is why we need to see Lord Jaru. I will tell you what I can. But Jaru is the keeper of the ancient records. There are things only he can tell you."

Vale took a deep breath and began. "Drexelon is the immortal Devil King of the Demon Zone. It is a terrible place filled with horrors, no one would dare to dream of. The dead and those unlucky enough to be captured are taken there, never to be seen again." Tears began to flow again. I could not help but gently wipe them away.

"I told you, I will do everything I can to help you."

She leaned into me, and I could feel her lips coming upon my neck, to which I carefully shied away from. Vale was surprised and stared a moment... I broke the silence.

"Princess, I have lost a lot of blood these passed couple of days. I am starting to feel the affects. If I could just have a little time to heal."

She looked at my cut hand with the cloth around it. She also saw the weakened way I held myself in her presence. Vale thought for a few breaths. With both her knees planted in the red satin seat next to me, she took my head in her arms, saying, "I'm so sorry. I have put you through so much." My face rested heavenly for a few moments, on her soft breasts. She continued speaking, "I have taken so much from you. You seem so strong, I simply forgot you might be hurt or have needs."

Vale pressed me into her perfect, shapely supermodel's body. I was immediately struck unprepared, with a weird energy that emanated in harm slivers, from her very core. I gasped when the peculiar force penetrated me layer by layer. Strangely enough, the princess started to slowly rub herself sensually against me. (I really wasn't complaining.) Gently, she gasped as her breath grew heavier, and her passions awakened.

Losing control, my body intertwined with hers. My mouth longed to kiss her full, red, inviting lips. When I thought I might finally explode, the sensation ended, leaving the princess and me in a heated embrace. Panting, we each separated, retreating to opposite ends on the red satin carriage seat. It was then that I noticed, the aches and pains from my battles were completely gone. The cut I had made helping Swicer, giving him my blood, was totally healed.

"What just happened?" I asked, still out of breath.

"As a priestess, I have certain special abilities," Vale panted. "I have healed and restored you, Master Adam." My expression went wide-eyed. I felt around my chest and body. Then I felt a second time, for the aches and bruises I had earned. I was even more breathless to find, that they were indeed truly gone, every single one. "Is it always like that when you heal someone?"

"No," Vale blushed, "you are special to me," she said with a telling smile. Vale took a red mango-like fruit from the brass platter of food. She then held it out to me. "Take this. This ruby fruit has restorative abilities, especially for the blood. When you eat it, it will not take you long to recover your strength." I saw that it was the same kind of fruit, she had eaten back at Silvia's stables. "In Phantasma, it is also called vampire's fruit, and is a good pick-me-up to vamps. But nothing beats real blood," Vale said nonchalantly. I took a bite, immediately wanting to spit it out. Vale giggled. "I guess there's a reason they're called vampire's fruit, though I encourage you to eat as much as you are able. You may not enjoy the taste as I do. But its restorative properties are no less real for you. Think of it as medicine."

I started eating the nasty fruit, which appeared to please her. She grinned happily as I finished it.

Almost immediately, I started to feel better. Vale handed me a cup of refreshing amber liquid. I don't know what it was. But my taste buds were running around my mouth doing back flips.

"Better?" she inquired.

"Yes, much," I answered staring out the five windows of the carriage. Two were on each side, and one big, rear view window was in back. The scenery was absolutely awesome. We were thundering passed a collection of at least six sparkling waterfalls. They flowed into a crystal clear lake below. An eerie see-through mist glided across the surface of the water, looking like something from a fantasy. There were all these little specks spurring all about. Gazing more closely, I saw that they were actual fairies. (Ohh wow!) Each one was about three inches. They glowed with a brilliant, near blinding light. As some of the little beings hovered about lazily in the air, I also spied a red-scaled mermaid. She had long, flowing blond hair, while she swam above the perfect mirror that was the lake. The mermaid saw the four vampires on black steeds-escorted carriage. She disappeared in a ripple of flawless crystal clear water. The words slipped from me before I could think.

"What can I expect when we meet Jaru?"

Vale answered, "He is the Master High Priest of Greyveil. Having served only ten years, he is wise beyond his experience. His connection to the magic of Phantasma, is second to none among vampires. Jaru will surely know what these recent events mean, as well as how to control your power." I looked at her with a questioning expression in my eyes. Vale quickly added, "To get you home." *That was a little odd*, I thought. A bit of time passed, while I enjoyed the ride and the awe-inspiring scenery. I soon saw that Vale had moved to the middle, of the red satin carriage seat we were sitting on. She looked at me, her eyes roving over my body.

"Are you certain that you are all right now, Adam?" she asked.

I had a feeling I knew where this was headed. So I tried to divert her attention.

"Being a vampire princess and all, are you able to have sex? I mean, with the way we first met back on Earth. If we were to have sex, would I be executed or something? You are a princess after all."

"Only if you took that which was not freely given," she answered. Vale inched a little closer. Crap, this isn't working.

"You said earlier that the bite you gave me was some sort of claim. What did you mean by that?"

"That as long as I have a bloodbond claim on you, no other vampire can seek your blood. If they do, I will know and they will answer to me." The princess groaned sensually, "You are mine and I need you now, Adam."

Taken aback a bit, I tried very hard not to show it. Vale was looking more and more sexually aroused, which really isn't a bad thing. However, what's sexy for her, usually translated into a bloodlust for me. She gingerly crawled across the carriage seat, smiling as her fangs extended. Her tongue caressed her full, soft, red lips. When she slowly approached, my heart hammered nervously. I panicked, hurrying to the cushioned red satin seat across from us. Vale was frozen in place. She stared into the space where I had been. A few moments passed, and I was about to ask if she was all right, when Vale turned to me with an angry expression on her beautiful face. It was complete with red shining eyes.

"Why are you running from me?" she asked, though it was more of a statement. I opened my mouth to answer, but I was cut short, when Vale was instantly on me. She held me at my shoulders with an insane strength, which was impossible for her small, feminine frame. Her fingernails digging into my flesh, she declared, "You are mine!" Slamming me against the long, cushioned, red satin seat, and quickly taking a seat on top of me, Vale sat with her perfect thighs at my sides. Her soft, yet firm butt was parked possessively on my crotch, as if it were her throne. Then the second princess seemed to let all the tension out of her body. Shocked, I couldn't speak. She leaned towards my face. Her shining red eyes were mesmerizing. Slowly, Vale inhaled as though enjoying the very scent of me.

"We are bonded," she said softly. "You are not supposed to resist me, Master Adam. You are supposed to meet my needs. That is your duty as my bloodbonded mate." Her hands smoothly touched my face, and ran through my short, black hair. The princess brought her face even closer to mine, panting. "You're not supposed to have the will to fight against me. The bloodbond has made us one and the same. Submit!..." She took a long swallow then added, "I swear you will enjoy every moment of it."

I began to struggle and Vale slammed into me, holding my shoulders again, her fingernails piercing my flesh once more.

"I don't understand, why are you doing this? How are you doing this?" asked Vale. "Our bloodbond is supposed to make you want me, make you want this!"

I coughed a little saying, "Princess, the bond you speak of I cannot feel." Her red, shining eyes grew huge with surprise, then lost their otherworldly glow altogether. "Perhaps it is because I am from Earth, or a human."

"No, the bond has always worked, even on humans. The past ancient accounts on record are numerous. No, it is something else, something I don't understand." I saw tears welling up in her eyes.

Pulling myself up from underneath her, I told Vale to look at me and not look away, which she desperately wanted to do. When our eyes met, I softly and gently told her, "No, there is nothing controlling me, making me desire you."

Vale opened up and the tears flowed freely. My heart broke and I tried to console her. "No, no" I said as kindly as I could. "I feel no bloodbond, Vale. But that doesn't mean I don't want you, or care for you. The desire in my heart is the same desire that has always been there." She stopped crying with those words and looked upon me sweetly. I let myself relax. "I have dreamed of you every night for two months. How else do you think I knew your name, when we first met? I loved you before you even stepped into my world. I ask you, Princess, bloodbond or not, do you really believe I could love you any more than that?"

Vale collapsed into my arms, and I embraced her for all I was worth, hugging her like the lost part of my own soul, I had somehow only just recovered. Then lightly kissing her, I spoke softly into her pierced ears. "I do not know what a bloodbond is, or even what it truly means. But I am sorry that I ran. I didn't know that it was so important to you." My eyes couldn't look at her. "I thought that maybe, I was only a meal to you, Princess."

"No, the bond is much more than that. You are a part of me now, and I a part of you. That is why your rejection hurt me so deeply."

I took a deep breath and exhaled. "It is not right that I shied away from you like that," I said. This caught her attention. She looked at me almost in shock. "If I have a duty to supply your needs, then I will do so." Vale came to me, placing her hands on my chest, leaning into my body. I slid my hands around her shapely rear, and she smiled devilishly, when BOOM, CRASH! I looked out the speeding carriage window, seeing the misshapen, twisted, dead warriors from the night before. Only this time, there were a lot more of them. They were furiously galloping up behind us, on a vast, open plain. It was filled with bizarre but beautiful flowers, while Reev's ominous, black, horseless carriage approached in the distance. The Honor Guard started to drop back on their dark steeds, to meet the threat. I turned to Vale.

"Are there weapons that we can use?"

"Yes!" she said, lifting up one of the red satin carriage seats, which opened into a kind of chest, that revealed a small cache of odd, almost medieval-looking weapons. There were swords, spears, and axes. My eyes widened with glee, when I found powerful arm mounted slingshots. Something deep inside was telling me these would be most useful. I hurried searching through the opened chest of weapons. "Where is the ammo?" I yelled frantically.

"We don't need any. They work by the magic we channel through them. But only powerful, skilled magic users can operate them."

Instantly, I handed her one of the dangerous weapons, and we took our places, me at the left, Vale at the right of the wide rear window, of the unpainted wooden carriage. The priestess-in-training fired a quick barrage, hitting two twisted corpse warriors, one of which fell from his tainted horse. I pulled my slingshot back, focusing my energy into it. Then I fired at the numerous wicked horde.

There appeared to be so many of them, as they steadily gained ground. I was totally taken by surprise, when the energy I shot blew up on impact. It took down three undead riders and their steeds at once. The winged vamps hesitated, looking to the crumpled warriors, then to me. I stiffened at their baffled gazes. Then, giving a great battle cry, the Honor Guard continued to fight even more furiously, their swords clashing with tremendous force, as they toppled their half zombie, half mummy foes. However, more undead warriors were galloping up, closing in on them. I had to hand it to the deathreaper: When he brought the pain, you really did feel it. I channeled less energy into the slingshot, firing in time with the princess, trying not to hit Swicer or his brave brothers in battle.

We seemed to be doing well. Vale and I picked off quite a few corpse warriors. The winged vamps too, seemed unstoppable. Somehow energized, they cut down and held the enemy at bay. I hadn't even noticed the rotten, bug-covered rider that came up beside us. He tossed a roughly cut ball of dark blue crystal into the speeding carriage. Vale and I both looked back, hearts pounding. My first instinct was to take it, and toss the object back out the window, before it exploded or something. I reached for the dark blue orb. Vale motioned to stop me, but it was too late, I had touched the crystal and was immediately paralyzed. A freaky image of the deathreaper appeared in the rough cut, round orb.

"Reev, what have you done?" Vale demanded with a horrified expression on her face.

"Worry not, Priestess, I only wish to talk with the boy. What is your name, traveler?" he asked me. I said nothing.

Reev smirked in his little, round crystal. Then I felt a terrible shock flow through my body from the orb. I couldn't move and my eyes rounded up into my head.

"Nooo!" Vale screamed. "His name is Adam Westlin!"

Reev slowly peered at her, looking absolutely depraved and amused. The shock stopped, but I was still paralyzed.

"Good, Princess; where is he from?" The reaper asked.

Vale was silent and Reev's brow furled. "No, wait, wait! Adam is from a place called Earth." Reev put a hand to his pale chin. "I do not recognize this place. Where is it located, Priestess?" Vale looked as though her mind was running a mile a minute.

"Aaaaaahhh!" I yelled as an even more powerful shock coursed through my body.

"It's another world, I swear!" she began to cry in earnest. Vale slumped on the carriage's red satin seat. "He somehow brought me there, and opened the way back," she sobbed. Reev's face seemed to open up. He looked curiously towards me.

"You are a human," he said to himself. "That power, the one you used back on the mountain. What is it called, boy?"

"I don't know. I only just learned I even had it."

Reev took a moment...then said, "Stop your carriage. Throw down your weapons and surrender...or I will detonate this crystal. Killing all of you," he finished coldly."

Vale looked completely defeated. She was about to gave the command to stop the carriage, when I began fighting the crystal's power, with everything I had. Gradually, I started to move again, taking the magical object with both hands. Then channeling energy over the rough cut, dark blue orb, I tried to focus it into a protective bubble, between my hands and the crystal. Vale watched frozen, like she had somehow fallen under the spell, of the thing herself. Reev's voice was coming in hot and heavy.

"This can't be! No one can..."

With all my might, I tossed the dangerous object from the vehicle. It hit the ground, rolling through the battle taking place behind us, to strike the side of the deathreaper's fast approaching heavy, black, horseless carriage. KA-BOOM! Reev's conveyance was totaled for the second time. The remaining twisted undead flocked to his damaged transport. And I heard an inhuman scream of frustration, "Aaaaaahhhhhh!"

We thundered away, the vampire Honor Guard taking their former positions, around the carriage. Soon, I could see us coming upon what looked like a small city. There was a great white castle at its center, looking as if it were built into and around a gigantic, impressive, white stone bat with outstretched wings. It was truly a wondrous sight against the setting sun.

Chapter Six

The driver slowed our approach, as we neared the vampire city of Greyveil. I could see that he was coming to a small, white, wooden check-in station. It had a tall metal gate before it, stretching in both directions, looking like a prison sentry tower, only much lower to the ground, with a small square building attached. I could tell the structure was reinforced from the inside and sturdy.

When the carriage stopped, a good ten feet in front of the building, outside the gate, the driver quickly dismounted from the high front seat of the carriage. Giving a little salute, he reached with his left opened hand to gently touch his right shoulder, in a very vampire-ish motion. The driver then handed over a rolled up brown parchment, that must have come from Aldett, to a weary, thin, tall vampire soldier. He was wearing the same dark gray shirt and slacks, (clearly a uniform) that Aldett's men were wearing. Only his had the gold threaded letters G.V., which I instantly knew stood for Greyveil. They were sewn into the upper left-hand chest of his shirt, as well as on his upper left arm. The tall, thin vamp's comrades watched us like hawks, from inside the dimly lit, cramped check-in station. The tall vampire soldier then looked quickly over the parchment, and waved an okay to the other soldiers. Three of them stepped forth out of the station's entrance, raising in their fists what looked like three different colored crystal pendants. They each hung on gold necklace chains. With a swift, stiff motion of the jewelry above their heads, there was a crack in the air, sounding almost like thunder. Then there was a weird bubbling of white energy in front of the gate. It disappeared in a quick two seconds. After that, the soldier closest to us stepped aside, waving us into the city.

"All of Greyveil is protected by powerful magical forces, Adam. No one may enter without using the pendants, or at least knowing the magic that protects us," Vale told me. The carriage lunged forward, and we carefully entered the vampire city on an old, white cobblestone road.

The first thing I noticed was all the military people. Nearly every street and road had at least one or two soldiers on it. The second thing I noticed was that, while there were obviously many vampires in Greyveil, there were also many other creatures. A nearby vamp couple on a public bench, particularly caught my attention. The two of them were romancing the evening away. As they leaned into each other passionately, I watched, unable to tear my eyes away. Their lips almost touched and in a split second, the brown shorthaired woman in a red dress bared her fangs, sinking them deeply into the well-dressed gentleman's neck. I gasped as he embraced her intimately with a lazy moan. It appeared to give him a great deal of pleasure, letting her hungrily suck the blood from him. I was nearly hypnotized by the sight of them, when we slowly passed their little scene. The female vampire's red, shining eyes instantly found mine. I gave a small, startled expression, and inched away from the window, averting my eyes, finding that Vale had been watching. She placed her hand on my shoulder with feeling, giving it a little rub to comfort me. As I was saying, seeing the sights of Greyveil, I noticed that along with vampires, there were also many other creatures inhabiting the city. The farther into the old English styled, little houses we went, the more I saw odd-looking creatures, and breathtaking bird women gossiping at shops.

"They're harpies," Vale said nonchalantly. Then I spied what looked like a tall, lanky werewolf.

Seeing him, the princess only nodded her head, yes, as if knowing what I was thinking, while he did some heavy lifting with a few dusty, old crates. Next, I noticed an armed, rather large, naga snake woman. She was slithering on patrol with some vampire soldiers. But there seemed to be a lot fewer of the other creatures, than the vampires. Rolling on, I saw that most buildings in the city had large canopies, and shelters in front of them, which really didn't surprise me; I mean, they are vampires after all.

So it makes sense that they would love the shade. I was however caught unaware, when the many canopies began to slowly recede. All at the same time, they exposed the busy walkways to the early, double moonlit night sky. Goodness, I still can't seem to get over seeing two moons there in the sky. They were a constant reminder that *hell yeah! I really was on a strange, new world!*. I started to see less soldiers and more well dressed men, women, and little vampire kids. They were of every type and age, all having a weird sort of timeless afterglow about them. It made them look almost magical.

Clearly, they didn't get much sun here. Also, it was painfully obvious that the vampires were just another race of people. Simply put, most vampires in Phantasma were born that way, not turned—or whatever Vale was talking about. I saw that their children ran around playing like any other kids, only with amazing toys, that seemed to shift and move all on their own. They had bouncing balls that appeared to follow their directions. There were dolls that danced independently for little girls, and little, flying propeller thingys that hovered about, preoccupying their gleeful little eyes. As we passed a nearby shop's windows, I saw what I thought might be televisions. But as we got closer, I quickly realized they were actually large crystals of some sort. They were held ingeniously in decorative stands and boxes for display. In passing, I sadly thought to myself, *It sure would be nice if I could see my family right about now.* As though the mysterious objects had magically heard me, they quickly displayed a super clear image of my sorely missed family, somehow pulling it from my mind. Grandma, Grandpa, and Tannon stood happily in a green, sunny, flower-filled meadow waving joyously back at me. In that moment I missed them so much, that I was finding it hard to choke back the tears. Suddenly, I felt the princess once again lightly place a hand on my shoulder.

She watched the crystal displays, and I completely let myself give in to her tender touch, leaning into her just a little. The closer we got to the palace at the center of Greyveil, the more modern the city appeared. Two and three-story high buildings with working lights reached into the sky, some having little walkways that stretched over the busy streets. A few walkways even had small café tables situated in their centers. Everywhere I looked, I could see crystal powered streetlights. They illuminated the newly formed, now starry night sky. The more I saw, the more closely it resembled any other city, though for some reason, except for the palace, the buildings never rose above four stories. There were also a few twists, of course, here and there, that made it totally unique. You know, like if rush hour had been at 8:00 P.M. and filled with creatures and monsters. We soon passed through a large, very busy plaza. It was populated with, what I could only assume were more harpies, werewolves, a few nagas, and some other creatures I simply didn't recognize. I saw that they were all busy buying, selling, and trying desperately to keep the interest of whatever beings, were around them. *What a strange place*, I thought to myself. Leaving the plaza, we went down a long, winding street, eventually coming upon a well-guarded courtyard, surrounded by an impressive white, metal gate. It was huge, about as long and wide as two football fields, as far as I could see. It had an armed vamp soldier on duty, about every twenty-five feet or so.

"Welcome to Greyveil Palace!" declared the princess. When we neared the gigantic, white, fairytale-like castle with the huge, looming stone bat built right into it, I noticed it had many great, lofty towers and tall, beautiful, dark windows. I also saw that the front entrance, slanted into the white cobblestone driveway. The front impenetrable-looking doors were actually below ground level. Everyone exited the carriage approaching the tall, thick, aristocratic, wooden doors. There were many detailed, little carvings etched into them. Vale led the way, followed by myself. The four winged vampire soldiers, who had escorted us took up the rear, while the driver stayed with the carriage. No sooner than the princess had stepped to the huge double doors, did they fly open, revealing a wide, spacious room with red carpets and high marble columns. It had a twenty feet-high ceiling with wondrous crystal chandeliers. They shone a gentle but strong light. Vale motioned to me to follow her, reminding me kindly to stay close. The four members of the vampire Honor Guard stayed behind, immediately taking positions to guard the entrance. Up a few steps, and through a normal sized doorway, we entered into an eye popping white hall with gold trim. Then we ventured into one of its many doors.

Inside, we found a kingly living area, filled with soft, fancy furniture. Big chairs, couches, expensive looking tables, and large, silk pillows were everywhere. I took a few steps inside while enjoying the view. Vale walked further into the impressive room. She checked the doorways on the far side. As I turned around and round, to look at the awe-inspiring place, I had the crap scared out of me by a young, red-haired, blue-eyed vampire boy wearing a vamp soldier's uniform, and a little gold skull necklace. Only, his uniform looked much better: It seemed to be made of a shiny, silk material. The young vampire boy was standing very close, eyeing every last inch of me. I swear, I thought I saw him sniff me once or twice. His face was only two inches away, when he grinned. Then the little vampire was simply gone. He just seemed to disappear. I started to look around, my eyes wide with a startled gaze.

I slowly turned to scan the rest of the breathtaking room. I nearly had a heart attack, when I saw that the little vamp kid with shaggy red bangs was standing just one foot right behind me. Instantly, I was knocked right on my butt in total surprise.

He giggled innocently, then happily asked, "Have you seen my sister?"

I looked at him, refocusing my eyes and trying to recover, from nearly pooing myself. "Who is your sister?" I asked him.

He glared at me with a little smirk on his face. Then said, "Princess Vale, of course, Silly."

What the hell! She hadn't told me she had a little brother, I thought. I was just about to tell him she was over by the doorways, on the other side of the room, when I saw Vale hurrying over to us.

"Adam," she said, "this is Rem, my dearest little brother. He is only twelve years old, but quite advanced in his studies. I am afraid in all that has happened recently, I had forgotten to mention him."

The little vampire gave his older sister a displeased look, and her face reddened with embarrassment.

"Adam, you may want to be wary of him. Rem is something of a...," She paused a moment. Then said, "a practical joker," shooting him an unpleasant glower.

"Sister Dailania has returned from her studies abroad," he said, elated in his response. "She is looking forward to seeing you." Rem had a devilish look in his eyes. Vale's reaction to his words wasn't very happy; that was putting it mildly.

She instantly told me to come with her, which I was more than happy to do, had Rem not stuck his foot out, making me trip clear over a heavily cushioned love seat. *Great*, I thought, *there is a little vampire version of Tannon running around the palace.* Vale took in a heavy breath and gave a long exhale. With a swift hand gesture towards Rem, the princess caused a mini whirlwind to materialize, making it whirl around and around him, messing up his shaggy red hair. He then lost his balance, landing on his narrow seat. Vale and I took that as our cue, to hurry through the open doorways, on the far side of the room. Down another gold trimmed hall, we slowed a bit, and Vale talked to me.

"You remember what I told you about my sister Dailania, don't you?" I nodded my head yes, as I walked alongside her. Vale's expression went hard. "My sister is a very strong-willed vampire. She has a way of, well…taking anything she pleases." (*Translation: she's a real bitch*, I thought silently to myself.) "Only father has ever really been able to control her," Vale continued. "We must go to see Darkdancer now, so that she will know of our bond, and my claim on you. If we avoid her, and I would really like to, she will only seek us out and hunt you down, Adam. But if you stay close to me, and I inform her that we are bloodbonded, she should leave you alone."

A sliver of fear shot through me. "Should?" Up a flight of red rugged stairs, we came to some beautiful, white, wooden doors. Vale opened them and we stepped inside. It was a big, but not gigantic dining room.

Like the one that I for some reason was expecting, it had white linen tablecloths and expensive looking plates, forks, spoons, and knifes. A huge, pink crystal chandelier lightly glowed above it all.

The walls were made of a highly polished brown wood, which I could almost see myself in. I was completely mesmerized, when I saw the gorgeous female vampire. She had pale skin, much like her sister's and little brother's. Long, brown hair with three pointy bangs hung down in front. It was tied in a low hanging long ponytail in back, with a big, red, glittery bow on it. The sexy vampire was wearing a pink tank top, with puffy, see-through shoulder sleeves. The shirt had a ruby pendant at its center breasts. She also wore a pink mini skirt, and what looked like red leg warmers, complete with pink dancing shoes. Vale's sister was dancing, swaying, and moving to ethereally beautiful music. She hadn't even noticed us. As Dailania danced, I saw a few of those little, magic-powered music players, like Silvia's music disc, only smaller. These were made of shiny gold and glittering jewels. They floated magically in the air around her, along with some nice smelling exotic flowers. It was an incredible sight, as Darkdancer lost herself in the almost hypnotic music. I could see that every move and gesture she made, unleashed a small amount of magical force. Soft, translucent energy waves seemed to ripple out gently from her. They lightly moved and shifted the objects floating in her presence. Then Darkdancer began to contort and shift her body, in time with the increasing tempo of the wonderful music.

The air in the room instantly kinda changed, sort of like it had been charged up, or somehow electrified. I began to have chills, feeling wave after wave of mysterious force hit me. Dailania, who was facing away from us, turned around, having her eyes closed, while she absentmindedly listened to the music. She started to dance more and more feverishly and wild. The tempo picked up even more. Her motions lashed out and she oozed sexuality, as she found a new rhythm. I could feel the force pulsing from her slender, tall, curvy body. Darkdancer whirled and twirled, moving more and more sexually. She started to rub and touch her body, continuing to dance, as if the music itself was now making love to her. Then opening her blue, cat-like eyes, which weren't like a real cat's, of course–they were only slanted with a beautiful, feline shape—Darkdancer stopped, and a rush of magical force escaped her startled body, nearly blowing both Vale and me off our feet. Expensive plates and silverware flew everywhere.

"Ahh, hello Sister. I hadn't noticed you come in. Always a pleasure to see you well." Her blue, cat-like eyes found me, and she sort of froze in place for a split second. Walking over to us, I noticed Dailania was a good two inches taller than me, at least, which put her at around six feet tall. "Well, well, well," she said. "I didn't know you were bringing me a gift tonight, Little Sister." She stopped in front of us, and introduced herself formally. "I am Dailania Shadowwind, also called Darkdancer. I am the First Princess of the Kingdom of the Vampire Territories" she declared with pride. "But I am sure you already know that," she said, looking to her younger sister. Darkdancer held out her delicate hand, which I took and immediately released back to her. I saw the tiniest glimpse of disappointment in her eyes. The tall vampire showed just a little hint of fang in her wide smile.

Vale displayed an emotionless face and proclaimed, "Adam is not a gift for you, Dailania. He and I are bloodbonded."

Dailania's smooth brow furled just a little. She folded her sharp red nailed fingers onto her chest. Vale continued speaking.

"We are here on urgent business to talk with the head high priest."

The shapely, tall, slim vamp laughed. "Ha, ha, ha, ha! Ahh, so you are here to see the master priest, are you, Vale? Well, I am afraid that Lord Jaru is very busy, and cannot be disturbed tonight," she said smiling at me. "He has locked himself in my study, and is pondering the alignment of the stars. Jaru has told me, he believes Phantasma is entering into a time of great change," Darkdancer revealed a little too happily, while she continued to eye me. "He seeks to find a way for us to use this knowledge, to our people's advantage." Dailania reached out a hand to my shoulders. Then began to sensually touch me in a very female way, declaring, "If you should ever find yourself desiring more um…mature company, I am certainly available, Sir Adam."

Vale simply glared at her, as if by doing so, she could hurt her big sister somehow. It really surprised me to see, the big female vampire was actually backing down at her younger sister's angry, piercing stare. Clearly, Vale wasn't kidding, when she told me she had problems with her older sister. Dailania took a couple of steps back, taking a deep breath, then cocked her hip.

"So why do you need to see Jaru any way, Vale?" she inquired meanly.

Vale said nothing, but narrowed her eyes and looked away. At that moment, I saw Darkdancer draw her hand back as if to slap her younger sibling. (Wow, she really is a bitch.) Thinking fast, I moved in front of Vale, catching Dailania's flying palm. Then, gently, I kissed it. Darkdancer jumped from the little electric shock my lips gave her. She was taken aback at first, but quickly relaxed. Vale turned to us, thoroughly mortified. I spoke kindly, trying to melt the bitch ice around Dailania's heart.

"Dear Princess, your sister has told me much about you." I said looking into her impossibly blue eyes. Darkdancer's expression grew a little angry. "I am only a visitor, and a stranger in your breathtaking land. Though, I have seen the strife of your people, your sister has promised to help me, to find a way home. I, in turn, have sworn to aid her in any way I can against her enemies. It would be most beneficial to myself and your kingdom, if we were allowed to see the head high priest as soon as possible." I softly rubbed the tall, slender vamp's hand in mine. She walked in very close to me, our bodies nearly touching as she ignored Vale. Her eyes deeply explored my light bronze-skinned features. Darkdancer told us to wait in the impressive, but now cluttered dining area, as she switched from the room. I turned my attention to Vale, quickly finding that she was not one bit happy. The expression on her face almost made her look ugly.

"Why did you do that?" she asked upset.

"Do what?" I questioned her.

The pupils of her eyes started to glow a soft pink and her anger rose.

"You were all over her just now!" Vale accused me.

"Not at all" I reassured her. "I only saw that Darkdancer was getting ready to attack you. I stepped in to keep things from getting ugly. After all, what would the king do if he thought, I had brought discord and unrest to his house?"

"Believe me," Vale continued, "discord and unrest were here long before you arrived."

I laughed and the second princess joined me. Her giggles were clear and wondrous. It was hard to believe she had been so cheerless moments earlier. Vale showed a radiant smile towards me. I walked to her, placing my hands upon her hips, and we drew our bodies close. Smelling an intoxicating perfume on her, I couldn't help myself. I nuzzled her ear, taking in the sweet scent. Then, I lightly caressed her cheek with my lips. Vale gave a small shutter, and just as I was working my way to her full, red lips, the dining room double doors opened up. Darkdancer was standing there with an exasperated look on her flawless face. She was holding a big copper key in her hand.

"Aahh!" the tall female vampire said. "I can't leave you two alone for a second!"

Vale only looked at her like the cat that ate the canary, and I tried my best to appear innocent. Dailania looked as if she was going to swiftly strut right back out the door. Then she stopped, looking over her shoulder at me. "You know, I can appreciate a man with large appetites," she said with a quick, little wink. "Now, if you two can tear yourselves away, from trying to make the next generation of baby vampires..." The both of us turned a bright red.

"I will take you to see Lord Jaru."

Chapter Seven

We followed Vale's older sister out of the marvelous dining area, through a good amount of the impressively sprawling castle. As Vale and I both hurried after her through the kingly halls, we passed a couple of young harpy ladies. One was with green feathers and the other with red. They looked over the many papers in their arms, deep in conversation over a subject that I could not quite overhear. They both had a little startle, when their eyes fell upon me. Transfixed, they could not look away, while our little group speedily rushed passed them, down the immaculate, long halls. Sneaking a small glimpse of the somewhat stunned harpies, I saw they had bird talon-like feet and beautifully feathered wings. Before going out of sight, I could feel their eyes never left me, until we disappeared around the nearest corner, where I was surprised to see Rem strolling down the next white, gold-trimmed hall. He had an absolutely astonishing dessert cake, on a really expensive plate. Rem seemed content to trot along as we rushed passed. Suddenly, on the corner of my eye, I saw the mischievous little vamp spin around behind us, stretching the amazing cake back in his arms, ready to toss it right at me.

Without turning around or even hesitating, Vale lifted one of her hands in a quick turning motion.

Instantly, a small mini tornado formed around Rem. He lost his balance trying to catch the fumbling cake, and it smashed right into his young face. I stifled a little giggle and we hurried away.

"How are you doing that?" the little vampire demanded.

The girls didn't even slow down, though I did hear Dailania ask to no one in particular, if Rem would ever grow up.

We soon came to a spiral staircase surrounded by soft, white benches. They were standing on golden curved legs, in the middle of the gold trimmed, white hall. The staircase went straight up about four floors. I could see it led to the top, of one of the many fairytale-like castle towers. When we finally reached a simple, wooden door at the apex, I noticed that a furry, orange, black stripped cat with huge, long ears appeared to be on guard duty, in front of the door.

I jumped when I immediately heard, a strong voice full of authority coming from Vale's older sister. It said, "Spectra, come girl!"

The furry, little beast sprang from the door, and shot right into Dailania's waiting arms, purring happily. Darkdancer gave the cat's fur a little stretch and rub. I tried to get a closer look at the sparkly red-eyed, otherworldly animal with five-inch long ears.

Spectra hissed viciously, taking a swipe at my extended hand, with her sharp claws. Vale's big sister gave a hateful little laugh.

"Careful, Adam, this familiar likes only me."

The mean-hearted cat hissed in total agreement with her. Darkdancer used the large copper key in her hand, to open the door to the tower. Inside was a large sixty-feet across circular room. It had a second story of walkways around the curved, grey stonewalls. On every level above and below were bookcases filled with scrolls, books, and old tomes. In the center of the lower level were many tables of varying size, each one having beakers, pots, little odd machines, weird plants, and even little cages. As I peered through the clutter, I saw a man hunched busily over one of the tables. It was filled with nothing but old scrolls. We walked into the strange room, and Dailania's familiar gave a little hiss. The man's head sprang up. He turned to us with a warm smile on his face. Somehow, I could feel an air of wisdom in his presence. Walking over, he addressed the princesses. They both seemed pleased and comfortable hearing his words. Jaru was about six feet one, with white hair slicked back into two points, each reaching out at an angle in back. He wore black pants and a black shirt with a grey front. The grey went down his chest in a V shape. Jaru also had on high tan boots that covered his knees. He wore a long, dark gray cape that had pointy, white fur above each shoulder. It was split about three feet up the back. When his eyes came to me, his body stiffened and his expression faltered.

"Who are you, young traveler?"

He reached his hand out to touch my face. His brown eyes shone with an odd, soft blue light. It totally weirded me out. Instantly, I stepped back.

Noticing, Jaru immediately apologized, saying, "I am sorry, young traveler. But I have never seen anything like you. The magic of Phantasma is swirling all around your being, more strongly than I have ever seen before."

"Lord Jaru," Vale spoke. "You should know that Adam Westlin," she motioned a hand to me, "has saved my life a number of times on my recent journey. First, when his blood healed an undead's poisoned wound." Jaru listened intensely to the beautiful princess. "Second, when facing the deathreaper, Reev, of the Ravenos Mountains. Adam used an unknown power, to throw him from a dangerous mountain pass."

Darkdancer gasped, putting a hand over her mouth with a smile, as her familiar, Spectra, purred. Vale continued: "I have bloodbonded with Adam."

Jaru gave a little nod, looking serious.

"Through that bond, I believe his touch is able to boost my priestess powers. I have experienced this only once, when riding my great white bat, Wingrider." The two listening vampires seemed nearly floored by her words.

Then Vale looked around the room, her eyes settling on her tall, older sister. She hesitated a little, then finally spoke. "As I was investigating the Crimson Plain..."

Jaru interrupted her saying, "Young Priestess, you know your father has forbidden you from leaving the castle, unescorted in these troubled times." He gave her a stern look, and Dailania let a laugh escape her. Spectra hissed angrily, swiping her paw at Vale, and the red-haired princess continued speaking.

"As I was saying, when I was investigating the occurrences in the Crimson Plains, I was in some manner, pulled into another world called Earth."

Jaru staggered back, looking like he was going to have kittens. He quickly went over to his old scrolls and books on the table, from which he was searching like a mad man.

"It was Adam who somehow opened the way between the worlds," Vale said.

Jaru's body relaxed as he stared into an old, stained stroll, saying, "So the boy is human then."

"Yes," Vale simply stated.

The head priest instantly walked over, examining me like a deranged doctor. Once again, his eyes glowed with a weird blue light. He looked over my body, then deeply into my eyes for a moment. I thought maybe he could somehow see my soul. Jaru lightly held my chin, so that he could better position my face, while he looked at it.

"The boy definitely has an air of destiny about him, that much is certain," said the priest. Jaru stared off into space, going into deep thought. Then the priest quickly broke out of it. He went over to one of the tables with all the curious equipment on it. Once again, he shuffled things around like a mad man, eventually finding a small glass container, of what looked like clear water.

Gently and very carefully, he brought the simple-looking liquid over to me. "This is the water of Ellu. It will help us to know the level of magic to which you are capable, young Adam."

Both the princesses had expressions of wonder in their eyes. Darkdancer was looking way too interested in the proceedings for my comfort, as though the head high priest was holding a lot more, than just an ordinary container of clear water. Sure enough, when I reluctantly placed my finger in the container at Jaru's request, the liquid changed colors, bubbling slightly around my finger. First, it turned blue then red then purple. Jaru looked truly surprised as he watched the reaction. The liquid continued to change to a funky black. I could see fear awaken in the head high priest, showing in Jaru's face. The liquid changed again, this time to a shining gold. Jaru's expression lit up with curiosity. The water of Ellu glowed stronger and stronger until…the little round glass container burst, in a golden white shower of wetness.

Spectra ran from Dailania's arms with a furious "Meeooowww!" She took shelter under one of the study's many wooden tables. Everyone in the room glazed wide eyed at me for a few breaths. Suddenly, Darkdancer shot me a wicked smile. She had a look that I really didn't like. What was her problem anyway?

"What does it mean?" Vale asked no one in particular.

"Only that young Adam here, may well have the most magical potential of anyone in Phantasma," Dailania answered.

Vale's eyes widened, and she put a hand over her mouth astonished.

"Has the boy ever had any magical training of any kind?" The priest inquired.

"No," Vale answered, looking at me as I nodded a no to her.

"Then he must start as soon as possible," the priest said.

"Training?" I said, not believing this. "I am not looking for training. I was only hoping you might be able to help me find a way home," I revealed.

Jaru looked me in the eyes for a few moments and took a deep breath.

"I take it you mean home to this Earth world," he said.

"Yes," I replied.

"Then, I am afraid you must endure the training, young Adam," he answered. His white hair and kind expression made him look wise beyond his years. "Not only is it foolish to allow someone with your potential to go untrained. It is incredibly dangerous, you could accidentally harm yourself or others" the priest added. I slumped on my feet, feeling like someone had just stabbed me in the heart. Seeing my less than positive reaction, Jaru spoke. "Please understand, that we vampires take a great interest in the molding of young minds, dedicating even a portion of our very palace, the nerve center of our kingdom, to guiding future vampire leaders, as well as the young up and coming leaders of other lands.

"Greyveil Palace is perhaps, the greatest magically advanced learning establishment in Phantasma.

"Students come from all around, working extremely hard just for a chance to be accepted here. It is quite an honor to sit in class next to princes, princesses, and the great future leaders of our world. Don't you think, Adam?"

"I only wanted to go home. Why is this happening?"

"Young traveler, you should probably know it is very likely in all of Phantasma, you are the only one with the ability to cross the two worlds, though you do not yet know how. Also, know that I am likely one of the only teachers, who can give you the knowledge you seek to find your way home."

I drew a little hope from his words and looked at him.

"I will start you off slowly, and give you the chance to increase the number of classes, if you choose. Your first class will begin at three o'clock tomorrow, in the castle classroom 104. Please, do not be late."

Oh God, it sounded like he had just enrolled me in a school! A school for monsters on another world—hell no! I had already graduated a year earlier, because I was so far ahead of all the other kids at my academic level. I thought I would at least have another year to fool around, and figure out what path I wanted to take in life. I felt light headed, and my stomach was full of butterflies.

Vale stood next to me, giving me a small nudge. "Don't worry, Adam," she said, "I will be there with you." She took my hand, giving it a little squeeze.

Darkdancer snorted and laughed. "Maybe I will see you two around the palace," she said. But her eyes only looked at me. Jaru walked over holding an odd little crystal container. It had a small, clear needle on its top.

"Adam," he said, "if we are to find proper answers, we must explore every possibility. I will require a small sample of your blood for study." I looked to Vale, and she gave a little nod. With her approval, letting me know it was safe, I rolled up my sleeve. The priest stuck me in the arm, with the needle of the crystal container. Slowly, my blood trickled into the clear vessel. The surrounding female vampires watched, mesmerized. As the blood pooled inside the container, it gave off little dim ripples of light. *Okay*, I thought, *that's never happened before?* Then I saw that the two young ladies were edging closer and closer. They seemed to be smelling something. And by the looks of it, it's something really good. I could see the fangs in their mouths and the desire in their eyes. With a slight fidget, I called Jaru's attention to them both. When he saw the two girls, he took the needle out of me and grabbed my arm. We both hurried away from the predatory sisters, to one of the wooden study tables at the far end of the room.

Jaru rubbed an icy-feeling blue ointment on the place, where the crystal needle pierced me. Instantly, the small puncture healed like it had never even been there. We calmly walked back over to the now not quite so excited ladies, though I could tell, they were very interested in the blood, Jaru was carrying. Still, they both tried very unsuccessfully to hide it.

"I think everyone here could use a little rest," Jaru said brightly. "After all you have all traveled far, some farther than others." He shot Vale and me a knowing glance. "I will continue my studies here to find answers. Young Priestess Vale, I trust you can find suitable quarters for brave Adam, here in the castle."

She nodded, and with a heartfelt thanks to the head high priest, we both walked for the door, stopping dead in our tracks to find Darkdancer, leaning in the doorway.

"Adam Westlin," she said, "I hope you will enjoy your stay here at the castle. I think you will find yourself most welcome here, no matter where you venture," she continued with a little, swift wink. "I certainly hope you and I can be the closest of friends." With that, Darkdancer slowly switched away, Spectra scurrying after her.

When Vale and I walked outside the door, Dailania was already gone.

"You are going to have to watch out for her," Vale told me. I shook my head in agreement. Once we both got to the bottom of the four-story spiral staircase, I heard my cell phone ring.

Ring, ring, ring, ring,…ring, ring, ring!

I quickly reached into my side pouch, retrieving my little cell phone. I flipped it open, expecting to hear from Grandma or Grandpa. I was almost dumbstruck to find that it was actually Tannon.

"Hey there, Big Bro, I haven't seen you in a while, so I thought that I would call. You know, checking up on you." Totally surprised, I said nothing. "Yeah, well, when exactly are you going to be coming back home? We really miss you around here, Adam. And Grandma and Grandpa have really been piling on the responsibilities lately. If you don't get back soon, I am afraid, I am going to have to fill your shoes with pudding mix." I was about to say something, but Tam Tam continued to speak. "I hate to say it, but you're pretty important around here, and I really miss you, Big Brother." Vale smiled as she listened to Tannon. "Well, get your butt back here soon. And I guess, I will catch you later, Big Bro."

"Tannon wait!" I cried only just stopping him in time. "I am sorry I cannot be there. But there isn't much I can do about it right now."

"Hey Adam, is all that horse crap about you being in another world really true?"

"Yes," I told him.

"Wow, that's cool Bro! You think that maybe sometime you can bring me along? You know, for back up."

Vale stifled a giggle, and I couldn't help the wide smile on my face.

"Ooo, ahh, yeah, sure, I think I would like that." I heard a muffled "YES!" over the phone. Then my little brother said, "I'm glad you're okay. I hope you come home soon. Goodbye, Big Bro!" Tannon hung up the phone. I was amazed how much better I felt, having heard his voice.

"What is that?" Vale asked as she gazed at my cell phone, having a puzzled look on her face.

"This?" I said. "It is only a cell phone. We use them back on earth, to stay in contact with other people."

Her eyes seemed like they might pop from her head. When I handed Vale the cell, she looked at the little screen playing a recorded video, of me lifting weights with a scrawny Tannon as the dumbbell. (There's a metaphor in there somewhere.)

"Truly a wonder," she said and I completely agreed with her. I still hadn't figured out how I was talking to my family back on earth. No way is anyone's service this good! I saw the princess really liked it, so I told her, "When I get back to earth, I will buy you one."

Vale was absolutely beaming, and she handed me back the cell phone.

"Come on, I had better show you to your quarters," she said. We walked through the huge castle, down a long corridor.

Eventually, we came to a red, wooden door with a bass knocker. It was at the very end of the hall. Inside was a large room with white carpet, a bed big enough for two, expensive furnishings, and a writer's desk.

"This is one of the guestrooms," Vale said, walking over to the right side of the room.

The princess peered out of one of two tall windows, to the well-kept courtyard below.

"If you have need of anything, please let me know."

"Well, I could use a shower" I told her.

She walked over to another red, wooden door on the left side of the room. Inside was a bathroom with a tub, shower, sink, and toilet all with working water. It surprised me, they had all the things that we had back on earth, although it worked in a freaky, otherworldly way. Everything just seemed to operate in a really silent sort of magical way. I couldn't even hear the faucet, when I touched the round crystal on its top to turn it on. I guess at some point, I thought I would have to go without the normal comforts of home. Glad to see that I was wrong.

"If that will be all, clean clothes are in the closet. I will see you tomorrow, Adam," Vale said.

"Thank you," I told her and Vale left the room. After a relaxing bath, I found some clean, orange silk pajamas. I quickly put them on and got into the soft bed, beneath its warm sheets. Then, touching a round, red crystal on the stand next to me, the few magic crystal powered lights in the room went out, and I drifted off to sleep.

Chapter Eight

I awoke the next morning, thinking maybe it had all been some wonderful dream. No such luck, as I looked around the well-furnished, regal guestroom Vale had put me in. I quickly got dressed in a white loose fitting shirt, brown pants, and tan boots. Soon, I found a young werewolf girl stationed outside the door. She was about 5'9" with brown, tan skin and long, brown hair halfway down her back, though the long bangs hanging to the left in front were white. Her eyes were large, beautiful, and of an amber color. She had cute little lips and ears like a wolf's, which were positioned a little higher than a human's, on the sides of her head. I realized for a werewolf she wasn't hairy. She just had strong wolf-like features, but she was still very cute. Speaking of animal-like features, I could tell that her body was very fit and well muscled. I could see it, even through the long, brown cloak she wore.

"Good morning," I told her, "my name is Adam Westlin. What is your name?"

"Taya" she answered. "Jaru thought you might rise a little earlier than your vampire hosts. So I was sent to help you with anything you might need. Also, I will be taking you on a little tour of Greyveil."

I was very happy to hear that. "Thank you very much," I said with a bit too much enthusiasm. After all, how often does a person get a chance to truly experience, a real magical city? I stepped out of the doorway, giving a little motion for her to lead the way. As she walked in front of me, Taya told me that food has been prepared for me, in the east dining hall. If I wished, I could eat before we ventured into the city.

"Sounds good to me," I said.

Taya led me to a large, brilliant dining room. It was slightly bigger than the one, I had met Darkdancer in the night before, but otherwise the same. She put a hand out towards a pulled out chair, asking me to please sit in front of an already set plate. As I sat down, I noticed a wheeled cart with a monumentally large dome covering on it. The metal dome had a small, square, yellow crystal on it. It glowed for a split second when Taya touched it. She lifted the big, long covering to reveal a seven-course meal, with all the trimmings, which smelled incredible.

"No way I can eat all of this," I said more to myself than anyone. "Won't you please join me?" I asked Taya. A little surprised, she gingerly sat in the chair to my left. Setting a place for herself, she first put portions of everything on my plate.

Then she prepared her own and poured an amber liquid. I recognized it from Aldett's war camp as really delicious. Taya filled two goblets that she had retrieved, from the second shelf of the cart. She then motioned to my full plate, saying, "Please, begin."

I grave a little prayer of thanks, and noticed that Taya was staring at me. "I always give thanks for what I receive," I told her. "I am alone in this land, and to be thankful is the least I can do."

She smiled and waited for me to start eating. I thought that was a bit strange, so I quickly started eating. I mean, I didn't want her to starve or anything. The food was amazing, even if I didn't know what it really was. Everything was fresh and pleasant-tasting, especially the meat, which was some sort of bird, like chicken, only way more delicious. I took a swallow of the amber liquid in the shiny goblet and was in heaven. I closed my eyes, enjoying the sensational taste. It was like nothing I had ever tasted before. Reopening my eyes, I saw that Taya was happily inhaling everything on her plate. Then, she took big gulps from her goblet. She caught me staring, and slowly put her spoon down.

I smiled warmly at her and asked, "So where are you from?."

She continued eating. "The Lunar Forest, Kingdom of Tearra Zan," Taya said.

"Is it nice there?"

"Oh yes, there is lots of fresh air and wolves to ride."

I nearly spilled the goblet I was drinking from.

"'Wolves to ride'?" I asked, coughing mildly.

"Well, yes; in the Lunar Forest, there are huge wolves. Some stand as high as six feet tall on four legs. They protect the land, and we sometimes use them as riding steeds, though they are far from tamed. It is only with our inner bestial will, that they allow us to ride them. If we are strong enough."

"What do you mean?" I asked.

"A wolf prime will not allow a weak were or person, for that matter to ride it. The last outlander to try was eaten alive," Taya said, snapping up a big piece of meat and chewing. "But once they bond with you, they are very loyal. Just be certain it is well fed."

"Wow, where I come from, wolves don't get nearly that big. But they command respect all the same."

"And where are you from, Sir Adam?"

"A place called Earth," I told her. "I'm trying to find my way home. The master priest of this castle is helping me."

"This Earth place, I have never heard of it. Where in Phantasma is it?"

Swallowing the food in my mouth, I told the cute werewolf, "It isn't in Phantasma. I am from another world call Earth."

Taya stopped eating. "So what are you, if you are not from Phantasma?"

"Human" I told her nonchalantly.

"That is impossible. Humans don't exist, they never have."

"Well, that is a surprise to me," I said.

"But you can't be human," she continued. "Legend says they were the ones who..." Her eyes met mine and she froze.

"What?" I inquired.

"It is probably better that I don't say anything. It will not be good, if I overwhelm you with too much information. I am sure you will be informed very soon." As Taya spoke, I noticed terrible scars going up both of her arms. Right then, I wondered if that was the reason, she wore the brown cloak. I reached out, touching the nasty scars before I could stop myself. She froze and I could feel her muscular body tensing.

"How did you get these?" I asked in a soft voice.

"It is an affliction that I suffer from. Some years earlier, I tried to save some of my people from a demon attack. While it was through much effort, I did prevail. I was struck with an unnatural wound, that is slowly eating away my body. In a year's time, I will die, Adam. I could not bear to make my family suffer alongside me, so I left. They have enough to worry about."

A single tear dropped from her large, amber eyes, and my heart overflowed. I could feel something deep inside of me. It came from my very core, traveling down my arm to the terrible scars on Taya, which I was still touching.

"Aahhh aahh!" she gasped. Her large eyes looked at me, and she closed them, as if enjoying some irresistible, heavenly force. My hand warmed against her skin, almost burning. I looked at the place where I was touching the cute werewolf. To my amazement, the ugly scars were disappearing, to the faint sound of ghostly screams. I tried to let go, but I couldn't. Taya drew more and more energy from me, while she continued to gasp. When I thought that we might finally pass out, the contact broke, and we both slumped to the dining room floor, panting.

"Are you okay?" I asked.

"Yes, yes!" she answered trying to catch her breath. "What was that?" Taya asked.

"I don't know!" I replied.

When I looked up at the attractive werewolf girl, she was examining her arms. She was running her hands over the smooth, new, brown tan skin where the scars once had been. Taya immediately tore off the brown cloak she was wearing. Underneath, she wore a tight red shirt with no sleeves, blue, high cut shorts and red shoes.

Man was she ripped! Taya looked as though she could bench press a small car. Quickly, she spun around, lifting the back of her red shirt, to show a body-builder's flawless back. Really excited, the werewolf asked, "Are the scars gone?"

When I peered at her strong female back, I saw the last of the terrible scars disappear into nothing.

"Yes," I told her, "the scars are gone."

Taya fell to her knees with tears streaming down her face. I gave her a little hug, and she sat there whimpering on the dining room floor.

Taya sniffled a bit and said, "You really are human, aren't you?"

I hugged her all the more. As the day went on, Taya and I had become fast friends. We explored the city just as she promised, first riding in a horseless carriage. I asked her, "How is it that the carriages in the city, can roll without horses or engines?"

"I do not know what an engine is. But the carriages are powered by crystals, and the crystals are powered by magic. As are most things in Phantasma," Taya told me.

"So magic is pretty much how most things work here," I puzzled.

"Yes," she said. "However, there are many things that do not use magic. To the dismay of many, there really is no substitute for hard work."

We both laughed and the attractive palace carriage, pulled to the side of the white cobblestone road. When we exited the odd vehicle, I saw we were in the busy plaza that I had seen last night. Only, it wasn't so busy anymore. There were only a few shops and stores open.

"Things only get going around here, at about one o'clock in the vampire city. The vamps are mostly late risers and are really nice. As long as blood is not around," Taya told me with a serious look on her face.

"So, what's in there?" I asked as we walked into the nearest shop. It was called Weapon's Master. Its inside was very small. It was filled with knives, swords, and arrows. They were of every otherworldly type you could ever imagine. Much of it looked like it came out of a barbarian's wildest dreams. I picked up a small knife with a green center to its blade. I recognized the green as being made of magic crystal. When I looked more closely at the little knife, it flashed with a bright light, blinding me. I stumbled around trying to find something to hold onto, so that I didn't fall. My hands caught a hold of something soft and round. It seemed solid enough. So I steadied myself against it. Cautiously opening my eyes, I saw that I was holding the rather large breasts, of a red-feathered harpy lady. She was blond and had pretty red-feathered wings with blue trim, attached to her arms. She wore a one-piece green dress, that draped over her large breasts in a v-shape. Its lower half looked something like a short toga.

I quickly took my hands away from the swishy mounds, mortified. The harpy lady's face changed before my eyes, morphing into something that looked more like an angry griffin, with pointy ears, a high ponytail, and bangs.

The sexy bird creature gave a loud caawww! And Taya instantly began a low growl. Her big amber eyes started to glow. The harpy backed down.

"I am certain you realize it was only an accident, Lanerva. You will have to excuse young Adam. He is a visitor in our land, and does not yet understand our ways. Please, you need not worry. I will compensate you for your trouble."

Lanerva's face went back to that of a beautiful, blond, ponytailed woman's. She huffed at me, and walked behind the counter on taloned bird's feet.

Outside the little shop, Taya laughed so hard I thought she might lose her balance, falling flat on her lean butt.

"What?" I said, laughing too.

"Are you that good with the ladies where you come from?" she asked me.

I gave her a little nudge, and she laughed even harder. This time, Taya did fall on her lean butt, giggling away.

"Okay, okay," I said, helping her up out of the Weapon's Master's front lawn.

We explored the plaza a little more, visiting many shops and stores. The werewolf girl seemed to be growing more fond of me, with each passing moment. Eventually, we stopped at a pleasant-looking establishment, called the Crescent Moon. It was run by a tall, lanky werewolf with greying brown hair. He looked like a normal enough guy. Only, his hair was a bit rough, but in a nice, stylish way. It was a rugged sort of look. I recognized him as being the same werewolf, who was lifting dusty wooden crates last night in the city.

"Hi, Zeno," Taya said, and the mature were wearing a button up blue shirt, and what looked like jeans (Wow, did they have jeans on another world?), peered to the door and smiled wide.

"Lu...ahh, Taya!" he said. "Where have you been hiding yourself, young lady. I was starting to worry."

She blushed a little, answering, "Things have been a bit busy at the palace lately. Dailania has returned from her studies abroad. As usual, she has brought trouble with her."

Zeno laughed a little and shook his head. "Who has she bitten now?" he asked.

"One of the castle's staff. It's a young male vampire so he should be okay."

The two werewolves saw the horrified expression on my face, and Taya asked, "Is everything well, Adam?"

"Yes," I said. "Only, I had just met Darkdancer last night, and she was acting a little strange."

"Strange?" Taya asked. "How so?"

"She was acting, well, like she wanted to suck my blood, among other things." I gave them both a revealing glance and Taya gasped.

"I think she might be hunting you," the female were swiftly added. Zeno nodded his head in agreement.

More than a little worried I asked, "What should I do?"

"I have just the thing!" Zeno blurted. He walked to the backroom retrieving a small golden box. Sitting it on the counter, he opened it up. Inside was a solid silver necklace. It had a tiny, glistening wolf's head hanging from it.

"Silver is a powerful deterrent for many of the creatures of Phantasma," he said.

"Vampires and werewolves being among them." Taya plopped down two gold Phantasma coins, and I put the necklace on, underneath my loose fitting white shirt. "Well, at least that is some protection. But you must understand the silver alone is not enough. You must use your will, channeling it through the wolf's head for the charm to truly be effective," the lanky shopkeeper revealed.

"Thanks a lot, Zeno. So how is everything back home?" asked Taya.

The tall were looked grim.

"The defenses are holding, but it would go so much better, if you would only speak with your father."

Taya looked deep in thought for a moment. Then she lifted her arms, showing them to the lanky werewolf. His face paled as his mouth flew open. Immediately, he jumped across the counter, nearly falling flat on his face. Zeno then stood before Taya with wide eyes.

"But how can this be?" he said, lightly touching her smooth skin.

"The visitor, Adam, healed me somehow. He is a human."

Zeno gazed at me, and immediately bowed with tears in his eyes.

"Oh, Adam, you do not know what you have done. Your actions have given hope back to the people. Should you ever have need for anything, you only have to ask, and we will be there for you."

"Okaaay," I said, taken aback slightly by his enthusiasm. "You know me, if I can help I'll do anything I can," I told them with a smile. "It's the way I was raised."

They both looked at each other then back to me. I felt like the biggest dork on Earth. Oh, sorry, make that Phantasma. Outside the Crescent Moon, I saw two shady looking vamps. They wore all black, and were standing across the slightly busier white cobblestone street. The vampires appeared motionless like statues. I saw an awful bug scurry across one of their faces, then jump into the other's ear. I thought I might be sick. Hoping I wouldn't meet any more vampires like those, I hurried Taya along back towards, the white horseless carriage we arrived in, which was a block or two away unfortunately. As we walked, I saw that the bug infested vampires were not following us. Suddenly, Taya stopped short. I bumped right into her. Turning around to face forward, I immediately saw the elf women Vale and I had battled yesterday. My God, they're still alive!

One had long, red hair and bangs. Another had green short spiked hair, and the last possessed a long, purple ponytail. Their eyes all matched the color of their hair, and they all wore leather tank top suits, with thigh-high likewise leather boots, each suit was the same color as their hair, in the places that weren't leather, mostly the lower half of the tank tops.

"It's the Serpent Riders. The redhead is Sparkle, the leader. The one with short green spiked hair is Flare, Sparkle's right hand. And the one with the long, purple hair is Ember. She has strong elemental powers," Taya told me. "They are the Weird Sisters, and the fact that they are here can't be good. We should probably go back to the castle before…"

The elven redhead shouted, "There he is!"

Her sisters looked our way, and both pulled really sharp-looking, shiny swords. When they started over to us, Taya threw something at them. It burst into a really bright flash of light. While the Weird Sisters were blinded, Taya and I ran down an alley going behind the Crescent Moon. I could hear the elves shouting, "Split up, they must not escape us!"

Behind Zeno's store, Taya pulled two swords from a very small, square, barred window, at ground level.

"Weres always prepare for any emergency," she said.

Swords in hand, we hurried down the alley, taking a quick right—only to come face to face with Sparkle.

She would have looked quite attractive, if she didn't have a crazed look in her eyes.

"So you are the one who violated the elven air space above our land."

"Aah, maybe you have me confused with someone else."

"No mistake stranger, I would know that aura of yours anywhere." Sparkle started walking towards us. "What exactly are you, and what is your connection with the vampires?" she asked.

I said nothing, too terrified by the fast approaching blade she held. Taya gave a low growl, and the elf smirked at her, thrusting her sword. Clang, clang! the metal swords clashed.

Sparkle deflected Taya's blows, and roundhouse kicked her into a pile of old wooden crates. The elf woman turned her attention back to me.

"Perhaps, you did not hear me, stranger, so I will repeat myself." A red, five-pointed, star-shaped mark appeared on her right eye. *Oh crap, why does this keep happening to me?* "What are you?" the elf asked again with a lot of anger in her voice.

I lifted the sword Taya had given me. With three quick slashes, I proved to be no match for Sparkle. She flung the blade from my hand, and it hit the ground.

Petrified, I could only stare at the exotic-looking woman. She grabbed me by the shirt, fisting it.

"You're going to tell me everything I wish to know. And you are going to tell me NOW!" Her right star mark covered eye gave off a weird, pink glow. I just stared at her. "What are you? Where do you come from? Tell me, tell me now!" Sparkle fisted my white shirt even harder. Shocked, I could only continue to stare. Her grip loosened and she stepped back. "You are able to resist my elven stargaze!" she said with wide, surprised eyes. Smack! Taya had walked up behind Sparkle, and hit her in the back of the head doublefisted.

"Come now!" Taya yelled. "We don't want to come across the other Weird Sisters."

Running through the back alleys, I could tell that we were headed in the direction of the palace carriage. Then something wrapped around my legs, tripping me. I looked down to see what it was, and saw a potted plant. It was growing like crazy around and around my brown pants legs.

"It's Flare!" the female werewolf told me, peering a block away in the direction we had just came from. Flare's green hair blew in the wind, while she made binding gestures with her hands, on top of a small shop. Taya quickly went back, retrieved her sword from the ground of the dirty alley nearby. She slashed the vines with it, and we ran as fast as our legs could carry us. I was surprised to see that I was keeping pace with a werewolf, when a bolt of purple lightning exploded off the brick wall next to us. I turned seeing Ember running straight for us, down an adjoining alleyway. Taya flung her sword as hard as she could.

It closed the distance, hitting Ember with its hard metal handle, right between the eyes. The blow was so strong it lifted her up off her feet. Not waiting to hear the thump of Ember's body on the hard ground, we bolted. Coming to the white, horseless palace carriage, we did not wait for its driver to open the doors for us. Taya threw the door open, hurrying inside, and I followed after her.

"Back to the palace as fast as you can! There is trouble in the plaza!" the young werewolf yelled with excitement. The driver took the steering controls, that looked like a couple of levers. And the carriage sped away, just missing Flare's big, monstrous plant trying to grab the vehicle from underneath.

Chapter Nine

We made it back to the huge, fairytale-like white castle with tall, dark windows. A truly impressive, giant stone bat overhead accompanied more red capped towers, than I remembered. I saw that Vale was in the courtyard holding two ruby fruits. It appeared she was waiting for us. Taya and I exited the carriage. The princess stood in front of me with her arms crossed, and a displeased expression on her face.

"Where have you been? The city is a very dangerous place, especially for the only human on Phantasma."

I saw a nearby vamp guard's eyes widen, as he overheard her words. Turning my attention back to Vale, I told her, "I realize that. But Jaru sent Taya to show me the city, while you were resting. I found it to be an incredible and wondrous place. Well, until the Weird Sisters showed up."

Vale was shocked. She asked, "What happened?"

I told her, "The she elves were in the plaza looking for us. Their leader said something about violating the air space over their land."

"Damn elves think they own the very skies above us," I heard Vale say in a low voice. "But there is more to it than that," she continued. "They probably hoped to ransom you for the Book of Kron, a human artifact they believe the vampires stole from them. No doubt, the elves would destroy all of Greyveil for it, if they could."

"The sisters chased us down and attacked us, but Taya protected me," I told her.

Vale's eyes shot to the long brown-haired werewolf with white bangs. She just stared with her eyes roving Taya's muscular body. In a flash, Vale slapped the female werewolf, and Taya took a single step back. The princess was angry.

"Did you bite him?" She yelled. "Did you taste his blood?" Her eyes glowed red. I swear, I could see Vale's fingernails growing long and sharp. Taya's big amber eyes started to glow as well.

Her brow furled and swiftly, I stepped between them, facing Vale. "Taya did not bite me," I said. Vale gave a mean sneer at her.

"How then is her affliction lifted? There is nothing in all of Phantasma, that could cure the curse which was upon her."

I gasped in shock. "It was cured, when I touched her earlier this morning in the dining room," I revealed.

The beautiful vampire seemed to settle down a little. But her mind was racing as she thought. Vale simply tossed me one of those nasty vampire fruits, she had been holding. Still not taking her eyes from Taya, "Eat up!" Vale said, "we have classes soon."

As we hurried along, Vale told me she would take me to all of my classes. She added, she didn't like my going out with Taya without her. She said I might catch fleas or something. Jealousy didn't look very attractive on her, so I quickly reminded the princess that, Taya might well have saved my life back in the city.

Vale let out a long breath and kept walking along. Deep inside the dungeon-like bowels of the castle, we came to room 104. Once inside, I saw that it was only a little bigger, than a normal-sized Earth classroom. It simply had fewer desks in it. There were about twelve desks, in the whole forty-feet-by-forty-feet classroom. I noticed it was about the size of the guest-room I was staying in, if you counted the bathroom with it as a whole. Strange things like models of dragons, posters of odd-looking fairies and a desk, with what looked like a vampire's skull sitting on it, were inside on display. I could tell by the long fangs the thing had. Vale and I sat down. She was sitting on my left. Then the other students poured into the classroom. There was everything from vampires, to werewolves, and nagas.

Heck, I even think I saw a kid I could see straight through, for an instant. They all took their seats. A tall lady with light blueish ultra pale skin and super puckered lips, was wearing a form-fitting blue dress. It made her look like a walking vase when she came in. Her hair was done up in a golden sort of elongated, upside down, triangular hairdo. She wore a tiara, which made her look like she had insect antennas, almost. Her dress also had huge, square shoulder pads, and an even bigger yellow collar, to kind of even out her really wide hips.

"My name is Adreiel. That's A-drei-el, and I will be teaching this class for the foreseeable future. I have been asked to give a small history lesson, for the benefit of those who shall remain nameless." She shot a small glance my way. Then Adreiel motioned a pale, blue hand to a small stack of books on her desk, saying "Crystal, if you would please..."

A young, ivory-skinned female vampire with small breasts and big, blue eyes sprang from her seat, in front of the princess. She wore a black form-fitting outfit and a tight, pink miniskirt, with matching pink shoes and an eleven-inch dark brown plait, standing straight up from the back of her head. It had a red ribbon tied in a bow around it. Crystal took some of the books in her arms, and passed them out to the nine waiting students.

"Please turn to page 375, the teacher instructed us."

The book was mostly filled with text and a few small drawings.

"I will be reading this small chapter aloud, and will take any questions you may have afterwards," Adreiel continued. "Please touch the red mark next to the chapter on the page."

When I tapped the mark, the inanimate book sprang to life, showing a moving hologram that was displayed in 3D over its pages, though I could only make out shadows and shapes that told the story. Obviously, that was just the way this particular chapter was made.

Adreiel began: "In eons passed, there was fought a titanic battle for the fate of all magic. It was one great power against many. An arrogant race powerful and blessed above all others, wielded a might that ripped worlds apart. Led by the wicked being, Zorath, they were cruel beyond all imaginings. The most gifted magic users in existence, they devastated their world. With reasons only they could comprehend, these beings saw all others as unworthy in their sight. They oppressed and enslaved all." The magical hologram showed an awful image, of many different kinds of shadows writhing in pain. Adreiel continued to read. "Then, using an almost god-like power, these formidable beings created the indestructible, immortal Drexelon to enforce their will. The greatest of their destroyers, he was immune to all harm. Accomplishing their wicked goals and ruling without peer, soon, these most unique of creatures grew unsatisfied with even that. The beings then decided they would not share, this most magical of worlds. They would instead cast all others from it entirely, into a world of their own making, where magic is forever beyond the reach of their enemies. In that place, the unworthy would be eternally trapped. The wicked beings pooled their great knowledge, and devised a way to make their dark vision a reality. However, in the casting of the spell, somehow, it all went wrong as evil so often does." Adreiel looked around the classroom warily. "The arrogant and foolish race was fittingly swept, into the prison they intended for others. Their vicious leader swore his return. With his master gone, Drexelon fell into the deepest of sleeps. Much time went by, and the story faded into legend. That is, until about seventeen years ago, when the immortal beast awakened. With him, he brought a plague of demons that poisoned everything, creating the place we now know as the Soulless Lands, and the Demon Zone. Can anyone tell me the allies of the demon devil king, Drexelon?"

A fat, green kid with red hair, dressed in brown kind of like a monk, was sitting in the desk to my right. He raised his hand.

"Cloven Demairaskiet," the teacher called.

He stood up saying, "The deathruler, deathreaper king, and his people are the allies of the spirit beast."

"Correct," the pale, blueish teacher told him. "Now, what is the name of the arrogant race, who was swept away and imprisoned in a magicless world, that they themselves created?"

A way too perky, cute naga snake girl with a Latin complexion like mine and short, brunette, curly hair wanted badly to answer. She possessed B-cup sized breasts, and a green dress that had baggy short sleeves. The young naga raised her hand, then shot up four feet in her seat on the thick, yellow bellied, light blue with red diamonds snake half of her body.

"Ulee," the teacher called.

"The name of the arrogant race was the humans," she said, smiling joyfully.

I felt a little knot in my stomach.

"But with all the humans gone, wasn't Drexelon supposed to sleep forever or something?" I blurted before I could think.

"Good question, Adam. While the humans were said to have created the demon devil king, it has been long believed that only their leader, actually controlled him. Some say he may have finally returned," Adreiel said grimly. "Can any student please tell me the name of the humans' ancient leader?"

Ulee quickly raised both arms, looking like she was about to burst. I even heard a rattle of excitement, as she bounced up and down on her snake tale. Adreiel took a breath and exhaled. She motioned to Ulee with one pale, blue hand saying, "If you please."

The excited snake girl spewed the answer from her lips. "The wicked human's name was Zorath," she revealed beaming.

In that instant, my head was splitting. I saw the image of a white-haired man, standing in wrathful flames.

"Beware the rise of the white dragon," he said. Though his shoulder-length hair was white, he appeared young. Maybe twenty-five years old or there about, sort of like the Head High Priest Jaru. "You must stop the Darksires," he solemnly continued. In his eyes, I could see an endless dark void. It terrified me like nothing else I had ever known, as I watched two worlds collide and destroy each other. "Serpentina wakens soon," the godlike voice of the man finished. The vision then ended abruptly.

When I snapped back to reality, I saw that the entire classroom was staring at me. "Are you alright, Master Adam?" the strange teacher asked. "Do you need to go to the infirmary?"

"No," I told her. "I'm fine."

Vale gave me a worried look, and I motioned my hands in her direction to reassure her. The class continued on. As I tried to listen to the teacher's words, something smacked me in the back of the head. I ignored it, again trying to listen to Adreiel's lesson. Smack! There it was again. I spun around in my desk and nearly had kittens. One desk right behind me sat Rem, with a wide smile on his face. Vale noticed us and gave an unpleasant glower towards her brother. Rem shrugged his shoulders, and she turned back around, her attention once more on the teacher. I reluctantly did the same, wondering just how long it would take him to make his move. The teacher read on about how some believed, there were still humans somewhere on Phantasma. Every now and then, a sighting occurred, but it would be quickly dismissed as a hoax; or a werewolf who had a little too much to drink. A strong wind blew the back of my neck, and I heard Rem's devilish laughter. Crap! I hadn't even seen him come in. Trying to ignore it, I heard the fat, green kid named Cloven. He was sitting to my right, choking back a giggle. I noticed that Ulee was watching, too, in a space cadet sort of way. Smack, something popped me in the back of the head. I spun around again, just in time to see Ulee's thick light blue with red diamond designs snake tail, thump Rem right in the back of his redhead, with her yellow rattle. Rem held the back of his head, and looked one desk over to his left at her in shock. Ulee reached into her flower-covered red bag sitting next to her, pulling from it a small, round, yellow melon. Her lips slowly slid over the somewhat sizable fruit. As Rem watched transfixed, it went down her throat and chest, with nothing stopping its slow descent. The fruit then rested in her stomach, with a little plop as a circular bulge. Ulee pointed to Rem then to the bulge in her belly, cutting an index finger across her long, but normal length neck, while giving the little vampire a kinda crazy expression. His eyes faced forwards, and he cradled his hands on his desk. He looked like an angel… a very surprised angel. I glanced at Ulee with a small laugh. She grinned, giving me a little wink.

"Lord Rem, I am so glad you could finally make it to class. Are you sure you wish to grace us with your royal presence?" Adreiel said sort of gliding across the class to him.

"Oh, yes!" Rem croaked, looking very uncomfortable. "You know I always enjoy your teachings Mistress Siren," he finished, trying to look very innocent.

Adreiel took the book she was reading from, closed it, and promptly smacked Rem on the top of his head. The impact made her long gold earrings swing from side to side.

"I want six pages on the history of humans in Phantasma and Greyveil. Do with my next class in two days."

Rem slumped in his chair, and Adreiel glided away, reopening the book and reading from it. When class let out, we all met in the halls. I walked up to the brunette haired, perky naga who had helped me and introduced myself.

"Pleased to meet you. My name is Adam Westlin."

The naga turned her attention away from talking to the slim girl vampire, Crystal.

"Oh, hi there, you're that kid Rem was picking on. I'm Ulee."

"Yeah," I said, "I guess he doesn't like me very much."

"Don't worry about it. There's definitely something wrong with that boy. Maybe he didn't breastfeed as a child."

"Yeah, maybe," I said.

Suddenly a tall, good-looking, young man with a feline-like stare walked up to me. He wore a grey dress suit with coat tails, brown gloves, and boots. His hair was white and spiky, and his skin was a light grey. It was the same kid I thought I could see through, at the start of class. "Greetings stranger, my name is Rafe," he said looking at me with creepy white eyes. You could still make out his irises though.

"I am called, Adam," I told him.

"Yes, I noticed you the moment I entered the classroom today. Sorry about Rem, we all still think the little prince needs a little time to mature."

Ulee shook her head in agreement.

"I noticed your strong aura," Rafe continued. "Especially when you zoned out in the middle of class, showing those freaky gold, glowing eyes. It's like its slowly growing stronger or something."

"Yeah, that was weird," Crystal said, just sort of appearing out of nowhere. "You're new, right? Where are you from anyway?" she asked, chewing her pink fingernail a bit with her exposed fang.

"Well, I come from a place called Earth."

"That's the Phantasman word for soil, where is that, exactly? I have never heard of it."

I was about to tell her, when Cloven butted in. "I think I have heard of that. Isn't that a tiny island kingdom to the north?"

Vale cut in, "We were just about to have a little something to eat. Would you all care to join us?"

"Oh yes, nothing like a good meal before self defense class," Rafe said.

Everyone agreed. In that moment, I saw Rem silently walking off alone.

"Hey, Rem!" I yelled, "where are you going? Aren't you going to come with us? I'd love to know more about what it's like to be a vampire, here in Greyveil."

The devilish, little vampire smiled and joined the group, while a little bookworm of a male werewolf passed him by, out of the classroom. As we all walked through the dungeonesque innards of the castle, I had to ask.

"So why do you love causing so much trouble anyway?"

The odd, little vampire just grinned happily, as he walked along with us, so I grabbed him and gave him a little nuggy, messing his hair. It seemed to lighten the mood; everyone relaxed and laughed a bit.

After ascending from the lower levels of Castle Greyveil, we surfaced in an incredible, sunbathed garden. It was as if I had found the Garden of Eden.

"Wow!" I breathed, and Crystal absentmindedly blurted.

"It's not like we haven't all seen a pixie garden before."

I walked gingerly with my mouth wagging open.

"Ah, yeah, there's a pixie garden on the castle grounds?" I asked not be-lieving it. "Well yeah, how else do you think we get such good melons?" Ulee said.

A little, winged pixie flew right in front of my eyes and zipped away. It ap-peared to be made only of blue energy, in the outline of a tiny, winged human. I then saw that there were actually, quite a few of them in the garden. Oddly enough, Rem started running about, flailing his arms and yelling, scaring the little creatures away. Everyone seemed exasperated with him, exhaling and making tired noises.

Finally, Vale flung her hand at Rem, and a strong wind blew from it, messing his hair yet again. Rem looked at his sister and she folded her arms, while everyone stared at him. He immediately stopped chasing the super fast pixies, and rejoined our group. Three pixies zipped out, changing to a red color, and laughed at him for all they were worth, then quickly zipped away in a shower of pixie dust. When Rem rejoined us, Rafe shot him an unpleasant look, and he sulked a little. Feeling bad for him, I gave his shoulder a little rub of encouragement. Instantly, he perked up again.

"So, does anyone know why the weird history lesson today in class?" Crystal asked.

"You know, that was really strange," Cloven blurted. "We went from potions and spells, to studying about some fictional race, that probably never even existed."

"Humans existed," I told him.

"Yeah, right, maybe in that little island kingdom you're from. But in the real world, we don't exactly have time for ultra magical super beings," he laughed.

Vale's eyes met mine, while I processed his words. She shrugged her shoulders with a small grin.

"Hey y'all, I'm really starting to get hungry. What do you say we talk a bit less and get a move on. I'm so hungry I could eat...a vampire." Ulee said, giving a little kiss towards Rem, who ran behind me frightened, saying, "Don't let her get me, Adam!"

I just smiled at her, while he shook with fear behind me. I had gone from prey to protector all in less than twenty-four hours.

Chapter Ten

The second princess led the way.

"We'll have to hurry, if we want to get good seats!" she exclaimed. As our little group walked through a series of beautiful archways, I saw that they stood on thick, golden poles, each pole having flower and vine designs, going up their forms. Through side-by-side double doors, I entered a huge, impressive cafeteria with row upon row of long tables, and red cushioned seats.

"This is the main dining hall," Vale said. "All students enrolled at Greyveil Palace come here to eat."

"The food's free as long as you are a student," Ulee blurted out.

I sorta figured she would know about food. I mean, she threatened to eat Rem twice. We walked through the crowded, gigantic square building to one of the busy lunch lines, where we were each handed lunch trays. Everything looked great and smelled even better. But I didn't recognize a single food. It was like being invited over to Dr. Suess' for lunch. I really would not have been surprised to see, green eggs and ham sitting around somewhere. I took a bit of this and a little of that. The meat looked good. But to a carnivore like myself, meat always looks good, and boy, was Ulee packing it on. Princess Vale stuck with the fruit. Rafe had the soup, and Crystal took a red liquid in a goblet with fresh pastries. Cloven had a big bowl of some sort of stew, while the little vampire, Rem picked up a plate of weird, orange slugs. They appeared to slowly move around on his plate, on trails of orange slime. We all took cups of a purple punch, and sat together at an unoccupied table, in the middle of the dining hall.

"Oh, I am not looking forward to self defense class. That damn Darkdancer's a real bitch. No offense," Crystal said to Vale.

"None taken," Vale replied nonchalantly, eating a bit of fruit.

"She really rubs me the wrong way," Rafe added, sipping his purple punch, while Crystal gawked wishfully at his handsome face.

"Burp! O-yeah, that's the good stuff!" the fat green kid dressed like Friar Tuck said. Everyone looked at him.

"What?" he asked, "it's the highest of compliments."

"Compliment uh," Ulee replied, stretching her long snake body over the dining hall table. Directly in front of Cloven, she did a brief pause. Then let fly, "bbbbbbbbbbbbbbbbbbbbuuuuuuuuuuuuuuur-rrrrrrrrrrrrrrrrrrrrrrrrrrrrrrrrp!"

The force of her release actually flew Cloven's red hair back. He swallowed a few times in disbelief. Rem watched like he had just seen someone rise from the grave. Ulee gave the little vampire a quick wink. He slowly slurped down one of his orange slugs, with wide eyes.

Cloven blurted, "I think I'm in love!" He then fluttered his eyes at Ulee.

I heard an immediate rattle of her tale, and she went back into her seat.

"She wants me," Cloven declared.

Ulee glared at him, shooting daggers with her eyes, to which Cloven repeated, "The highest of compliments," then winked at her, blowing a big wet kiss. In that moment, we realized that the entire dining hall had witnessed, Ulee and Cloven's little show. They both turned bright red, looking as if they just wanted to die. The dining hall hesitantly went back to business as usual, with a few disturbed students glaring at the odd couple.

Vale asked, "So, Adam, have you had much experience in self defense?"

I gazed at her like she was from Mars.

"I mean, before now. Did you have any lessons or anything of that sort?"

"No," I answered. "I have only managed to get myself out of a few scrapes, here and there."

"Well, this is extremely important in our world, Adam. We are at war with an indestructible evil. If you cannot fight well…" Vale stopped and a worried expression came over her face.

"What's wrong?" I asked.

"Self defense class, that's what. Jaru isn't known for his gentle touch," Rafe spoke.

"I don't think that Dailania's going to go easy on you either," shot Ulee.

"How do you know?" I asked her.

Time seemed to stop and the whole group, including Vale, stared at me.

"O, sugar, you really are new. Darkdancer doesn't take it easy on anyone. I think it's the way she's wired."

"Bitch," Vale said.

Everyone nodded their heads in agreement, while they ate.

"So, tell me more about Jaru," I inquired.

"He's the teacher of the self defense class. And I am sure you already know, he is the master high priest of the entire vampire city," said Crystal.

"Jaru takes his work very seriously. If you are not careful, you could end up with broken bones or worse," added Rafe.

"That's probably why it is Dailania Shadowwind's favorite class," Cloven interjected over a big spoon full of stew.

"Oh, it really sounds scarier than it is. The palace infirmary is the best in the land, sugar. If anything happens, they would fix you right up," said Ulee.

That did not fill me with confidence. Suddenly, I found myself not wanting to go to my next class.

"Adam you don't have to worry. I will be there in class with you," the princess reminded me. Rem simply looked around the long table at everyone, enjoying the drama as he slurped slugs. We all finished eating, and had a few minutes before the next class began.

Ulee looked off into space for a second, then said, "Dang, I forgot my bow and arrows. I'll meet y'all later, okay. I really want to get in some practice today with class. Master Jaru says that he's going to teach me to improve my focus."

"We all know if there is anything you need, it's focus," Cloven added.

Ulee gave a warning rattle of her tail and slithered away.

"What's her problem?" the fat, green kid asked. I stifled a small giggle, and he smirked at me saying, "Well, we better hurry or we will be late."

"Why did Ulee call Jaru Master just now?" I quietly asked Vale.

"Because here in Greyveil, the teachers are the masters of their classes. You may wish to remember that, Adam."

A little later, we walked into a wide, open outdoors area. It was in the midst of many wooden and straw practice dummies. Dailania was already standing at our destination. She had her hip cocked in front of a circular ring with a soft, white sand floor. It was surrounded by a thick, yellow rope held in place by eight wooden posts. This ring was a lot like the one in Aldett's war camp, only with weapons racks holding every pointy weapon imaginable, on each side of it. As everyone gathered in front of the ring, I noticed a few new faces. Most were young male vampires. They all seemed really tall and strong.

Deep inside I told myself, "Oh, great, this is going to be good. I think I will focus on trying not to get killed."

Jaru appeared out of nowhere in a dim shimmer of light, at the center of the ring.

"Welcome, my students! Welcome to self-defense class! As many of you may have already surmised, we have a new student. Adam Westlin, please step forward."

When I did so, Jaru continued.

"Young Adam may well be very important, to the future of Greyveil. So treat him well, and everyone, put your best foot forward."

All the tall, young vampires roared with applause. I had no idea what he was talking about.

"Now, then, with that bit of business out of the way, I think we should begin, don't you, class?"

"Yes, Master Jaru!" they all said.

"So, have you all remembered to do your daily exercises?"

"Yes!" everyone answered. "Have we all been practicing with our weapons of choice?"

"Yes!"

"Then, it is time to see what you have learned. I know you will all make me proud!" the white haired priest said. He walked from the ring and stood next to Darkdancer. "Reyon and Teshin you're up!"

Jaru motioned for them to enter the ring. "We will start with unarmed combat!" Jaru's voice rang out.

The two tall, pale, white skinned vampire kids did as he had requested. Each one of them looked handsome and confident, when they took places on opposite ends of the ring. Reyon had long, blond hair and a beauty mole on the right upper side of his lips. He wore a white shirt and tight black shorts.

Teshin had short, spiky, black hair and a gaze that could stop a clock. He was a whole new kind of intense. He had on a black shirt with white, skintight shorts very much like Reyon's.

"BEGIN!" Jaru said, and they both went into defensive stances. Their knees bent, their legs apart, and their hands in front of them. The two vampires clashed in a test of strength, with Teshin quickly gaining the upper hand.

He tossed Reyon over his broad shoulders. The blond landed on his feet, and caught Teshin in the gut with a spinning heel kick. Teshin staggered back with a confident smile on his face. He put down his defenses and stood there, looking Reyon in the eyes with a fearsome gaze. The blond ran directly at him, and he jumped straight up about eleven feet, coming down on Reyon's shoulder with a crushing elbow.

"Aaahh!" the longhaired blond yelled, then hesitantly returned to his feet. They both stood facing each other for a moment. And in an explosion of motion, they were once again fighting, with fists so fast they made the wind whistle with every blow.

"You're not going to win, Teshin, not this time!"

Reyon swept the black-haired vampire's leg. Then, in one movement, he grabbed Teshin by his black shirt, slamming him to the ground with truly excessive force.

"The match is ended," came Jaru's strong voice. The two vampires faced one another, touching their right shoulders with their left opened palms in a vampire salute. They both then exited the ring in an orderly fashion.

"Very good, gentlemen. I look forward to your next showing," said Jaru.

Ulee came slithering up carrying her bow and arrows. The priest peered at her, with a little disappointment in his eyes, saying.

"Glad you could make it, Mistress Naga. I will be helping you with your lesson momentarily."

Ulee gave Jaru a bashful smile, and his voice rang out over the class, "Rem vs Enzo!"

Rem shyly walked to the circular ring entering the arena, and Enzo did the same. He was another tall, well-put together, young male vampire, and he absolutely towered over Rem. Ulee put a hand over her mouth, and gasped at the sheer size of Enzo. The skinhead vampire looked like, he had muscles on top of his muscles. They each took their places on opposing sides of the ring.

"Begin!" commanded Jaru.

Enzo ran straight for Rem as he growled. But when he reached the small vamp, Rem just seemed to disappear. My mouth nearly hit the ground, watching Rem now standing behind Enzo, hardly paying attention. He was looking at his fingernails, as if he needed a manicure. Enzo turned around, his muscles bulging. He was about to punch the young vampire prince, in the back of the head, really hard by the looks of it. Suddenly, Rem wasn't there anymore. Enzo blinked his eyes in surprise and Rem laughed. The huge vampire tried to spin towards Rem to grab him. Right before he could, the little vampire jumped into a sideways backwards flip, catching Enzo right in the face with his foot. Enzo roared in frustration, throwing a mighty punch. Rem easily stepped to the side with an incredible speed. No wonder I hadn't seen him enter Miss Adreiel's class earlier today.

The little devil of a vampire is super fast! Enzo pulled his other fist back, about to take another swing, when Rem immediately moved right in front of him. Bang, bang, bang, bang, bang! Little Rem had hit the large skinhead several times in the head at high speed. Enzo fell to his knees, then to the white sand below, as Rem quickly dodged his descent.

Jaru pointed two fingers at the unmoving Enzo and shouted, "Infirmary!"

Two other big vampire kids grabbed Enzo, and carried him off to the castle.

Rem gave a little bow, before scurrying from the ring.

Jaru's voice ring out again, "Adam vs Rafe!"

The light grey-skinned, young man with white, spiky hair made his way to the ring, to the delight of nearly every girl in class. Some of them actually swooned at him.

I crossed the ropes soon after Rafe, and he looked at me emotionlessly.

"Begin!" said Jaru.

I ran up to Rafe with a flying kick. He stepped to the side, sticking his arm out. It caught me right under my chin with a clothesline. I hit the sand. Quickly returning to my feet, I threw many punches, but none connected. He simply backed away out of my reach. Then, I tried a spinning kick, Rafe kicked me in my standing leg. Crap, this guy is good! I staggered a bit, and I realized he was reading my every move. I motioned like I was going to sweep his legs, then rushed forward to catch him in the jaw, with a stiff left cross. I heard a lot of ohhhs and ahhhs coming from the crowd. A thin ribbon of blood ran down Rafe's nose. All the girl vamps in class hissed with excitement, especially Crystal.

"Well, now, you are full of surprises, Adam Westlin," Rafe said, wiping the blood away.

Instantly, he went into really fast punches and kicks. I barely blocked them in time, trying a spinning back knuckle, which he unfortunately dodged. Rafe took a step back studying me for a second. When I was about to attack, he disappeared like a ghost. I looked around the ring and saw nothing. So about to leave the fighting area, I suddenly caught a powerful punch in the gut.

"Aaahh!" I let slip, taking three more invisible punches to the face. "Crap" I said in a low voice and lashed out wildly, with spinning punches and kicks. Just then, I felt one of my kicks connect. Seeing an impact in the white sand, I immediately jumped into the air. And I mean just as high as Teshin had, when he fought Reyon. I landed with a strong knee, but I was too late, the impact outline was empty. Looking around the ring, I tried to find footprints or something. But there were none.

Instantly, I felt arms around my neck from behind. They were squeezing the breath from me. I gasped as the crowd cheered. Using all my might, I tried to break the hold of Rafe's invisible arms. Employing every ounce of my strength, I could feel an energy building inside. Before I knew anything, a terrible force exploded from me, knocking Rafe off my back. He reappeared when he hit the white sand, disoriented.

"This match is ended. Well done, Adam. However, If you would indulge me, I would have you in one more match. If you feel up to it, Master Adam," said Jaru.

Supporting my weight on my knees, as I stood panting, I gave him a thumbs up and grinned. He promptly said, "Miss Ulee, if you would please enter the ring."

Oh hell in a handbasket, I thought. *I can't fight a girl!* Ulee slithered onto the sand, and her tail gave me a warning rattle.

"Miss Ulee vs Adam! Begin!"

Ulee slithered forward. "Let's see what you got, Kid-o!" she announced.

I swallowed hard and Ulee whipped her snake tail, trying to hit me with its girth. Smack, smack, smack, her tail hit the ground. I flipped and rolled in the sand to avoid it. Then I ran straight for her, while she quickly braced herself. Soon Ulee's eyes opened, looking around in surprise, only to find me on the other side of her.

"Are you making fun of me?" she asked a little upset.

Like a dork, I hesitated, "Uuummm no."

Ulee made a displeased face and dived for me. I was able to move and push her away. She fell face first into the white sand... The naga arose, shaking the sand from her cute brunette hair and face. I actually helped her up, dusting off her green dress a bit.

"You are making fun of me!" she said. Her tail reached behind me and with a snap, it hit the back of my legs, sending me to the sand. I hit flat on my back. Before I could move, I felt the weight of Ulee's warm, heavy, snake-tailed body on mine. She coiled up with all of her girth and strength, holding my arms and legs down. Man, was she heavy! Slowly I saw Ulee's bulbous, round ass eclipsing the sun, as I gazed up from the white sand. Wow! Her rear really hadn't looked this big, when I was standing upright. It just spread out more and more, when she bent down towards me. "Not so funny now, is it?" Ulee said, and sat right on my helpless face, with her pillowy rear neatly perched on top of my cranium. Suddenly, I heard an odd sort of bubbling from deep inside of her. *This can't be good*, I thought and started struggling. To my surprise, I seemed to sink farther into Ulee's rapidly spreading, round cheeks. She gave a lady-like grunt, then fidgeted to get more comfortable. Most girls usually have a problem letting others know they're heavy. Ulee didn't seem to have that problem. The class just kinda stared, and a few stunned mouths dropped open. My God, why would they just let this happen? It almost seemed like I was being swallowed, by Ulee's amazingly soft, female ass. I desperately hoped that wasn't the case. Then I realized she wasn't even wearing panties! Now that I think of it, how would they fit her? Oh well, at least I knew by the not so bad smell, that she washed thoroughly. It really wouldn't have been so bad, pressed under the two warm, round, female cheeks—if the naga hadn't totally farted, while I was down there. This wasn't one of those cute, little, girly farts either. This was an apocalyptic, attention-getting sort of unleashing, of the repugnant winds of war. Faaaaaaaarrrrrrrt! her backside tooted. The whole class instantly erupted in laughter. And I went limp underneath the smelly naga. Not my proudest moment by far. I guess I should probably be happy, the attractive snake girl didn't take a huge dump just now.

"This is ended!" Jaru said, trying not to laugh. "You may let him up now, Miss Ulee!"

"Oh, shoot! I was just starting to get comfortable. I think he was juuusst starting to head north. If y'all know what I mean," she squeaked in a funny voice, snuggling her rather large buttocks against my face.

I could really use some fresh air right about now! I think the perky naga girl really needed, to lay off the red meat for a while, too. It was making her really gassy. As Ulee got up, she loudly passed gas on my face one more time, to the class's amusement.

"Miss Ulee, please refrain from using your uum, attacks, when the matches are ended!" demanded Jaru.

"That will teach you to make fun of a lady," she said, then slithered out of the ring. I got up with my face stinging, from Ulee's powerful...attacks. I dusted myself off, feeling super embarrassed, and Jaru spoke.

"I don't understand. You did so well against Rafe. What happened?" the priest asked.

"I was taught to never hit a lady," I told him.

"I see. Well, we will certainly have to work on that. After all, I cannot allow your face to be a seat, for every girl in my class."

I slumped on my feet, and the class roared with laughter. When I got back to our little group, my friends were trying desperately not to laugh. Rafe looked me in the eyes with a smirk saying, "Good job!" while busily fanning the air. I pushed him with a grin. Instantly, all my new friends giggled uncontrollably, and I laughed with them. What else was I supposed to do? You take the bad with the good, I guess.

"Sorry about that," Ulee told me. "After your great match with Rafe, I thought you were just making fun of me."

"I would never do that," I told her. She hugged me, and gave my back a little pat.

"Your face really is quite comfortable though," the snake girl added. I laughed and gave Ulee a good-natured shove to the shoulder.

"Next up, Vale vs Dailania the Darkdancer!"

Chapter Eleven

Darkdancer entered the ring first to complete silence. Then, Vale made her way to the cheers of everyone. As they took their places, Dailania spoke.

"I hope you don't expect me to go easy on you, Little Sister."

"I wouldn't dream of it," replied Vale.

On opposite ends of the ring, they both readied themselves, taking their stances.

"Begin!" came Jaru's voice. Darkdancer just smirked at her sister.

Vale went on the attack, throwing a flurry of claw-like punches. Her sister swatted them away, still smirking. Vale then unleashed a combination of furious kicks with her punches. The last one grazed her older sister's face. Dailania took a step back, looking surprised.

"You're actually a little faster, Sis!" she said.

"Let's continue Dai Dai! Maybe you will find that I am a lot faster, than you think."

Darkdancer gave a quick, little laugh. Then, she shot forward with her own combination of punches and kicks. Vale managed to parry them away before impact. Darkdancer was looking more and more surprised.

"Well, I see that Adam's blood has a few perks to it," she said.

Vale's expression changed when she heard Dailania's words. The older sister gave her a knowing look, while she slowly nodded her head up and down. Instantly, Vale shot forward with a punch, and Darkdancer grabbed her arm. Vale recovered it before her sister could do any harm.

"Yelp, definitely faster!" the taller female, three banged, brown pony-tailed vampire said.

"Adam is mine! I'll never let you have him!"

"Oh, Vale, it's not like you could ever stop me!"

Vale was about four inches shorter than her sister, but she stood her ground, like she was just as big. Dailania tried to punch her. This time, Vale caught it; then the other fist when Darkdancer threw it. They stood locked in an estrogen-filled female vampire test of strength, nether one giving an inch.

Suddenly, Dailania broke free and hit Vale straight in the face. In that moment, something strange happened. The impact from the blow shook Vale's done up, red hair a loose. It dropped to her shoulders and seemed to grow several inches. If she was a ten before, she just hit twenty on the knockout meter. Along with her long, red hair, Vale's skin radiated an almost angelic glow. Jaru watched speechless, with his mouth wagging open, when he saw the beautiful, goddess-like young vampire. There were gasps throughout the watching crowd.

"Oh, yeah, I got to try me some of that!" Dailania proclaimed.

"You will not!" Vale shot back at her, then hit Darkdancer with a strong right.

The older, brown-haired vamp smiled. Blood dripped from her lower lip, and her pink tongue lapped it up. Dailania raised her arms above her head, cocking her hip. I heard music begin coming from the ring. Darkdancer must have one of those small, gold music players that I saw with her in the dining room, when we first met. A terrible wind started to swirl around Vale, and dark clouds began to form overhead. The priest watched the angry sky, then turned his attention back to the two fighting princesses. Dailania danced with dreadful rage and graceful moves. With every shake of her hips and gesture of her hands, she sent devastating energy exploding around Vale. But her little sister stood her ground, attacking with powerful, offensive wind spells. Sending forth her hands, Vale caused the wind to concentrate into a kind of shields, blocking Darkdancer's terrible waves of energy. The two rival sisters were completely destroying the ring.

Jaru's voice rang out. "This match is concluded! You may stop now!"

The two sisters didn't budge an inch.

"You have destroyed my ring, and now am I correct in thinking, that you two ladies wish to defy me openly, in my own class! The priest's voice was downright frightening.

The skies cleared and the music stopped. The two princesses hesitantly turned away from each other, and exited the devastated ring. When Vale returned to the group, she was absolutely the most beautiful girl, I had ever laid eyes on. Her red hair was halfway down her back, and she was stunning.

Cloven spoke, "Wow, that was incredible!"

"It looked like some kind of transformation," Crystal chimed in. "So do you feel any different?"

"Yes," the princess said. "I feel very different, stronger and more powerful."

"Truly, that's great, Vale! Maybe we can finally dethrone the bitch queen, and make things a little better around here!" Ulee said.

"Hear, hear!" everyone joined in.

Darkdancer eyed me from across the crowd of students. Then Jaru walked over.

"Hello, young students! I would like to speak with Princess Vale, if you don't mind."

The princess walked over to him, and they talked right in the midst of us.

"Youthful Princess, I noticed the change which fell upon you, just moments ago. Are you all right? How do you feel?"

"I am fine," Vale said.

"With your permission, Princess, I would like to examine you."

"But I can't leave!" retorted the female vampire.

The priest cut her off with a wave of his hand.

"I am certain that Master Adam, can get along fifteen minutes without you, Young Lady."

Jaru looked to my new friends, and Rafe blurted, "Don't worry, we'll keep an eye on Adam for you, Vale."

"Thanks!" she said, then Vale and the priest both walked towards the castle, with his hand guiding her shoulder.

"Oh, and class, I leave Princess Dailania in charge in my absence," the priest said before hurrying off.

The entire class let out a collective, sad sounding, "Aaaawwww!"

With Jaru and Vale gone, Dailania stood in the destroyed ring, saying, "With no sparring area today, we will simply practice with our weapons of choice."

I saw Ulee rush to pick up her bow and arrows, from the grassy ground. Her face was actually bursting with excitement.

"Remember to practice caution, class, and try not to inflict any mortal wounds," Darkdancer finished.

She then stepped out of the ring, starting to assist a skinny, green kid, who needed help with controlling his spear movements. Everyone went over to the weapons racks on each side of the ring. Rafe retrieved a slender sword. Crystal was holding a foil. Cloven grabbed an iron ball and chain, while little Rem wielded double swords. I walked over to the rack, deciding to keep it simple. I chose a slender sword, exactly like the one Rafe chose. The group all began to limber up, swinging their chosen weapons around. I joined them and was shocked to see Ulee, swinging at the air with her bow. She appeared very serious. Apparently, they are good for more than shooting arrows. I sliced through the air a few times with my sword, and heard a little laugh.

It was Rafe, watching me in the company of a shyly grinning Crystal.

"What?" I asked.

"You may want to develop a proper stance, first," the grey-skinned kid told me.

"Oh yeah," I said mockingly to him, then taunting him with my sword.

Rafe shook his head and exhaled. He walked over to me, and we crossed our swords. As we stood motionless, Crystal said, "Ready, begin!"

Rafe swung his sword, clashing with mine. When he did his strike, he quickly closed the distance between us, knocking me right on my butt. He gave me a hand up, saying, "You see, with a proper stance, that would not happen so easily."

Right then I was thankful I hadn't fought Rafe, when he had his sword. I think it would have played out a lot differently.

"Again," he said, and I lunged at him with my sword. Clang, clang, my blade flew straight up out of my hand, and Rafe caught it. "You have a lot to learn, Master Adam," he said.

"Be nice, Adam is new. It's going to take time for him to adjust," Ulee blurted.

"Yeah, they can't all be as good as me," Cloven said, whirling his heavy ball and chain over his head. He let go of it and I stared in amazement. The weapon was still whirling above his head. With a flick of his chin, Cloven sent the black ball and chain careening into a wooden practice dummy, totally destroying it. I stood there with my mouth gaping open. Rafe gave Cloven a joy-filled high five, and they both laughed good-naturedly.

Crystal gazed at them. "You boys," she said. "When are you going to learn?" A small, glowing spark lit on the end of her pink fingernail. She flicked it onto a straw practice dummy. It was instantly consumed in raging flames. "As I was saying, when are you going to learn, that anything a male can do, a female can do better," she said, plunging her foil into the ground to stand on its own.

The two male students went over to Crystal, patting her on the back and congratulating her.

Rem danced around the flames, and Darkdancer walked into our little group. She looked at the two destroyed practice dummies saying, "Showing off a bit, I see."

"We were just showing Adam a few tricks," Cloven said.

"Don't bother, if Adam wants to learn something really useful, he only needs to come see me."

Dailania brushed her hand through my short, black hair.

"Hey! You can't do that!" said Ulee.

"Who's going to stop me?" replied the tall vampire princess.

Ulee's snake tail gave a warning rattle, and Darkdancer focused on her.

"Sitting on people might have worked for you earlier." I turned a bright red, and my friends stifled their giggles. "But I am a whole other bag of tricks, Lard Ass," the princess said angrily. Ulee opened her mouth in surprise and froze, mortified. I swear I thought something was going to fly into it. Cloven cut in, playing the role of peacemaker.

"Ladies, ladies, please, you are both far too beautiful to act so ugly."

"Butt out greeny, I'm talking to little Miss Snake Butt," said Darkdancer.

Ulee hissed at her, and the cute naga's mouth stretched super wide, just like Miss Silvia's, while her tail continued to rattle.

"That's your answer to everything isn't it? Oh, I'm upset, eat. People don't like me, eat. I have a big, snaky lard ass, eat even more. Is there anything you won't eat, little Miss Naga?"

"Well, you're so nasty I doubt I could keep you down, Dai Dai. But I am willing to try," proclaimed Ulee, opening her mouth impossibly wide again.

"Don't call me that!" Dailania's eyes shone red under her three pointy bangs. She was just about to attack Ulee,when a super fast pair of hands caught hers.

It was Rem. The little vampire stared into the eyes of his older sister, as she towered over him.

"What do you think you're doing, Rem?" Dailania asked nastily.

The little vamp clutched Darkdancer's hands even tighter. "If you hurt my friends, I am going to tell Father."

Dailania snatched her hands out of his grip, looking at him meanly, while he stood in front of her straight-faced. She then sneered at our group, and walked away to supervise two big vampire jocks.

"I reeeaaallly hate her!" came Ulee's voice.

I spun around to see tears coming down her sweet face.

"Don't cry," I told her. "Darkdancer is just saying that to get under your skin. As snake girls go, you are the perfect weight," I lied. "Believe me, I know."

Ulee gave my chest a little smack and laughed.

"Wow, what crawled up her butt?" the fat, green, redhead kid dressed like Friar Tuck asked.

"I have no idea," answered Rafe, jabbing his sword into the air a few times, practicing.

Rem chimed in, "Don't be too hard on her. Father puts a lot of pressure on Dailania. She is dealing with it the only way she knows how."

Totally surprised, everyone looked at Rem's sad face.

"That's no excuse to be a bitch," Crystal said, playing with her dark brown hair.

"That's right," Ulee added. "She doesn't have to walk all over everyone the way she does," we all agreed, and Rem seemed to give up. I could only wonder what kind of pressure, the king was putting on the tall, brown-haired princess.

"Hey, you want to do something with us later after class?" asked Ulee.

"Sure," I said. It's not like I had anything else to do. We all practiced a little more. I was astonished to see that Ulee was really good, with her bow and arrows. The girl never missed. I don't know what all that stuff she was saying about focus was for.

"Hey, Ulee," I called to her.

She instantly jumped at the sound of my voice. The arrow she released flew wildly, and skewered a straw dummy savagely through the head.

"Ooowww, sorry," I told her, and she gave me a displeased glare.

"Don't mind her," Cloven said. "Our little naga needs to learn a bit more control."

Ulee licked a twelve-inch tongue at Cloven, and it actually scared me a little. Then I noticed Ulee's eyes. They were focused on something behind me. I turned to see what it was, and saw Jaru returning to take control of his class, with Princess Vale still crowned in her golden, jeweled tiara not far behind, walking in our direction.

Not thinking I blurted, "You're the most beautiful thing I have ever seen!"

The princess stopped cold with surprise on her face, and blushed bright red.

Crystal and Ulee's faces both lit up, as they looked at each other. Rafe and Cloven each laughed, patted my back, and rubbed my head.

"We kinda knew there was something going on between you two," Rafe said.

"It's just good to hear one of you admit it," Crystal interjected, raising an eyebrow at me.

"Yeah, well, we are bloodbonded, after all, I said."

Everyone's mouths flew open with shocked expressions on their faces.

"Adam, you are bloodbonded to a vampire princess?" asked Crystal, looking like she was going to explode. She peered at Vale, then to me.

"Uuh, yes," I answered her.

Then Crystal did explode into giddy giggles, hopping up and down. She grabbed Vale's hands and laughed in celebration.

"Tell me everything!" she said, "when did you taste him?"

Vale turned an even brighter red, and Rem giggled happily along with the rest of us.

"So you like them fanged, do ya?" Rafe asked, giving me a roguish look.

"I suppose I do," I told him.

Everyone soon paired up, and started to practice with our weapons again, talking all the while about the relationship between Vale and me.

When class finally let out, Vale told us she needed to see her giant bat, Wingrider, in the palace stables far across the field, from where the self-defense class was being held. Our friends all offered to come with us, and we made our way to the stables. In one of the two long, amazingly clean buildings were about twenty stalls. Hay neatly covered the floor of each one. In about half the stalls were either powerful looking horses, or huge, big eared bats.

As we walked passed each compartment, the horses snorted, and the large bats gave high-pitched, little screams.

"Those things give me the creeps!" I was shocked to hear Rafe say.

"Really, why?" I asked him.

Rafe looked at me like I was a ghost. "It's a giant bat!" he said.

"Now that I think about it, that is pretty damn scary" I told him.

He nodded his head in agreement, while the group arrived at Wingrider's stall. The huge, injured and bandaged white bat screeched a greeting to us, and Vale entered his compartment. She rubbed the beast's head.

"My poor alpha bat," she breathed.

So that is what they are called, I thought.

Then Vale spoke into his large ears, "*Sen nuw sa la wen, te aosh nuw malu.*" The great white bat became completely docile.

"I love it when you do that priestess speech," said Crystal.

"It is okay for you all to touch him now," Vale declared.

Everyone patted and rubbed the soft white fur of Wingrider, but Rafe.

"What is wrong?" the princess asked.

"I have a thing about giant bats," Rafe replied.

"He will not bite, I promise you," Vale reassured him.

"No, no, I will just wait here," Rafe said, looking like he was one hair away, from bolting right out of the stables. Vale turned her attention to the bandages on the big white bat's wing.

They were clean and well maintained. "This must have happened when Ember's spell collided with mine," Vale spoke to herself. She began to remove the bandages.

Crystal automatically said, "That really doesn't look good."

Ulee shushed her, and gave Vale an apologetic look.

"Is there anything we can do?" Cloven asked, seeing what was underneath the well wrapped bandages, and making a sour face.

"No, just wait and watch," said Crystal.

Vale appeared to hug the great white bat. Pressing herself into the beast, she also spoke these words, that seemed to comfort him. "*Ho su sel lu, yu ni co re,*" the princess told Wingrider. Then, she pressed her hands into the ugly, fur-less wound on his massive wing. The huge bat screeched in pain. Everyone but Vale jumped back, and Rafe was no longer anywhere to be found at all. Wingrider soon relaxed, as Vale pressed more and more into the wound.

Watching her hands, I saw the offensive burn injury slowly vanishing. Holding on tightly, Vale pressed again into the burn, then even more, finally letting go with a gasp. She supported herself by clutching her knees, then panted.

"Are you okay?" I asked.

"Yes, yes," she said.

"Only, that took a lot more out of me, than I thought it would."

"I can go get you something from the main dining hall, if you like," came Cloven Demairaskiet's voice.

"No, no I will be all right."

The princess gave Wingrider's newly healed wing a caress, and exited the stall.

Ulee laid a hand on Vale's shoulder. "Are you sure you're okay?" she asked.

Vale smiled at her and said, "Maybe I could use a little something from the dining hall."

"Then it is settled. To the dining hall!" Cloven commanded.

"Don't you think you have spent enough time in the dining hall?" proclaimed Crystal, looking at his round belly.

Cloven stumbled to a stop then declared, "Hey, where I'm from, bigger is better, baby! You can never spend enough time in the dining hall!"

"Hear, hear!" said Ulee, and Crystal huffed at them both.

"Well, we had better get going then!" I told them all.

When we reached the large double door entrance to the stable, I nearly jumped out of my skin. Rafe had just reappeared from being invisible. He stood in front of us looking very embarrassed.

"You know Rafe, I have never seen anyone run from the stables, as fast as I saw you do a moment ago," said Cloven. The grey-skinned, white, spiky-haired kid looked mortified. Cloven continued, "You didn't really run, you sort of flew from the building."

The girls laughed and everyone kinda surrounded Rafe.

Hey, if he bolted again, there was no telling when we would see him. Not to mention the whole disappearing, reappearing thing, scared the crap out of me. So we comforted him, and told him it was okay.

"You know, I am afraid of heights," I lied, trying to make him feel better, as we walked to the dining hall. It's really just a glorified lunchroom, but hey, the food's good.

Chapter Twelve

Inside the dining hall, the princess was looking a bit worse for wear.

"I will be right back," Cloven said and hurried off. After he left, I felt a small nudge behind me on my left. I thought nothing of it. Then it almost knocked me over. I turned to find Crystal making little head motions, for me to go over to Vale.

The Second Princess of Greyveil caught Crystal coaching me.

"That is quite all right," Vale told the skinny, young vampire. "I will be okay, Cloven's coming back with a little pick me up."

Crystal settled down and the big, green kid dressed like a monk, soon handed Vale a big goblet. She immediately started to drink from it. By the red that pooled around her mouth, I knew that it was blood. The princess drank all the red liquid from the goblet. Then she looked at me with an embarrassed expression on her face.

"Feeling better now?" Cloven inquired.

"Yes, I am fine," Vale answered.

"Well, I am glad you are feeling better and all. But we really need to get going. The master high priest has us on an errand for him," spoke Ulee.

With a quick few swallows, Vale asked, "What sort of errand?"

"He wants us to collect fiblings for him," said Rafe.

"Fiblings, what are those," I asked, puzzled.

"It's hard to explain," answered Cloven.

"They are evil," Crystal blurted out, cocking her hip.

Vale spoke up, "They're not really evil."

"But they're pretty damn close," added Rafe. The princess glared at him.

"Hey, has anyone seen Rem?" I asked. Everyone looked around.

"That is just great," Rafe huffed. "The one time he could actually be useful and he disappears."

"Kinda like what you did in the stables there, Mr. Phantom," came Ulee's voice.

"So, Rafe is a phantom," I said to myself. The well-dressed, light grey-skinned kid turned pink and snorted at Ulee. We all laughed and I asked, "So where are we going?"

"To the Dark Forest," Vale answered. My eyes grew to the size of saucers. "Don't worry, Adam, it is just a name. It's really just Darratessa Forest."

"Great, just take all the mystery out of it for him," said Cloven. He took a bite of what appeared to be a turkey leg. I hadn't realized he was holding that. "We will take my ride," the jolly, green kid said. A short while later, the group arrived at what seemed to be the equivalent of a parking lot.

There were mostly those horseless carriages, which I had gotten so used to seeing, as well as a few carriages that still had horses. Walking over, I was expecting more of the same, but was struck speechless, when I first laid eyes on Cloven's wild-looking vehicle. It looked like a dump truck and one of those horseless carriages, somehow had a baby. I swear it was the ugliest thing I had ever seen.

"There she is," the fat, green student declared. "Isn't she something?"

"'She'?" I asked.

"Oh yeah, this here is Darma Lee. She is one of my dad's modified carriages. We really think they're going to take off. Just wait till they see one of these babies in action. You treat her right and she'll never let you down."

Where had I heard something like that before? Crystal rolled her eyes, "You actually named that thing? I knew you were weird, Demairaskiet, but wow!"

Cloven bent down close to his ride, "Don't worry baby, she didn't mean it. The skinny vampire's just jealous of what we have together."

I can't be sure, but I think I saw him give his modified carriage a little smooch.

"That's just wrong," Crystal commented. Cloven's vehicle was built like a carriage, only lower to the ground, more like an earth vehicle. It's about the same size as normal earth automobiles too, only a bit longer. It was black, having six side windows, six wheels and headlights. Just as we were going to enter the odd contraption, a brown sack of something hit me, and landed on my feet. I peered in the direction from which it flew, and saw Rem lugging another brown sack.

"Rem, where have you been? You shouldn't disappear that way without telling anyone," said Vale.

The little vampire shrugged his shoulders and picked up the sack, which rested on my feet. Inside the modified carriage, there was plenty of space for everyone. Cloven and Ulee sat up front. Everyone else sat in the two spacious, orange-colored back seats that faced each other. When we rode in the fat, green redhead's ride, we all learned some things that were very important: Number one, Cloven loves speed; number two, he is in terrible need of driving lessons; and number three, Darma Lee has no seatbelts. We swerved around every curb. I think he was actually trying to hit the mailboxes, and strays that crossed our path. Zoom! the vehicle flew over the steep hills like a rocket ship. I tell ya, I would sell tickets to this ride, if I thought anyone would survive it.

"Oh, God, how much farther!" I yelled.

"We're almost there!" screamed Ulee. The modified carriage soon spun out and screeched to a halt.

"There now, that wasn't so bad, was it?" our jolly driver asked.

Rafe immediately reached over, and smacked him in the back of the head. Once the doors opened, I pushed my way out of the carriage, falling on my hands and knees to the leaf-covered forest floor.

"What's wrong with him?" Cloven queried, getting out of the driver's seat.

Everyone glared at him, as if they too wanted to smack him in the back of the head.

"Where did you learn to drive?" Everyone asked at the same time.

"My father taught me," the green student declared proudly.

"Umm, how about you let me drive us back when we are done here?" said Rafe.

Cloven was about to protest, when Vale cut in. "I think that is a good idea. Everyone, do you think Rafe should drive us back?"

We all said, "Yes!" so loud we scared ourselves.

"Okay, then, now that that is settled, I think we should get to work. Don't you?" Ulee asked, looking to me.

Crystal passed out butterfly catching nets, telling everyone to be careful and show no mercy. Rem played with his net, waving it around so fast, he mistakenly netted himself. I giggled a little, and Crystal shot an unpleasant look my way.

"This is no laughing matter, New Kid. The fiblings will chew you up and spit you out!"

"Okay, okay, I think we may be getting a bit too serious!" Rafe interjected. "Adam, be careful and everyone else do the same."

We all gave Rafe a quick nod, then started into the forest. Boy, did it live up to its name. The trees were twisted and scary. The canopy leaves and branches were so high and thick, they sort of blocked out the sun. It was so eerie, walking though such thick darkness this early in the evening, though strong patches of sunlight and red grass, dotted the forest floor here and there, making it all look so much more alien. In a forest—any forest, really—you could always hear birds, animals—even the wind. But here in this alien place, you could hear none of that. It definitely gave me the creeps. I could see why it was called the Dark Forest. We walked into its depths for what easily felt like hours, seeing the occasional bright, luminescent, little bats, four-horned deer, or weird looking phoenix-like bird. Eventually, horribly quick, scurrying grubs shot across the forest floor.

"We're in luck," said Rafe. "Do you see those grubs?"

I nodded yes.

"Well, the fiblings eat them. If they are around, the fiblings can't be far behind."

As we approached cautiously, I spied a small, hairy creature rooting through the leaves. It appeared to be a round ball of fur with long, hairless, monkey-like arms. Its circular, shiny, black eyes were spread really far apart. And it had tiny, round ears on its head, which was also its body.

The little being scurried about on cute, little feet, and possessed a really thick, fur-less tail in back. I waved my arms swiftly to get the group's attention. They all looked in my direction. I pointed silently at the long-armed fur ball. It was about the size of a grapefruit. Everyone quietly nodded, and we closed in on the little creature. Stealthily, we approached it from behind. With a slight rustle of leaves, its tiny ears sprang up. Three of us lunged forward with our nets, but the fibling was too fast. It raised its long arms in the air and ran away screaming, revealing a row of big, shark-like teeth. Rem dived for the small being with his net. The fibling jumped about five feet straight up, bouncing off the little vampire's forehead to avoid it. The odd little creature then ran into an opening, at the base of an old stump.

"Well, I guess that one got away," I said.

Crystal, Rafe, and I helped each other up from the ground, and started looking around for any other fiblings. We got maybe ten feet from the stump, when the little creature came marching out humming a tune, as though we weren't even there. We all looked at each other, then shot out after the weird, little being. Again, we missed and it scurried away screaming, its long arms high in the air. This time, it was Cloven who dived for the fibling, without a net and arms extended. The small fur ball quickly hopped while he was in midair, onto his head, then to safety. The green teen instantly got a mouthful of forest goodness. (Also known as dirt.) Ulee was waiting for the little fibling once it escaped Cloven. It stopped right in front of her. The cute, brunette, green-dressed naga tried to swat it with her heavy, light blue, red diamonded tail. Smack! the fibling dodged; smack! it dodged again. Frustrated, Ulee threw herself trying to land on it. The little beast launched itself at her, catching hold of Ulee's short, brunette hair.

"Aaaahh!" she yelled as the fibling swung from her curly locks, by one long arm. We ran to help her, and I knocked the little creature from her hair. It landed on the forest floor protesting, making little hops up and down at us, its toothy mouth open and arms raised high, grunting.

"This is so over!" Crystal proclaimed. She hurried over to the fibling, and with a snap of her well-polished fingers, Crystal created a small flame and flung it. It ignited into a roaring fire when it hit the fibling.

"No!" yelled Cloven.

Crystal folded her arms and smirked at him. The powerful flame died down, but the devilish, little creature was still there, hopping up and down.

"Oh crap!" Cloven blurted out as the small beast started to throw fireballs at us. We of course made a sound tactical retreat, while the little fibling gleefully tossed hot, flaming death. All seven of us ran deeper into the Dark Forest, chased by the little creature. Finally, we came upon a clearing full of dead leaves.

When we stopped to catch our breaths, the fibling entered the clearing. We readied ourselves, but the fibling seemed to lose interest completely. It started to root around in the leaves again, looking for grubs.

"Oh good," Cloven panted, "it wore off!"

"What? What wore off?" I gasped, still trying to catch my breath.

"Fiblings are creatures that are resistant against magic. They can throw spells back at their casters," Cloven said, clutching his net and turning to the skinny, young vampire. "So would you please not do that?" he yelled at Crystal. There was an instant rustling of leaves all around us. When we looked towards the edges of the clearing, we saw a buttload of fiblings emerge from their hiding places.

We were surrounded.

"Somehow, we have gotten behind enemy lines!" Rafe said.

Rem giggled and tightened his grip on his net. Ulee started to look really worried.

Vale commanded, "Nobody use any magic!"

We all readied ourselves, again holding our nets. And with the only sound in the entire forest being the little fiblings, I let fly the command, "Now!"

We all ran after our own individual fiblings. Vale actually caught one under her net. Unfortunately, while holding it down, two other fiblings ran up and jumped on her now long, beautiful red hair. The princess yelled and stumbled around, as the little creatures pulled her hair. I saw Rem covered with about three fiblings, running at super speed through the leaves, giggling. Rafe and Cloven were back to back, punching and kicking down the little monsters, when they jumped to attack. Crystal had lost her damn mind. She was screaming, chasing whole crowds of the little fur balls around the clearing. It was total chaos. Then three fiblings jumped on me, knocking me to the ground. When I looked up, I saw two of them marching around happily on my chest, with the third cheering them on. I smacked the furry beings off my body, and I swore. I heard them say "Weeeeee!" When they flew through the air, and landed clutching at Ulee's green dress.

"Sorry!" I told her, and the naga went wild. She flicked and tossed them from her, then shot out after the little creatures when they ran, cornering a crowd of five or six.

The little things all grunted at her, and Ulee pounced on them. She had actually caught the little monsters. I was about to go over to congratulate her, and help with their retrieval, when Ulee stood up and turned to me with empty arms. I saw a couple of bulges heading south, from her lady-half to her snake rear. Then Ulee burped quite loudly.

"Never mind," I told her, and started looking for more of the little creatures.

Crystal was now surrounded. One fibling would distract her, while another grabbed onto her tight, pink miniskirt. She was really starting to lose it, so I rushed over and chased the little monsters away, kicking one clear into the leafy canopy. It laughed like it was insane the whole way up. When I turned to Crystal, she collapsed into me.

"Are you all right?" I asked.

Crystal froze for a moment, stiffening at my neck. She breathed deeply then pulled herself off me.

"Yeah, I'm all right," she told me.

We turned back to the creature-filled chaos, to find Vale standing there watching us. Crystal cleared her throat looking at Vale for only a second, then ran to help the others. Vale stood there staring at me.

"It's just Crystal!" I told her. "Nothing would have happened."

Vale flicked her long, red hair back, and we both rejoined the madness.

"This isn't working," Rafe said. "We are going to have to retreat."

It was like the fiblings understood his words. Each one raised its arms and cawed. Yes, like a bird, they all cawed in victory. Crystal grew upset and was about to torch them again, when Rafe grabbed her hands, stopping her.

"Are you insane?" he asked. "Don't you remember what happened the last time? Stop it with the flames!" he commanded. Crystal looked sheepish and began rubbing her left arm innocently. The little fiblings closed in around us. Suddenly, Rem appeared, using his super speed.

He was carrying his two brown sacks. He tossed one out, then the other. Where they hit the leaf-covered forest floor, many little cupcakes spilled from the bags. The fiblings saw the sacks of treats and immediately swarmed them. More creatures than I could count overtook the bags of cupcakes.

"You had those all along? Why didn't you say anything before?" Rafe asked.

Rem answered, "Well, we were having so much fun." Rafe started towards him with clinched fists, looking upset, but a very big Cloven stepped into his path, stopping him.

"Hey, at least he brought the cupcakes. I didn't know fiblings liked cupcakes, did you?" The fat friar-look-alike peeked into his eyes.

Rafe calmed down and turned his attention back to the fiblings. We easily managed to catch some of the little monsters in our nets. They were a lot less trouble when they were eating. And Ulee was more than happy, to scoop them up by the impossibly wide mouthful, gulping as many as she could down her elastic throat. Everyone just sorta watched in morbid curiosity, while Ulee forgot we existed, and downed most of the little fur balls, enacting some strange form of revenge on the little creatures, I guess. Or maybe they just tasted really good to her.

By the time she was done, the snake half of her body was maybe three times as big as it had been, if not larger. Ulee wiped a little dirt from her mouth and flipped over onto her back, laughing on the forest floor with a mighty burp. Cloven and Rafe helped her up. She gave another loud burp and looked embarrassed.

"That's okay," Cloven said, "I like a girl who can put away her food... He stopped and thought for a moment. Then added, "And just about anything else for that matter."

"Wow, you're heavy!" Rafe complained.

Ulee stared at him unpleasantly.

"What's wrong, Rafe, can't handle the extra lovin'?" Cloven declared.

Ulee turned to the green gen gratefully, then faced forward as we continued on through the strange trees, that blocked our path. When we eventually arrived at Cloven's modified carriage, Rafe immediately retrieved the keys from the psychotic former driver.

"Remember to pat the seat before you sit down. Darma Lee likes it when you do that," Cloven said.

"Ah, sure," replied Rafe, and did as the fat, green kid requested, to his everlasting shame.

We all entered the vehicle this time, with Rafe and Cloven up front. Everyone else was in the back with the fiblings. Ulee sat over stuffed next to me. She was eyeing the fiblings we caught, while they grunted at her. She smacked her lips and reached for one of the tied nets. When Ulee reached forward, the bloated naga passed a little gas, but I think only I heard it. Instantly, she froze with a bewildered look on her face. Ulee then quickly sat back in her seat with wide, surprised eyes. I don't know why she was so embarrassed. Earlier, she give me a firsthand demonstration, of the inner workings of her colon, for crying out loud. After a moment or two, I whispered to her, "See what happens when you eat too much."

Ulee turned red. I smiled at her and whispered in an even lower voice into her ear. "Don't worry about the smell, I'm used to it."

The cute, gassy girl naga snorted and stifled a laugh, while she remembered back to our little self-defense match.

"Excuse me, Rafe, I would like for you to let Adam and me out at the plaza, if that is not too much trouble."

"Not a problem, Princess," said Rafe.

When I looked at her, Vale told me there were some things, she wanted to talk to me about. Crystal looked as if she was going to burst, then made a small kissy face at me.

Chapter Thirteen

Rafe let Vale and me out at the plaza, as the princess requested. I told all my friends I would see them later, probably in class. Then Cloven's modified carriage pulled off back towards the castle. Vale and I walked slowly down the somewhat busy sidewalk. She appeared deep in thought, not even noticing the harpies and big, horned, black and red dogs that passed our way.

"Princess, is everything okay?" I asked.

Vale turned to me about to speak, when—ring, ring, ring—it was my cell phone. I really was surprised to hear it ring. By now, I thought for sure the battery would be dead. I flipped the small phone open, and my Grandma's voice called out to me.

"Adam, Adam are you all right? I am so worried, please speak to me!"

"I'm here Grandma, and I'm doing fine."

The princess folded her arms and waited, simply peering in a different direction.

"Is everything well? How is Tannon and Grandpa?"

"Oh, they are fine. I just needed to talk to you, Son. We miss you so much, please come back home."

"I would if I could, Grandma, but don't worry. I have made wonderful friends here, and they are going to help me get home."

I heard her exhale over the phone.

"That is good news, Adam. I know that I should not worry. You have grown up, and you are a strong, young man now. But I do, I do worry about you!"

Grandma started to cry, and it made me start to cry in turn. Hot tears flowed down my cheeks.

"Please, come home safe," she said and hung up.

I looked away from the princess, and wiped the tears from my eyes. Vale lightly touched my shoulder saying, "It's okay, Adam. It sounds like she loves you very much."

I turned to face the female vampire.

"I can tell that you love her as well," the princess finished.

Vale placed a delicate hand on my face. I could only think that her long, red hair and pale face were the most beautiful things, in the whole world. As she looked at me, her expression hardened. Vale turned away, taking a few steps.

"Adam, have you ever considered?... Have you ever considered maybe not going back?"

"What?" I said completely shocked.

"Your grandmother is right, you know. You have grown into a fine, young man, and if you stay here, you could be with me."

"Ooohhh, Vale!" I breathed to her.

"Would it really be so bad?" she asked, still looking away.

"No," I told her, "it wouldn't be bad at all."

I walked up behind the princess and gently rubbed her arms. She turned her head towards me with her eyes closed, enjoying my touch.

"So, why then," she said softly, "why go back?" Vale took a moment, waiting for my answer.

"Princess, my family needs me and I need them. Surely, the Second Princess of all the Vampire Territories can understand that."

"I understand it Adam. It's just that I think I may need you, too."

Immediately, I kissed the beautiful vampire, more deeply and more passionately than I ever dreamed possible. When my lips pulled away from her, she was limp in my arms. I caressed the pale, white skin on her attractive face, running my fingers through her long, silky, red hair. She began to stir, and gazed up at me like a child, while I held her close.

"Princess," I said, "I know that you want me to stay here with you. But you must understand, there are things I simply must do. I feel somehow strongly driven to do them." I stood her up on slightly wobbly legs and continued speaking. "Like on the day we first met, I dreamed of you night after night. I knew you were in trouble. And I knew that I had to do whatever I could to help you.

"That we met was not by chance. I even dreamed of the deathreaper who pursued you."

The princess reached up to touch my face, and I took her hands in mine.

"I don't understand, Adam. How could you know such things?" she asked."

"I don't know," I told her. "But ever since we came to Phantasma, I feel like there is something growing inside of me, and it's getting stronger. What is happening to me, Vale? I just...don't understand."

The princess hugged me softly, and I pressed into her, breathing in the strong scent of exotic flowers.

"Adam," she said, "humans are the most magical creatures Phantasma has ever known. I cannot be certain what is happening to you, but I do know that it is nothing to be afraid of. Remember back in self-defense class, the change that I underwent. I am positive that it was a benefit of drinking your blood."

My brow shot up as I listened.

"Your blood changed me and made me stronger, Adam. I believe that is what's happening to you now."

I looked at her a little dizzy. "I think I need to sit down, Princess. You've given me a lot to think about."

We both hurried over to a not-so-busy restaurant called The Biting Fangs. It had a big glowing sign with actual biting fangs on it. Large tinted windows were in front, and a huge canopy covered six outdoors café tables. Both of us slowed down walking under its shade. We sat at one of the unused café tables deep in the corner, underneath the huge, yellow canopy. I was hyperventilating a little. Vale called a really thin, blond vampire waitress from inside The Biting Fangs.

"Evening to ya," the waitress said. "What can I…" the thin vamp stopped and bent over close to me, inhaling the air deeply, like she was smelling a hot apple pie. I saw two small fangs extend from the sides of her thin lips. Vale gave her a serious look, and she snapped out of it.

"I'm sorry, what did ya say ya wanted?" asked the thin blond.

"Two honey meads, please," the princess said.

The thin waitress sashayed back into the restaurant.

"She will just be a moment. Is there anything I can do?" Vale asked.

I reached for her hand on the café table and gave it a small squeeze, smiling reassuringly to her. Our waitress returned with two big, ice cold glasses of amber liquid. She asked if there was anything else we needed, before promptly returning inside. The thin blond gave a devilish fanged smile to me, when she left. I quickly chugged the delicious drink, downing half of the big glass in my first sip.

Vale took a small sip from hers and I asked, "So, what about the bond between us?"

The young priestess was taken aback by the question, saying nothing. I then told her I was feeling pretty bad today.

"I think you needed me, and I wasn't there for you. When Crystal pushed me forward in the dining hall, I should have gone to you." Feeling a terrible sadness come over me, I continued, "But sometimes I feel so weak."

Vale chimed in, "That is normal, Adam. It is why I gave you the ruby vampire's fruit to eat. You felt better after eating it, right?" she asked.

"Yes," I nodded. Actually, it tasted so bad that I hadn't really noticed.

"As long as you eat the fruit, it will quickly replace anything I take from you, keeping you healthy and strong."

I thought hard about that, nodding again in understanding.

"What about the bloodbond," I repeated.

The priestess retreated from me a little. "Well, what do you wish to know, Adam?"

"I am afraid that I still do not completely understand it," I told her.

Vale took a deep breath, looking very uncomfortable. She came close and held my hand, caressing it lightly.

The vampire then gently spoke from her full, red lips. "In our world, when vampires find someone they really like, they bite them. Through that bite, a deep bond is made linked by powerful magic. However, not every bite creates a bloodbond. That is a choice made by the vampire himself, or herself. Usually, the being bitten becomes enamored, with the vampire who bit him or her. Again, that is only if the vampire decides to bond. Vale looked guilty, fidgeting a bit.

"We don't have to worry about that," I said, "I loved you long before you ever bit me, Priestess."

She stopped fidgeting and continued, showing a radiate smile.

"The bloodbond makes the person bitten, subservient to the dominate vampire."

"Wow! I really didn't know that, Vale," I said, puffing out a really long breath, starting to hyperventilate again.

"Oh, Adam, you need not worry. That part of the bond had no affect on you."

"What do you mean?" I asked.

"It's true; while I can feel you and know where you are, I cannot will you to do what I want. If I could…"

The beautiful redhead looked guilty again. I had a feeling I knew what she was thinking. Looking deep in her sparkling green eyes, I told her she doesn't have to will me to do anything for her. She had only to speak, and I would gladly do whatever she asked. The princess swallowed a few times, as if her throat had just become really dry. A bewildered expression came over her attractive face. Vale's mouth hung open absent-mindedly, while she thought and peered into space.

"Are you all right, beautiful?" I queried. Her eyes met mine and immediately, she moved her chair so close, there was literally no space between us. The scent of exotic flowers came strong and hard. Gazing at her perfect face, her sparkling green eyes roved over mine. "Are you really so surprised, Princess? I told you, I would help you any way I could."

I saw fangs extending from between her full, scarlet lips. They seemed a bit larger than before. I gently ran my fingers down her flawless, pale cheek.

"Anytime, anywhere," I told her. Vale reached out to me, her warm hands feeling all over my face and neck. Soon, her fingers started to roam my muscular chest as well. The princess looked at me, her expression a little questioning. Then Vale opened her mouth, exposing her slightly bigger, pearly, white fangs. I turned my head and braced myself. Vale lunged for my neck.

"Your bill," came our waitress's voice, and the princess stopped just short of tasting me. Vale looked up and hissed angrily, her eyes shining red at the thin waitress. The blond hid behind the platter she was holding. Cautiously, she retreated a few steps. I very carefully and lightly touched Vale's chin, bringing her furious gaze back to me.

"It will be okay," I told her. "We can always find a more private place."

The princess's eyes turned back to their sparkling green selves. She quickly slapped a single gold coin, on the bill that lay on the café table. Vale took my hand, and we hurried through the busy plaza sidewalk.

"Where are we going?" I yelled so that Vale could hear me.

"Some place more private!" the red-haired vampire told me.

We entered one of the alleys, that lead behind the many plaza stores. It would not have been my first choice, but I didn't think anyone would disturb us back here. I panted, trying to catch my breath. Vale stopped motionless, facing the dead end, she led me to. I stared at her seductive, curvy, female shape. When the priestess turned to face me, I froze at her red eyed, shining gaze. She looked away, ashamed of her desire and the face she'd shown me. I went to her, softly caressing her lovely face with the outer palm of my hand, telling her she has nothing to be ashamed of. Vale embraced me, holding me tight at the chest—so tight that I knew I wasn't going anywhere, unless she wanted me to. The princess swallowed a few times, and I saw that her thirst was getting the better of her. She breathed deeply of my scent.

"Ohh!" Vale said, "do you know how good you smell right now, Adam?"

"It must be because I really want to give my blood to you, to give you what you need, Princess."

My hands lightly rubbed her back. Vale seemed to go limp against me, hearing my words and feeling my touch. I caught her in my well-muscled, light bronze colored arms, and I could feel her body quivering... Then, embracing Vale for all I was worth, I soon felt her fangs sink deeply into my neck. She moaned in ecstasy. There was a swift pinch, then I felt no pain. Actually, I could feel warm waves of pure pleasure, emanating from her delicious bite.

"Aaahhh, ooohh," I moaned, listening to her swallow mouthful after mouthful of my life's blood.

Vale's grip tightened around me, and my hands started to explore her goddess-like body.

"Yes, YES!" I told her, with wave after wave of pleasure flooding every inch of my being.

Vale and I momentarily lost our balance in our passion, circling around and round behind the plaza store, while her powerful embrace bound me to her. Finally, we landed against a tall, wooden gate, which surrounded the property behind the store. Vale was holding me as though she'd never let go, but the swift impact shook the princess, out of her vice-like grip. She gazed at me possessively.

With no thought at all, I kissed her soft, full, red lips. Her hands ran warm under the white, loose fitting shirt I was wearing. I followed suit, my hands pulling up and searching diligently beneath, her purple silk blouse that had runes going up each arm. I could feel that her white skin was totally smooth and flawless. It was almost like touching a work of art. As I massaged her c-cup sized, soft breasts to her delight, Vale's breath was heavy and hot against me. She raised a single sexy leg around my waist, clutching me tightly to her still fully clothed loins.

"Princess," I asked, "are you sure this is what you want?"

Vale sexily licked my lightly bleeding neck. With a big lap of her soft, wet tongue, she swallowed and reached into my brown pants, grabbing my manhood.

"Ooh!" I gasped.

Guess that answers the question. She first took it rough, as though it were her property alone. Then gently massaging it, with a sexy female moan on her part, we stared at each other a moment. The princess lightly bit her lip, showing sizable, white fangs with her smile. I grinned at Vale, and she curled her silky, red hair around her finger, peering at me hungrily. Our faces slowly approached each other, and I gave Vale's fully fanged mouth two soft kisses, before again kissing her deeply. As our lips touched, her mouth opened and she sucked my tongue into it. At first, I was a little caught off guard. But fearlessly, I explored the inside of the vampire princess' beautiful, but dangerous mouth with my tongue. I wasn't surprised at all, when she got excited and finally bit me. Again, the priestess held me possessively in a vice-like grip. She sucked my bleeding tongue insatiably, French kissing me at the same time. Then, Vale began rubbing her lower regions against me, while she lost herself in the ecstasy of the moment.

I really wasn't complaining. Faster and faster than harder and harder, she rubbed. I could feel nothing but pleasure, first from my neck, then from my very busy, bleeding tongue. Soon, Vale's grip grew so powerful, I thought she might hurt me. I forcibly grabbed her by her firm, round buttocks, lifting her up onto my still clothed manhood, which ached so desperately to be released. My hands ventured deep into the irresistible mounds, of the vampire princess's curvy, perfect ass. She sexily and hungrily seemed to try, and swallow my bleeding tongue right out of my mouth. When we slammed into the tall, wooden gate around the property behind the store again, I finally tried to drive my bloody tongue, all the way down the princess's dainty throat. Her eyes flew up into the back of her head, and her lower regions jumped, quivering. I could feel a strong pulse going through her body, emanating from her very loins. Yes, it is true, Vale Shadowwind, the Second Princess of Greyveil, just had an orgasm and there was no penetration—well, other than her sucking on my bleeding tongue. *Must be a vampire thing,* I thought to myself. Vale slid down the wooden gate to the ground, laughing happily. I took a seat next to her.

"Oh, you are going to make one fine vampire," the princess told me.

I took a few breaths. "But I don't want to be a vampire," I told her.

Vale instantaneously looked at me a little shocked, and her brow furled slightly. I peeked back at her.

"What do you mean?" she asked, seductively licking the blood from around her lips.

"I told you, Princess, I intend to go back home."

"But why, what is back there that I cannot offer you here?"

"Family," I said.

"I don't know if you realized this yet, Adam, but I am of the female persuasion."

"I noticed," I told her.

"Then you also know, that I am well capable of supplying you with a family. A really big one," she grinned, looking devilish.

I laughed, then told Vale, "It's just something I know I have to do. But there is no need to worry," I quickly added. "Once I find out how to cross the two worlds, I would come back, and I hope that you will come to my world. You know, just for a visit. I'm sure my folks would love you."

There was a weird feeling between us. I could tell Vale felt it, too. She laughed and answered, "I think I would like that," and we kissed passionately. The princess slowly lowered herself, laying on the white cobblestone ground, watching me excitedly, with only her head still supported by the gate. I climbed on top of her, positioning myself between her heavenly thighs. The strong scent of exotic flowers was driving me wild, and Vale smiled in anticipation. We happily kissed again, and my hand clutched the princess' red, v-shaped belt, unsuccessfully trying to remove it. Vale's soft hands stopped my futile attempt. She was about to take the belt off when two shady-looking vampires, wearing all black, walked into the alley, looking at us lifelessly.

Chapter Fourteen

The two vampires were as still as statues. The princess and I quickly recovered from our compromising positions. Then, for reasons I can't quite figure out myself, I put a fist over my mouth, coughing quite falsely. I tried to look as innocent as I could. Vale saw my reaction, and just stopped herself from laughing out loud. Upon getting a closer look, I realized it was the same two vamps I had seen earlier, in front of the Crescent Moon. With that realization, a few horrible bugs crawled over their blank faces, going into their noses and mouths.

The princess' expression was terrified. A shaky hand went over her open mouth in shock.

"Lastan, Lastan, is that you?" she called to the brown-haired vampire on the right. The two statue-like figures simply stood there.

I swiftly asked, "Princess, who is Lastan?"

"He worked in the palace kitchen a long time ago. He was my good friend."

I could tell she was trying not to cry.

"Adam, Lastan has been dead for more than two years," the princess revealed.

My face went completely surprised, and the two vamps opened their mouths. Inside was an appalling swarm of terrifying, black insects. The bugs crawled all over them.

"By the twin moons," Vale breathed, "they are possessed!"

The two all-black-wearing dead closed their mouths. Two more statue-like, blank-faced vampires walked out of the alley to stand beside them. I heard the sound of thunder, and it began to rain, as if it were a sign of the horrors to come.

"I really think we need to get out of here!" I told Vale, but when I looked back to her, she scared me more than they did: Her eyes shone a powerful new red, that I had never seen before. It was like red vampire eyes times ten. When the frightening new deep-red color spread over the whites of her eyes, Vale's hair seemed to blow in a rain-filled breeze, that only appeared to touch her. She held her hands like claws, her fingernails growing long and sharp before my very eyes. The princess hissed fiercely, revealing long, piercing fangs.

The black-suited vampires simply stood there, unafraid and emotionless in the downpour. Fear and adrenaline welled up inside me. I really didn't know who the more frightening enemy was. One of the dead vampires walked forward, his wet arm extended, trying to grasp for me. Seeing that it was Lastan, I crouched defensively in the rain. Before I could do anything else, there was a swift swipe, and Lastan's arm was gone. Filthy, black bugs poured from the severed limb. Lastan, still totally without fear or emotion, looked where his arm once had been. Then he gazed at the hellfire mad princess. He opened his mouth again, showing the gross swarm of bugs.

Vale hit him with a windspell. It had such force, it knocked Lastan up against the brick wall of the store, tearing away the remaining limbs from his body, along with his head. The three other dead vamps pulled knives from their soaked shirts and attacked. Vale sent a claw-like hand deep into one of their sides. The strength of the blow, carried the dead vampire she struck clear into his partner, who was about to slash me. They both hit the nearby brick wall and crumbled, striking the wet ground with a nasty thump. The remaining bug-infested vamp pulled out a long, jagged dagger from inside the back of his black shirt. He flew into a dreadful onslaught of slashes. I batted his lethal blade away barehanded, trying desperately to avoid being cut. Finally, I swiftly kicked him in the gut. His wet hair flew forward, and the impact caused him to hesitate, standing in the pouring rain. It was all the princess needed to rush over, and tear the head from his body.

I watched her wide eyed and awestruck. As she dropped his insect-covered head into a newly formed puddle, Vale appeared to hiss frighteningly at me. I literally froze with fear. She moved like a total predator through the rain. There was no wasted motion at all in her movements. Time just seemed to slow down with her beautiful, goddess-like body moving towards me. My short life flashed before my eyes. Vale reached for me, and all I could do was accept my fate. But as I watched helplessly, I saw Vale's sharp, red fingernail polished claws shoot passed me. I spun in time to see the two dead vamps, she had knocked against the brick wall of the store. They were only about three feet away, brandishing their foul looking knives. With a single powerful stroke, the princess disarmed both of them of their knives and their hands. Oh, God it was totally horrifying! The emotionless dead looked at their missing hands. Vale grabbed them both by the throat, lifting them up off the ground into the downpour. I stared in amazement, as she tossed them into the air, hitting them with a single mighty wind spell. On impact, the two dead vamps shattered into a shower of filthy, black bugs. The princess turned to me. Seeing the fearful expression on my face, she stopped cold.

"Adam I..." She took a step forward. I took two steps back. An awful sadness seemed to envelop her.

Tears started to pour down her beautiful but monstrous face. I could see them even in the rain. Mere moments later, her expression hardened. Vale walked strongly and confidently to me. I knew I had no chance of escape. I shut my eyes expecting death, as she approached transformed into a complete predator. With Vale nearly upon me, I waited for the end, soon finding that it never came. I opened my eyes to see her standing right in front of me in the rain. She would not look me in the eyes, and I simply didn't know what to do. Suddenly, the princess spoke, still looking down at my chest in the downpour.

"Adam, I don't understand. Why are you afraid of me? I love you, I would never hurt you. I am only trying to keep you safe."

I began to move, but before I could, Vale started to cry in earnest. As the tears came down, she pleaded.

"Why can't you accept me? I have done everything right. But the blood-bond will not fully work with you." Vale looked at me with the same powerful, dreadful, red eyes she showed our enemies. I knew then that the princess didn't want to hide secrets from me anymore. "It is your blood that makes me strong, you know. This is what you do to me. You have changed me," she said as rain streamed down her face, mixing with her tears. Vale looked down at my chest again. "I am strongest right after tasting you... Why can't you understand, Adam. You gave me strength." She lifted her arms in the air around me, as though she was going to embrace me. But her arms just hung there still and motionless in the rain. "I will use this strength to protect you, Adam...and to make you mine," she added, tears still streaming down her face. "Why can't you be mine, Adam? Why?"

I hugged her lovingly, and she jumped at my touch. Using a gentle hand, I lifted Vale's totally vamped out face to peer into her frightening, totally red eyes.

"I do accept you," I told her. "But this is a whole new world. Everything works so differently here. Once in a while, I need a little time to understand, and really come to terms with what I have seen. You ask me why I can't be yours? But I was yours since the first night you showed up in my dreams." I took her claw-like hand. "Oh, Vale," I breathed, kissing her forehead, then French kissing her completely fanged out mouth. "There is so much I don't understand. It just takes a little time." I hugged her passionately in the rain, accepting the girl, the vampire, and even the monster.

"That is so touching. I think I may cry," came a wicked voice.

Vale turned around, once again becoming the predator. I looked to the alley, recognizing that voice. There stood a tall, muscular vampire in the downpour. He had a blue, roughly cut crystal orb around his thick neck. The malevolent Reev's face showed within it and spoke.

"Greetings, Princess! Did you know that deathreapers could turn the clock back, so to speak, on a long dead corpse, giving them the appearance of what they looked like before they died?" He gave a sinful smile as it thundered and the rain continued. "Have you enjoyed your little reunion with Lastan?" he asked. "He looks great, but I am afraid his sandwich-making skills have suffered greatly. Still, I think he may have been my best work."

The princess hissed angrily, showing her long fangs, looking even more dangerous than before. Reev gazed at her carefree from inside the little blue orb.

"That time of the month again, Princess? I was hoping there would be better timing for our meeting, this time. Oh, well, as long as the cramps don't kill you, I suppose it's okay. After all, that's my job," he grinned.

Reev then turned his wicked attention to me.

"Adam Westlin, the great traveler! The great 'human' traveler!" the deathreaper said, still smiling in the rain. "The only being able to cross the two worlds." The big dead vampire approached, stopping halfway towards us. "Drexelon will surely be pleased. I'm going to enjoy finding what makes you tick," Reev said, looking at me with a psychotic intensity. It was then that I realized the blue orb around the big vamp's neck, was the same kind that totaled Reev's carriage in the flower field, outside the city of Greyveil. Fear filled me, and Vale positioned herself protectively in front of me. It seemed all hope was lost, when a long, sharp blade immediately pierced through the tall, muscular vampire's chest. Taya stood behind him in her long, brown cloak, noticing Vale's new form only for a second. Quickly, she took the necklace with the blue orb, and flung it over the wooden gate, to the empty property behind the plaza store.

"What? No, you will not escape me again!" roared Reev.

With a swift motion of her brawny arms, Taya cleaved the big, unliving vampire in half. The creepy crawlies inside poured out like water in the rain.

"Hurry!" Taya commanded, clutching her sword with fury in her large amber eyes. We all ran speedily from the dead end behind the plaza building, and—BOOOM! The deathreaper's blue crystal exploded, turning the property and the wooden gate into little more than toothpicks.

We were all blown clear across the alley, to land ungracefully behind a long chain of more stores and restaurants. The path was boarded up into one long, puddle-filled straight run.

"I saw you two from the Crescent Moon, when you were at The Biting Fangs!" Taya said. "I knew you were in trouble, when I saw so many creepy vampires watching you. Once they followed you two into the alley, I gathered as many weapons as I could find."

"Thank you," I smiled. The amber-eyed, brown tan skinned werewolf put her hand on mine, smiling.

Vale looked away from us as it poured. If I didn't know better, I would say she was jealous. But now was not the time. As we all recovered, picking ourselves up, we found we were face to face with a truly enormous female naga. She had long, shiny black hair down to her waste and a short, red dress hugged her midsection with a silver breast plate. She also had grey scales and stood about nine feet tall, while she crawled low on her belly after us. The scary, female naga was the biggest thing I had ever seen. I mean her butt was almost to the ground as she crawled, and she was still nine feet tall. I stared stunned, and the big snake lady opened her mouth shockingly wide, to show hundreds of filthy, black insects scurrying around her insides. *Oh yuck, she's dead*, I thought transfixed.

Taya grabbed me, pulling me away from the gross spectacle. I snapped out of my weird trance, and the three of us ran as fast as our legs could carry us. When the giant dead naga pursued, her snake tail whipped ferociously, destroying crates and other properties. Taya pulled two more swords from her long, brown, wet cloak, tossing them to Vale and me... We both caught them, as more dead vampires started climbing over the plaza's gates, to get to us. We all ran through the rain for our lives, cutting down as many dead as we were able. Vale slashed so strongly, she cut cleanly through two dead, and beheaded a third in one smooth strike. Taya cut down one approaching vamp that made it over the gates, then used her claws to rip the face off another that lunged for her. The dead vampires hit the ground with a splash and dissolved into wet, foul heaps of filthy bugs. The big snake lady thumped her tail against the ground with awesome force. When she did a dangerous spray of razor sharp scales launched from her thick tail. We barely managed to dodge them. I hit the wet ground in the nick of time. Taya jumped for cover behind some old garbage cans, and Vale made a shield out of a couple of walking corpses. At this point, I was so hopped up with adrenalin, that I couldn't think. All I knew was instinct, slashing the head from one vampire. I quickly hit another with the hilt of my sword. His face disintegrated and horrible filth poured out. The huge, pursuing naga lashed her tail mightily over her head. Without thought, I slid across the ground, through the rain to avoid it. Vale and Taya each did awesome simultaneous backward flips over it. Upon landing, a couple of dead grabbed and held Taya. As she struggled, the massive naga hissed, stretching her huge mouth open, then shot straight for the female werewolf. Seeing what was happening, I ran for the two dead who were holding Taya down. I could feel something inside of me surge, and my speed was nearly instant. I chopped the heads from the two dead vampires, grabbed Taya, and sprinted forward, just in time to see the two headless, bug-infested bodies get simultaneously swallowed by the furious, giant, female naga who pursued us. When the gross bulge sank into her depths, I snatched up a second sword in the downpour from a dead attacking vampire, at the same time cutting him across the chest and neck, slaying him, as lightning flashed frighteningly in the background. I then jumped from the rain-drenched brick wall of a nearby store, to gain extra height—not that I needed it, because to my surprise, I found myself upside down maybe twenty feet straight up, looking down on Vale and Taya's stunned faces. When I saw the huge snake lady finished swallowing, she slithered and coiled. I concentrated magic like never before, focusing, then threw the dead vampire's twisted sword. It dimly glowed gold with a strange force. Not only did it hit its target, it blew the mighty snake lady apart in a shower of gross, black ash. I landed and there was no time for congratulations. The overwhelming dead immediately swarmed me. They were really vicious and way too close. I hardly could fight back against the crowd of emotionless corpses. Clang, clang our swords crossed wet in the rain as thunder clapped loudly. Soon, I could see Taya and the princess hacking dead carnage, to reach me though the downpour.

"Adam, Adam we're coming!" Vale yelled with both a hacking sword and slashing claws. Taya appeared angrier and angrier, I could see the muscles in her arms bulge and flex forward more and more, when her brown cloak flew back with each swing of her sword. It looked as if I saw her body literally grow a little when she growled, losing herself in the battle. We fought bravely, yet more and more dead joined the fight. Even Vale's spells did not seem to be enough. For every two destroyed, three more would block her path. The dead were slowly overrunning us, as it poured down raining.

CRASH! BOOM! CRASH!

Cloven's ugly modified carriage burst through the wooden gate, that blocked us from Greyveil Plaza, plowing down many of the foul corpses that stood against us.

"Get in the carriage! Hurry!" demanded Ulee, sticking her head out the front window. Feeling hope anew, the three of us sliced through our remaining foes, fighting back the undead crowd, while it grew even more. We all made it into the odd vehicle, with Vale's appearance swiftly going back to normal, when she entered it.

"We have to get out of here!" I told them.

Cloven reached under his seat, retrieving a corked beaker of glowing multicolored liquid. He blurted, "You never mess with a gen's friends! I think these guys are in need of a serious lesson!" He rolled down his window, and threw the glowing beaker, into the crowd of insect covered, wet dead. Not waiting for impact, the modified carriage instantly burned rubber in reverse. The beaker broke against the head of one of the many dead. Its multicolored contents spilled out onto the crowd. A weird light started to shine from the liquid. And the potion erupted into a swirling mass of cloudy blackness, immediately sucking in and swallowing up the crowd of horrible dead.

"What was that?" I asked.

"A banishing potion," replied Cloven, swerving out into the wet street. "A gen's best friend," he added. We sped off towards the castle through the intense rain. In the back of Cloven's vehicle, things were still a bit heated.

"We can't leave you two alone for a minute! What was going on back there?" Crystal inquired.

"The deathreaper!" I answered struggling for breath. "The deathreaper's minions have followed us. They have found a way to walk right into Greyveil."

"We must get back to the palace. Jaru must be informed as soon as possible," the princess demanded.

To my great regret, the fat, green kid heard her and floored it. We hit warp speed all the way back to Greyveil Castle, bumps, hills, mailboxes, and all. Back in the castle parking lot, the rain had all but stopped. We hurried alone, with Rafe and Crystal helping a still very overstuffed Ulee. In the halls of the wondrous palace, we soon found the head high priest. Upon hearing the news, Jaru had us follow him to his office. Through thick double doors, the room was spacious. It had four lamps, one in each corner, with cold, grey stonewalls. There was a large, expansive desk with two chairs in front of it. Many other cushioned seats lined the walls. We sat a big bag of fiblings near his desk, then walked over to a well-lit corner of the room, which had many empty chairs. The priest gestured with one hand for us to sit, and we all obeyed; as Ulee plopped down in her seat, her bloated body gave a little fart.

"Sorry," she smiled weakly, and a few members of our group tried not to laugh.

Jaru stood with his hand to his chin, peering down at us.

"Now, tell me what has happened," he said.

Vale stood up. "The minions of the deathreaper, Reev, have infiltrated the city. Adam and I barely escaped with our lives."

I added, "If our friends had not been there to save us, we would not be here warning you," then gave Taya and the rest of my friends thankful nods. Seeing that they understood, I turned my attention back to the white-haired priest, Jaru.

"I have received no word from Greyveil's gates of any attack, or a breach of any kind," he said.

"Reev has found a way to make the dead who serve him appear living," I told him. "They are walking in right passed the guards."

"Lastan attacked us behind the plaza," Vale said, clearly, wrestling with her emotions.

Jaru walked over gently hugging the princess. "I am sorry," he breathed. Then he turned back to us, appearing very serious. "How many did you see?"

The faces of everyone in the room peered at the priest, looking both fearful and grave. I could almost see the chill go up Jaru's spine. He instantly turned, speedily walking to his grand desk. He pulled a small one of those magic crystal displays from it, which I had seen my family in, when I first entered the city. Cloven stood up, adding that he had used a banishing potion to destroy the enemy.

"But there may be more," the green, red-haired fat kid said. Jaru quickly sat the crystal in a wooden box display on the desk.

"Answer, answer!" he commanded, touching it only once.

"Is there anybody there!"

"Swicer here, I thought I might check the outer defenses. Is there anything wrong, Lord Priest?"

"Yes, the princess and several of her friends have been attacked within the city gates."

"I know," the winged vampire cut in. "The Weird Sisters have already been ejected from Greyveil."

"That is not what I speak of," said Jaru.

Swicer stood at attention and called out, "Sir!" giving a vampire salute.

The priest continued: "The deathreaper, Reev, has a way to mask the appearance of his dead minions. They now appear living."

"Except that they have no emotions," I told them.

The priest added, "Except that they have no emotions. Allow no one entry into our gates. I will send special lenses to you. With them, you will be able to see the aura of the living, and its absence in the dead. Wait for my courier, and search the city for any of the deathreapers servants."

Waving a hand over the crystal to turn it off, the priest walked back to us and asked, "Is there anything else?"

We all looked at each other.

Vale replied, "I think that's all."

Our group then filed out of Jaru's office. On the way, I felt the high priest's hand pull me back. I turned to find both Vale and him waiting.

"Adam, there is a special class I wish you to attend. It will take place at eleven o'clock in Dailania's study, tonight. We will learn more about your abilities, and look for the answers you seek."

"Thank you, Jaru." I gave a little bow. Then Vale and I joined the others in the hall.

Chapter Fifteen

In the palace halls, we caught up to our worried, overly-excited friends.

"Just what in the void is going on around here?" asked Crystal. "Yeah, yelp, really!" they all agreed.

I took a deep breath and exhaled, deciding to come clean.

"I am really human," I told them simply. "And Reev followed Vale and me here."

Everyone immediately stopped walking and turned to stare at me. Rem giggled wide-eyed, and blew out a slow breath of amazement from his mouth.

"I thought you said you were from one of those little northern islands," said the fat, green gen.

"Actually, you said that," I corrected him.

"He's got a point," exclaimed Ulee, looking a little worse for wear.

Cloven slumped his shoulders and appeared glum.

"How did you know to show up there and save our bacon?" I asked.

"What's bacon?" asked Rem.

Staying focused, I continued. "What I mean is, how did you know we were in trouble?"

Rafe looked at me with his white irised eyes.

"Well, Miss Ulee needed something for her...situation." The full naga fidgeted a little. Rafe gave her a kind look, then turned back to me. "So we tried getting some medicine for her stomach, at a nearby potions shop."

Crystal cut in on the conversation. "After a while, Rafe started getting this weird sensation. It pulled his attention towards that alleyway, where you guys were."

Rafe in turn interrupted the skinny vampire. "It was the same feeling I get when I am near deathreaper magic. Trying to find the source, I eventually saw Adam. He was flying straight up maybe twenty-five feet in the distance."

I heard a few gasps from my friends, while Taya and Vale's eyes met with knowing expressions.

"Adam tossed a sword that appeared to explode," said the light grey-skinned phantom, "though I couldn't see that part so clearly."

"That's enough to get anyone's attention," proclaimed Cloven. "But now that we know you are human, it all makes more sense."

"Speak for yourself," demanded Crystal, "though I will admit that the history lesson in Miss Adreiel's class, is adding up now. But humans are extinct, if they ever really existed at all."

"How can you say that? Everyone knows that the humans created Drexelon. If he exists, then they exist, it's common sense," declared Cloven.

"That's only a bunch of legends. No one really knows where the great demon beast comes from," Crystal said.

Cloven was completely exasperated, shaking his head in disbelief.

Ulee slithered up in front of me, staring really hard. "So, you're a human," her eyes looked me up and down. "Where in Phantasma did you come from?"

Vale stepped forward. "He comes from a place called Earth, exactly as he told you when you first met. I brought him here through a gateway, he somehow opened up."

"Why in all Phantasma did you do that?" inquired a very bloated and uncomfortable Ulee. Vale's face reddened, while she tried to hide her naughty smile. Ulee's face instantaneously went surprised. "Oooh," she breathed. Crystal smiled along with her, and they stifled giddy female giggles.

I wonder just what I am missing in all this? I felt an arm around my upper body and chest. Whoever it was clutched me close to him or her. I turned slightly, seeing Rafe.

"I knew it! I knew it!" he said excitedly. "All those weird sighs, the aura, the glowing gold eyes, that strange magic you used to win our self-defense match. I knew there was something special about you!" the handsome phantom said, laughing.

"So why spill the magic beans now?" asked Rem, looking a bit shy.

Everyone looked at him, then back to me.

"Yeah, why tell us now?" asked Cloven. "I mean, you have kept the secret this long."

"First of all, I am the only human on Phantasma as far as I know. I am not completely sure what that means. But I do know that I probably shouldn't let everyone know right away. I do already have a deathreaper coming after me," I told them.

"I guess that makes sense," said Ulee.

"Second, you are my friends, and you just saved our lives. I would really like to trust you, if you give me a chance."

"I think that is something we all would appreciate," declared Cloven. "I also believe we have a unique, golden opportunity here to find out a lot more about humans. This is not something that happens every day."

Everyone agreed and the princess appeared a little worried. I was starting to wonder if this had been such a good idea after all. Outside, the rain had completely stopped. Within the castle grounds, on the other side of the two long stable buildings, where prying eyes could not see, our little group decided to gathered. They all formed a circle around me and the questions began.

"Why is Reev after you?" asked Rafe.

"I believe he was actually after Vale," I told him. "But having saved her from him more than once, I think he wants me now, too."

The group looked at the beautiful Vale. She gave a little nod of verification. They took a moment to think about what I said.

"How did you stop such a powerful enemy?" inquired Crystal.

Vale stepped forward. "Adam Westlin has very strong magical powers. Even the deathreaper cannot withstand them."

Cloven nearly choked, "Oh I think we are going to be very close friends indeed!" the fat, red-haired, green gen said.

"Ditto," Rafe added with a smile.

"I noticed that Jaru has taken an interest in you, Adam. I even overheard something about, a secret meeting up stairs in Darkdancer's study," blurted Ulee, peering at me slyly. All my friends focused on me waiting for my answer.

"There is no secret meeting. It's only a class he wishes me to attend," I said.

"A class where you and the princess are the only ones present? A little strange don't you think?" Ulee continued.

I really didn't know what to say.

"Adam, there are no classes that take place in Darkdancer's study. She is too much of a bitch for that," the naga proclaimed.

"I told you," said the princess, "Adam has very powerful magic. However, he has no understanding of how it works, or how to use it properly. The high priest has agreed to teach Adam, and help him find the answers he needs, to find a way home."

"Let me see if I can understand this," interjected Cloven. "Adam is strong enough to cross the two worlds, but he has no idea how he did it."

Vale nodded in confirmation, and the jolly, green kid couldn't hold back his laughter. "Wow, that is the most awesome thing I've ever heard! But don't worry, Adam, I have always wanted an apprentice," he said happily.

"Ditto," added Rafe.

"Okay, okay that is all fine and good. But what if there are more of those dead guys running around the city?" asked Taya. "As Adam's Daylight Guardian, I am a little worried."

Vale eyed her curiously for a moment, then said, "I believe Jaru and Greyveil's soldiers are well capable of handling the situation."

Cloven placed a green hand to his chin. "Adam here seems to have amazing potential. However, I believe it is a serious liability that he has no real training. The situation with the deathreaper only makes it that much worse. I know that Jaru has promised to instruct Adam. But this cannot wait. The more he knows about his abilities, the safer he will be. Princess, I think that Adam would benefit greatly from a few friendly, crash practice sessions with Rafe and me."

Vale hesitated, again appearing worried.

Rafe looked very tired, all of a sudden. "It will be all right. We will both protect him, Princess," he said.

Vale relaxed and reading her reaction, Rafe and Cloven told everyone they would see me back, to my guestroom in the castle afterwards, to prepare for Jaru's secret class. With that, we were off across the wet, well-maintained grass. I walked away with the green, fat gen and the handsome, grey phantom leading the way. I didn't know where they were guiding me to. But I took the opportunity to ask a few questions along the way.

"Cloven, I heard you say that you were a gen."

"Of the Geni Empire, what of it?" the fat, green kid asked.

"Did you mean like a genie in a bottle?"

"Genies are females, gens are males, and the hold bottle thing only happens, when one of us breaks one of our more serious laws. The elders are a bit harder on males however, they even change the spelling of gen G-E-N to jinn J-I-N-N, as a sign of great disgrace."

"So, being in the bottle is a punishment?" I asked.

"I will put it to you this way," said Cloven, "Would you want to live in one?"

"No way!" I blurted and the green kid smiled, as we entered the white fairytale-like castle.

"Oh, then there is you, Rafe; are you really a phantom?"

"Well, that is what my mother tells me. I am a loyal subject of the spector king," he said.

"You said you could feel deathreaper magic earlier. Why is that exactly?"

"Probably because deathreapers and phantoms are related, though no one really remembers how."

"Ooh," I told him, completely fascinated, while we hurried up a few flights of long, zigzagging stone stairs. At the top, we entered a small, wooden dungeon-like door. Once inside, I realized that the word dungeon didn't just describe the door. It also matched nearly everything in the spacious room, except for the bookcases and worktables, all sitting at the front of the grey, stonewalled room, within some sort of strange drawings on the floor.

When I bent down closer for a better look, Cloven stood over me, saying, "That is a seal of protection."

"What do you mean?" I queried.

"Anyone standing in the seal is protected from any dangerous, or out of control magic," he answered.

"Well, here we are," said Rafe. "This is the testing room. The walls are so thick and protected by such strong magic, that even dragon's fire cannot penetrate them."

"Let's get to it then, shall we," said Cloven.

The two of them stood together and gestured for me to stand before them. I did so, and they immediately began to speak, with Rafe going first.

"Adam, in our world, the first thing I wish you to know is everyone doesn't start out with great magic. Some of us are never attuned to it, thus cannot use it. But even those who are attuned to magic, usually only find out at puberty. I have no idea why. We'll simply chalk it up to the will of the ancients. But there are also those rare exceptions, like Prince Rem, who show impressive abilities from a young age. They usually come from families with a strong magical lineage, and must take up immediate training. To those with the gift comes a great advantage in life. Those without often occupy lower positions here. It may sound bad, but there are many exceptions, because I find that the greatest and most useful magic any being can possess, is simply hard work. With enough of it, you can accomplish almost anything."

Rafe stepped back, and it was Cloven's turn. The fat, green gen crossed his arms and spoke.

"All magic in Phantasma starts out as a kind of energy. It is our ability to channel and carry that energy, that is the beginnings of magic." Cloven held up a single finger, and a small ball of light appeared on the end of it.

"You see," he said, "By channeling energy through my arm and concentrating it, I am able to produce light."

The light went out, and he uncrossed his arms. "Now, let's see if you can do it."

I loosened myself up, held up a finger, and tried to channel energy into the tip. Nothing happened, and Cloven looked a little disappointed. I tried a bit harder, my fingertip burst into a mighty light. It blinded everyone but me, I guess because I was the one who created it. Rafe and Cloven dropped to the floor trying to shield their eyes.

"You can stop now!" yelled the fat, green kid.

Automatically, I made the light go out and put my hand down. "Is there anything I can do for you?" I asked.

"No, no, it's fine. I think our sight will come back soon," Cloven said, trying to find the front worktables to steady himself on.

I felt terrible hearing him say that. After five long, embarrassing minutes of me trying to help, they recovered their sight and we were at it again.

Still squinting, Cloven told me, "I don't think you have a problem storing magical energy."

Rafe cut in, "If anything, I think you need to practice moderation."

Next, they told me they wanted to test the strength of my magic. They setup one of those wooden practice dummies from self-defense class, putting a filthy, gold-scaled armor on it.

"What is that?" I asked.

"Dragon scale," said Rafe, "the most magic resistant thing in the palace."

This time, they both stepped behind the protective circle, which was carved in the grey stone floor, in the front of the dungeon-like room.

"Okay, we're ready! Take your place. Gather and compress the energy inside you!" Cloven instructed, "then channel the energy through your arms, releasing it from your hands in one big burst."

I did as he instructed, standing in front of the armored, wooden dummy. I started to draw in energy. It sent electric waves though my tense body. Then, channeling it through my arms, it spewed from my hands, decimating the armored, wooden dummy. The singed armor hit the floor smoking.

Rafe and Cloven watched with huge saucer eyes.

"Woh! That's what I like to see, pure, raw power! You know, Adam, projectile spells take a lot of power," proclaimed Cloven.

"For that reason, many can't even use them, unless tapping a secondary source of energy, such as an alpha bat mount or some other riding beast," added Rafe.

So that's why I haven't seen many spells flying outside of aerial combat. They both walked from behind the protective circle, with excitement on their faces.

"Wow, that was great, Adam, and from a guy with no magical training! You don't even look winded. I sure am glad you're on our side!" said Rafe, patting me on the back in congratulations. I laughed along with him, glad it went as well at it did.

The green, red-haired gen tried to pick up the armor for some reason. The now attractive-looking armor burned him.

"Ow!" he yelped.

"Why does it look like that now?" I inquired.

Rafe replied, "The blast you hit it with cleaned two hundred years of dirt and grime from it, Adam."

"Wow, it really looks amazing!" I blurted.

"It was a real piece of crap before." They both looked at me, starting to laugh, and I joined them. After a little more intense coaching from both of them, the light grey phantom kid suddenly appeared very tense.

"Okay, time to get serious," Rafe said. We know that you are capable of strong magic. But you must adapt, learning to use it in any and every situation. Remember not to second guess yourself; stay fluent and flowing. Time for a little magical sparring," declared Rafe.

We each took a place on opposing sides of the large, grey, dungeon-like room. Cloven commanded us to begin from behind the protective circle.

Immediately, Rafe flew at me with amazing speed. He threw a barrage of punches and kicks, I barely was able to block.

"Good, good!" he said, giving me a wicked look.

Suddenly, he moved even faster than before; so fast, in fact, that multiple copies of himself seemed to travel after him. In a flash, Rafe darted behind me, sending a magically charged punch to my kidneys. I stumbled forward, falling to one knee on the hard, grey stone floor. Cloven watched with intense interest.

"You need to empty your mind," the phantom told me. "There is no time for thought in battle. You must learn to act and react instantly. All that separates you from death in combat, may only be a fraction of a second. You must learn to use it to your advantage."

Not waiting for me to stand, Rafe ruthlessly attacked. He kicked me in the stomach and kneed me in the face hard, sending me to the cold stone floor. I looked up at him in shock.

"In battle, there is no waiting, Adam. Your enemies will show you no mercy. The reapers are death itself personified. You cannot hesitate, not even for a moment. You do and it will all be over." Rafe said grimly.

I charged at him, and he promptly disappeared all together. Stopping immediately after my missed punch, I looked at Cloven, who shrugged his shoulders, and smack! I felt a punch across my jaw.

"Stay focused on your opponent!" the unseen phantom said.

A little peeved, I instantly went into a series of furious, spinning kicks and punches, moving as quickly as I could, while I executed them towards the sound of his voice. I felt a kick connect, then heard Rafe hit the floor.

"I fall for it every time," he said reappearing.

I gave him a cocky smile, and he told me to just let go, to let the magic of Phantasma flow through my entire being. At the time, it seemed like a really good idea. Right away, I could sense the energy filling my body, making me stronger. I truly started to feel more powerful, and as my eyes met Rafe's, he stiffened and looked at Cloven. The fat, green kid gave a half smile, shrugging his shoulders. Instantly, I punched Rafe so hard he flew six feet, hitting the floor.

"Stay focused on your opponent!" I told him.

He stood up wiping a little blood from his bleeding lip, which immediately healed. *Oh, crap!* I thought to myself. We ran straight for each other, punching, kicking, and ducking.

With the magical energy welling up inside me, I was moving faster, jumping higher, and hitting harder than I ever dreamed possible. I wasn't thinking at all, I was simply letting it happen. Our battle was like some terrible, choreographed dance of death, where we each scored mighty blows trying to maim each other. Rafe suddenly caught me from behind in a full nelson.

"This is over!" he snarled, starting a strong run for the far, thick stonewall. He was going to smash me into it, like I was a battering ram. As we approached the wall, I ran my feet straight up it, flipping free of Rafe's grip. Magically charged, I flipped a couple more times in mid air over his head, then landed right on top of the grey-skinned phantom, with all my weight focused into a knee. Rafe hit the floor.

"I guess you were right," I told him. "It is over."

I stood up victorious, utterly pleased with myself. Turning to Cloven, I expected him to be thrilled.

What I really saw was a look of horror on his green face. I followed Cloven's worried stare back to Rafe, finding him cradled into a ball, writhing in pain. He pressed a hand to his back.

"Oh, no!" I said.

Fear for Rafe quickly replaced my feeling of victory. Cloven rushed to his side, trying to move him.

"We have to get him to the infirmary!" he said.

"No, wait!" I told him. "I think I can heal him."

"What! Only a priest or a priestess has the power to heal! No way!" Cloven exclaimed.

I pressed my hands into the young, grey phantom's back. Rafe stopped squirming painfully and seemed to calm down.

"You are full of surprises, my young apprentice," Cloven said with a smile.

"Yeah, I hope that's a good thing," I told him. A little after making certain Rafe was okay, both my friends started to stare at me really hard.

"What is it?" I asked.

"Your eyes, Adam, they are glowing again," said Rafe.

"What? What is happening?..." I asked.

In that instant, I was transported to a foul place, where the very walls and floor appeared to move and shift, in a very disgusting sort of way. Looking up, I found that I stood before Drexelon, the horned demon king himself. Petrified at first, I soon realized he could not see me. I then felt the touch of my friends' hands on my shoulders and arms.

"Adam, Adam what is the matter?" I heard them say.

Immediately, they too, were transported as well.

"By the twin moons!" they both said at the same time, looking stupefied as they peered at the mighty, armored, two-horned, fifteen-feet beast. He had a deadly devil's tail, with a wicked plate on the end of it that whipped around. A great, white, spiky mane of hair was atop his head, stretching down his back. Drexelon's lower face was covered with a bandana-like cloth, like that of an old west bandit's. And he wore a foul, red cape with huge, metal shoulder pads. The thigh-high armor on his legs was solid silver, and his spirit did not seem rooted in his body. The beast was also covered in living shadows. Having silver armor plates on both his forearms, he possessed sharp claws for hands and long, dragonesque feet.

"Don't be afraid," I told my friends. "I don't think he can see us; this is just a vision. I have had them before." I threw my chin towards the terrifying creature, directing their attention. And we all watched as the deathreaper, Reev, reported to his dreadful master.

"Great Drexelon," the deathreaper said, "I have infiltrated the vampire city. It is only a matter of time before it falls. The princess and human boy...

The horned juggernaut interrupted him, "Human, you say? There is a new human presence on Phantasma?" he asked. "You must bring him to me immediately."

"What of the princess?" Reev asked.

"She is of no importance. The human boy is all that concerns you now. What is the name of this boy?" the beast asked.

"Adam Westlin," replied Reev.

The great demon king swelled up, with tremendous power flowing from him. I saw the frightening deathreaper cowering in fear.

"Destroy the city and bring him before me. I shall send my undying shadow, to aid you once you are inside Greyveil," the beast commanded.

The vision faded, and we were back in the testing room. We all looked at each other, shocked. My friends stared dumbfounded, their mouths wagging open. I suddenly felt really weak, falling to the stone floor. Rafe and Cloven instantly picked me up, supporting my weight.

"What's wrong? Are you okay, Adam?" they both asked.

"I will be all right," I told them. "I guess when you came into my vision, it drained me a little."

Cloven peered into my eyes, more serious than I had ever seen him.

"Adam, we must report this to the High Priest Jaru. It cannot wait; we have to tell him what we have seen."

"Go on," I told them, "it will be okay. I'll go back to my room and wait for you there."

We exited the testing room. Rafe and Cloven hurried with genuine excitement in one direction, while I went the other.

Chapter Sixteen

As I walked the breathtaking white halls with gold trim, I soon realized I had no earthly idea where I was. I also knew that Greyveil Castle was truly huge and sprawling. I guess I wasn't thinking too clearly, after the boys entered my vision. It somehow drained me of my strength. When I peered down the long corridor, I couldn't help but think, this could take a while. Both tired and weak, I took a turn here and a left there. Walking wearily, I hoped to find someone to ask directions.

Ring, ring, ring…ring, ring, ring!

I retrieved my cell phone from my pocket, which showed a totally dead battery. Yet, somehow, it was still working. I was too tired to question it, so I simply answered.

"Hello,"

"Gal dang it Boy, fun is fun but when are you going to bring ya narrow ass back home, Son?" It was Grandpa.

"Sorry," I told him, walking along the impressive halls lost. "But I am working on it. I'm afraid it could be a while."

I heard him step away from the phone, and start cursing in the background, sounding like a pissed off lone ranger. When he returned to the phone, I quickly asked if everything was well at home.

"Of course, everything's all right. I'm only missing ma first in command. Not to put down ya little brother, Tannon, or anything, but that boy couldn't find his ass with a GPS, two hands, and a roadmap. I swear it's like keepin' company with a giant gerbil or something."

I gave a small giggle and told him to "Give it time. He'll eventually get better."

"I hope ya right Boy, cause I am missing you a powerful good bit right about now. Do you realize when I asked Tannon to trim the flowers in the front flowerbed, he did it with the dang lawn mower. Between you and me,

115

I'm about ready ta hogtie that boy, and toss him in a lake somewhere. I think it would probably help him put a few screws back in place. If you know what I mean."

I knew Grandpa was only kidding.

Boom! Crash!

I heard something over the phone.

"Dear Lord, give me the strength not to tar and feather my grandson," Grandpa said. "I gotta go, Youngster, while there is still something left to save. You stay safe, and come back to us now."

Grandpa hung up the phone. Hearing from my family always made me feel better. And right about now, wandering the halls of this huge palace, I really needed it. I snapped the phone shut, putting it away as I continued to walk. Eventually, I entered an area of the castle that was dimly lit for some reason. I walked along at a snail's pace, laying eyes on Spectra, the orange, black stripped, long-eared familiar of Darkdancer. She was quietly giving herself a bath, licking her fur in front of a large, open doorway, that a gentle light poured from. I merely waved to the strange cat, continuing passed the doorway in search of help. Suddenly, I heard a sensual voice call my name from inside the room. Slowly walking through the large double door portal, I found Dailania wearing her pink tank top with puffy, see-through shoulder sleeves, a pink mini skirt, and red leg warmers. She was standing inside with her hip cocked.

"Oh, hi, Princess Dailania. I am a little lost. Can you help me find my way back to my room?" I asked.

She said nothing, walking up then circling me. I was so tired I could barely think. She used a quick finger, to break and toss away the silver wolf's head necklace around my neck. Taya had given it to me for protection. Well, so much for that. The motion Darkdancer made was so fast and I was so weary, I barely even noticed it.

"What are you doing here?" she asked, looking at me with cat-like blue eyes underneath three pointy, brown bangs.

"Um, I'm lost," I told her.

"Where is my sister and her friends?"

"They are reporting important news to Jaru. It concerns a possible attack on the city."

It was like I was talking to her, but at the same time, I wasn't. She seemed to be in her own little world, as she circled me like a shark.

"An attack is very important news, indeed!" Darkdancer said, stopping right in front of me. She leaned forward, inhaling my scent deeply for some reason. Crap! I had a feeling I knew where this was headed. But in my weakened state, I didn't think I could escape her. "You look tired," Darkdancer said. "Please sit and rest a moment, while I keep you company."

I sat on a long, red couch. It was in the middle of a square, white room with gold trimmed walls. Four lamps with white shades were placed in each corner of the room. An expensive, thick, red rug with gold designs laid on a grey stone floor under the couch, in front of a large magic crystal display, that showed the perfect picture of a roaring fireplace. It wasn't a really big or spacious room. There simply wasn't much in it, so it seemed bigger than it was. Darkdancer sat next to me.

"This is my favorite room in the whole palace. I come here when I want to think or be alone."

"I am sorry. I really didn't mean to disturb you, so I will just be going." I attempted to stand, but Dailania immediately caught my hand.

"NO, WAIT! Please stay, I don't get much company. I would really like it if you stayed."

I sat back down and she relaxed.

"So is it true, you have bloodbonded with my sister?"

"Yes, it is true," I told her.

"Then you truly must serve Vale well. I have never seen her happier."

"What do you mean, 'serve'?" I inquired.

"You know, she is your mistress now. You have no choice but to do as she commands. Till she turns you, that is, oh young love."

"It's not like that at all!" I blurted.

Darkdancer stiffened then looked very interested.

"Please tell me how it is, then."

"The princess needed my help, and I was there for her. I care for Vale deeply, but I am not her slave."

Dailania looked puzzled. She thought about my words, brushing her three pointy brown bangs back.

"But Vale did bite you, didn't she?"

"Twice," I told her.

The tall princess appeared completely dumbfounded.

"How can you be bitten twice and still not belong to her, heart, mind, and soul?"

I shrugged my shoulders and gave her a blank look. She puzzled and puzzled over it, finally saying, "Unless…Vale hasn't claimed you at all."

Darkdancer slowly inched forward a little. I could see sharp white fangs extend between her full red lips. The scent of exotic flowers strongly overtook me.

Oh, God, that smell! She is trying to seduce me, I realized. It must be some sort of vampire allure. The whole time I simply thought that smell was perfume. But her scent is so much stronger than her sister's, it now seems obvious. Darkdancer was so beautiful, looking like a larger copy of her younger sister. She had long, brown hair tied by a red, glittery bow in a low hanging ponytail. Her eyes were a magical blue, as deep as any ocean.

"It's amazing, no vampire has truly claimed you yet, Adam. You've also penetrated the protective barriers that limit movement in the palace. It must be fate," Dailania told me.

"I didn't see any barriers, and that's not it," I said. "I am bonded to Vale, but our bloodbond works differently from the usual bond. She seems to draw power from my blood, but she cannot control me. Vale cannot will me to do what I don't want."

"Typical," Darkdancer said. "My little sister can't even do the bloodbond right. As usual, it looks like I am going to have to show her how it's really done."

I tried to stand, but Dailania was on me, before I even knew what happened. She pressed me into the couch cushions and moaned sexually.

"It will be okay," she said, giving my face a long, sexy lick of her soft, pink tongue.

Wow, the first princess was actually tasting me.

"Wait!" I told her. "Vale can still feel where I am, and if I am in danger."

Darkdancer giggled, snugging against my warm body on the couch. She gave my face another sensual lick before standing and telling me. "You look so cute when you are worried. I could see why my sister wanted you so badly."

A strange, otherworldly music started seemingly out of nowhere. Dailania began swaying, sexually moving and throwing her hips around in time with the music. I couldn't help but notice that they were really nice hips, too. As she danced, Darkdancer turned around, lifting her pink mini skirt to proudly show me her well-proportioned, muscular butt, half concealed in red silk panties. Its double teardrop shape was almost hypnotic, while it swayed and bounced in front of me. With her every move now, I could feel pleasure oddly flowing into me, like from some irresistible outside force, I was powerless against. My body warmed and God help me, I started to lust for the tall, brown-haired vampire. I wondered briefly what in Phantasma was Dailania doing to me. She continued to dance seductively, and I was unable to stop myself. My hand slowly rode up her perfect, long legs.

"Oh, Adam, I knew you were a bad boy at heart!" she laughed. "Just let yourself go, and I will show you things my sister never dreamed of."

I seized her mesmerizing circular ass, in front of me, and she gave a little whimper.

"Oh, yes, Lover, that's what I like," Darkdancer declared.

She lowered herself into my lap. Her exquisite, soft ass slowly and sexually began grinding harder, and harder into my still clothed manhood. She moaned more and more in ecstasy. My God, she was so hot! Dailania turned around, taking long, deep, sexy breaths. Then, spreading her legs, she mounted my very excited body with a gasp.

"You are even more gifted then I thought," she said, feeling me hard against her.

Her round, firm buttocks and thighs were warm in my lap. Darkdancer then pressed her c-cup-sized, soft breasts into my face, laughing. I grasped mighty, heavenly handfulls of her chest, as she smothered me. The scent of exotic flowers was overpowering. It seemed to sort of make me go numb inside. This was nothing like with Vale. What the hell was going on? The music still going in the background, Darkdancer arched her body and threw her head back in time with it. In every movement, I felt more and more pleasure penetrating me. Stopping suddenly, Dailania eyed me hungrily.

"By the void, you smell good and I'd bet you taste even better!" she said. I saw her open her fanged mouth.

And I somehow found the strength, to push her away onto the red rugged, hard castle floor. The music stopped and I stood up.

"This…this is wrong!" I blurted out. "I don't know what's happening here, but I do know that it is something I didn't choose. I'm leaving, Princess!"

I turned to wearily walk out of the room, and felt Darkdancer's hands around my neck. She was holding me from behind. Then, lifting me from the palace floor entirely, Dailania tossed me back onto the couch.

With a cock of her sexy hips, the double doors shut and locked. I was totally trapped in the room with no escape.

"Where do you think you are going? Adam, don't fool yourself, you are going to be mine. You're much too fine a specimen to belong to my little sister. A vampire prince of your caliber can only belong to me."

"But I am not a vampire or a prince," I told her.

"Two things I can change easily enough," she replied.

Darkdancer's eyes shone red, and she flew to me with incredible speed, catching me with a single hand by the throat. Immediately she pressed my lips to hers, kissing me savagely. Still weak, I could hardly make an effort to resist.

"Perhaps, you do understand after all." The princess said, kissing me more sexually with a moan, as her eyes turned normal again. "I love a mate who knows his place," she continued.

Her hand entered my loose-fitting, white shirt, touching all over my light bronze, muscular chest. She then ripped the shirt completely from me. I hardly had the strength to stand, and Darkdancer at this point was all business. Her hands were everywhere, carefully exploring my body. The princess' lips locked on mine, and I could do nothing, but experience her kissing me, with her fangs piercing my lips and tongue. Falling to the castle floor, the female vampire followed me all the way down, never removing her lips from mine. Her tongue whipped around wildly inside my mouth, while she greedily sucked the blood from me… When Dailania finally came up for air gasping hard, she mounted me once again. Then the sexy vampire caressed her belly and licked her lips.

"Oh! I just want to swallow you whole!" she said, staring at me with her blue, cat-like eyes as I lay there helpless beneath her. "I have never tasted anything like you," she added. "It's like drinking power itself!" Her tongue licked the remaining blood around her full, red lips and fangs, then Dailania sucked gently at her fingers. Her incredible blue eyes seemed to pierce my every defense. Only after a short moment, when time seemed to stand still, did Darkdancer plunge deeply into my neck with her fangs. It was so forceful, I jumped in surprise beneath her weight, while I lay on the hard castle floor.

"Mmmmm!" she moaned, sucking my neck with a ferocious intensity Vale never showed. For a moment, I thought she might take more than just blood. God, I really didn't want to die.

The princess' large, shapely, female body relaxed into mine. Hot on top of me, she pinned me to the floor, never letting up on my neck. Darkdancer then placed my hands on her round, muscular ass underneath her red silk panties. "Yes, yes! That's it!" she breathed with her fangs still penetrating my neck.

She started to rub her body and breasts forcefully and sexually against me, continuing to drink my blood. Full of desire, Darkdancer reached into my brown pants. Suddenly, the locked double doors were blown apart. A furious Princess Vale stood in the doorway. She was so upset, she was shaking. Dailania stood up, wiping the blood from her mouth and licking it. She cocked her hip.

"Well hello, Little Sister," she said.

Vale struck her with a wind spell, so fast and hard that she hit the white, gold-trimmed wall six feet up above the crystal display, cracking it before hitting the grey stone floor below. Vale gazed at me in my sorry state. Seeing that I could hardly move, she rushed to my side, picking me up. Vale was really strong for a girl, apparently, or even a guy. I guess it's another vampire thing. She placed me in a neighboring large ballroom. It had six-feet-tall windows on its far side, overlooking two dazzling moons in the night sky, with the palace courtyard three stories below. Vale turned to walk back and attend to her fallen sister. But when she looked up from me, Darkdancer was already in the ballroom doorway.

"Your bloodbond has failed, Little Sister! Adam is to be mine now!" she demanded.

"He will never be yours!" Vale snarled.

"He already is," Dailania said, licking her lips sexually, sucking my blood from her index finger."

Vale grabbed her older sister, throwing her with a great fierceness into the spacious, empty ballroom. Darkdancer landed on her feet, laughing.

"Oh, Little Sister, you were never a match for me."

Vale's eyes shone red with intense anger. "Things change!" she replied, running at Darkdancer with unbelievable speed, to lock hands with her older sister in a female vampire test of strength. They pushed and shoved at one another. But neither one budged an inch. Their grip finally broke, and Dailania punched her younger sister in the jaw. Vale took the punch, following it up with one of her own. Darkdancer appeared stunned, and the two vampire sisters exchanged blows. Moving like something other than human, they fought as though the battle had been somehow planned in advance. Both sisters seemed to know and counter every move the other made. Vale would punch, Darkdancer would dodge, going into a powerful kick, which Vale then flipped over. They were actually pretty much even, and they both realized it, stopping the battle.

"You've gotten pretty good, Little Sister," said Dailania.

"If you think that was impressive, just wait," said the smaller, red-haired princess. Vale moved with her vampire speed. Fearlessly clutching Darkdancer, she flipped the taller female vampire over her shoulder, with such forcefulness that the slam broke the floorboards of the palace ballroom. Instantly, upon landing, Dailania did the same to her younger sister. And they took turns smashing up the floorboards with each other's bodies. After about three slams each, Vale and Darkdancer just sort of circled one another like hungry wolves.

"Adam is mine now!" Dailania said. "You are too weak to bind him properly to you!"

"The human belongs to me, and I will not allow you to have him, Sister. You have always taken what is mine, but it won't happen this time," Vale said.

"It's not like you can stop me, Vale," retorted Darkdancer. The red-haired princess screamed, "Aaahhh!" They traded blows once again. Vale was punched in the mouth, and Dailania was struck in the eye. They stared at each other with a terrible hatred.

"I think it's time I ended this," said the bigger sister. She dropped her hands, striking a pose. The moment she made her magical motion, the plaster exploded from the walls, and the glass from the windows did the same. A powerful wind began to swirl around Vale. Her eyes shone a terrifying complete red, while her nails extended long, and her fangs grew even longer. My God, she was once more becoming the predator. I had once seen its fury back in the plaza alley. Darkdancer cocked her hip, and threw her long, brown hair into the wind. Immediately, many sharp shards of glass and plaster started to rise swirling from the floor. They floated suspended in the air all around us.

"Any last words?" Darkdancer asked as her blue eyes narrowed, and small chunks of glass and plaster started to hit Vale.

"Yes, Sister," the red-haired princess said. "Goodbye!"

Vale shot forward so fast I could barely see it, hitting her older sister so ferociously, she flew head first seven feet across the broken floorboards, then out the broken six-feet windows to the castle courtyard below. The floating pieces of glass and plaster dropped from the air. I could hear the guards below.

"By the two moons! It's Princess Dailania! Someone go and retrieve the high priest!" Barely conscious, I watched Vale slowly revert back to her normal self. She walked over, peering out the broken windows. Then everything went dark.

Chapter Seventeen

I awoke on a soft bed in a sterile, white room. It had at least twenty more beds in it, some occupied, some not. I turned my head forward and to my horror, I saw a large, alien box jellyfish floating above me. Its tentacles roved silently over my exposed chest. Every caress somehow made me fill a little better.

"Don't worry, it's called an *avzorvis*. They feed on negative energy, usually speeding up the healing process."

I sat up looking to see where the voice was coming from, soon laying eyes on Cloven and all my friends, except for Vale. They made their way to my bedside, being careful not to disturb the big, floating jellyfish. On arrival, they wasted no time.

"You look awful, what happened?" asked Ulee.

"I ran into Darkdancer in the halls," I told them.

Rafe and Cloven immediately stepped forward.

"It's all our fault," declared Rafe. "We were so scared and excited by your vision, we really didn't think to stay, to protect you."

"It is okay, I told you to go."

"But we knew that bitch would probably be hunting you," replied Cloven.

"Oh God, that's right!" I remembered. "Where is Dailania?" I asked.

Everyone suddenly got quiet.

"It took a while to clean her up. Jaru could only do so much. They're bringing her in now," said Rem, looking nervous.

No sooner that he had said that, four vamps dressed in white wheeled the female vampire in on a stretcher. As they passed us by, totally focused on the tall, brown-haired princess, we all got a glimpse of Darkdancer. She was conscious and one side of her face was badly battered. She also had a broken arm and leg. My heart sank and I felt terrible. I never meant to be the cause of so much trouble, especially between family.

"Will she be all right?" I asked. Everyone looked at me a little stunned.

"They are not sure yet," said Crystal. "But Dailania is strong. If anyone could bounce back, it would be her."

I watched the four vamps in white take her, to the furthest left-hand corner of the room. Pulling white curtains around the bed, they placed her in.

"So tell us what happened, Adam, not that we can't guess. But what exactly was she trying to do to you?" Ulee asked.

I tried to get my thoughts in order, taking a deep breath, then I spoke.

"Darkdancer found out that the bloodbond between Vale and me, wasn't working properly."

"What do you mean?" asked Crystal a bit surprised.

"Well, that the princess doesn't have the power to will me, to do what I don't want."

The skinny vampire with the dark brown plait sticking up in back gasped. "But how is that possible? The bond has always made the bitten subservient to their vampire masters!"

I looked at her completely bewildered. "So am I supposed to be Vale's slave?" I asked.

Crystal looked a little sheepish, then answered, "Well, yes!"

"Ooohh!" I breathed. I know Vale told me earlier, but I was still more than a little shocked.

"So you're saying that you're not her servant, slave or whatever?" questioned Rem.

"No, I am not," I told him.

He put a hand to his red-haired forehead and stared into space, while everyone else did the same...

I looked at my friends, wondering what their problem was?

"The second princess claimed you, but you are not bounded to her," said Crystal. "Darkdancer found out, and tried to claim you for herself."

"That's bad right?" I queried.

"Well, that is one of the ways vampires choose their mates on Phantasma," Crystal exclaimed. "Whether or not it is a bad thing depends on your point of view. There are those who accept it as a gift. There are also those who are chosen as slaves, or are made vampires against their will."

Without thinking, my hand reached up rubbing my sore neck. Everyone stared intensely.

"What?" I asked.

"She bit you, didn't she?" asked Rafe.

"Yeah, she did," I answered. My friends sort of stood there in limbo for a moment, thinking. "Someone going to tell me what's going on?"

"Sorry, it's just that when a more powerful vampire bites a bloodbonded person, it is possible for the stronger vampire to steal that person away," Crystal answered.

"So what you guys are really telling me is, that the bloodbond can be bad. But it's really just vampire love."

"Yes, but there are times when love doesn't even come into it. It could be just control. I cannot be sure, Adam. But it is possible that Darkdancer tried to bring you into slavery," Crystal told me.

Ulee started to cry. "Adam, we are so sorry, some bunch of friends we turned out to be."

I took her hand, rubbing it gently with my thumb.

"Don't beat yourself up," I told her, "sometimes these things happen. All we can do is learn from it, and try to do better the next time."

The naga cried freely, showing her concern. She hugged me, and I hugged her in return. Then I saw the head high priest enter the large, sterile room. He was pushing two big bowls of red mush, with two cups of water over to me.

"I see you are awake, Adam," he said, stopping at the bedside while the group parted, allowing him in to see me.

He shoved a big spoon of mush in front of my face. I immediately swallowed its contents and wished I hadn't. My eyes watered, my face scrunched up, and I wanted to hurl.

"It is only ruby fruit mush," he said. "It will help you heal and replace the blood you lost. It's really not that bad."

Oh, God, yes it was! But I said nothing, and I saw a few of my friends giggle wittingly. Well if medicine tasted good, it wouldn't be medicine, I guess. So I relaxed and accepted my fate. After several big spoonfuls of awfulness, Jaru told me he had spoken with Vale, and he knew what had happened. He seemed to get a little depressed. Turning away, he asked if I still cared for Vale. I answered, absolutely; nothing had changed. A bit surprised at first, I then saw him grin. He turned back to me.

"Adam, in light of what has happened, I think it best that we postpone our meeting, til a later date." I completely agreed.

Jaru smiled again, and told my friends to make sure I eat as much mush as possible. My heart sunk at his words. The priest grabbed his cart, wheeling it to the furthest bed on the left, going behind the white curtains where Dailania lay.

"So I guess we better get you better then," declared the fat, green redhead. "Open wide," he said.

I am ashamed to admit, the whole eating mush thing did not work out well for me. It took much longer than anticipated. After about half a bowl, they actually had to physically restrain me, and force-feed me. In my defense, the stuff was foul. And I don't think they would have won, if Taya hadn't been holding me down. Wow, that werechick is strong!

Everyone said it was for my own good, but I think they enjoyed it. That's right, pick on the poor, defenseless human. I could be wrong, but I really believe it may have been a revenge thing. Rafe was enjoying himself way too much. Don't they know you're supposed to be nice, to the hurt and hospitalized? When the deed was done, and the bowl was empty, Vale appeared in the infirmary doorway, not making eye contact with anyone. All my friends suddenly looked tired. They yawned, yes, all of them—at the same time. Then they told me they were going to go get some rest, and I should do the same. They all reluctantly funneled out of the room, passed a distant Vale. Clearly, she was worried about something. The red longhaired, beautiful princess sat next to me looking dreadful. She would not look at me.

"What is wrong?" I asked.

She just sort of sat there a moment, finally saying, "I won't let her have you, Adam. Darkdancer believes she can take what is mine. But not this time, I will never allow anyone to have you, but me. We will be happy together, Adam. You and I will make a wonderful future for ourselves," she proclaimed. A tear rolled down her cheek. I weakly reached over and took her hand. Vale's body tightened up at my touch. She immediately engulfed me in an overly passionate hug.

The princess couldn't hold back the tears, as she smothered me. "Adam, I thought Dailania may have stolen you away from me. She always takes everything," Vale snorted. "I could feel you were in danger. If only I had been faster," she cried.

I softly rubbed her back and hugged her lovingly.

"I am right here, and I'm not going anywhere," I told her.

Vale looked at me kindly, with tearful eyes that immediately stopped on the bite, Darkdancer had given me. Her eyes flashed a quick red for an instant, then got as big as saucers.

"She bit you!"

"So?" I said. "I'm fine. I feel a little drained, but otherwise, I'm okay."

Vale stifled a giggle, then got serious. "You don't feel attracted to my sister at all?"

I looked her in the eyes, and I couldn't keep contact. The tears started coming, and I did my best to reassure the princess, I didn't belong to Dailania.

"I am not her slave or anything," I told Vale. "Your sister simply looks just like you, only bigger with brown hair and blue eyes. Yes, I find her attractive, how could I not? But I am a one-woman-man, and you were here first," I told her.

She giggled a little and we kissed.

"Good! All this time I thought that maybe I did something wrong. That perhaps that was the reason I hadn't bonded with you completely; the reason I couldn't control you, making you completely mine, Adam." She blushed, showing a little fang. "I am glad that Darkdancer is also unable to completely claim you as her own.

Vale started getting a bit too excited. She kissed and lustfully touched my body. When she climbed onto me, I gasped in pain. "Oh, I am sorry, I didn't think it would hurt you," she said, retreating.

I put on a brave face trying to smile at her. Vale quickly relaxed, regaining her composure. She sexily blew me a kiss walking away, saying, "Get well soon," while she exited the infirmary.

Wow, I really enjoyed watching her curvy body leave. After a bit of time had passed, the lights went out so the patients could get some rest. Swicer had entered the building just prior to that. He was on guard duty, protecting Darkdancer. Laying there in the dark, I began to think. Dailania only did what she did out of love. She believed the bloodbond I had with Vale wasn't there or something. The more I thought about it, the more I believed that it was flattering, really. There are worse things than to be desired by a beautiful woman. Even if said woman is a vampire. I sat up at my bedside, gently brushing the swaying tentacles of the *avzorvis* away. I then walked through the silent, dark infirmary passed a few sleeping patients.

Once I had arrived at the white curtains that surrounded Darkdancer's bed, a very serious looking Swicer loomed over me, asking.

"Why are you not in bed, Adam?"

"I believe I can help the princess," I told him, "as I once helped you."

He seemed caught off-guard and thought for a moment.

"You would do this, even after what she did to you?"

"Yes," I nodded to him in the shadowy darkness.

The big, winged vampire with the wavy, brown hair and the tattoo down his right eye hesitantly stepped aside, allowing me through. I slipped quietly behind the white curtains. Above Dailania was one of those big, floating jellyfish. It was busily caressing her body. As I approached her bedside, Darkdancer opened her eyes.

My heart was broken, seeing her hurt so badly. It was like staring at a terribly injured, larger copy of Vale. I truly believed Dailania only wanted love. And vampire love is pretty rough any way you slice it, with the blood drinking and all. Who was I to judge? I kindly brushed her three-pointy bangs out of her eyes. She silently watched me, unable to speak.

"What you did was not good, Dailania," I said. "But I do understand it. I never wanted you to get hurt. Or to cause trouble in your family." I noticed Swicer's shadow on the corner of my eye. It came closer, falling upon the surrounding white curtains. He was listening intensely, motionless, and without a sound. I lovingly looked deep into Darkdancer's blue, cat-like eyes, paying him no mind. "I tried to tell you," I continued. "The control part of the bloodbond, for whatever reason, has no affect on me." A single tear rowed down her battered face. I gently wiped it away, caressing her soft, white skin. "You are amazingly beautiful," I admitted. "Anyone can see that. If I hadn't met your sister first, I would be proud to be with you. But I did meet her, and I must honor that relationship. I don't want you to be angry with Vale, Dailania. Because she has told me, you've taken nearly everything that was ever hers, her whole life. I see by the way you treat others that it is true." The tall, beautiful, broken vampire started to cry unencumbered, when she heard my words,

though she still couldn't speak or move. I leaned down, gently sitting her up. Putting my arms around the first princess, I embraced her affectionately, and simply let her cry it all out, while I held her protectively. The whole time, I could sense Swicer's eyes now peering into the white curtains. "You don't have to be strong all the time," I told Dailania. Laying her back on her pillow, I saw that snot was everywhere. Glimpsing the embarrassment in her eyes, I didn't want Darkdancer to feel bad. So I reached over to a cloth and washbowl, that sat next to her bed on a small table. I wet the cloth and wringed it out. Gently and without judgement, I cleaned Darkdancer's face. Her heavenly blue eyes watched me through the tears. I couldn't help but to lovingly cradle her beautiful, battered face with one of my hands. I then stood up, not making a big deal, and cleaned her snot from my shoulder. "I know that you have lived your lives like enemies," I continued, "but whatever is in your pasts, you should forgive and forget. Otherwise, it will drag you down your whole lives." I softly rubbed a little wetness from her forehead, kissing it. Then I lightly brushed her hair back with my hand. "I don't believe you want to be miserable. Do you, Princess?" Darkdancer only looked at me. "You are sisters after all!" I exclaimed, "two halves of the same whole. You must not hold grudges, your enemies are too great. You should be helping each other. It won't be perfect, but I promise you will be much happier for it. If you will think on this, I will help you. Will you do it mighty and powerful, First Princess of Greyveil?" She struggled and gave a little nod. "That's my girl," I told her. Placing my hand upon her head, I channeled all the power I could into healing her, just as I had with Rafe. Her back arched, and her eyes rolled up into her head.

Swicer quickly entered the white curtains that surrounded us. Watching with great concern, he didn't appear to know what to do, as he pulled a small crystal display from his cloak, clutching it tightly in his hand. Soon, I heard the princess' broken bones, snapping back into place all over her body. They mended while she groaned from my magical touch. Once again, I was unable to let go, until the healing was complete. When my grip finally broke free, we were both breathing hard, trying to catch our breaths.

Filling weaker than ever, I immediately turned away, to retrace my steps through the darkened infirmary, not even noticing Swicer's slack-jawed expression in front of the unmoving, but clearly healed, princess.

I climbed back into bed. As I lay there beneath the soothing tentacles of the *avzorvis*, I noticed Darkdancer was already standing over me, looking unbroken and gorgeous. Peering up at her, I couldn't keep my eyes open. Against my will, I drifted off to sleep.

Chapter Eighteen

I opened my eyes quickly looking around, expecting to find a very sexy, possessive, tall, female vampire. Instead, there was no one, and I could see that it was now morning. There was a blond cat girl nearby dressed in purple. She looked like a nurse, attending to the few patients in their beds. I yawned tiredly, then noticed Taya coming towards my bedside. She was dressed in her brown cloak pushing a big, covered platter on a wheeled cart. When Taya removed the lid, underneath was the most deliciously aromatic, hot food I had ever smelled. The female werewolf told me to please eat. I was more than happy to oblige.

I don't know if the food was really this good, or if I was just hungry as hell. But I was inhaling it with no signs of slowing down. As I stuffed my face, the pretty werewolf with long, brown hair and white bangs told me, I had been asleep for two days. I nearly choked. No wonder I was so hungry. After two days, I could probably eat my own shoes and enjoy them. If I actually still had them, that is. Taya watched me, smiling. I was a little embarrassed at my lack of manners.

"Oh, don't mind me; we werewolves see absolutely nothing wrong with a healthy appetite," she said."

I continued to eat, and Taya brought me up to speed on what I had missed.

"Darkdancer has mysteriously recovered completely," she said. "It is as if she had never fallen three stories from the palace."

I gave her a swift "Hmmm," still eating.

Taya peered at me suspiciously. I knew that she knew I had healed Dailania.

"Vale wasn't too happy about that," Taya continued. "The two sisters have been ignoring, and avoiding each other for the passed two days. But that's not the weird part: Dailania has been acting very peculiar—not simply towards Vale, but towards everyone. I am not certain, but she seems to have changed."

"What do you mean?" I asked.

"At times, she seems almost nice, if I didn't know better."

"That is good," I said. "I think everyone deserves a second chance."

Taya started looking at me suspiciously again. I concentrated on my food. She stared as if waiting for an answer to a question she hadn't asked. Ignoring her, I finished eating. Taya finally gave a small exhale, giving up. The brown tan skinned werechick then promptly reached under the cart, retrieving a not so big bowl of vampire fruit mush. All traces of happiness immediately left my face. She stirred the bowl and smiled to my dismay. So, after a mighty battle of wills...I ate the crumby mush.

"Is it just me, or does this stuff taste worse every time I eat it?" I asked Taya.

"This was concentrated, so it actually tastes worse," she answered, wheeling the cart away with a smile. "I am going to notify your friends that you are awake. They said something about a girl's day out. As your daylight guardian, I think it will do you good to leave this place and stretch your legs, so to speak. You may follow me back to your room. There you will find clean apparel and a shower."

Back in the guest-room where I had been staying, I found a nice red shirt and blue pants, just as Taya said, laying on the bed. I took a relaxing shower and put on the new outfit, slipping into some leather black boots, I found in the closet. When I had finished getting ready, I heard a knock at the door. It was Taya. She had a yellow rose in her brown hair. The appealing werewolf was wearing a flattering, short cut dress. It was the same yellow color as the rose, with matching cute shoes. She looked amazing, and I was speechless.

"Your friends are waiting down stairs," she revealed. "I will take you to them."

Following the attractive werewolf with big, beautiful, amber eyes, I eventually descended a long, white stone staircase to see Vale, Ulee, and Crystal all waiting for us. Wow, the girls all looked fetchingly lady-like in their new dresses. They all held their cute, little matching purses. Reaching the staircase's bottom, Ulee spoke first.

"Whoa! Adam you're looking lots better, raaarrr!" She sexily growled her approval at me. "I guess that nasty mash did the trick," Ulee added as she showed off her shiny, new, green dress.

"Yes, I must say you clean up nicely, human," said Crystal, sporting a purple, long cut dress with matching bangles.

Vale was merely standing there in the midst of them, appearing as a total vision of loveliness. She was wearing white, three-inch heels, gold bracelets, and an amazing, above–the-knee-length white dress. It had a low cut front and back neckline. The revealing dress nearly floored me.

"Greetings, Princess, you and your friends are looking truly lovely today. I really like your dresses," I said looking deep into her eyes.

"Thank you. I thought you might like to join us today, Adam. It could not have been good, being cooped up in the infirmary for so long," Vale said.

"Yeah, come see how the girls have fun!" interjected Crystal.

"We promise we won't try to beat you up, like the boys did," said Ulee with a smile.

"Hey where is Rafe, Cloven, and Rem anyway?" I inquired.

"Oh, they're off doing boy things… I think they may have gone off in search of better personalities," proclaimed Ulee. They all laughed and I stifled the urge, only grinning.

"Okay ladies, let's go out on the town," demanded Crystal, raising her arms in excitement as she did a little jig.

Nearing the front entrance, our mostly female group came face to face with Darkdancer and Spectra, when they entered the castle. She and Vale froze for a moment, gazing at one another. The tall, brown-haired vampire then looked at me and spoke.

"Good evening, Lord Adam, I am glad to see you up and well. I hope you will excuse my earlier behavior. I'm afraid I misunderstood the nature of things."

I didn't remember ever becoming a lord. But I guess I'll roll with it. She acknowledged Vale and the others a little stiffly. As the tall female vampire walked away, I blurted, "Would you like to come with us, Princess?"

Darkdancer stopped in her tracks and turned back to us. All the girls had befuddled looks on their faces, including Darkdancer.

"Drexelon's spiky, tailed ass, she will!" said Vale in a huff.

Dailania fearlessly approached and faced her younger sister.

"You should know that what happened two days ago, only happened because you surprised me, Vale. Now that I know what you are capable of, it will never happen again."

"Are you sure about that?" asked the red-haired, smaller princess with a pinched brow.

"I believe that Lord Adam has invited me, Little Sister. If it is his wish that I accompany him, then I intend to do so," declared Darkdancer.

Vale's eyes suddenly shone beyond angry, to the scary, predatory red they were the night that Dailania was hurt. To my surprise, Darkdancer's eyes shone the same frightening red. Holy crap, they were both vamping out! I noticed the other girls gingerly backing away. I threw myself between the two princesses. Their chilling eyes each returned to a regular upset red, then became fully normal.

"Will you two please stop this!" I pleaded. "It's like you are not family at all. Why do you hate each other so much?" I asked. "You know what, it doesn't matter! Whatever is in your pasts, forgive it and forget it. You two are going to be sisters for the rest of your lives. You can't change that, so please accept it. You are two halves of the same whole. Ladies, you almost look like twins. I would hate to come between you. Dailania, I am with Vale. It is not going to change. Do you understand?"

"I understand, Adam. But I need for you to understand. I know that you choose my younger sister. However, should she relinquish her claim on you, or let you go even for a second, I will be there to snap you up. Let's just say you will be staying in the family."

Vale hissed her disapproval towards Darkdancer. The tall, female vampire simply stood without fear, gazing at her sister.

"Okaaayyy, fair enough I guess. Now, can we please stop being at one another's throats?"

They both slowly nodded.

"As long as she remembers that you are mine!" exclaimed Vale, looking Darkdancer in the blue eyes.

"Now, shake hands!" I told them.

When they did it, I hugged them both.

"Now, this is how family should be!" I proclaimed.

I was glad they seemed to take it well. For a moment, I thought they might tear me apart. I'm so glad it went the other way. I really hated that the princesses despised one another so. We left the castle at last. Outside was a white horseless carriage with gold trim waiting for us. The ladies and I all entered, sitting uncomfortably. The tension was thick, and the two sisters were eyeing each other. I think everyone was expecting firework…so I reached over, rubbing the attractive siblings legs, reassuringly.

"Girls, it will be all right. It is better to be friends than enemies, you will see."

They both relaxed a little, and the carriage pulled off. I did all I could to keep the young ladies happy, and their minds off their long-standing hatred. I told them about my home life, and many misadventures with my little brother, Tannon. It kept things interesting. The ladies laughed all the way to our first destination, which was of course shopping. The carriage stopped in front of the Weapon's Master shop, that Taya and I had once visited. Leaving the carriage, we all entered the little store.

"Ah, hello girls, welcome to the Weapon's Master! I am certain you will enjoy our new selection of weapons. You can't be too careful, you know. Demon attacks are on the rise these days," said Lanerva. The red-feathered female shopkeeper with blue trimmed wing, finally noticed I was with them. She froze, staring for an instant.

Then Lanerva walked over to Ulee, to offer advice on a few new items.

"What's with her?" asked Crystal.

"I am afraid she is a victim of Adam's earlier charms. He has quite a way with the ladies," said Taya.

She and the three vampire girls huddled together. I knew that Taya was spilling the beans, about the earlier incident with Lanerva. I pretended to be interested in a few little knives, that lay on the shelf in front of me. Suddenly, a dark shadow fell over me out of nowhere, while I hunched over. I looked up to find the big-breasted shopkeeper with arms folded, tapping her finger.

"May I help you, Young One?" she inquired.

I turned to her, knocking over the entire box of knives.

"Oh, um, yes, I mean no, just looking for right now." I clumsily picked up the box of knives. The blond haired, red-feathered harpy with blue trimmed wings walked off. I heard lots of devilish giggles behind me. The girls all ran over. They affectionately touched my red shirt wearing chest, and back with their gentle hands, teasing me.

"Oh, Adam, you are so smooth. How could we possible resist you?" they all said.

I smiled and the girls laughed as Ulee slithered up. Crystal began whispering into her ears. The naga smiled and started making kissy faces at me. Our trip had only just started, and I was already blushing so hard, I could probably signal spaceships, if any were up there. In this place, I wouldn't doubt it. The girls selected their accessories, and I even helped a little, being the guinea pig for Ulee's demon spray, which she accidently sprayed me with. Thankfully, it only turned my black hair green. Afterwards, Crystal told me she liked it, but I didn't believe her, on account of the stupid smile, and dumb look plastered across her face.

Vale was trying out an odd, little five-inch metal stick. She waved it around trying to get it to work. I walked over to help, and the thing extended to about five feet long, hitting me in the center of my forehead. I picked myself up. Looking into the reflective surface of a nearby shield, I saw a big, bright, red dot the weapon had made. The girls tried not to laugh, but Crystal and Ulee were soon rolling in the aisles. I told them that it was okay. I concentrated, focusing my magic and healed myself. Lanerva stared amazed, and all the girls, even the princesses, started laughing. I looked at my reflection again in the shiny shield. The red dot was gone. But my hair had gone rainbow-colored, red, yellow, green and orange.

"Don't worry, Lord Adam. I think it's cute," said Dailania.

I relaxed a bit, and decided to see what Darkdancer was looking at. Walking over to her, trying to strap together some dignity, I saw she had a silver shield, with little lightning bolts going around its gold trim. As I approached her, a small thunderbolt instantly shot out from the shield, striking me. I awoke to two giant breasts hovering over my face.

"There, he is awake," Lanerva said, corking a little potion bottle she used like smelling sauce. "You girls may want to be more careful. At least til he learns a bit more about how things work around here. Adam is still a bit too green to let go unattended," the harpy warned.

They all agreed and we soon left the Weapon's Master shop, with a few shopping bags in tow. Back in the carriage, they all asked if I was okay.

"I'm fine," I reassured them.

The carriage hurried off to its next destination, which was the Crescent Moon. When we entered the store, Taya and I were greeted warmly by Zeno, the tall, lanky, mature werewolf storeowner with brown, graying hair.

"Good evening Princess," he said, looking towards Taya. She was mortified…

"Ah, we are over here. You know, the Princesses!" Dailania corrected him.

"Oh aah, yes, sorry about that," Zeno said. "I am getting older, and I sometimes get a little confused these days. But please, ladies, look around. I have received a large variety of potions that are sure to please."

All the girls immediately fanned out in search of good bargains, while Taya and Zeno walked whispering among themselves, over to the counter. The big, amber-eyed werechick did not look happy. By the time she walked away from Zeno, he looked totally defeated, as if he had just been scolded by his mother.

That's weird, I thought. Then, an over-excited Ulee seemed to appear out of nowhere.

"Adam," she said, "you have to see this!" She dabbed a bit of potion on her wrist. Instantly, her curly, short, brunette hair turned to living snakes. I shot out of there so fast, I'd like to think I left a dust trail. Ulee just stood there, saying, "What?" One of her hair snakes actually bit her. "Ow!" she jumped.

So hiding on a far aisle, I mean reassessing the situation, I didn't notice Crystal come up behind me.

"Hey, Adam, could you tell me what you think of this?" She sprinkled a little yellow liquid from a small bottle, onto the backside of her hand. Nothing happened at first, then Crystal's a-cup sized breasts expanded to size double D. "What do you think?" she asked, jiggling from side to side.

I said nothing, completely speechless. I could only stare with my mouth wide open, on the edge of a wet dream. Soon, I felt a hand on my shoulder pulling me away from perhaps, what I believed was the greatest invention ever made. Surely, humankind could benefit from its use for centuries to come!

"Get over it,Lover Boy, it's only an illusion. You try to touch those things, and you're in for a 'small' surprise."

Snapping out of my daze, I saw it was Taya's muscular arm that pulled me away. Crystal hissed at the bossy werewolf.

After a bit of distance, Taya released me, telling me to be good.

"Yes, ma'am!" I told her.

She walked away, silently watching from afar. Looking down the aisle she left me in front of. I noticed Dailania poring her attention over an item. Walking over to her, I asked.

"Hey Princess, what cha got there?"

Darkdancer nearly jumped right out of her skin. I thought her reaction was odd, until I saw the many love potions in front of her, and the one clutched in her hand. I felt a dumb expression appear on my face. I stiffened and simply walked away, coming face to face with Vale. She peered at the love potions, then to her older sister. Darkdancer smiled innocently, and put the potion back on the shelf. Still watching her sister, Vale guided me towards the other side of the store, where she started to smile, getting a bit intimate. She coyly showed me a tiny, brown bottle.

"What is that?" I asked.

Vale moved in close, whispering, "It's a fertility potion."

Instantly, I saw everyone in the Crescent Moon, stop what they were doing, and stare at Vale and me. We both turned bright red. The princess quickly walked off, to rummage through more of Zeno's stock. Thankful for the save, I went up to the front counter.

"Hello Zeno," I said, then nodded to Taya. "I hope Taya didn't hurt your feelings earlier." She tensed up, glaring at me in surprise. "I know from my vampire fruit mush experience with her, that Taya can be very bossy, downright forceful, really. And I saw her lay into you earlier. Are you okay?"

He paused for a second and answered. "Yeah, it was my fault. Sometimes, I wonder why she even bothers with an old wolf like me."

Taya looked on him with loving eyes. Then I noticed the girls starting to come up front with their items.

I could only guess at what terrible things, were concealed in those little bottles. When Darkdancer's turn came, she spread maybe fifteen or more items across the counter. Zeno rang them up, while Taya eyed the tall, brown-haired princess suspiciously. When the lanky werewolf was finished, Dailania had spent a small fortune. Taya hurried over, bumping the first princess as she took her bags.

"Oh, sorry," Taya said, "you know us weres clumsy, clumsy!"

Dailania snatched her bags, saying, "Yes, you are!" then hurried out the door to the carriage. Once she was gone, Taya sat a small bottle of love potion on the counter.

"Darkdancer had this tucked away in her dress," revealed Taya.

The girls gasped, and Vale just looked plain angry.

"I didn't sell her that," breathed Zeno.

"I know," replied Taya. "Remove the love potions from the selves. If she comes back, tell her you're sold out." The female werewolf walked to me adding, "Adam, outside the castle, I am charged with your safety by the High Priest Jaru. If anyone endangers you, even by something as foolish as a love potion, they will soon regret it. Even a princess of Greyveil," she warned.

When we returned to the white carriage with gold trim, it was getting dark, and Darkdancer was in a good mood. She suggested that she choose our next stop. Vale drew her fist, moving forward. But I stopped her, calming her by rubbing her shoulders.

"Please," I offered, "where do you think we should go next?"

A diabolical smile came over Darkdancer's face, and soon, the carriage pulled in front of The Biting Fangs. A 3D moving hologram of the restaurant's fanged, glowing sign was projected into the night sky, and the tall, brown-haired vampire led the way. Inside was a mundane eating establishment, there was a kitchen area, that seemed way too large for such a small restaurant, from what I could see through the order window. The place had a bar and seven tables, with six booths lining the walls. After we entered the restaurant, a thin, young male vampire about my height walked up, and hugged Dailania.

He had black hair, and he was wearing an aristocratic, red dress coat that had metal, pointy shoulder pads. His pants were black, and tan boots were on his feet.

"Hi, Val!" Darkdancer said, "they are with me."

"Ah! Any friends of yours are welcome here anytime!" said Val.

"Have you gotten any better, with those twin banishing pistols of yours?" Dailania asked.

Instantly, the red-coated, black-haired vampire pulled out two shiny, metal, weird-looking firearms from his coat. With amazing reflexes, he took aim at an ugly, standing cardboard cutout of himself, firing off two shots almost faster than I could see. The cardboard cutout was covered in the same swirl of blackness that appeared, when Cloven used his banishing potion. Then, the unflattering advertisement disappeared altogether without a trace.

"We can't all be as blessed as you are with magic, Princess. But I am a god, as long as I have my two little ladies here," Val said, waving his twin deadly weapons.

Darkdancer gushed a little, and they walked passed the kitchen entrance, to a big, iron door in the back.

Val put away his pistols. "I never liked that cutout, it just didn't capture my inner bad boy," he said. The red-coated vampire then had a really big, well muscled vampire unlock the heavy door. The instant it was opened, loud music poured from inside. When we walked in, Val declared, "Welcome to The Biting Fangs!" That huge kitchen is making a lot more sense now!

Chapter Nineteen

The Biting Fangs was a huge, open, dimly lit area. It had many dazzling lights here and there. As well as many dim, little, fairy-like, floating lights all around. A spacious dance floor was at its center. And a few vamp waitresses came from a second kitchen entrance, working the many round and square tables surrounding the dance floor. The high ceiling supported artistic balconies, and there was also a well stocked bar counter. It was positioned in the left-hand corner as we came in, having eight red bar stools. Straight forward from the entrance door, passed the dance floor was a small, curtained stage area with many filled seats in front of it. Beautiful women danced lustfully there. I noticed because the curtains were see-through. All the dancers had huge breasts and well-developed asses.

This can't be real, I thought to myself. One of the dancers was tall, ivory skinned, and wearing gray. She had the same color beautiful, long hair that sort of looked like peacock tail feathers. Another dancer possessed copper-colored skin and a high, tight, white-haired ponytail with two pointy bangs in front. She was wearing blue, though they both had on very little, G-strings and bikini tops mostly. They also both sported big, transparent wings. The peacock's wings were grey outside and red inside, while those on the dancer in blue were pink.

"See anything you like?" Darkdancer asked in a low voice. I cleared my throat, feeling a little embarrassed for watching the curvy ladies. "Careful," she continued, "they are dark fairies. Male vampires tend to like their um...assets. But be warned, their bloodlust is just as great as any vampire's. Actually, some are considered to be vampires by many," Darkdancer told me.

"But I saw some fairies earlier; why are these so much bigger?" I asked.

"Once certain fairies drink the blood of another, they take on their attributes, usually size being among them, not to mention that the fairies become addicted to the taste of blood, not that there is anything wrong with that," Dailania finished.

The fairy wearing blue looked at me, and I swiftly looked away, as we shuffled over to a table. Moments later, I peeked a little and saw that the fairy was still watching me. *This can't be good*, I thought to myself. We pushed two square tables together, sitting in the back, not too far from the bar.

"Hey, how about I get everyone a few drinks?" Darkdancer blurted.

"That would be great," I told her.

She speedily rushed over to the bar.

"I wonder how long it's going to take the princess, to realize she doesn't have the love potion anymore?" I said.

The girls all choked back a laugh, as we listened to the awesome music that played.

"Hey ladies, I don't know much about dancing, but would anyone care to dance?"

"I thought you would never ask," said Ulee.

She took my hand, practically dragging me onto the dance floor, through the beautiful, fairy-like lights. On arrival, Ulee swayed to the music, her arms bobbing up and down while her yellow-bellied, blue snake tail with red diamonds lashed from side to side.

Here we go, I thought, starting to pick up the rhyme. I simply moved, dancing in time with the song. Then I grabbed the snake girl, lowering her close to the floor and bringing her back up, as we continued to sway and enjoy ourselves. Ulee was laughing,

"This is fun!" she said. "If you weren't already Vale's, I might have to make you my little lunch box, Adam."

I just laughed, secretly curious about how true that was, and wondering. What the hell was a lunch box? As we danced on, I jumped from right to left, dodging Ulee's powerful tail when it swept across the dance floor, undulating with joy. I even saw a few of the surrounding dancers, actually bounce in reaction to its considerable weight, as her tail thumped against the floor a few times. Also, Ulee unwittingly hit more than a few people, while we were dancing... But who is going to complain to a giant snake? Everyone just seemed to grin and bear it. A quick snap of her thick tail, and a good fifteen percent of the watching crowd went down. Ulee didn't even notice, lost in the music. I quickly got in close behind her, holding her curvy hips to me as we danced. Ulee took a lustful breath, and her tail undulated between my legs, while I held her. Let's face it, I think this may have been the only safe place, on the whole dance floor. When the song ended, we returned to our table.

Dailania still had not returned, and Crystal was waiting for me. She took my arm, pulling me towards the dance floor again. A bit caught off guard, I looked at Vale.

"You are the only boy with us," she said shrugging. Back on the dance floor, the skinny, small-breasted vampire was like a whirlwind, spinning this way and that. I could barely keep up with her energy, as Crystal left little fires floating in the air while we danced, at every snap of her fingers. The excited girl vampire soon placed my hands on her hips, and told me to hold on. She jumped into the air, going between my legs with me still grasping her. I pulled Crystal back up, and threw her high into the air again. Catching her, I spun to the right then the left, with me passing her behind my back twice. It was like having my very own set of living vampire nunchucks. I threw the little fire bug straight up, catching her one more time, and gently setting her on the dance floor. We continued dancing and speedily spinning to the music. The whole place had noticed us, gathering around. And a trail of flames suddenly ignited across the floor, under Crystal's spinning body. It was quite a sight, seeing the overjoyed vampire have fun. She broke out of the spin, grinning and standing before me like a woman possessed. Then the song ended.

Heading back, Darkdancer still had not returned with our drinks. And, of course, Vale was standing there in her amazing white dress, waiting for her turn. The music slowed down, and a love song played, as fairy lights swirled above. On the dance floor, I lovingly waltzed with the long, red-haired princess. It was like heaven. I don't know if it was the music or the setting, but my feelings for her seemed to overflow in the moment. I held her close, and could hear women swooning all over the dance floor, while I gently touched her angelic face. Then, Vale seized me, as though claiming me for her very own. We gracefully danced slowly across The Biting Fangs, looking one another deeply in the eyes. I lifted the princess up into the air, never breaking eye contact. We spun around and around to the lovely song that played so clearly. She appeared as an angel above me, and as Vale descended into my waiting arms, I hugged her far more emotionally than was appropriate, ending the dance in a kiss so profound, that for an instant, we seemed to become one. The surrounding crowd applauded, and a few ladies fainted. We took a bow and returned to our table. Upon arrival, both Taya and Darkdancer simply grabbed me, heading back out onto the dance floor. They dropped me in the middle of the cheering crowd. Then on each side, they circled me to a hard rocking kind of music. Dominantly, Darkdancer grabbed my shoulders, starting to dance with me. Boy, she really liked skin on skin. For a moment, I thought she would rip my clothes off right there. Soon, I felt her nipples hard against me, when she did her sultry dancing. Taya walked up, spinning me around. The gorgeous were also began dancing, and she wasn't shy. After a bit of close quarters breasts to chest dancing of her own, her brown, tan hands seemed to travel every inch of my body. The amber-eyed werewolf then actually let me grind against her well-toned ass, to the crowd's delight. Dailania pulled me away, and Taya pulled me back. Somehow, I soon found myself dancing with both of them at the same time. I moved like mad trying to keep up, first grabbing Darkdancer, spinning and dancing around and round to her enjoyment. When I put the tall she-vamp down, I caressed her soft cheek and immediately went to Taya, dancing super hot and close together. Our bodies almost seemed to get lustfully tangled up in each other, while we danced. Eventually I pulled myself free, to Taya's small protest, then tossed her into the air.

Surprisingly, her fine, athletically muscled legs wrapped around my head. We spun around and round like a propeller to her gleeful laughter, with Taya finally letting go, going into a midair backwards flip. When she landed on her feet, Taya stood tall and confident, looking to Darkdancer as if to say, "Top that!" The tall, brown-haired princess cocked her hip, and the fairy-like lights and crowd were magically pushed away, making more room on the dance floor. Dailania looked at me with her blue, cat-like eyes and I froze. She magically glided across the dance floor to me. I could see an intense longing in her eyes. As we danced, Dailania was more passionate than I had even seen her. Moving and swaying, her hands roved all over me, when she circled. We began dancing more and more intensely, the dazzling lights flashing around us. Soon, our very feet lifted from the dance floor. I was filled with a gentle pleasure, not forceful like before, when her magic tried to control me, and Dailania took my blood. We continued to dance to the music, ascending gently into the air. Enjoying every moment of it, we flew higher and higher. It was such an incredible experience. Nearly to the ceiling, in the upper shadows of the club where it was hard see, Darkdancer asked, "Do you know why I am called Dailania, Adam?" Tiny sparks of light lit gently in the air, created somehow by the female vampire's power. They came down before our eyes like beautiful snowflakes, so we could gaze upon each other. The first princess continued, "I'm called Dailania, because it is the name of the vampire goddess of justice, that I am named after. She is very passionate and very loving," the sexy vampire said, running her fingers through my hair. "She always gets what she wants," Dailania finished, holding me possessively. Then, looking me deep in the eyes and quietly leaning forward, Darkdancer told me she loved me. Before I could react, she hugged me close, kissing me passionately where no one could see.

We quickly descended back to the dance floor. There, Taya clapped along with the rest of The Biting Fangs dancing crowd. Darkdancer took a little bow, making her way back towards our table. The long brown-haired, white-banged werewolf asked if she should get us a wedding gift?

"Big-eared mutt, I suggest you keep your mouth shut, if you know what's good for you!" snapped Dailania. Taya just gave her a look that said, "Oh, really!"

They both headed to our waiting friends, returning to the table, through the fairy-like, floating lights. Vale looked a little lost as she stared off into space. I sat next to her, hugging her and rubbing her arms all at the same time.

"It's only a dance," I kissed her.

Thirsty from all the dancing, I quickly gulped down the drink Darkdancer had gotten for me, and nearly had a heart attack. Coughing and wheezing I asked, "What was that?"

"I think it's called Dragon's Fury," answered Vale.

"Good stuff!" I replied, patting my chest trying to restart my heart.

Vale and the other girls giggled at me. Being brave, or stupid, depending on your point of view, I requested, "How about another?" This time, it arrived promptly.

I guess Darkdancer didn't bother looking for the love potion with this one. I swiftly downed the Dragon's Fury. It warmed my insides. After picking myself up off the floor, I looked around telling the girls, there were a lot of pretty women at our table, and it was great to have five dates.

"Ulee," I said, "that snake butt of yours…" She gave a little warning rattle.

"Looks amazing!" I finished. "You're going to make some lucky guy or dinosaur very happy. Crystal, you're a lovely 'little' lady." She looked at her small breasts and back to me. "Please, don't set me on fire," I added. "Taya, I have always liked dogs." They all sort of laughed, and the pretty female werewolf gave me a puzzled look. "Dai Dai," I said, looking to Dailania. "You are awesome, like some wonderful dream…or nightmare. I've got the fang marks to prove it. Then there is Vale, a goddess come to life. Have mercy on me, dear goddess, for I am only a man," I requested.

They all looked at each other and Ulee exclaimed, "He's drunk!"

"Already?" asked Crystal.

I nuzzled Vale's long red hair, informing her that she smelled great for a deity.

Then Val visited our table. "You all really know how to party," he declared. "It is my pleasure to inform you, that the house is offering a free lap dance, at the dancer's request."

I peeked over to the stage area, seeing the same white ponytailed, pink-winged, blue-wearing fairy that eyed me earlier. The girls were about to protest, when I hopped up out of my seat, yelling, "Party! Party!"

The thin male vamp with black hair and a red dress coat led me to the stage, going to a small room on its right. It had red-cushioned love seats lining the walls, and a single cushioned chair at its center. Val sat me down on the chair, and I forgot why I was there, along with my own name. As I sat there waiting, the gorgeous, copper-skinned, white haired, pink-winged dark fairy walked into the room.

"Hi, my name is Aleeta," she said.

Her bikini-topped breasts and sizable ass, both stuck out a bit more than normal girls, but not in a gross way. It was more in an attractive, instantly attention-grabbing, sexy sort of way. It didn't take me long to be at full attention, if you know what I mean.

"Whoa, your butt and tits are gigantic!" I told her.

"That's not a problem, is it?" Aleeta asked.

"No, I think they're awesome, and I think you're awesome!" I replied.

"How sweet, I think the same of you," she smirked sensually taking a seat, facing me warm in my lap. Her eyes were pink and large. She had a strange, unnatural beauty about her. "Your aura is like nothing I have ever seen before. What are you, handsome?" she asked, lightly massaging my ear with her tongue.

"I am a human being," I slurred with a hiccup, enjoying her lady-like touch.

First a bit shocked, slowly, Aleeta started to sexually press and rub her nether regions into me, moaning. She guided my hands over her shiny bubble butt, where I was more than happy to take a few mighty handfuls, of the impressive mounds. Aleeta then began carnally moving up and down, gently straddling my body. Still laughing drunkenly, I simply enjoyed the show, unable to stop myself from softly moaning a little in delight. Aleeta was a professional after all. She pressed her overly huge bosom into my face, and I sank between them, breathing deeply of her candy-like scent. Then, crushing me between her mighty melons for a while, and feeling me up thoroughly, she gasped in ecstasy. Aleeta suddenly threw one long, curvy leg over my head, spinning around to show me the juicy ass, that I had so gleefully been massaging. Her otherworldly buttocks began softly stroking and nuzzling against me, slowly working their way up my body and pressing into my flesh, while Aleeta used her mystifying hips. When she could go no farther, her hands grabbed my head, plunging me deep into the g-stringed depths of her ass. She seemed to enjoy it, moaning and groaning sexually as she rocked from side to side, holding me there. Finally, the fairy allowed me some air, from the presence of her well-perfumed butt cheeks. Aleeta then decided to sit her sizable rear on my overexcited, swelled manhood. Merrily, she rubbed her big bubbles hard into me, while she clutched my hands to her over-grown breasts. Still way drunk, I told her that her wings (which were like large insect wings, yet oddly a bit batwing-shaped.) were beautiful, just like she was. Aleeta outstretched her glorious, transparent pink wings, and I smiled at her. That was all the excuse she needed. Her lips parted, and I could see fangs every bit as big and sharp as Vale's.

"You have a pretty mouth, just like my girlfriend's," I said, drunkenly.

Aleeta gently ran the point of her fangs against my neck. When she was about to bite, she froze. Slowly, the dark fairy hesitantly stood up in front of me. I looked to the open doorway, seeing both Darkdancer and Vale looking pissed. As they walked over, Aleeta was lifted, choking from the floor by Dailania's power of magical motion. The two sisters stood on both sides of the ensnared fairy, each firing off powerful, spinning jump kicks, that Aleeta's head was sandwiched in the middle of. Her eyes rounded up into her head, and she fell unmoving to the floor.

"Never liked these damn fairies!" Vale said. She then examined me carefully, declaring, "The fairy didn't bite him. We made it just in time."

Darkdancer looked out the door onto the busy dance floor. "By the void, I think it would be best, if we got out of here, Vale."

The red-haired princess threw me over her shoulder, going over to her older sister. Looking down, I had a great view of Vale's perfect, yet plump, round ass. I patted it like bongo drums, then plunged my face between the circular mounds, thinking I was still in the lap dance.

The princess jumped, blurting, "Ooh!" I giggled mirthfully.

"Shhhh!" Dalainia demanded.

Vale simply shrugged her shoulders, stroking the back of my legs. We shot out swiftly passed the fairy lights and stage, across the dance floor. Drunkenly, I waved to all the people we passed by.

Back at our table, the princesses promptly told the others what happened, and that we had to be leaving.

They all retrieved their purses, and we saw two big vampires checking the back room, where we left the unconscious, white-haired fairy. One of them immediately sprang from the room, calling to two more big vamps.

"Oh crap!" Ulee and Crystal both said at the same time.

We hurried though the crowd, going though the heavy, metal door while two large, muscular vampires pursued. But Val was waiting with two more huge vampire bouncers, on the other side. Our little group stopped right there.

"Why in such a big hurry, ladies? I do hope you were enjoying yourselves," said the thin vampire with the red dress coat. I told him his hair looked great!

Two more vampire bouncers burst through the heavy door behind us. Ulee quickly coiled around them, squeezing. As big as they were, they were both totally immobilized, Ulee giving one of their cheeks a little wet lick, while eyeing Val.

"What is going on in here?" demanded Val.

"Your fairy tried to taste my bondmate!" snapped Vale.

Val appeared stunned. Then he asked the two vamps Ulee was squeezing, if it was true. They nodded their heads yes, and Ulee gave them another squeeze.

"Ladies, ladies, please! I am sure this is only a misunderstanding. I assure you that the parties responsible will be dealt with. Also, please know that with your next visit to The Biting Fangs, all drinks and food will be half priced."

Ulee and Crystal gave silent little "Yays!"

"Now, which of you felt that your bloodbond mate was in danger?" asked Val.

Vale and Darkdancer both raised their hands. Everyone in the restaurant's empty front stiffened. The two vampire sisters looked at one another.

"You felt that Adam was in danger?" Vale asked her sister.

Dailania simply and slowly nodded her head up and down. Vale and all the other girls' eyes grew to the size of saucers. Val said nothing, only taking a deep breath and pulling a small crystal device from his pocket. He then went over to me. I was still draped over Vale's shoulder. Wow, she really was strong!

"That is a nice coat, can I try it on?" I asked Val as he stood before me.

"No, but I like your hair. Rainbow is so in right now." Val pressed the device to my forehead, and watched as it turned a weird gold.

"What?" he started, then blankly told the princesses, "This will verify your bloodbond, and if the boy was truly in danger."

Val walked over to Vale, holding out the little device. She pressed a finger to it. After a moment, it glowed sky blue.

"Positive," he said. Vale's shoulders slumped and she exhaled in relief. To her surprise, Val reset the small device, once again pressing it to my forehead. It turned gold, and he held it out in front of Darkdancer. She pressed a finger to the gadget, and it felt like an eternity...

Finally, the little device glowed sky blue again.

"Positive!" proclaimed Val. The two vampire princesses looked at each other, shocked, which quickly turned into a wicked grin on Dailania.

"You are both telling the truth," said Val.

"But no one has ever been bloodbonded to two vampires at the same time," said Crystal.

"It's impossible!" declared Vale, while Darkdancer smiled with her mouth open in glee.

"I don't know. It's the first time I have seen it myself. Maybe it is because you are siblings," said Val.

"But this has never happened before, even between siblings!" snarled Vale.

"Look, I only wished to find the truth, and we have done that. You are all free to go, ladies! Clearly, there is much for you to talk about."

Reentering the carriage, I was still feeling the effects of my Dragon's Fury drinks. I sat between Vale and Darkdancer, as they eyed one another.

"What a great party! I hope these pink elephants never go away. I call that one Fredrick!" I told them with a hiccup.

"What's an elephant?" asked Taya.

Everyone shrugged their shoulders.

"Hey Ulee, were you really going to eat those guys?" I asked. "Because I bet it's nice and comfy in your belly, all warm and soft. In fact, open up, I think I'd like to check it out."

Ulee simply smiled, looking at the two vampire royals, then to me. I got up from my seat, and the two princesses pulled me back down. Hitting the seat, I giggled. "I see, I went and left the vampires out!" I slurred. "Well, I think you ladies could use a drink. So come on, I could take all of you, I have had plenty of yucky mush." I laid back in the seat, and told them to go for it. Drunkenly giggling my head off, I saw them both ever so slightly licking their lips, while Crystal simply sat there, like a fence post, looking left out. Vale and Darkdancer both started forward, stopping when each one glimpsed what the other was doing. I laughed trying to focus my eyes. "I guess that just leaves you and me, Taya," I proclaimed. "How about a bone," I offered, showing her my naked, light bronze-colored leg. I saw a glimmer of amber light shine through Taya's large eyes, then I passed out.

When I reopened my eyes, I saw that I was being dragged back into the palace by the girls. They suddenly stopped, and I heard a familiar voice speaking. Looking up, I saw Aldett with a bit of worry on his face.

"Princesses, I need for you to prepare yourselves. The king will be arriving sometime tomorrow," he said. "The human is expected to be presentable."

I stood up, stepping forward. "I am presentable," I told him, falling flat on my face, with my butt up in the air.

"I would sooo bite that right now, if you weren't here, Vale!" exclaimed Darkdancer. Then I drifted off into unconsciousness.

Chapter Twenty

The next day, I opened my unfocused eyes to the horrid sight of a fat, green, red-haired woman in a purple cloak, laying next to me.

"Aaahhh!" I yelled. "Oh God, what did I do last night?"

She quickly sat up in bed confused, while I tried feebly to explain, getting to my feet. "Ahhh, Miss, I am really sorry, but I was very drunk last night. I am afraid, I don't remember a thing."

A light gray hand grasped my shoulder, steadying me. My vision cleared, and I saw that it was my phantom friend, Rafe. He was laughing as hard as he could. Not understanding, I hesitantly looked back to the bed, seeing a big-bellied Cloven Demairaskiet grinning at me. He fluttered his eyelashes and tried to look sexy. I nearly barfed, but managed to stop myself. It had been the green gen all along.

"Did you enjoy yourself last night?" he asked in a high-pitched voice, caressing his man boob.

This is so not working for him, I thought. Rafe was literally rolling on the floor, giggling madly. "All right, all right!" I said. "What are you guys doing here? I am pretty sure I did not bring you here from The Biting Fangs, last night."

"You went to The Biting Fangs last night?" asked Rafe finally regaining a little control.

"Yeah, Dailania got us in!" I told him. The two boys looked at one another in shock. "What?" I queried.

"That is the most popular place in the city. Most can't even get in," said Rafe.

"Yes, they're very selective about who they allow to enter. Everyone also says, that Val guy who runs the place is really bad news. Something about him being wrapped up in Greyveil's criminal underbelly," the fat, green gen interjected.

"Yes, everyone believes he is a really big player in Vampire Territories crime, Adam. But no one can prove it," the handsome grey phantom added. Thinking hard about their words, I noticed that my hair was no longer rainbow-colored. I looked in a nearby dresser mirror, running my fingers through my black hair.

"Oh yeah, we fixed it for you. The King of the Vampire Territories, Sevorift Annadraus Shadowwind has arrived, and he requests an audience with you as soon as possible," revealed Cloven.

"Yes," continued Rafe. "They sent us to help get you ready. A word to the wise: Say as little as possible, and you will be fine."

"Oh and they also want you to wear this," Cloven held up the most aristocratic dress suit I had ever seen. It was white having gold, leafy vine designs on its sleeves and coat chest, complete with a blue silk shirt and matching white shoes.

"One more thing," the fat, green gen breathed. "We have to do something about that hangover. You are in bad shape. How much did you drink last night any way?"

My head was throbbing, and I held up two fingers. The boys instantly both doubled over, laughing. "That's right," I told them, "pick on the poor, hung over human." They tried to control themselves and broke out in laughter all over again. "Okay, let it all out!" I instructed. A few minutes or so later, I was fully dressed and looking good.

Rafe held a small glass of foul, grey, lumpy liquid up to me. "Drink this," he said. "It's not honey mead or anything. But it is the only way to get rid of a hangover fast enough, to get you ready for the king."

They both paused waiting for me to drink it. As I tipped the glass over into my mouth, I saw their expressions go from normal to pure wonder. After gulping down the grossness, I licked my lips, asking if they had any more.

"That was the nastiest thing, I have ever seen," said Rafe. "I've seen worse," added Cloven.

He stepped forward to straighten my collar. And I burped the yuckiest burp imaginable right in his face. "I stand corrected," Cloven said. "I am truly impressed." Then he turned away, gagging. "That stuff is a creepy kind of nasty," he declared.

Pleased with myself, I hurried over to the bathroom, washing my mouth out. Moments later Rafe and Cloven led me through big, white, elaborately decorated doors, to a large throne room. It had gigantic, white columns extending all the way up, to the twenty-five-feet high ceiling. Beautiful, long, red banners hung from the columns, with the gold letters G.V. The floor was a shiny, scarlet mirror, that seemed to slightly change red shades, as I walked. And wondrous crystal lights lined the outside of each big column. Aldett, Jaru, Vale, and Dailania were present, along with all my friends. They were gathered around a yellow seated, golden throne, which supported a big, tall, long-red-haired, emerald green and gold armor clad, oily-bearded vampire. He had triple shoulder padded, pointy shoulders. When the boys and I approached, I heard Aldett telling the king, that the elves had been successfully repelled. However, he was able to gain information, of a possible coming attack on the castle. Aldett didn't think there was anything to it, but was here nevertheless.

"Ah, hello, Young One!" King Sevorift said with his blue eyes somehow piercing deep into me. "I have been looking forward to finally meeting you, Adam Westlin. I am told my beautiful daughters have kept you on your toes, so to speak. Not only that, you have also pulled a distant Vale from her protective shell, and survived my Darkdancer, I hear they both regard you as quite the prize."

"Father!" the princesses both bleated.

He finished by saying, "Impressive!"

"Thank you, Your Majesty," I retorted, blushing a bright crimson.

The king then requested, "Please tell me about these visions of yours, Adam."

A bit overwhelmed by his impressive presence, I just couldn't get it together. "Well, aaahh, you see, ummm...," I stuttered a little, frightfully.

Cloven and Rafe both bravely stepped forward, with Cloven humbly saying, "Forgive us, Your Majesty. But I and my classmate were both present, at the time of one of Adam's visions. When we touched him in the midst of the experience, we too were drawn into it, and peered at the Demon Beast King Drexelon himself."

Ulee, Darkdancer, and the others froze with serious expressions on their faces, gasping. Then they continued to listen, silently.

Rafe cut in, saying, "Not only that, but we also observed the deathreaper, Reev. He was planning a coming attack on the palace with Drexelon."

"But was that not three days ago?" the king asked.

The high priest gave a modest nod.

"Why then has he not attacked?" Sevorift continued.

"We cannot answer that, Your Majesty. We can only tell you what we saw," Cloven said.

The king took a breath in frustration, then turned his attention back to me saying. "I am told that you are bloodbonded to my young, Vale."

"Yes, Your Majesty. I care for her greatly," I informed him. He seemed a little puzzled.

Darkdancer stepped forward, "Father, I too, am bloodbonded to Adam."

My jaw nearly hit the mirror-like, crimson floor. The king's unwavering face grew surprised. Talk about bad timing. My mind immediately flashed, *why yes, Mister King, I am two-timing your princess daughters. Just thought you'd like to know.* I didn't even know if that was true, still unable to remember much of what happened last night.

"How can that be?" Sevorift asked, snapping me back to reality. "No being has ever been bonded, to two vampires at the same time. The stronger bond always destroys the other. It simply isn't possible!" he proclaimed, looking directly at me.

Darkdancer told him, "I don't know, but I have a claim to Adam, Father."

Vale hissed at her sister, cutting it short when Annadraus looked at her. He stared for an instant at them both. Then, he ran his green-armored hand through his long red hair.

"Do you both truly care for this boy?" he asked. Both princesses sincerely and silently nodded yes. He again thought for a moment and said, "I am sorry girls, but this has never happened before. I am afraid you must work it out amongst yourselves."

I could see Vale's heart sink, while Darkdancer began staring at me with hungry eyes. Surprisingly, I then noticed a heartless, almost wicked look. It was deep in the king's eyes, towards his oldest daughter.

"Dailania, stop ogling the boy, and show some strength like I taught you!" the king demanded. "You are the First Princess of Greyveil. You don't have time for foolish, little love games! I expect much more of you than that child. You must be a pillar of strength always, in these trying times."

Wow, I thought, *this guy really needs to pull that stick out of his butt*. He hard-heartedly started towards her. Darkdancer swiftly stood a bit straighter, stiffening. Immediately she took on the bitchy attitude of old.

"Yes, Father," Darkdancer said, trying to sound strong and confident.

But her voice cracked in fear, and for the smallest instant, I could see, she wanted to cry. Sevorift stopped walking towards her and promptly left the throne room, with Aldett in tow behind him as he spoke.

"There are urgent matters that I must attend to. Please, excuse me!"

After he left, everyone relaxed. It was as if someone had magically sucked all the tension from the room. I slumped, exhaling and breathing easier. A still high-strung Jaru appeared before me.

"Adam," he said, "now that you are well, I wish to see you in Dailania's study within the hour."

I nodded my compliance, and he quickly followed behind the king. With only my friends left in the throne room, they quickly gathered around me, but I instantly went straight to Dailania. Spacing out, she jumped a little when my hand fell upon her puffy, pink, see-through shoulder sleeve.

"I am so sorry," I told her. "I never would have guessed, that your father was pushing you so hard."

Everyone was watching me in astonishment. Then they were completely blown away, when Dailania clutched me to her soft breasts, and openly cried on my shoulder. I rubbed her back softly as the tears came down, telling her it would be okay.

"You must respect your father, but understand that it's all right to be weak sometimes. People who always need to be strong only hurt themselves."

She lifted her head, gazing at me with her blue, cat-like eyes, looking awful.

"We all need rest at some point," I told her. "So you must understand that it's okay for you to relax, Dailania."

She placed her head back on my shoulder, continuing to cry. "We are your friends. It's okay for you to be yourself around us... We won't let him hurt you," I said. She hugged me to herself even tighter, sobbing as if I were life itself. I tried to loosen her grip, but her embrace grew stronger still around me, and she quietly continued to cry. "Don't worry," I told Dailania gently. "If you ever need me, I will be there." Her arms suddenly slackened, and she slumped to the mirror-like, scarlet throne room floor, weeping with her hands covering her face. Ulee and Crystal gingerly helped her up, with Taya instructing them, that she'd guide them to Dailania's quarters.

The moment I turned from Darkdancer, Vale was right there in front of me. She smacked me hard in the face, asking, "Why?"

"Because it's not her fault," I said. "I can't be sure, but I think your father has molded and manipulated her all her life. I saw him, Princess, and he scares her." I peered into Vale's beautiful, green eyes, softly saying, "She needs help, Princess. She is alone, and Darkdancer needs someone to be there for her."

Vale turned away as tears came down. "What about us?" she asked.

"Nothing has changed, Vale. I still love you, and when I say 'be there for her,' I am not just talking about me." I saw her body release its tension, and Vale simply followed after her sister.

Once the princess was gone, "Whoa! Wow!" Rafe said, with Rem softly giggling.

"That was like thunder!" the phantom kid exclaimed.

"Really loud thunder!" said Rem. He did his best impression of a thunderstorm.

Rafe then informed me, "She smacked you so hard, I thought it was going to break your neck."

"She could do it too," Cloven interjected.

They both nodded their heads up and down in agreement, while Rem added, "and get away with it, too."

"You are all exaggerating," I told them.

"Adam, there is a big, red, princess-sized hand print on the side of your face," bleated Cloven.

I reached up to touch it, and it stung painfully. The three goof balls started laughing, with Rafe saying, "It's never boring with you, is it?"

I held my sore cheek, rolling my eyes at them, and we headed for the palace infirmary. On the way, Rem was running around, with his arms out like an airplane circling us. I wondered if he even knew what an airplane was? Arriving at the infirmary, we were greeted by a cute, blond cat girl in a purple nurse's uniform. She was only a shade less muscular than Taya. It was the same cat girl, I had once noticed before. Her hair was down her back. She had mismatched green and blue eyes. Long bangs were on her forehead, also going down beside the pointy cat ears on top of her head. Rem started acting odd. I thought he turned a little pink, standing there staring at her, with a dumb smile on his face.

"Hi, Pan Pan!" Rafe said. "Adam here has had another unfortunate mishap, with another vampire Princess of Greyveil. I think we are going to need something to take care of this." He motioned a light grey hand to my bright red, hand-printed face.

Pan Pan first told Rem, "Welcome back," with a wink.

The pink on his face immediately turned to candy apple red. When the feline female finally saw my face, she was instantly taken aback a little.

"Wow, that princess didn't hold back!" the perky cat girl declared.

Rem gave a light giggle, shyly looking elsewhere when Pan Pan's eyes met his.

"Which one was it this time?" she asked.

"The redhead," Rafe replied.

Her eyes widened in surprise. "I thought for sure it would have been the tall, brown-haired, wild one again," she said.

The cute, blond cat girl then led the way down a sterile, white hall to the right of the infirmary entrance. I hadn't noticed it before. At the end of the hall, we walked into a new part of the infirmary area, passing many individual little examining stations, with all sorts of weird, otherworldly remedies on their many surrounding selves.

"Here we are," Pan Pan said, while gesturing to the examining station to the far left. I sat on a white-sheeted bed, where Pan Pan started to take a closer look at me. Roughly, she felt my arms and legs, then quickly took the clothes from my back.

Not understanding, I told her, "Um, the hand print is the only thing we need to fix."

She looked at me with her mismatched eyes and laughed. "Oh, I am sorry," she said. "You are due back here today for a full examination, by order of Lord Jaru. So as long as you are here, we are just going to get this out of the way."

"Okay, but shouldn't I wait for the doctor?" I said.

Pan Pan looked to Cloven, "What's a doctor?" she asked.

The fat gen shrugged his shoulders, and she focused back on me.

"Adam, this is my infirmary, one of the best in Greyveil. In this place, I am second only to High Priest Jaru. As Head Caretaker, if anyone is going to examine you, I assure you it's going to be me." She then turned my head from right to left, and licked my sore cheek, hard. Totally surprised, I stared at her with saucer-sized eyes.

Cloven quickly interceded, telling me that "Pan Pan's tongue has the ability to detect, diagnose, and even sterilize some infections."

I should have realized something like that. The naga Miss Silvia also had similar abilities.

"That's it!" The blond cat girl said.

"There are some chairs next to the hall, gentlemen. You may wait for young Adam there. Please, exit the examination area now," she demanded.

As my friends walked away, Pan Pan pulled white curtains shut around us.

"Now maybe I can get some work done," she breathed, taking up a nearby clipboard. "Of what descent are you?" she asked.

"Uummm, aah?"

"What are you, Adam?"

"Oh, I am human."

"Really," she said, writing it down and asking many other tedious questions. Eventually, Pan Pan did treat my injured face, fixing me up good as new by using some weird, wet, little pads she laid on my cheek. They smelled like a monkey's backside. No pain, no gain, I guess. When she was done, Pan Pan blurted, "Well, let's get to it." She had me spit into a small glass container, took a little of my hair, and told me to take off all my clothes. I simply stared at her, unmoving. "Any minute, Mr. Westlin," she said.

Well, she is their head doctor, or whatever they call it here. I took off my white pants and dropped my silk undies, which were so generously provided by my hosts. Pan Pan pulled up a few pages and started writing. She looked all over my body in deep thought, as I silently stood there. Suddenly, the cat-girl froze, when she peered between my legs. Realizing she had stopped, I followed her gaze, and I was nearly floored. I was big! I mean, I was always well off in that department. But now, wow! You'd think I would remember growing a third leg. I wonder how I had missed that? Pan Pan was mesmerized, so I faked a cough, to get her to snap out of it.

"Oh, ahh, yes," she said. "I am going to need you to turn around, and place your hands on this shelf."

I complied to her request.

"Now, please spread your legs and bend over."

"Wait, what?" I said, looking back to the blond cat girl. She was busy putting on rubber gloves, oiling up her fingers with some kind of liquid. Fear shot through me. "OH! Uumm, the high priest has requested my presence!" I blurted out. "I am sorry, Miss Pan Pan, but I really have to go." I grabbed my clothes and got the hell out of there, first running through the white curtains around the bed. I then streaked passed the other examination areas, where a few sick vamps and other creatures, perversely watched my little show, as I passed. When I reached Rem and the others, they only seemed to freeze, staring at my nakedness.

"We have to go!" I told them. They peered behind me, seeing a slightly befuddled Pan Pan, with a greased up rubber gloved hand, fast approaching. Hurrying into my underwear and pants, I shot for the door. My friends instantly ran behind me, and we promptly exited the infirmary like bats out of hell.

Chapter Twenty-One

When I was certain, I was far enough away outside, I ducked beside the palace, thinking I would be out of sight. Unfortunately, a lot of young vampire girls were there to ogle my shirtless body, over their text books.

"Hey, isn't that Adam?" One dark-skinned, black ponytailed girl said.

"He was at The Biting Fangs last night," said another ivory-skinned girl with a long, brown brad.

"He is incredible! Adam dated five girls last night, AT THE SAME TIME! I'll bet he tastes amazing!" blurted a shorthaired blond, with too much makeup over her eyes. I quickly turned back, to find a better place to finish dressing, when I realized they had all stopped studying and began to follow me. I looked back, and the cute schoolgirls smiled toothy, fanged grins at me. Ah hell! Instantly I broke into a run, quickly shooting passed Rafe, Rem, and Cloven. As they finally caught up, a stampede of young vampire girls ran behind me.

"I will meet you in Dailania's study!" I yelled, trying to stay ahead of the small mob.

The vampire girls started to gain on me, in the well-maintained castle courtyard. I ran and began to feel enthusiastic fingers, pinching sharply at my backside. Glancing back, I saw yet another overjoyed, heavily mascaraed vamp blond wink at me. She slowly licked her wet tongue across her top lip, to the giddy giggles of all the other pursuing girls. Good golly! I had better think of something quick. I saw one big, busty, brown-haired vampire chick pull out a white, finely braided lasso, that she twirled over her head. Wow, they were prepared for every possible contingency. Good for them!... I wonder if that means they had planned this, hmm? Luckily, I remembered the affect Phantasma's magic had on me. With two she-vamps now on each side, and a big vampire cowgirl in front, I began to channel magic through my body, while many female vampire lips started to part, showing sharp pearly whites.

Jumping amazingly high, I latched onto an unlit street lamp. Looking back only a moment, I listened to the wanton pleas of the many young vampire girls. The busty, fanged cowgirl missed the mark, throwing her lasso. And boosted by magic, I jumped to the top of, one of the nearby palace buildings, where I was able to enter the castle, losing the cute vampire girl mob.

"You can't escape the Black Rose Society, this isn't over!" I heard them say.

Later, in front of the winding staircase that led to Dailania's study, my friends were waiting for me. They stood up from the surrounding white benches, they sat on.

"Adam, are you okay?" asked Rafe.

"They didn't catch you, did they?" queried Cloven.

Rem simply watched, curiously.

"No," I said. "I am fine."

They all started laughing. *I really should expect no less by now*, I thought.

"Adam, your entertainment value is endless!" Cloven told me. "What did you do to them, to make them, all come after you like that?"

"Nothing! I was only trying to find a place to put on my clothes, unmolested."

"You failed miserably," Cloven and Rafe both said with huge grins.

"We really wanted to help, but you were moving like a super-charged red stallion," Cloven added. "Rem was the only one fast enough to catch you. But he is too young to know much about female vampires. I am afraid he would not have been much help," Rafe interjected. Rem blushed brightly.

"That's okay. It all worked out fine, and I am here now."

The two boys stood before me with arms folded, glaring. "Just what is it with you and girls anyway?" they both asked.

"First you take five of them out at the same time, to the most popular place in Greyveil. Now this," added Rafe.

"I don't know," I answered.

"Well, they all seem to want a piece of you. So try to keep your shirt on in front of them, would you," demanded Cloven.

We started up the four-story spiral staircase, which led to Dailania's study. At the top, Darkdancer's familiar, Spectra was standing guard. She merely purred, stepping aside, allowing us entry.

"Good kitty," I told her. She purred happily at me.

Inside the large, round, grey-stoned, two-story room that was filled with nothing but bookcases, on every wall above and below, there were many wooden tables covered with papers. Lots of weird devices also cluttered the lower level. Jaru was feverishly poring over his old strolls and tomes. He only noticed us, when the simple wooden door closed behind us, making a small thump. Jaru peered over his shoulder.

"Ah, Adam, welcome! I expected you a bit earlier, Young One."

"Sorry, but Miss Pan Pan said you wanted me to have an examination."

"I see," he said. "And did she complete her examination?"

"Afraid not," Cloven cut in. "She seemed a little too interested in Adam's hind quarters." I stared at him, and the gen winked a brown eye at me.

Jaru looked at Rafe questioningly. The light grey-skinned phantom kid gave a single nod of compliance.

"Yes, I would rather not have her feeling around the inside of my rear!" I told him looking really disturbed.

He stopped himself from laughing, saying, "Yes, I believe we can dispense with that part of the examination. I will be sure to inform Miss Pan Pan."

Rem took a seat, and started playing with some weird, little objects on a nearby square, wooden table. The priest then walked to me saying, "Adam, we really must do something about your inability, to battle the opposite sex. Greyveil and indeed Phantasma itself can be a very dangerous place."

"We know," Rem said delightfully as he played, then popped himself in the eye with one of the little objects, he was fiddling with. Rafe and Cloven laughed, but choked it back, when Jaru turned to Rem and looked at the two older boys, displeased. Cloven rolled his eyes as if to say, "Oh, well." Then he told the white-haired vampire, that I had been chased by a mob of young female vamps, not fifteen minutes ago.

Jaru took a deep breath exhaling, "Adam, you do understand that by nature, vampires are predators, correct? If they think you are weak, or that you will not fight back, it only makes you an easy target."

"Yes Priest," I said, and Rafe stifled his laugh, while I tried to look serious, giving Jaru my undivided attention.

"I have taken the liberty of speaking with Princess Vale," he continued. "She, too, believes that we must quickly address this problem."

"I understand," I told him. "But Priest, you should also know that, while I do not seek to harm women, I assure you I will strike down a real enemy, even if it is female. I simply do not find it necessary to hurt my good friends, if I can help it. No, I won't needlessly hurt women. I have no wish to harm them or anyone else, really."

Jaru continued, "I only wish for you to understand, in our world hesitation can equal death, young Adam." I could see the sincere concern in his eyes. "Every girl you meet would not be as forgiving as your friend, Ulee." He smiled and the boys snickered, listening from the table behind me. I turned bright red with embarrassment. Jaru then told me, that I was to have special classes facing off against female opponents, starting tomorrow, to help me get over my little problem. I agreed.

Also, the priest added, "I was informed some days ago of your ability to have powerful visions."

"Yes, but I never know when I will get one," I told him.

"Your friends tell me you pulled them into one of these visions."

"They touched me as I was having it," I said.

"I see. They also tell me that you saw the demon, Drexelon, instructing a deathreaper to attack Greyveil."

"Yes," I replied.

"Adam, are you aware that the most talented seers on Phantasma, are only able to see the smallest of details, concerning the great demon king?"

I gazed over, seeing the wide-eyed expressions on my friends' faces. Turning back to Jaru, I told him, "I had no idea."

"You have a great gift. Should you receive any more visions, anything at all, please inform me immediately."

"Yes," I said.

Jaru continued. "Adam, I am certain you now know that humans are very magical creatures on Phantasma. Are you also aware that the powers you possess, will only grow stronger with time?"

"But what are these powers? And why do I have them?" I asked.

"As I have told you, humans are highly magical creatures," said the priest. "The growing magic you feel is natural. They are the powers you have always had. Only now, you are tapping into the magic of Phantasma, which is far greater than what you are used to. Understand that though all humans are magical in our land, or so the scrolls tell me, there is something more about you."

"What do you mean?" I asked.

"Your abilities appear greater than any human's in the ancient records."

"Wow!" blurted the boys' voices coming from the wooden table and bench, where Cloven and Rafe had planted themselves.

"King Sevorift also requests the use of your abilities, in aiding and protecting the city of Greyveil."

"Of course," I said, "anything to help."

Jaru smiled telling me, "Two o'clock tomorrow, please try not to be late. That is in addition to any other classes you may have." He handed me a scroll saying, "Your schedule, Master Adam." Weapon wand training 101, introduction to surviving mystical creatures, and protecting against corruption—those are just the first three. I noticed a locked metal cabinet holding shiny swords and other weapons, with removable wands built right into them. Could those be weapon wands? I had a vivid vision of myself causing havoc in Greyveil, spell-casting and simultaneously slashing vampires with the mystical, wild weapons. Um, maybe I'll tell Jaru later, I thought to my self. The high priest gestured a hand to the door, and we all exited.

As we reached the bottom of the winding four-story staircase, I told my friends, "I don't know about you three, but I am a little hungry. Is the dining hall open?" I asked.

"Now, you're speaking my language," said Cloven. So we headed for the food.

I was surprised to see that it was quite busy. A few werewolves, nagas, phantoms, and harpies were all present, among some other creatures I did not recognize. As we walked up to the buffet style counters, manned by quite a few lunchroom workers, I noticed there were no vampires.

"It's still a bit early," Rafe said, as if knowing what I was thinking.

"The princesses and the prince are only awake to greet the king, and welcome him back to the palace."

"Yes, I wonder how Princess Dailania's doing?" I said, taking up a bowl of renweed stew, or so the little label said. The two teens did the same, but faltered a little when I said her name. Rem pointed to an odd food, to the far left of everything else. One of the many dining hall workers, was more than happy to retrieve it for him. I grabbed some weird, pink bread and honey mead, then went to find a table, which was easy enough, being that all the vampires were mostly asleep. I sat at a table in the middle of the huge hall. The green gen sat to my left and the phantom to my right. Rem, the twelve-year old, red-haired vampire parked himself right in front of me. Unfortunately, his choice of breakfast food looked like a bowl, of shiny moving eyeballs. Every now and then, I think they winked at me.

Cloven wasted no time taking a bite of his pink bread. He bluntly asked, "Why are you so concerned with Darkdancer?"

Everyone seemed to be waiting for my reply. "I think she may not be as bad as everyone thinks," I told him, starting on my stew, which looked gross but tasted awesome.

The two older boys loudly grunted, shaking their heads. Rem just sat there playing with his yucky-looking living eyes. Boy, this kid is weird.

"I am serious," I told them. "I think her father is making her do those terrible things."

"The king?" they both asked.

I gave a little nod, and they each broke out laughing.

"Oh, yeah, she is the biggest bitch in Greyveil, because daddy made her do it," proclaimed Rafe.

"What you are saying is highly unlikely, Adam," added the fat, green gen.

Suddenly, a loud thump got our attention, when both of Rem's fists hit the table.

"Adam is right," he said. "Father controls almost everything Dailania does. He believes that he is helping her, trying to make her stronger. But...but..."

"What is it, Rem?" I asked. "He is hurting her!" the little vampire told me. He started to cry. "She tries to be so strong. But when she is alone...my sister cries herself to sleep almost every night."

"How do you know that?" I inquired.

"Because I can hear it, Adam. My hearing is better than most other vampires, and I sometimes listen outside her door," Rem said wiping away the tears. "She puts on such a good show that father does not suspect, and is completely blind to the way she really feels. It's like she's not even his daughter. More some sort of monster he's trying to create."

I touched Rem's fisted hand, and he looked at me with sparkling blue eyes. "I am sorry," I told him. "I will do everything in my power to help Dailania, and try to pull your family together."

His hand grasped mine, and he gave me a heartfelt "Thank you."

Rafe and Cloven finally clammed up finishing their breakfast. Then we headed for Dailania's room, guided by the red-haired, twelve-year-old vampire, Rem. When we arrived outside her room, he casually rapped on the red double doors. Ulee answered, appearing a bit stunned.

"Oh, what are you boys doing here?"

"Adam was a little worried. He wanted to be certain that Dailania was all right," spoke Rem.

"She is fine," Ulee said, "now get out of here!"

"No, let them in," came Dailania's voice.

Ulee let all the tension flow from her body, seeming to give up. The naga slithered aside, allowing us in. When we entered Darkdancer's room, I was astounded. It was huge, maybe sixty or eighty feet squared. There was expensive furniture of every type all over the spacious dwelling, just out in the open, leading in a spiral pattern to an enormous, soft, orange, silk-sheeted bed. It had many comfortable-looking pillows on it. The average height ceiling was lined with four rows of light crystals. And there were tall six-feet windows, on the right hand wall as you entered. Vale, Taya, and Crystal were all gathered around Darkdancer, with concerned expressions on their faces. Ulee made her way back to the huge, beyond-king-sized bed.

"Welcome to my quarters, Lord Adam. I am glad you came," Dailania said.

"Yes, I wanted to make sure you were okay, Princess."

She rubbed her arm, looking a little ashamed.

"I am fine," Darkdancer said, not looking at me.

"I also wished to ask you about your father."

She turned her head, lifting her magical, blue, cat-like eyes. "If that's okay," I added.

"It's fine," said Vale. "We were just speaking about that."

"Just what is it that he is trying to do?" I asked Dailania.

"My father believes that the only way to stand against the devil king, and save our people, is through the strongest of leadership. He has trained and molded me since I was a child, much of the time not very kindly." She seemed to lose herself in thought a bit. Then Darkdancer quickly looked back to me. "But he wasn't always this way, Adam. At least that was what my mother, Ooray Shadowwind, used to tell me," she said, cradling her forehead against her intertwined palms.

"What happened to your mother?" I asked.

"We do not speak of it. The memory is far too painful," interjected Vale.

"She was claimed by the earlier years of the war," Darkdancer told me.

"I am sorry," I said.

"Thank you," she replied.

"So what you are telling me is that your father, is so bent on making you this strong leader, he has basically forgotten, you are only one vampire, and more importantly, you are his daughter."

She nodded, trying to hide the tears, that started to well up in her beautiful eyes.

"Please don't cry, Dailania. It is always darkest before the dawn," I breathed.

"But he just gets more and more consumed by the war. It is all he thinks about!" she cried. "I love my father, Adam, but at times, I don't even think I know him."

I pondered a moment, then asked, "Vale, what do you think of your father, the king?"

"Father has always been kind, though a little distant at times."

"Ah," Darkdancer scowled. "What does she know? Father has always protected his poor little Vale! He always shielded you from everything! While I slaved learning war and politics, scheming and killing, what did you ever do! Frolic in fields and think poor little me," Dailania said.

"My life was never so simply, Sister," retorted Vale. "As you learned from father, Jaru was the only parent I ever knew. While you and father left me alone for months on end, I too had to learn of war and politics. Only, I see now that I may have had a kinder teacher. Be that as it may, still, I would have loved to have spent just one of your trips, getting to know my father. Do you know how it feels to be raised by a complete stranger, Dailania? I assure you that I do!"

"You don't know what you are talking about," Darkdancer said under her breath.

"My life was not easy, Sister," said Vale.

"At least you had a life!" shouted the tall, brown-haired vampire, getting to her feet. "I am nothing but his puppet! You had it all, then Adam just up and falls into your lap! Oh, no, Little Sister, I deserve a little happiness too in this life. By right of the Royal Bloodbond, I claim Adam as mine."

"I too have a bloodbond with Adam, and I claim him, Dailania," said Vale.

"I will never relinquish my claim!" shot back Darkdancer.

"Nor will I!" retorted Vale.

"Then, I guess Adam is as much mine, as he is yours," the older sister said.

The two princesses stared each other down, their eyes beginning to shine red. Our friends just seem to back away from the two warring vampires. Not that I blame them. Wind blew violently throughout the room, as Vale grew angrier and angrier. Meanwhile, with a cock of her hips and a move of her hands, Darkdancer made the furniture in her room start to float, spinning swiftly in midair. Seeing the battle about to take place, I grabbed the first thing I could find, which was a drawer from a spinning dresser. I smashed it on the floor. The wind stopped blowing, and the furniture fell from the air. Both princesses peered at me with their shining, red eyes.

"You girls just think you can pass me around, like some object you own? I am afraid that I am not your slave, and if all you are going to do is kill yourselves, then I want nothing to do with any of you!" Speed heightened by magic, I ran out the red double doors, slamming them behind me. I really meant what I had said.

I rushed quickly through the castle semi-crowded with students, towards my room. After heading west, I passed a few more happy teens, watching a magical 3D hologram of a roaring, green dragon, somehow projected from a wall portrait. I turned one corner then another, seeing fewer young people. I was really upset, running down the now empty, luxurious halls. I passed a single cute, little, redhead vampire girl at high speed. She speedily spun around, kicking me with her heel square in the forehead, as I ran right into it. The impact knocked me from my feet, and I hit the floor, hard. Looking up, I saw the little vamp teen grow and morph, into the pointy-eared red-headed elf, Sparkle. "No one escapes the Weird Sisters," she said. I went out like a light.

Chapter Twenty-Two

I regained consciousness still a bit dazed in a dark, damp, depressing place. I was chained to a cold, stone column and sitting on a filthy, wooden stool. Light poured through cracks in an old style, thick, wooden door. Through the darkness, I could see I was in a large, dungeon-like room. It was filled with dusty potions, strange, dangerous-looking machines, and crazy, otherworldly weapons. Close by, I could hear familiar voices. They were coming from right outside the old style wooden door, about ten feet in front of me.

"We have delivered you the boy, Deathreaper," said Sparkle's stern voice. "Now, when the vampire city falls, make sure you remember that the spoils go to the Elven Nation."

"Ladies, I guarantee that when the dust settles. You will all have everything that is coming to you," graciously retorted Reev. "Simply have your elves in place, to allow the entry of my forces at the appointed hour, and I assure you that your vampire enemies will be at your mercy. Well, if you had any mercy," the reaper added.

"Yes, I still can't believe how easy it was. With all the vampires looking for you and your undead minions, they didn't even notice us," said Sparkle. "Well, I do love a bit of misdirection."

Reev laughed wickedly. The wooden door creaked open, with the deathreaper telling Sparkle, and I can only assume her sisters, to stand guard outside. As he entered the miserable room, four crystal lights illuminated the darkness. It wasn't an improvement. Reev stood before me every bit as frightening, as the first time we had met. An eerie force seemed to emanate from him, filling me with dread. He had silver eyes and blue wind-swept hair, culminating in a point in the back of his head, in a really expensive haircut sort of way. He was wearing a black robe pinned shut over his heart, with way stretched-out sleeves that drooped down at his wrists. Black pants and brown boots finished out his attire.

"Finally," he said, "we have a little time to get to know one another. Adam, I am not such a bad person. I only seek a little information," he finished.

"Yes, so you can bring me back to your master, Drexelon," I said.

"That thing is not my master!" the reaper quickly shot back.

"I saw you taking his orders," I blurted.

"How could you know that, human?" he asked.

"I told you, I saw it. I also know that the demon king frightens you, deathreaper."

Reev looked stunned, then immediately composed himself asking, "What do you mean, boy? How can you see such things?"

"Visions sometimes show me things. But I don't always understand them."

"Interesting," said Reev. "Can you prove this, Adam?"

"You're supposed to destroy Greyveil, and bring me back to the horned beast, Drexelon," I said.

A sharp dagger instantly materialized at my throat, in a swift shimmer of liquid silver.

"What makes you so sure, human?" he asked.

I looked at him fiercely. "I know," I told him."

The deathreaper lowered his blade, slightly puzzled. "I must say that is most interesting. If nothing else, you are quite brave, Adam Westlin. Tell me, are you smart as well? Tell me, why does the great beast want you so badly? I could have reduced Greyveil to ashes by now. Yet when we found that you were recovering in the infirmary, from that bitch princess' bite, Drexelon had us to wait, even pull back the forces we had already deployed.

"All for the moment we could ensnare you. Why is that, Adam Westlin? Being a powerful seer is considerable. But it hardly warrants such extreme actions."

"I don't know," I told him.

Immediately, his fist punched me across the jaw. Then he came back with a backhand on the other side. Oh, God, that hurt!

"Do you know what it is like to explain, why you can't kill to an army of bloodthirsty elves?" Reev smacked me again, hard, with the back of his fist. I could taste blood, and my vision started to blur. "Not fun at all little human," he breathed. "Let us just say, I was glad I had my own undead army with me at the time, which reminds me. I have heard that the princesses, along with nearly every other female in Greyveil, are fighting over you. As I recall, I think I may have interrupted a little something, between you and the redhead back behind Greyveil Plaza. Don't you know they plan to make you a vampire, boy? Perhaps that is your plan," said Reev.

"I don't want to be a vampire!" I snapped.

"You have a funny way of showing it. Now, tell me, why you are so important to the beast?" Reev commanded.

"I don't know!"

He quickly kneeled, placing a cold hand against my chest. As he twisted it into me, I could feel a sensation of silvery, cold serpents painfully entering my body. They forcefully somehow began to drain the very life from my being. It was the most excruciating thing I had ever felt. I could feel myself growing weaker, becoming unable to withstand it, as I screamed in purest agony.

"Make no mistake, boy, I am death, and there are none who can stand against my divine might!"

"What...about Drexelon?" I asked.

Caught off guard, he broke the hold. Hesitating only a moment, Reev cruelly began to choke me with an iron grip.

"His day will come, little human... For death comes to us all!" the deathreaper said.

My eyes started to roll up into my head, and I began to lose consciousness. Reev let go just short of killing me. I coughed violently trying to catch my breath. This guy was serious, and if I wasn't careful, I was going to end up dead, orders or not.

"Reev, please," I pleaded, "you know that I am new to Phantasm. How can I possibly know anything? If the beast has plans for me, then only he knows them. I am only trying to get home," I said.

The reaper smacked me again, making the dreadful room spin. He looked away, facing the dusty stonewall, thinking a moment...

"We will continue this another time. When I have more questions...and there will be more questions," he breathed.

Reev then sidekicked me in the face with terrifying force. Everything was suddenly ripped from me. I could see nothing but darkness, and I could feel no pain. It was quite peaceful, considering where I had just came from. Time didn't seem to exist here in this strange void. I wondered if this is what it's like to die. And I slowly seemed to fade away in this eerie place, with no pain, no thoughts, and no desires.

"Adam," came a voice I thought I would never hear again. I tried to find it, but I could not.

"Adam," it came again. This time, I felt the warm hand of a friend on my face.

Opening my eyes, I could see Darkdancer right in front of me.

"Adam, wake up," she said. "Please be all right. I am so sorry. This is all my fault. I didn't mean to drive you away."

"Hi there," I said.

She hugged and kissed me all over.

"Ow, Ow!" I protested.

"Oh, sorry. I have already freed your hands. Just hold still and I will heal you, Adam."

Before I could do anything, the tall vampire stood me up, pressing my body hard into herself. Darkdancer's slightly taller body enveloped mine, while her arms wrapped around my form, squeezing and possessing me. I felt a mighty power flash through my being. I was completely immobilized, with

Dailania starting to nibble my ear. She breathed heavily, moaned momentarily, and reached for my white dress pants, which were now totally ruined. This was so not the time. Her power soon touched my very core, and its hold on me broke. Darkdancer lightly suckled my flesh without breaking my skin.

"Princess, Princess," I said, "How did you find me?" "Our bond, of course," she said running her fingers through my black, short length hair.

"Where is Vale?" I asked.

"She wanted more time with father, so I gave it to her," Dailania admitted.

"They and Adett are currently discussing the war, and impossible paths the kingdom might take to a better tomorrow—most of which involve murder, maiming, and deceit."

Not wanting to upset her, I simply said, "We have to get out of here!"

"Yes, sorry," the princess replied, "this way." Having just awakened from the death slumber Reev tortured me into, I was not thinking too clearly. I left the weapons-filled room that imprisoned me empty handed. Come to think of it, I didn't see any weapons on Darkdancer, either. When I stepped outside the old style, thick, wooden door, we entered into what looked like some horrible nightmare, of an underground maze. It was ancient catacombs. Soiled skulls and bones were scattered everywhere.

They even appeared to be used for decoration. Roots hung from above, and the walls were blackened, decaying and cracked with filth. The place looked like it was at least a few hundred years old. The more I thought about it, the more I believed, this really is the kind of place death would hang out. I hear a weird sort of clicking, and a thump in the far darkness. Luckily, we ran swiftly in the other direction, with Dailania leading the way. I saw twisted hemp after twisted hemp of undead zombie bodies, all crawling with foul insects. Apparently, the princess had been busy.

"You didn't come here alone, did you?" I asked.

"Of course, Adam, I am your bloodbond mate after all!" she said proudly.

I wasn't going to argue. We needed to get the hell out of here, and I mean like yesterday. We followed the ancient, curved and decaying walls. Undead warriors soon burst from their crumbling mortar. There were six of them, three from each wall. They weren't like the other undead I had already seen. They were a whole new kind of foul, totally rotten with no flesh at all in some places. What little flesh they did have was putrid and gross. They looked like walking diseases come to life. The smell alone was enough to make me retch. I kicked the skull from one, and instantly smashed the head of another into the weak tunnel wall. Darkdancer spun around a few times, using moves I had never seen before. Hell, she was actually dancing, and every movement was deadly. Each swing of hips and pose of her hands, smashed them against the walls, crushing their vile bones. Darkdancer had defeated all four by herself. But one gross corpse peeled itself from the wall. It was coming up behind her. Acting quickly, I channeled magical force though my hands, blowing the evil thing apart. The princess looked back in astonishment. Our eyes met and she told me, "Thanks."

We hurried through the hauntingly dark tunnels, lit only by a few magic crystals here and there. The few undead left were of little consequence, blown apart or crushed by Dailania's dance. We came upon branching tunnels, and Reev appeared seemingly out of nowhere.

Dailania danced fast and furious. The deathreaper only stood there, taking the impact of all of her spellbound moves. When the brown-haired, tall vampire stopped, Reev moved to her swiftly, slapping her so hard, the momentum made her fly up against a nearby wall, breaking it to pieces with her head and upper body. The princess fell to the ground and was knocked out. Reev turned his attention to me.

"Play time is over, you pathetic human dog! I grow so tired of this… Now you will learn why, the blademaster race of the deathreapers is to be feared. You will see the horror that all living things fear. Now, know my power and tremble!"

A wicked, unnatural shadow crept over the deathreaper. The awful dread that poured from him was amplified tenfold. As we stood there in the growing darkness, in front of the many branching, dreadful tunnels, I could soon hear the sound of hundreds of lumbering, walking dead. Then I could see their malevolent, twisted faces while their mangled, and warped corpses approached from the shadows, in every direction. It was truly the stuff of nightmares. Completely surrounded by the horrible dead, the reaper simply laughed.

My mind raced, flashing on images and remembering all that Reev had done to me. The torture, the imprisonment, and the fact that I thought I had died at his hands.

Somehow, I had snapped inside, no longer thinking. Now feeding off the growing power inside me, the dark didn't matter. The dead didn't matter. The only thing that mattered was him and me. I calmly and without fear walked straight up to Reev, standing before him through his evil presence and aura. He intensified its might, and the malign power hit me like physical force, nearly bringing me to my knees.

The grotesque dead neared the unconscious body of the princess. Looking at Reev straight into his now totally silver, soulless eyes, the deathreaper told me to beg for mercy. I used all my magic, hitting him with an awesome stream of energy, unleashing as much force as I could possibly muster.

The reaper actually screamed, as the golden inferno of white-hot power smashed him, into the dilapidated walls of the underground tunnels, where I continued to shower him with merciless, glowing destruction. Reev sank into the molten wall, and with a gesture of my hands, the surrounding dirt and stone broke apart, burying the wicked death figure. I turned to the approaching foul dead pulsing with power, now engulfed in magical flames of destruction. They all paused, and merely fell to the ground lifeless, sinking back into the cold tunnel soil. It must have been because I defeated Reev.

Immediately, I ran over to the princess, shaking her feverishly.

"Princess, Princess, please wake up!"

"Oh, aah!" she said, opening her blue, cat-like eyes. "Oh, where is the deathreaper!" she asked, her eyes quickly roving the darkness.

"You need not worry, Princess, I have taken care of Reev."

Darkdancer's eyes grew wide and surprised. She quickly got to her feet, peering around the empty catacombs. Dailania soon found the molten grave, I gave the reaper.

"Yes," I told her, "he is in there."

The tall vampire kissed me, taking me in her arms.

"Let's get out of here, this place really stinks!" I said, fanning away a bit of smoke from death's new grave.

Darkdancer laughed and we headed for the entrance. Outside, the two huge, twin moons of Phantasma were there to greet us. Never had I been so happy to see an alien sky. The catacombs that we had only just escaped, looked like a simple, small carved out entrance, in the bottom of a large rock formation, covered by forest trees on its top. Hurrying away from the awful place, we soon came upon a huge, furry, reddish brown bat. He was sporting a well broken in brown, leather saddle. I crouched in defense, skidding to a halt.

"This is Nightheart," Darkdancer said proudly. "He is my good friend, and steed when the occasions arise."

Waiting patiently, the great bat was enjoying some odd, new kind of fruit, I had never seen before.

"*Shinuk zen nu zalu lu*," said Dailania to the bat. Then she plucked one from the wild bush saying, "They are Kaya fruit. Here, you must be hungry. Try one." She tossed the long, curved, green fruit to me. I took a bite. It was neither sweet nor bland. But for some reason, I really enjoyed it, wolfing it down.

Apparently, I was really hungry. The princess simply stood there, smiling, after I made twelve inches of fruit quickly disappear, in maybe three seconds flat.

"I hope your other appetites are just as insatiable, Adam," said Darkdancer.

Giving a small cough of embarrassment, I asked, "How did you defeat the Weird Sisters?"

"Weird Sister?" she repeated.

Fear instantly shivered up my spine.

"Oh God, Princess, we have to get out of here!" I yelled.

A deadly orange spell flew to the right of my head, missing it by mere inches, shattering into a shower of sparks upon the ground. Dailania and I looked up into the fantastic alien sky, seeing the three Weird Sisters descending upon us from above, on their mighty winged serpents. The princess quickly mounted Nightheart, then reached back helping me up.

Once I was on the giant bat, we quickly ascended into the blue sky, which appeared to have been a mistake. The princess became woozy, unable to steer the winged beast, correctly. The blow she had suffered from Reev, must have hurt her more than I had thought.

As more of the elves' lethal spells whizzed by us, I yelled, "We have to switch places!" against the wind to Dailania. In midair, I swiftly swapped positions with her, taking the reins of Nightheart. At first, the beast panicked fighting me, but when I remembered and spoke the words, *"Sen nuw sa la wen,"* Nightheart quickly calmed himself, allowing me to guide him, though it was still a bit shaky.

While I tried to get the hang of flying, I soon realized the Weird Sisters were not alone. Three smaller flying beasts joined them, flying up from the dense forest below. They looked like large, white, featherless birds with reddish hawk-like eyes. They possessed leathery skin and long, whip-esque tails. On their backs were saddled lightly armored male elven warriors. The armor and helmets they wore were brass, and they had on dark brown ninja-esque uniforms underneath. Immediately, I flew at one of the pointy eared warriors. Nightheart's hind claw knocked him from his stingray-like mount. The Weird Sisters encompassed us. Now on all sides they fired multi colored spells of destruction. In all the aerial chaos, I noticed big, clear crystals strapped to the heads of their four, yellow, black slit eyed, purple winged serpents. The big jewels flashed orange and in an instant, the large winged snakes actually breathed fire. Right away, I dipped downwards with Nightheart, narrowly avoiding the arrows of the white bird riders. By instinct, I threw my hand up behind us. It fired an orb of gold energy, that hit the wing of one of the giant birds. It floundered in air, with Darkdancer finishing the creature using a long, purple, spear-like spell that skewered it through the heart. Spinning out and making a quick course correction, we soared for the enemy hundreds of feet above Phantasma.

"Get in closer!" yelled the princess. "I will fire to the left, you fire to the right!"

As we sped toward the Weird Sisters, I spun a few times to avoid their incoming deadly spells. And yes, it made me want to lose my lunch. Once upright again, I threw a golden orb at the green-haired elf Flare, while Darkdancer attacked Sparkle. Surprisingly, I felt the princess' legs tighten around the reddish brown bat, giving it a little kick. *"Ku tarra vin!"* she said, and Nightheart fired an awesome, focused beam of deadly sound. Its force hit the remaining white bird rider. Before falling, the bass-armored warrior fired a single arrow, that hit its mark in the shoulder of Nightheart. The reddish brown bat screeched in pain faltering a little from the air.

Only the Weird Sisters remained, and they turned the sky into an inferno, their serpent beasts belching flames wildly at us and into the air. The red-haired Sparkle and green-haired Flare also fired many spells, as if protecting their other sister. Ember the purple-haired elf woman was hovering silently behind them, charging up her elemental lightning attack. We flew up over, under, and through the sisters' defenses, firing our spells offensively. Nightheart only just dodged, having his expansive brown wing bitten, by one of the dagger-teethed serpents.

"We have to stop the purple-haired elf, before she can fire!" I yelled to Dailania.

"Fly above them, I have a plan!" Darkdancer shouted back.

We dived, avoiding the sister's many wicked spells and fireballs. Once passed them safely, I pulled up hard soaring above the Weird Sisters upside down. The princess dropped from the saddle behind me, falling through the air to land squarely on top of the purple-haired elf. Purple lightning shot in all directions, when they fought atop the mighty serpent. Flare and Sparkle were both hit, veering off, retreating to regroup. Taking two left cross punches and a kick, the purple-haired elf fell from her steed. The princess took control of the beast serpent, immediately firing an onslaught of fireballs.

While the remaining sisters were distracted, I flew straight for the green-haired elf woman Flare, striking her from the side. She was airborne before she even knew I was there. With only the redhead, Sparkle, left, the princess and I focused our attacks, trying to overwhelm her. It so was not working. Our combined attacks were completely blocked by a wall of serpent's fire. Two of Sparkle's spells streaked for each of us. We barely banked out of the way. I don't know if she had been holding back, or if she was just pissed that we deep-sixed her sisters. But this elf was really starting to get on my nerves. The princess and I both attacked at the same time. Her barrage of fireballs and a quick spear-like spell were all blocked, the elf deflecting Dailania's spear spell with her bare hand.

Once again, I tried plowing into the enemy. It worked before. As I impacted with Sparkle's winged steed, she quickly jumped from the beast, attacking me. The wild elf woman punched me in the ribs and threw me from the saddle. I caught on to Nightheart's saddle straps before I fell. Sparkle steered the great bat towards the serpent riding princess, firing off multiple deadly spells. Darkdancer did not fire back. I knew it was because she did not want to hurt me. I grabbed the elf woman's long leg, stopping her assault. Then I tried to pull her off Nightheart's saddle, while she struggled to stay planted. Able to pull myself up as I fought against her, Sparkle quickly proceeded to elbow my brains out. I guarded my face with my hands and arms, finally ousting the wicked elf female, with a quick burst of magical energy.

"No!" she screamed.

Pure hatred was in her red-orange eyes, as I watched her fall, to be sure of her defeat. I then flew to the serpent Dailania was riding. The princess immediately vacated the beast's saddle, rejoining me. Without a rider, the serpent simply roared and flew aimlessly away.

"We must go to Silvia's supply station," said Darkdancer.

"Just tell me which way to go," I told her.

Chapter Twenty-Three

It took a while to reach Silvia's home. On the way, we glimpsed many wonderful sights. There were volcanos with green lava, belching tremendous columns of illuminated smoke into in air, great sparkling lakes with mighty geysers at their centers, and the out skirts of a vast white sand desert. When we came to the forest-surrounded, sparkling lakes, where the rattler scaled naga Miss Silvia lived, inside a nearby small supply station. Well actually, it was really a small cottage. The sky was dark, and the princess seemed to grow weak, allowing herself to slouch, resting against me. We landed ungracefully in front of Silvia's odd, little cottage.

Nemm quickly flew from the round topped, wooden front door.

"Adam you're back! Miss Silvia and I missed you!"

As she zipped closer though the air, Nemm covered her mouth. The joy on her face turned to concern.

"Oh, no, no, no! What has happened? You are all hurt!" she squeaked.

The little house sprite quickly shot back into the cottage. Moments later, a much bigger Silvia slithered out behind her. Silvia first looked at me and I stared back amazed. She now stood seven feet from the ground, where she once was only five feet ten inches. How had she grown so fast? Silvia wore a nice one-piece yellow dress, with a matching ribbon tying her hair. Her scales were now a glossy white with yellow stripes. Swiftly, she snaked her way over, taking the princess into her sizable arms.

"She has been poisoned," the large naga said, slithering into the house, and placing Dailania on the comfortable couch, where I once laid not long ago.

"Nemm, specimen one-forty–three!" Silvia said.

The cute house sprite immediately retrieved one of Silvia's big jars. It had dark blue liquid and an infant-sized slug inside. Darkdancer shifted restlessly, grunting in pain as she got worse.

"Adam, there is no time, hold her down!" commanded Silvia.

Quickly opening the jar, the big snake lady clutched the unpleasant creature inside. It made an awful squeal. I held down the now seemingly unconscious princess, as Silvia searched Dailania's body, finding a nasty but not too deep small wound. It was under her tank top, on her upper left breast just above her heart. The naga gave it a single lick, then told me the girl had tasted my blood. Because of that fact, the injury would not kill her, but the wound still needed to be drained of its poison, just like before. Silvia placed the gross slug above the princess' heart, where it clamped down, sucking madly, whipping its tail and tentacles in all directions. Repulsed at the awful sight, Nemm immediately shot from the room, hiding her eyes.

Darkdancer sprang to life in terrible pain. Her eyes bulged and her fangs extended as she gasped. Her power of magical motion began to move and shift the nearby furniture, with every little jolt of her body.

"The slug, it's too close to her heart! We have to remove it!" the large now white, yellow striped naga told me. Silvia tried to pull the large slug away, but the princess cried out in agony, with tears falling from her eyes. Many of the objects displayed around us exploded, and were destroyed by the intensity of Darkdancer's unleashed power.

"Hold her tightly, Adam, I know what to do!" Silvia breathed.

I braced myself, continuing my efforts holding the struggling vampire, in all the ghostly chaos. The snake lady crawled onto the princess, taking the foul slug into her mouth, where she bit down hard. The creature squealed in pain, then disappeared behind Silvia's elastic, red lips. With one gulp, it was gone. Darkdancer fell motionless onto the couch.

"The vampire is badly hurt, Adam. I don't know if I can save her," said Silvia.

No, this can't happen! Not when she was only trying to save me! Immediately, I placed my hand on Dailania's chest, channeling as much magic as I could, trying to heal her. Her body arched towards the ceiling, and Silvia watched in astonishment. Once again, I could not break free until the healing was complete. The blood and wounds swiftly disappeared as Darkdancer braced, clinching her teeth together, gasping. The princess and I then both collapsed, she into the soft couch, and I into the hard, wooden floor.

"Ouch!" I leaned against the couch getting back to my feet.

The snake lady told me, "That was incredible. I didn't know you were capable of healing others, Adam."

"Myself also," I added. Silvia was stunned.

"Most incredible, indeed!" she said. "Why even bother to come here, if you are so capable, Adam?"

"The princess rescued me from the deathreaper, Reev," I told her. "I believe she may have thought, I would be too weak to heal her."

"But clearly, you were not too weak," the big naga said.

I looked over, seeing that Darkdancer was resting well.

"No, I was not…thanks to her," I replied. Then I asked Miss Silvia, "Why is it that you are now so um…"

"Large?" she added simply.

"Well, yes," I answered.

"This will take a bit of explaining," Silvia told me. "Adam, in naga society there are many kinds of nagas. I am, or was *Silin*, which are smaller and well-suited for things like, research for example. Well, a couple of days ago, when I had finished my tests on the large slug, that had sucked the poison from you earlier, um, once I had no farther use for it I, well…"

"You ate it," I finished for her.

"Correct," the naga said. "Perfectly normal. We nagas can stomach almost anything, and we waste nothing. So soon after devouring the specimen, I could feel the changes that your blood enabled. Quite amazing really. Adam, you have made it possible for me to change from *Silin* to *Sorvien*."

"Uh!" I said.

"I have gone from worker to warrior class within my society. Such a thing is unheard of in our world."

"Oh," I hooted like a true rocket scientist.

"Adam, you are amazingly gifted. I believe that in you may be the greatest discoveries Phantasma has ever known. Look at Vale's increased power, the older sister's resistance to fatal undead poison, and let us not forget myself. Adam, you may possibly be the most important person on Phantasma!"

Seeing that Silvia was really excited, I said the first thing that popped into my head.

"That is great," I told her, not fully understanding. "So when will we be able to make our way back to the palace?" I asked.

Silvia began reexamining Darkdancer. After a few licks of her tongue, and a minute or so later, she told me, "The princess is fine, but she is totally exhausted." Silvia still appeared a little befuddled by my healing ability.

Nemm reentered the room, looking around at the aftermath with wide stretched, brown eyes.

"Now, see if that power of yours will work on the bat, and you may leave in the morning," said Silvia.

"All right," I replied, while Nemm laughed girlishly for some reason. Maybe she knew something I didn't. "Hey, Nemm, you want to go outside and play with me a little, after I am done?" I asked.

The little flying sprite was very ecstatic, fidgeting about excitedly, so I told her, "Let's go while the princess gets a bit of rest."

Silvia smiled, saying, "I will clean up here."

Nemm and I then hurried out the door. I was instantly in awe, as I saw the two huge, glowing moons hanging there in the night sky, before me. I hadn't noticed them before. I guess they must have been to my back, when we first got here. It was as if I could reach up, and touch them if I wanted.

"What is wrong?" the little hovering girl asked.

"Oh, ah, nothing, I just have to heal Nightheart that's all."

"Oh wow, Adam, you can do that, Brother?" she asked excitedly.

"Oh sure, I'm starting to get pretty good," I told her. Then I thought about Nemm calling me "Brother." I noticed Vale calling her "Sister" the first time I visited Silvia's. I'm sure it's nothing, I pondered as we approached the mighty bat, who snapped at us, clearly not in a good mood, scaring the small house sprite. She quickly took refuge behind me, peering over my shoulder at Darkdancer's reddish brown, giant bat. Getting closer and closer, I spoke the words "*Sen nuw sa la wen.*" The beast immediately calmed.

I stoked the fine fur of his reddish brown head, finding the festering enemy arrow still stuck in place. I then told Nemm to back away, which she immediately did. Continuing to soothe and stroke Nightheart, I swiftly grabbed the arrow, pulling it from the beast in one fast motion. He screeched in pain, and I immediately started to heal him, before he could attack or anything. The great bat was completely immobilized at my touch, and so was I as power poured from me into him. Once my grip had broken, I was unable to stop myself. I fell to my knees before the large beast. Completely petrified, it really surprised me, when Nightheart gave me a mighty slurp of his tongue. I laughed so hard I nearly passed out. I had actually been afraid of him up til now. Well, at least I was afraid of his fangs, anyway. I hadn't had the best experiences in that department. And Nightheart's fangs were way bigger than Dailania's.

"Hey Nemm, let's see if you can catch me!" I blurted out. She giggled in glee, and the game was on.

Instantly, we ran passed Silvia's devil horned bullfrog pond, for the familiar trees. Nemm zipped through the air, and I ran at an incredible speed. The house sprite happily tried to catch me in the cool, late evening air, but I seemed to stay one step ahead, even yanking on her little, green dress every now and then to get her attention.

She laughed enraptured, and I soared through the night sky, jumping from tree to tree with ease. Nemm zipped here and there still trying to catch me. It was almost like being on the moon. Enjoying the rapture of it all myself, I lost track of the little sprite altogether. Gravity didn't seem to have such a tight hold on me anymore. I laughed, giggled, and flipped carefree high in the air. I had all but forgotten Nemm's effort to catch me, nearly jumping out of my skin, when the cute, little sprite flew right into my arms out of nowhere, giggling. We dropped from twenty feet up, with me landing effortlessly on my feet. Darkdancer was standing right there, she had watched the whole time.

"Oh, ah, hey, Princess, is everything okay?" I asked.

"Your human power is growing, Adam," she replied. "We need to get back to the palace, before I am missed."

"Princess, you are in no condition to travel. You nearly died, Dailania. Please, go back and get some rest. Miss Silvia tells me we can leave in the morning. Whatever comes up it's my fault, and I will deal with it." With that, the tall, weakened female vamp faltered a little, then wearily walked back to the cottage.

After playing with Nemm a bit more, the house sprite and I returned to the cottage as well. Upon entering, I saw that the place had been thoroughly cleaned. All the damage was somehow repaired. It was like the vampire princess' power never even touched the place. Miss Silvia was sitting patiently in the dining area, across the many curved archways of the living room.

With a single look from her, Nemm instantly flew to her room. Surveying the inside of the cottage, I realized Darkdancer was nowhere to be found.

"She is resting in Nemm's room," the large naga told me.

Geez, how do they do that? Am I so easy to read? Walking over to Silvia, I could see just how much she had grown. Her ample hips were hanging off the sides, of the now too small chair she sat in. It threatened to break under her considerable weight. After what happened with Ulee in self-defense class, I was more than a little worried.

"Please Adam, take a sit," she offered.

I sat right across from her at the dining area's café table.

"Miss Silvia, I was wondering why is it that Nemm now calls me "Brother" sometimes?"

She smiled. "It means she feels comfortable with you Adam; safe. When house sprites feel truly safe with a being, they consider them family. It's quite the honor really. If you should ever have need of her, she will be there, however she can."

"Wow!" I let slip before I could think.

"So tell me, Adam, have you given any thought to your safety in our land?" the snake lady asked.

"What do you mean, Miss Silvia?"

"I mean the fact that Phantasma is filled with predators and powerful beings, who would all like nothing more than to eat you, in one way or another," she said.

I was a bit taken aback at her bluntness.

"I don't mean to frighten you," the snake lady continued. "But if I didn't know you already, Adam, and a vampire princess was not with you, you would probably be in my stomach right now."

I stared at her intensely.

"I am only speaking the truth," she added. "There are many dangers all around you. Are you capable of protecting yourself, if need be, Human?" she asked with a flip of her big, yellow-striped, white-scaled, coiling tail.

"Miss Silvia, tell me: among these many predators you speak of, how high does Reev, the deathreaper, rank?"

"He is one of the most powerful on Phantasma, as I am sure you are aware by now," said the naga.

"He is dead," I told her flatly. "I killed him."

Silvia appeared to freeze in time for a moment. Coming back to her senses, she told me, she thought I had said, the princess had rescued me earlier.

"Dailania freed me, but the reaper knocked her out, and I had to face him."

"What happened?" Silvia asked.

"He raised maybe a hundred or more of his gross dead, coming at us on all sides." The big naga gasped. "His eyes had changed going completely silver, and an evil power came from him, it was almost overpowering."

"Then what happened?" Miss Silvia asked.

"I burned Reev alive with as much magic as I was able. He now rests in the molten grave I put him in. So, tell me, Miss Silvia, do you think I am unable to protect myself?" I held up my hand. It burst alight with the terrible flame I had used on the reaper. I saw the naga back away a bit, so I allowed my hand to go out, placing it on the table.

Her tensions eased, and she reminded me that I had once told her, if I could help her in any way, all she had to do was ask.

"Yes, I remember," I admitted.

Silvia smiled and quickly opened the nearby trapdoor leading to her cellar. Down in the spacious room, filled with wall-to-wall specimen jars and weird objects. There was now better lighting and long, wooden tables, upon which rested many papers and odd, fantastic machines.

"Adam, as you know I am a researcher or a scientist, as you put it, though, I am with a few more options now, thanks to you," the naga added. "Anyway, I have learned many things about your blood, and its affects in our land on other creatures. It appears to boost, strengthen, and even alter our physiology on a magical level. But, of course, there is still so much more to learn and…and…"

"You require samples," I finished for her.

"Yes," the big naga said, grabbing one of those pointy crystal containers, that were used for drawing blood.

Oh, swell, I thought to myself, but after Silvia had what she wanted, she appeared to be in a much better mood, working her weird devices, and fiddling with her new samples. So I asked, "Exactly what are you doing down here?"

"Adam, I am sure you know that all of Phantasma is threatened, by the great demon king, Draxelon. Well, I think being that the beast was created by humans, perhaps the key to destroying him, may rest with humans as well. So being that you are the only human on all of Phantasma, that I know of, this makes you very, very important." Silvia turned to me, looking most serious. "Adam, if you find yourself in danger from anyone or anything, I want you to know that you have a friend in me, and also in the nagas. I have already sent word of my discoveries back home. Should you ever need help or protection, we will be there," she told me.

"Miss Silvia, are you aware that the High Priest Jaru, as well as the Head Caretaker of Greyveil's palace infirmary, Miss Pan Pan, are also doing research on me and my blood? Probably for the very same reasons."

"No, I was not aware, but I did suspect. Only a fool would allow such opportunity to slip through their fingers. When I learn a little more, I would be sure to contact them," she said.

Then the huge white-scaled, yellow-striped snake lady quickly coiled around me. Clearly aroused, she came up from behind with a passionate hug.

I was completely surprised and unable to move. I asked, "What are you doing, Silvia?"

"Adam, are you aware that you are most attractive?" she asked, pressing her large, pillow-like breasts into my back, which threatened to pop out on each side of me.

"My friends, Rafe and Cloven once told me, there might be something between myself and the opposite sex here," I said to her.

"They were right!" Silvia breathed, licking a good portion of my face sensually, with her semi long forked tongue. She coiled around in front of me. God, she was huge! The woman could shallow me whole. I had better play this smart. Her large, soft hand slowly reached inside my blue silk shirt, where she tenderly felt the shape of my warm, muscular body.

"Adam, you could be a great asset to the nagas, and to Phantasma as a whole," she told me. "All I would have to do is get you back to Varanala, the land of the white sands." Silvia brought my fingers to her red-lipped mouth, playing with them, while she sexily lashed her semi long forked tongue between each one. The large snake woman then took my hand, completely inside of her warm, wet mouth with a sexy moan, slowly sliding it deeper and deeper down her massive throat. Silvia started to suck on it suggestively, as if it were a more sensitive and sexual part of my anatomy. She worked her way all the way up to my shoulders, stopping while she lightly hissed. I swear this would have been so sexy, if it wasn't scaring the crap out of me. Licentiously, Silvia lapped at the parts of me that weren't already inside of her. As she moaned, I could feel her warm insides undulating, moving, and inviting me inside. Growing a bit worried, I gave a little jolt. Silvia slowly retreated, freeing my arm. The big, curvy naga swallowed, licking her female lips and continued speaking.

"From the land of the white sands, you could help us all. With your assistance, we could overcome the great beast, Adam."

"I will help you," I told her looking into her green eyes, "but I am only seeking a way home, back to my world."

Silvia uncoiled a bit, backing away slightly. She looked at me. "But you are so powerful, Adam. Here, you can be a king."

"Maybe I will," I told her. "But I still need to return home. There are responsibilities that I must own up to."

The big naga held me close, and I sank between her sizable breasts.

"Oh, you are such a good boy. I could just eat you up, Adam Westlin," Silvia said.

"Yes, I believe you could," I told her. "But who would save Phantasma afterwards?"

The big naga laughed, easing her embrace. Her coils loosened and she let me go. "I bet you would feel so good inside me," Silvia breathed, allowing me to slip through her arms.

I simply smiled back at her, going up the cellar steps. Once back in the living room, I laid down on the comfortable couch, wondering which inside me she was speaking of—sex or her stomach? "Wow, aren't there any normal chicks on Phantasma?"

I immediately drifted off to sleep, thinking on the bizarre subject.

Chapter Twenty-Four

The next morning, Darkdancer and I said our goodbyes to Nemm and Silvia, after a quick but sweet breakfast of juice, and I'm really not sure what it was, but it was fun to play with, as it oozed around my plate eating the toast. The princess was acting a bit peculiar. She really wanted to hurry back to the palace for some reason. I was actually surprised she was even up so early in the morning. Vampires usually did not arise till at least twelve o'clock or later. We soon mounted Nightheart with Dailania at the reins. The newly recovered giant bat shot nose first into the morning sky, spreading its expansive wings. It was quite refreshing to be up in the air again, with the ever-blowing wind cooling our warm bodies. But I couldn't really enjoy it. The princess was totally, and strangely focused on getting back to the castle.

As we flew at breakneck speeds, the great white Greyveil Palace eventually came into view. It truly was like something out of a wonderful fairytale, located in the dead center of the vampire city. Its courtyards and grounds were well kept. Getting a better look, I saw that the land it sat upon was really the size of eight footfall fields, if four were sitting side by side, yard line to yard line next to four more. It was a lot larger than I had originally thought. That's not even counting the stables, which were a little to the side of the awe-inspiring castle. The palace walls were strong, and its many towers long and pointed.

They stood like majestic spears tipped with impressive, red caps. As we neared the castle, the eyes of the great white, stone bat glowed red, turning slightly towards us. It almost looked like the impressive creature was getting ready, to fire on us or something. But the eyes soon lost their brilliance, and the bat settled back to normal. Dailania landed Nightheart right in front of the castle's front entrance, which sloped beneath ground level. When we dismounted, a nearby soldier immediately took the alpha bat's reins, gingerly walking towards the stables with him. The vampire commander, Aldett, then stepped from the palace doors as we approached. Barrel-chested and having brown, slicked back hair he was wearing a sparkly, black, shoulder-padded suit. It had a red diamond shape on his chest, and a black cape with red inside lining flowed behind him. He quickly walked to us.

I tried to tell Aldett what I had heard in Reev's dreadful keeping, about the elves helping the reaper to enter Greyveil, but he threw up a black, regally gloved hand, silencing me as he went straight to the tall vampire princess.

"Where have you been, Dailania? The king is very upset," he said, scolding her.

Darkdancer paused a moment, then continued into the castle.

"I left to retrieve Lord Adam from the deathreaper," she told Aldett, walking speedily.

"What! How could you be so irresponsible, Princess. Going alone! If anything had happened to you…"

"The reaper is dead," she said plainly.

Aldett stopped right there in his tracks, pausing in the immaculate palace room.

"How is such a thing possible, Princess?" he uttered in total disbelief.

"The reaper attacked me, and Adam destroyed him with his power. The human has become strong, Aldett. I saw him myself."

I don't like where this is going, I thought to myself. The barrel-chested vamp looked at me, placing a hand on his chin.

"Is that so…," he said, peering into my eyes. Continuing through the sprawling castle, Darkdancer told the vampire commander, she had sent her little sister in her stead.

"Yes, I know," he said, "but you neglected to tell your father. I am afraid he is not taking it well, Princess."

She stopped cold in front of two big, white, impressively decorated double doors that lead to where the king dwelled. I could see the worry in her. She turned her sparkling, blue, cat-like eyes to me. Instantly, I realized it wasn't worry I was seeing—it was fear. Dailania pulled the great white doors open.

Inside sat the mighty Sevorift Annadraus Shadowwind, in his jaw-dropping, crimson-floored throne room. We calmly walked up, standing before him.

"Dailania, where have you been?" thundered the vampire king's voice, its very force making the princess jump.

Immediately, the vampire commander walked over to the king's side, whispering something in his ear. Both their eyes instantly landed on me, and I knew Aldett was telling the king everything we had just told him.

Sevorift swiftly stood, and walked slowly to the princess. He was truly intimidating, tall in his green, triple shoulder padded armor, now draped in a red cloak.

"Daughter, you dare endanger the future of my kingdom! And for what, a mere plaything! You are the crown princess! Must I remind you always child! Your importance is far too great, for you to act with such foolishness! You are my daughter, Dailania, and heiress to my throne!"

"I never asked to be!" Dailania shouted.

Now standing before her, the king drew his hand back. Before he could slap the princess, I used my magically accelerated speed to stand in front of Darkdancer, shielding her. Sevorift's armored hand struck my cheek, the power of which caused my face to bleed. Holy cow! I couldn't believe how hard he was going to strike her. Everyone in the throne room stared at me, totally surprised, but no one more so than the frightened first princess.

"This is all my fault," I said. "It is because of me and my carelessness, that the princess left the castle without permission. Please, if you must punish someone, punish me. Darkdancer saved my life, and I would gladly suffer any punishment for her."

Sevorift laughed in amusement, and the princess only gazed at me through watery eyes.

"Very well, young Adam Westlin," the king said, walking back to his throne. Sevorift looked to his commander, who gave a small nod. Then he told me that he proposed a small contest.

"No!" Darkdancer protested, but she was instantly silenced by a forbidding stare from her father.

"Both you and my Commander of Forces Aldett, are to do battle here and now. You may consider this a small examination, if you like, so that I may see these great abilities, that I have heard so very much about. I think that I may even be something of a fan, Young One."

The king pointed his green armored hand, to the space beside me. Aldett stepped out onto the huge, crimson throne room floor to fill it.

"I've been waiting for this Adam, ever since that time when you visited my camp. Don't disappoint me," he said.

We faced one another with Dailania backing away, to stand beside her imposing father. The king then commanded us to begin.

Instantly, I used my increased speed to clash with the barrel-chested vampire. It stunned me to find, that he was just as fast as I was. Could he have been holding back before? When we collided, the power of the impact caused us to rise into the air. With gravity being less of a problem for me now, we continued the fight at high speed, zipping, jumping, and battling all over the throne room. The vampire king laughed madly, enjoying the chaos as we pounded one another. Soon, we both grew more focused, each beating the other back. Aldett and I then took places eyeing one another, on opposing sides of the room. He gave a mighty battle cry and I did the same. We ran towards each other meeting in battle before the king, trading high-speed blows. I dodged the vampire's swift advance, flipping upside down to kick him in the head. Aldett stumbled back and smiled. *Yeah, I'm going to pay for that,* I thought to myself.

Once again, we fought a high-speed battle. This time, the commander gained the upper hand, like I didn't see that coming. After he absorbed a couple of my hits, Aldett punched me in the throat, kicked me in the stomach, and flipped me onto my back. I coughed as I got up, wiping away a little sweat from my brow. Before Aldett could react, I immediately slid across the floor, clipping his legs from under him. The vampire fell straight towards me, where I caught him with a stiff right cross punch. He hit the throne room floor beside me, and I quickly got back to my feet. Laughing a bit and rotating his jaw, Aldett arose, pulling out what looked like brass knuckles, taking them from somewhere behind his back. My mind flashed, *Where the hell did those come from?* I looked at the king. He said nothing, but the brown-haired princess appeared truly worried. When I turned back to the commander, he was already flying at me full force. I barely moved out of his way. His missed punch hit the Floor, resulting in a mighty shockwave. I was carried back a bit by its tremendous force. "I have the power to channel magical force through metal objects," revealed Aldett. I hadn't expected that, this was not good. The sparkly black clad vampire told me not to hold back, but not wanting to fry him like I did the reaper, I only used some of my power, which was more than enough to impress. My two fists lit with golden flames of destruction. The king and princess merely watched intensely with mouths agape. The commander attacked again. I met his magical, brass knuckled fists with the flames of my own. On impact, the throne room exploded in a grand show of flames, and vivid sparks of light. Again, we battled intensely at a blistering speed, with the barrel-chested vamp's every magical punch, exerting impossible strength. However, Aldett seemed a bit slower somehow. I could read his every move. Easily dodging his many punches and kicks, I spun around behind him. Back to back, I grabbed the vampire under his arms. Then, using all my might, I threw him with such ferocity, that when he hit a large throne room column fifteen feet away, a large portion of it cracked, falling to the floor. The vampire commander dropped to his knees. As he doubled over slumping to the floor, I heard his bones pop and crack. Still, Aldett stood up, running towards me. I could definitely see why this guy was the leader of the vampire army. Unable to think of anything else, my flaming fists struck him. First, I released a right to his chest, which burned his black, sparkly suit, then a left cross spinning into a backhanded right. It sent Aldett straight out of his brass knuckles, to land motionlessly on the shiny, scarlet floor with terrible face burns. The king stood, and was ecstatic as he clapped.

"Well, well, I believe you may have done something right after all, my daughter. This boy will be most useful in the coming battle!" said Sevorift Annadraus Shadowwind.

"But Adam has already killed the deathreaper!" revealed Darkdancer.

The tall, green-armored vampire froze, stunned for a moment. He looked at his unconscious commander. The king then laughed mightily.

"It appears Lord Aldett wished to test you, Adam Westlin, for reasons perhaps other than my own. Had I known you had already destroyed Reev, I never would have even bothered to test you. But whatever the reason, Aldett was correct about your value to Greyveil, and to the vampire people."

Darkdancer was so happy, she looked as if she could burst. Annadraus then continued.

"Yes, your value to us may be even greater, then I dared to dream," the long-red-haired vampire said, caressing his oily-looking beard. "It would seem that my oldest daughter has a problem, with the future I would gift her with."

Darkdancer's joy turned to worry in a split second, while the king spoke. "Perhaps, she has not the strength I had once believed. Perhaps, what I need is a young male heir."

Dailania cut in, "Rem, Father, Rem could..."

"The boy is too young and unrefined," the king's voice thundered. "I require one a bit more mature, and ready to face the battles ahead."

His blue eyes changed to shining red, as they looked at me. Baring his long, dangerous fangs, he spoke, "After two hundred long years, the day has finally come. You, young Adam, can make my vision a reality. Under my guidance, it is your strength that can save our people."

Oh crap; in trying to save Darkdancer, it appears this guy wants me to take her place! Did he just say two hundred years?

"Your Majesty, please, I will help you, but I only wish to return home to my family."

Sevorift caressed his oily red beard again as he thought.

"Are you not bloodbonded to not one, but two of my lovely daughters, Adam Westlin?"

"Yes, Your Majesty," I answered.

"Then worry not, boy, you are home."

The king hammered his armored fist down upon his golden throne. Four vampire guards appeared out of nowhere, not as fast as Rem, but having superspeed nonetheless.

"The boy is to be confined, until the ruby mooned night of transformation!" the king said.

"No, Father, please!" Darkdancer objected.

He simply looked at her coldly, then continued. "When Adam shall become vampire and truly join us, to lead our people to victory!... Take him away!" the king commanded. "Adam Westlin is most important to the future of our people."

Darkdancer wept openly, and I pulled away from the vamp guard's grip, walking to the still unconscious vampire commander, to kneel next to him. I placed a hand on his chest. With a gasp, he sprang back to consciousness. When his barrel-chested body arched towards the heavens, the guards started for me, but they were stopped by a hand gesture from the king. I could hear a few of Aldett's bones snapping back into place. His burns immediately faded away, and we both collapsed.

"Extraordinary!" King Sevorift said.

Aldett laid on the throne room floor completely healed and panting. The guards then grabbed me, taking me to a room which rested at the top of the tallest tower in the palace, sitting at its dead center. The room was large and of a circular shape.

There were six dark windows ringing the tower, facing out in all directions. The place also had a large, silk-covered bed with soft pillows, where a clean white shirt and black pants laid out of me. There was nice furniture, chairs, a dresser, and so on. To the right of the entrance was even a small bathroom. Were it not for vampire guards posted outside the door, I never would have known I was a prisoner. I sat on a well-crafted chair and healed my wounds, wondering where I had gone wrong. A little after noon, I was visited by the second princess, Vale, but after entering the room, she said nothing to me, merely taking a seat on the large bed, and staring out one of the many tower windows.

"Is everything okay?" I asked a little worried.

"No, everything is not okay, Adam..." She looked at me. "I would have gone after you. But after you left, Dailania was summoned. With all that passed between us in the argument, she allowed me to go to one of her meetings with Father, in her stead. I didn't know that something had happened to you. I...I thought you might need some time to yourself. The others said they would find you, and help to calm you down. It was only after being with Father a number of hours that...that I could feel your suffering, Adam. You have to know that I would have come. I would have saved you!" Vale turned from me. "But Father...I tried to tell him! I tried to get out!" Tears streamed down her beautiful cheeks.

"But he would not let me, no matter what I did!"

"Did he hurt you, Vale?" I asked, placing my hand on hers.

She reached up to touch her cheek, but said nothing. *That bastard*, I thought, taking her into my arms. Attempting to comfort her, my hands rubbed against her hourglass shaped body. As we embraced, I noticed the princess nuzzling my neck more and more. I grabbed her shoulders, pulling her away so I could see her. When I held Vale in front of me, she licked her full, red lips, swallowing a couple of times, appearing shy. Her stomach gave a wet gurgle, and I knew what she needed.

"Oh, I'm sorry, Vale. I had completely forgotten that you might be thirsty," I said. I opened a few buttons of the clean, white shirt I had only recently put on, after a relaxing shower. My neck exposed to the princess, I let her know that I was there for her. She opened her mouth, showing her perfect, white teeth. And as she watched me with sparkling, green eyes, I saw her so lady-like face slowly grow mighty, sharp, k-nine-like fangs. I playfully give her a little smile, touching a finger to her nose. Not wasting any time, Vale happily bit down deep, penetrating me with a mighty, female grunt. So much for foreplay!

"Aaahh!" I gasped, as electricity seemed to flow through me from her perfect lips. She laid me down on the sizable, silk-covered bed, sucking heartily at my neck. Was it just me, or were the pleasure sensations from the princess' bite, that much more intense now? Even her scent of exotic flowers seemed stronger than before. Vale took my hands and, to my surprise, she placed them on her soft, sensitive breasts under her purple blouse, where she vigorously rubbed herself excitedly. Oh, God, I only wanted to sate her primal need!

It never occurred to me, that she might have more than one! Now was not the time for this. I needed to find out more about my current situation. Hungry for me in more ways than one, the princess started gulping more and more of my blood, while she used my hands to stimulate her tender breasts, and rub her heated, curvy rear. Vale then released my neck, massaging my face against hers. She licked me slowly as if somehow, I would soon disappear down her lovely throat altogether. A jolt of some wonderful force hit me. *What the hell was that*, I thought? It filled my body, and my mind flashed on images of the princess, I couldn't quite make out.

"We can't do this right now, Vale, your father…"

"Don't worry about my father. Just relax Adam, this makes you taste so much riper." When our eyes finally met, Vale seemed to peer into my very soul. Our lips slowly approached one another, hot and wanting. The princess then promptly gave a little burp, before they could touch. Not quite so perfect after all, but wow she was sexy. I grinned in amusement, and she rolled her eyes, happily continuing to lick my face, eventually settling back into my neck once again. As her fangs sank back into me, it was a jolt of total pleasure. My body stiffened and an audible groan escaped me. I was nearly unable to take the pure euphoria of the moment. Vale also moaned sensually, continuing her feeding efforts. She lapped and smacked hungrily against my sensitive neck. Dear God, I think I could feel everything a thousand times over. I could actually see an image of Vale and Darkdancer in my mind. But it faded quickly. Wantonly, the princess resumed guiding my hands, not that I needed coaching. Faster and faster, the vampire started caressing me perched atop my warm body. The more Vale touched me, the more I could almost see. And the more hungrily she sucked from me. Finally, I held her tightly to me by instinct, and a little of my magic seemed to flow into her. Vale's back arched upwards like that of a cat. I could feel powerful pulses jolting through her. She gazed at me fanged mouth agape, seemingly frozen. Moments later the princess collapsed into me, laughing.

"Oh, I can taste the very power inside of you, human. What a wonderful appetizer," she said, "I can hardly wait for the main course." The princess reached into my black pants, and her face lit up like a Christmas tree.

"I knew you were gifted, Adam, but…"

"Yeah, I was going to tell you about that," I told her. She gave me a devilish look. "Princess, wait a moment," I pleaded. "I wish to ask, what is going on with your father? Why am I locked up like this?"

Vale exhaled, letting go of my more sensitive parts. Then sitting her soft, heated ass upon me, she spoke.

"Sometimes I think you really know how to ruin a good thing, Adam." She took another breath and continued. "When you defeated Commander Aldett, and Father learned that you had killed the reaper, he saw you as a possible savior for our people. Or at least someone to give us a fighting chance. Adam, the Demon Zone spreads constantly. Eventually, it will overtake us all."

"But why does he think that I am a savior?"

"Because that is what I believe!" the princess told me.

"How could you say that?" I queried, rubbing her perfect thighs as she sat so sexy upon me.

"Because that is what you are. The dreams and visions you revealed to me. You told me you were here to save me, Adam, when we spoke in the blood red grove of the Crimson Plains," she replied.

"But what about my home, my family?"

Vale lowered herself upon me so that her teardrop-shaped, soft, c-cup breasts rested upon my mouth, silencing me. Her green eyes were overpowering, as she gazed into my face.

"This is your home now, and I am your family," she said. "It was always meant to be this way. Why do you think I brought you here, Adam?" I just looked at her. "So that you would be mine, Human, and now you are," the princess answered giving my face one long, vertical slurp of her soft now scarlet vampire tongue. "Yes, we were helping you to find a way home," Vale continued, "but you are far too valuable, and special to me, to take a chance of losing you."

"But I would have come back, Vale!" I pleaded.

Her breasts engulfed me, while she hugged my face to her. "Now, you don't have to," she retorted. I could not help but to breathe in her lovely scent. Then, gingerly getting up from the bed, Vale walked to the door, knocking softly. The vampire guards opened it and the princess told me, "I will send Taya with your meal, and more ruby fruit to help your blood recover. Know that I also, will go to request leniency from my father on your behalf, to at least free you from this room, though you will still be under strict guard. For nothing must happen to the future Savior of Greyveil. When I return, we'll finish what we started here, Adam."

I peered at her and through my gaze, she knew that sex was the last thing on my mind.

The princess turned back to me sternly, "Adam, you are my bloodbonded mate!" she declared. "As such, you belong to me! You would already have known this, if the bloodbond worked properly on you," Vale added. "So I am telling you now, I am your mistress, and all that you are is already mine!... When I return, you should know that I will most certainly, have that which is mine!" she said, looking between my legs, "whether you be willing or not!" the female vamp finished. Then Vale stormed out, with the guard locking the door behind her. I couldn't believe it.

I simply stared at the door, expecting Vale to come back any minute, to tell me it was only a big misunderstanding. But as the minutes passed, I realized that the princess wasn't coming back to apologize. I was in deep crap, and I could sense danger, fast approaching my family back home, like it had somehow been long asleep, but was now waking. Oh, God, how could this have happened? Everything's gone so wrong. I pondered and pondered, hoping to see a way out. But there were no easy answers. Soon, my mind drifted to happier thoughts of me, my family, and just how much I loved Grandma and Grandpa. I would miss them so.

Hell, I was even going to miss Tannon. We didn't always get along, but there were some good times.

As the images flooded my mind, my heart ached so much I believed I could physically feel it. Oh, how I so wanted to go home! *They need me*, I thought silently so hard, that there were tears in my eyes. The desire built up within me, like nothing I could possibly explain. Then I heard it, the strange rippling sound, the same one I had heard when I first met Vale. A weird vibration began to happen, beating once again in time with my heart. It appeared first as a kind of wavy heat effect. Then in the blink of an eye, it opened up into a shadowy passage. I knew it led back to Earth. Standing before the strange portal, I hesitated only a moment, before I walked through it.

Chapter Twenty-Five

Making my way between worlds, my mind was stretched in every possible direction. Images of Phantasma, all the new friends and enemies I had made flooded my consciousness. I shielded my head, trying to stay coherent or at least sane. When I thought that I might finally go mad, suddenly, I found myself standing in front of the weird columns, and stunted trees of the clearing just west of my home. Tannon was nearby facing away from me. Crouched maybe twenty feet forward from where I stood, he was playing with a wild squirrel, he had somehow caught, to the everlasting horror of the squirrel, of course. Man, could he be any weirder?

Tannon turned his brown-haired, brown-eyed head, finally noticing me. The captive squirrel, seizing the moment, promptly escaped his grasp. Tannon gasped instantly, running straight for me, with his arms out as if to give me a big hug. He swiftly closed the distance between us. And our heads cracked together, colliding in terrible pain.

Yep! I thought to myself, *I'm definitely home!* Both of us doubled over in pain, I helped the little beast find his balance. Then, we started towards the two-story house with white siding that I called home. When we approached, Grandpa stepped outside onto the porch. Seeing me, he ran straight for us. At fifty-eight years old, the man could move when he really wanted to. He gave me a hug, and put his arm on my shoulders as we walked, saying, "Nice duds, son, what is that cotton? Boy, I sure am glad to see ya. It ain't been the same around here without cha, Adam."

I grinned proudly, then Grandpa told me that he had some work lined up for me. A tractor job, a little auto repair and of course, yard work. Yep, it sure was great to be home. As we entered the house, Grandma was at the sink busily washing the dishes. When she finally laid eyes on me, she dropped the plate she was holding, breaking it on the kitchen floor.

"Oh, Adam, you've come back!" she said rushing passed the kitchen table, to hug and kiss me on both cheeks.

"We tried to contact you, but we couldn't call anymore. We thought that maybe something terrible had happened."

That's right, I hadn't had any calls lately. *Hey, where the hell is my cell phone? That dirty damn deathreaper must have taken it!* I silently thought, giving Grandma a mighty hug, and kissing her sweet-smelling cheek. We all then headed left out of the kitchen, slash dining room, towards the living room, making ourselves comfortable on the soft, recently acquired living room set. In front of the likewise new forty-two–inch, flat panel television, which I myself graciously provided. In the brightly lit, medium sized, square living room, my entire family all started to pry.

"So, where were ya, Boy?" my Grandpa asked.

"I met a girl," I told them, "her name was Vale Shadowwind."

"Oh, that's wonderful, Son! So when can I meet her?" Grandma inquired.

I knew that I couldn't lie to her. Those damn blue eyes of hers wouldn't let me.

"I think we broke up," I told her instead.

"Oh Adam, I'm sorry, are you going to be okay?"

"Yes, Grandma, I will be fine."

"So how far did you get with her?" Grandpa asked.

Grandma became stiff as a board looking at the gray haired man, like he had just dropped in from another planet.

"I think I got to third base," I told him.

"Adam!" Grandma scolded, while Grandpa declared, "That's my boy!" Grandma then gave her husband a little rap on the head, and he protested.

"I'm only looking out for the boy's best interests. With all the bad luck he's had with girls, I was starting to wonder if maybe he had switched teams."

"What?" I said.

Grandpa immediately threw up his hands to calm me.

"Hey, I don't judge" he continued. "All I'm saying is that I want great grand kids someday." I settled down, still staring at him a little weirdly. Grandma asked, "So why did you break up with her, son?"

"She was a vampire," I answered.

Grandma made an expression that I couldn't quite place, and Tannon laughed, asking, "So do you mean like the ones with fangs?"

"Yes," I answered flatly, and the little ten-year old hit the floor, rolling in laughter.

"As long as I get my great grand kids, I'm fine with that," said Grandpa. *Okaaay, I really wasn't expecting that*, I thought to myself.

"Albert James Westlin, just what in the world are you going on about?" Grandma queried.

"Hey, now, the boy's having hard luck with all the normal fillies. I'll take what I can get," the fifty-eight-year-old retorted.

Tannon continued to giggle even harder on the floor, looking as if he was starting to have trouble catching his breath. Geez, I almost thought the little devil might croak.

"So, all that talk about being on another world…"

"Yes, it was true, Grandma."

"How did you get back?" she asked.

"I think that I always had the power, but I was only able to use it when…when I truly remembered how much I loved you all, and just how badly I really wished to come home."

Grandma told me, "That was beautiful, Adam."

Grandpa added, "Yes, that was beautiful, my grandson, the space alien."

Everyone laughed and life resumed as usual, with my family throwing me a welcome home celebration that night. A few friends of ours came over, and we all had a good time. There was Mr. and Mrs. Perkins, an old couple who I did a little work for every now and then. They couldn't keep their cars and tractor running for crap. There was also Miss Neely, a shut in who I was surprised was even here. And Gordy Myer, the most crooked man in Tinsdale. He once sold someone a car that had no engine. They were among other miscellaneous friends. Gordy owned a used car dealership, as well as a few other small businesses around town. He also brought his brood of five hell raisers with him. Actually that's not true. Kalin, the youngest, sixteen-year-old daughter was okay.

But Billy, who was nineteen, Russell who was eighteen, Jeb, who was fifteen, and Paddy, seventeen years old, were a whole other story altogether. They mostly caused trouble at the local high school and around town, harassing younger teens and just about anyone smaller than themselves. You know, pulling stupid pranks and committing petty theft. Paddy and I once were an item. That is, until a better-looking guy came along.

She dumped me without a second thought, and the guy she traded me up for, dumped her soon after. So Paddy's been kind of stalking me these passed three months, sort of eyeing me from a distance, but not approaching. I think she wants to get back together, but I don't think the girl really cared about me. Or anyone else, for that matter. I am ashamed to say that it took me a whole month to get over her. I can't believe I didn't see Paddy for the terrible person she was, earlier. And sure enough, as I enjoyed the music drinking my punch, "Hi Adam?" came her shrill voice. She was wearing an ugly, tight one-piece, multi-colored dress. It had tiny, little flowers on it, and what looked like wire scraps on its shoulders, with four-inch high platform heels. It resembled a tight shopping bag, with the bottom missing out of it. I wondered if maybe a circus clown somewhere, was missing his date for tonight.

"Oh hi, Paddy, you're looking nice this evening," I lied.

"Thanks, I wore this dress just for you, Adam." She gave a little twirl.

"Wow!" I said, then I quickly moved on before she could figure out, what I was really thinking. "So what brings you guys out here?" I asked.

"Well, we heard you had left Tinsdele, and that got me to thinking. Once you were gone, I really missed you, Adam. You're not like any of the other boys I've meet."

"Other boys?" I questioned.

Not answering, she simply blurted, "Why don't we go talk outside?"

Paddy tucked her long, blond hair behind her ear, grabbing my hand. We headed towards the front door. As I followed in tow behind Paddy's shapely, thin body, I saw Tannon giving the Myer brood a run for their money. When Billy and Russell stood up to speak with a couple of random girls, and boy, did they look suave, the little monster sat bowls of potato salad in their seats, quickly going over to Jeb, to find more devilry to get into. My God, he was smooth. The two older boys sat back down, and the look on their faces was priceless.

When Paddy and I finally made it to the porch, I was still trying to hide my ear-to-ear smile. She sat on the old, red, swinging bench. It was to the right of the front door on the edge of the porch. The blond patted the empty space next to her. I sat and there was no denying, the girl was cute, crappy shopping bag dress and all. She had flawless, white skin, blue eyes, and of course, Paddy possessed long, blond hair with nice b-cup sized breasts. If I didn't already know, I had all the worth of a stick of gum to her, and I hadn't been through so much already, I would have been all over the girl.

"It sure is nice out here tonight," Paddy said.

"Sure is," I replied. The thin blond shifted herself to face me.

"You know, I still think about us, Adam. You were always so good to me."

I simply gazed at her, thinking a moment. "If I was so good to you, why did you dump me, Paddy?" I asked.

"I...I made a mistake," she answered.

"Yeah, a mistake that lasted all of two whole months," I said.

Paddy looked a little shocked.

"Why so surprised? I heard what happened five months ago, just like everyone else in town. You got with Mr. Looks Good and after he got what he wanted, he kicked your ass to the curb."

Paddy slapped me and maybe I deserved it. But it felt good to get that off my chest. Feeling a little better, "I'm sorry," I told her.

She took my hand, squeezing it, gazing at me as I sat motionless. My head still turned the other way from her slap. "Adam, why don't we get back to-gether?" she asked.

I slumped, looking at her soft, warm hand in mine. "You hurt me, Paddy. I would have done anything for you, and you threw me away like I was nothing."

"I know and I'm sorry, Adam. Can't things just be the way they were, before all this?"

"No, they can't, Paddy. We can't go back, we can only move forward. And...and I am just not ready," I told her.

"Not ready! not ready!" She sprang from the red, swinging bench. "Adam, I gave you three months, because I was the one who broke it off! But not ready!" The irate bond paused, glaring at me. "You've been seeing someone else, haven't you? Who is she? Who is the bitch, Adam? I'll string her boney ass up by her own hair extensions!"

You know, the girls back in town often called Paddy the Dragon Lady. I think I know why now.

"Don't worry about it," I told her. "It's over between Vale and me."

"Oh, my poor baby." Paddy quickly said, coming to me with puppy dog eyes, and a slightly poked out lower lip. She caressed and touched my body. "I'm here now, you just forget all about that mean, old girl."

Which one— her or you? I thought to myself. But I have to admit, it was nice sitting there in the cool of the night, with my head resting against Paddy's soft, perfumed breasts. Still, I couldn't do this again, not so soon. I had only walked out on Vale around noon today. I removed my head from Paddy's breasts, escaping her arms as I stood up.

"I'm sorry, Paddy it's just too soon for me. I need a little time to sort a few things out."

Paddy took a breath, exhaling long and hard. She then stood up walking to me. Out of nowhere, the bold, thin blond kissed me penetrating my lips and mouth, to nearly send her surprisingly long tongue down my throat. When we separated, Paddy told me to take all the time I needed. (Translation, she'd be seeing me real soon.) Immediately, Tannon and Jeb shot from the front door, with a very upset Billy and Russell giving chase behind them. Both of the older boys were wearing a light coating of pork n' beans, when they stepped from the porch. Tannon whirled around, flinging ice cream from a spoon and bowl he was carrying, crowning Billy and Russell, making them both ala mode. I choked back a laugh, and the two big boys shot out after Tannon and Jeb. We watched the spectacle and Paddy asked.

"Don't you think you should do something, Adam?"

"Why?" I replied, "They're never going to catch him. I know, I've already tried. So, how fast is Jeb?" I inquired.

Paddy just looked flabbergasted, throwing her hands up in frustration. Then, clutching her purse, she switched off after them. I didn't much like being with her just now. But I loved watching her go. She knew it, too, when she turned back an instant, catching me look. I coughed, trying my best to appear innocent, and Paddy smiled, then continued after the boys. I tried to reenter the house, but I came face to face with Kalin. She was blond like her older sister, but she wore it short and tied back in a little ponytail. Her eyes were also blue, and she seemed a bit shy at times.

"Hey, Kalin, I haven't seen you in a while."

"Yeah, I've been busy trying to keep the rest of my family out of trouble."

"Well, that's a full time job," I said.

"Yeah, tell me about it," she retorted.

"So are you still volunteering down at the recreation center?" I asked.

"Every now and then, but Dad has me learning the ropes down at the dealership. Wow, Adam you look great!"

"Aaah. Okay," I replied.

"I mean, I heard you left town."

"Um, yeah, I guess you could say that," I told her.

"Well, I'm glad you're back!" The short-haired blond quickly hugged me and gave me a kiss, swiftly walking away.

I thought it was a bit odd, so I watched her trailing after Tannon and her family. That's when I saw Kalin do a little dance, like a football player in the end zone. A little bewildered at the sight, I simply went inside. Almost immediately, Grandma walked up to me.

"Have you seen Tam Tam anywhere, Adam?"

Oh, God, I wanted to say no so badly, but that sparkling, blue-eyed stare of hers... After hesitating a little, I told Grandma, "He's outside."

"Well, go get him, Boy."

"Yes, Ma'am!"

Forty-five minutes of hell ensued, with me trying to calm down Tweedle Dumb and Tweedle Dumber. Gordy and his brood did eventually leave, however.

After the longest goodbye, I had ever seen, I actually fantasized about kicking their Bronco, and crappy, little sports car down the street, just so I could go and get some sleep. Wow, I was really glad to see them all go! Better go make sure the silverware is still there.

Later, after a mild clean up job, we all got ready for bed. I watched my little brother dance through, brushing his teeth all the way to his bed. *Well, he's pleased with himself*, I thought as I heard happy humming, coming from his darkened room. Then, Tannon's creepy, circus clown-faced nightlight quickly illuminated the darkness. I knew for a fact he wasn't afraid of the dark. With something that creepy and ugly in his room, he couldn't possibly be.

Sometimes, I think he does things like this, just so I'll think he's weird. Settling into bed, safe in my room, I drifted off to sleep, dreaming of sweeter times. Later that night, clank, thump, thump, I open my eyes peering through the darkness. There, to my astonishment, stood Vale in front of my opened window. I clicked on the light. She instantaneously grabbed me by the neck, pulling me from my bed. Then Vale swiftly slammed me into the wall across the room with a thump, using only a single outstretched, stiff female arm. I struggled, and as her grip started to weaken, Vale commanded, "Stop it!" A strange feeling hit me. It wasn't painful; actually, it felt really good. I went limp in the princess' grasp.

She seemed to take notice, indecisively asking, "Adam can you feel me, the pleasure that I can give you?" Her body stiffened and I was flooded with euphoria.

"Aaahhh! Yes, yes, I feel it!" I told her. She suddenly stopped choking me, and her hand dropped away. Walking over to my bed, Vale plopped down into it. I took a few deep breaths, glad to have her hand from around my throat.

I asked, "What is this, Princess?"

"The bloodbond," she answered. "For some reason, I do not yet understand, it's working now."

"That's good, right? I mean, it's what you've wanted all this time."

"I don't know anymore, Adam! A part of me just wants to take you, and drain you dry, but!..."

"But?" I asked.

"Adam, why did you leave? I can give you everything, anything. Don't you understand that?"

"You were trying to take me away from my family, Vale."

"But I'm your family now!"

"I can't just throw away my family, Princess. I could never turn my back on them."

She seemed to slouch, depressed hearing my words, and her eyes started to tear up.

"But if you like, you can join them, Vampire."

She looked up to me, and a single tear trailed down her beautiful face. I sat next to her and Vale hugged me so hard, she nearly broke something. I looked at her and she gazed at me.

"So are you ready to finish what we started, Miss Vale."

She gave a fanged smile, that quickly turned into a very serious glare. "What is it?" I asked.

"The deathreaper has returned, Adam."

"But I killed him. I know I did!"

"I am afraid reapers are not so easily conquered. He lays siege to the city, and Greyveil Palace as we speak."

"What! Why are we sitting here talking?"

"You will help us then?"

"Of course, I will." I told her, caressing her pale cheek.

"After what we did I...I wasn't even sure I had the right to ask. But we need you, Adam, so much!"

"It will be okay, but we have to go now, while there is still something to save!" I started for the door and stopped. "How did you even get here, Princess?" I asked.

"I don't know. There was fighting, and so much destruction was happening all at once. I just started thinking of you, that in the hour of our greatest need, you weren't there. My heart ached and a shadowy portal opened up. I knew somehow that it would lead me to you. Once I was here, our bloodbond told me where you were."

"Then, that is what we must do. Focus on our friends and your family back on Phantasma, just like you focused on me. Remember how much we care for them, and how much they need us right now.

Focus all of your emotions, Vale, there is no time left! Just let them all flood out of us and become our power!"

There was a small boom followed by a weird rippling noise. A shadowy portal opened up right in my bedroom. Quickly, I changed into a black t-skirt, dark blue jeans, and black tennis shoes. Once dressed, I was more than ready.

Chapter Twenty-Six

We stepped through the maddening gateway, suddenly finding ourselves standing outside a burning Greyveil Palace, watching total chaos as elven warriors and undead corpses, moved like a plaque to destroy everything. The overwhelmed spell shooting, ax-weapon wand armed vampire guards were struggling, a few of them also using arm mounted slingshots to overcome the enemy, much like the one I used days earlier. But they were in obvious need of help. Some of the elves utilized special magic crystals to shield themselves, making the slingshots almost useless. Vale and I immediately joined the fight, taking down a couple of twisted dead.

We used swift attacks and stole their tarnished swords, which was a good thing, because we were soon ambushed by five pointy-eared, sword-wielding elves. They wore brown ninja-like outfits with brass, shiny armor and helmets. I ran head first to meet their threat. The princess used unnatural predator speed to circle around behind them. And we converged on the nimble warriors in battle. The elf soldiers were light on their feet, flipping and cartwheeling all over the place. I kicked one in the chest, leg swept another, and stiff-arm punched the third. They were out easily enough. I guess flips and cartwheels aren't everything. Vale clashed swords a few times with one overzealous, long blond-haired elf soldier, quickly coming back with her sword hilt across his face, to swiftly knock him out. It all happened so fast the last elf could only watch. Overcome with fear, he dropped his sword and made a run for it, but he was easily caught by Vale's speed. She held him by the back of the neck, lifting him from the ground with one arm, as her eyes shone a shiny red. Instantly, Vale caught the frightened elf in an iron embrace, opening her mouth to reveal two long, sharp fangs. She bit down hard into his neck, driving her fangs deep. Fascinated, I could only stare while the princess fed off the helpless elf warrior, sucking mightily at his open neck. His skin paled and his eyes rolled up into his head, with his body going limp, falling to the ground.

Vale spat the last swallow of his blood from her mouth, saying, "That wasn't nearly as tasty as you are, Adam."

I didn't know if I should be flattered or frightened. We both switched from the atrocious undead blades, to the better-made elf swords. I heard a familiar voice, locked in the sounds of combat, nearby. There in the night covered courtyard, outside the walls of the castle, fought a single, furious Miss Ulee, against a crowd of at least six elf soldiers and undead corpses. We were coming to help, but Ulee shot two elves in quick succession with her bow. Then her snake tail lashed, stretching impossibly long, to swat two gross undead, breaking them apart. The two remaining elf warriors gathered their courage, charging her with their sword and spear. Ulee instantly caught them in her light blue with red diamonds snake coils. As she squeezed, I could hear bones snapping. When the soldiers finally laid motionless in her embrace, the cute brunette naga opened her little, dainty mouth impossibly wide, while buckets of drool dripped from it. Oh crap, she was about to really ruin their night. I rushed in to stop the morbid scene.

"Ulee, no, don't do it!" I yelled.

She looked at me with her mouth still agape.

I told her, "If you eat them now, you won't be able to fight any more. They will weigh you down and make you helpless. We need you to fight Miss Ulee, please don't do this!" I pleaded.

She hesitantly closed her huge mouth, and released the now unconscious elves.

"You owe me a meal after this is over, Human!" she sneered, looking a bit peeved.

"It's a date!" I replied.

Vale asked, "Where is the Deathreaper?"

"He is somewhere inside the castle," Ulee told us.

We all entered the grand, burning structure together, soon seeing that inside, both Taya and Crystal were in a dire fight for life. The werewolf girl zoomed around the big, open, opulent room, slashing everything that moved with her somehow longer, seemingly unbreakable claws and fangs. Even the walls were damaged, and the banister broken by her slashes, as she flipped and jumped attacking from the dazzling, white staircase at high speed. My God, Taya was like some sort of living, feral wrecking ball. Her amber eyes in addition to pointy wolf-ears were absolutely beautiful, and a mark of two crescent moons, one within the other, glowed bright for a split second on her forehead in the chaos.

Meanwhile, Crystal protected herself in a teetering ring of spinning, deadly flame. The skinny vampire was tossing out hot, fiery death onto multiple enemies, helping the few grey-suited vampire soldiers present in the room. It was amazing, through all the death, carnage and flying daggers, they were actually able to clear the huge room, of a whopping nine enemy soldiers, with a little help from Ulee, who shot the last elf before he could throw his sharp, silver dagger to pierce Taya's heart.

"Thanks!" the cute werewolf girl told Ulee.

The naga gave a little nod in return.

"We have to find Reev and the Weird Sisters," I told everyone. "If we can take down the enemy leaders, the rest will either fall easily or surrender."

"I saw the deathreaper heading this way earlier. Follow me!" Crystal said.

My friends complied, and the vamp soldiers headed elsewhere, to clash in battle. Going through white double doors behind the white stone staircase, we passed a couple of empty rooms, then entered an open space where we assisted three more vampire guards, easily dispatching a small horde of undead. Once they had dissolved into piles of filthy bugs, Ulee led the vampire guards into the next spacious room, which had high up dark glass windows, where Flare, the short green-haired, tall Weird Sister attacked. The three guards were instantly struck with huge, flying thorn projectiles, collapsing to the floor. Unable to help them in the face of such a huge threat, we rushed into the room. The tall, green-haired elf woman extended a long, golden spear, laughing as she spoke.

"The book returns to us soon! Greyveil will finally fall before the Elf Nation of La Seeren. How I have dreamed of this moment!" she declared.

"Keep dreaming, Bitch!" came Vale's voice.

With amazing speed, the princess closed the distance, slashing with her sword, and Flare blocked her many blows. We all joined the fight, but we were stopped when huge, monstrous, thorny vines attacked from every direction. Crap, how had we missed those? I actually think I heard them roar, when they reached for us. What the hell kind of plants are these? Amazingly, Flare, in rare form was holding us all off with her atrocious vines, while she fought a furious battle with the vampire princess. Her spear skills were astounding as she blocked, parried, and hit Vale. I finally fought my way to their struggle, through the raging plants. The skilled elf still seemed to be a match for us both. Suddenly, the dark glass windows above all shattered! And the purple-haired Ember stood there, watching, as a great wind rushed through the room. We continued to fight Flare, with Vale scoring a left punch on the female elf. I then kicked the green-haired enemy in the stomach, causing her to retreat slightly. The moment Flare did, Ember struck the room with an awesome bolt of purple lightning. I was so not expecting that! All of us were blown from our feet. Everything around us was devastated... Coming to my senses a little later in the smoky aftermath, I peered around the room, and the two Weird Sisters were gone.

"Oh they did not just do that!" Crystal said. Vale coughed, "glad I wore my protective bloodstone necklace." "I am definitely having elf blood tonight!" the skinny vampire continued.

"Hope it's better than what I had," the princess added.

"I can follow their scent," Taya interjected.

"You girls, go take care of them. Vale and I will find the reaper. If I can defeat him again, all of his undead will be drawn back into the ground, changing the momentum of this war."

"Okay," said Crystal. "Just keep heading that way." She pointed towards more double doors. Then Taya, Crystal, and Ulee all leaped and slithered out the broken, high windows, enthusiastically tracking the wicked female elves.

Vale and I entered a half-destroyed, long, white, gold trimmed hall. It was strangely eerie as we warily walked. Then the undead seemed to appear from everywhere, and the ceiling started caving in to the sound of loud booms.

"What the hell is going on up there?" I said crossing swords with the blank faced, emotionless dead. I cut the heads from a few corpses, slashing and fighting. But more and more slowly threatened to overtake us.

Braced against the ever-growing, foul horde, I told Vale to run while I held them back. The princess' eyes shone red, then glowed a frightening crimson over the whites of her eyes.

"No, let them come!" she told me.

I pushed the dead back and swiftly ran behind the princess. A fierce wind seemed to come from nowhere, swirling around her, with the misshapen and twisted dead fast approaching. They brandished their sharp weapons and the beautiful, red-haired vampire quickly hit them, with her powerful wind spells. Vale screamed, enraged as they struck rapid fire against the dead. When the smoke had cleared and she was done, even the hall walls were gone. But I could tell that throwing so many spells at once had weakened her.

"I will take the next fight," I told her. "I need for you to rest and regain your strength for now, Vale."

Panting, she agreed and we slowly came to a red, gold-trimmed door. It was at the end of the destroyed hall. We reluctantly looked inside. The big, well-furnished room was empty.

"Finally, a bit of luck," Vale told me, flicking back her long, red hair. We passed opulent furniture and many weird looking, stuffed beasts. Griffins, dragons, and some creatures that I couldn't even began to describe, were all on display. The princess and I soon came to an unthreatening, simply, wooden door. Opening it, we were immediately blown back by a small explosion, that turned it into toothpicks. Inside the next room, Rafe and Cloven had their hands full, fighting the formidable vampire, Commander Aldett? Wait, did I just step into the twilight zone or something?

"What is going on in here?" I asked stepping into the large, wrecked, red chandelier-filled palace room.

"The elf, the redhead, she put a spell on him!"

Rafe said, blocking Aldett's mighty sword strikes.

"Yeah, we are trying not to hurt him. But I don't think we have much choice." Cloven added, holding a huge battle-axe. He then threw a small heap of debris at Aldett, with only a gesture of his green hand. The barrel-chested, black clad vampire brushed it aside, with a wave of one sizable arm.

"We could use a little help here," Rafe declared, blown two feet back by the force of the commander's magical brass-knuckled blows, when they collided with the palace floor. Two of the impressive, red chandeliers above fell from the ceiling, shattering on impact.

"Any minute now!" the phantom teen said, while Aldett slashed powerfully at his sword, then kicked the fat gen in the gut, when he tried to charge the powerful vampire.

I rushed in, clanging a furious blow off Aldett's sword. Glassy eyed, he stumbled back in surprise. In that instant, Rafe, Vale, and Cloven piled on top of him, quickly tossing his sword and brass knuckles aside. The barrel-chested vampire struggled beneath the weight of my friends.

Cloven asked, "Okay, now what?"

"Maybe I can heal him," I said. "He is not hurt, Adam. He is mind–controlled!" exclaimed Rafe, clearly uncomfortable under Cloven's mighty girth.

"Do you have a better idea?" I asked. He said nothing, and I placed my hand on Aldett's forehead.

Immediately, the commander's body arched upwards, tossing my friends from him like little more than soft pillows. He gasped and his eyes bulged as his fangs extended. When his healing was complete, we both hit the floor at the same time.

"You know, Adam, you could make a killing as a healer," said Cloven.

"Adam has a greater destiny!" retorted the princess, running her gentle fingers through my black hair while I panted, trying to catch my breath.

"Is he all right?" I asked, attempting to get a better look.

"He is unconscious," Vale said, examining him. "Will he be okay if we leave him here?" asked the princess.

"He's going to have to be," Rafe answered. "Where we are going he is just too easy a target."

I looked to a mound of debris and broken chandeliers, in the far corner of the room. "We can hide him in there till this is over!" I proclaimed.

Once Aldett was safely tucked out of harm's way, we continued through the sprawling palace, coming to a room where shiny wooden panels covered the walls, and beautiful, twin staircases curved reaching upwards. When we neared the bottom of the stairs, Sparkle, the red flame-like haired, leather-clad leader of the Weird Sisters descended. As she came down, she was holding twin elven swords. Our group backed off, and a red, five-pointed star mark magically appeared over her right eye, while she glared at us.

"You've come far," the tall elf woman said, "but it ends now!" With amazing swiftness, she placed a silver charm around Vale's neck. Instantly, the curvy vampire hit the floor, unable to move.

Cloven and Rafe tried attacking with their weapons, but Sparkle kicked Cloven in his round belly, gaining altitude to come down on Rafe, with two quick, sword-holding punches. Both of my friends now stunned, I rushed in, clashing swords, with the enemy elf blocking my every move.

"I remember you, Human!" she said. "I may not be a vampire, but I will drink your life's blood this night, for what you did to me."

"Try it!" I told her.

Quickly, Rafe and Cloven reentered the fight. *What is it going to take?* I thought to myself, as I experienced Sparkle's fighting prowess. The wicked redhead was fighting all three of us, and it still was not enough. Sparkle simultaneously split kicked the two boys, sending them to the cluttered floor. Then, she clipped my legs from under me with a swift kick. I hit the floor hard, and when I lay recovering, the pointy-eared elf mounted me.

"What was that you said about me trying it?" she asked.

Instantly Sparkle bit powerfully into my neck with no hesitation. Vale helplessly watched unmoving nearby, with tears in her eyes. I yelled, feeling Sparkle's painful bite. Rafe soon kicked her from me. When Sparkle got to her feet, she licked her lips, swallowing like she didn't even feel Rafe's kick. Once finished, she stared at me with an astounded gaze.

Immediately, Cloven attacked tossing a roomful of debris with a wave of his hand, quickly followed by a powerful battle-axe swing. Sparkle didn't even try to dodge. Instead, she flicked the debris and powerful blow away like they were nothing, quickly kicking the fat gen in his head. Rafe then attacked at high speed, appearing transparent with multiple aftershadows, when he tried to help his friend. The tall elf woman immediately caught him by the throat. Her grip was so strong that Rafe dropped his sword. Holding him to her face, Sparkle's red star-covered eye glowed pink. When she released Rafe, he was a glassy eyed zombie. Rafe slowly picked up his sword from the floor. When Cloven tried once again to slash the pretty elf female, Rafe blocked it. Totally surprised, Cloven hesitated. Instantly, Sparkle was on him, taking away his battle-axe with an overpowering, unnatural grip. She held the fat, green gen close, the same as she did with Rafe, before him. Once again, her star-covered eye glowed, making Cloven yet another glassy-eyed zombie. Oh hell, everyone was either down or zombified. When I tried to get to my feet, the redheaded elf kicked me so hard I flew backwards, landing on the shiny, yet messy palace floor. Helpless, the female elf woman mounted me again.

"Your blood is a true wonder, Human. I feel stronger than I ever have. I was going to kill you. But after this, I think Queen Sable will be wanting a taste, as will all my sisters. She opened her mouth to bite me again. But there was a loud smack, and Sparkle collapsed onto me. When I peered upwards, I saw the young vampire, Rem, holding a sword. He had knocked Sparkle out with the handle of his weapon. Rem tried to help me up. But Sparkle's long fingers reached around his throat, quickly lifting him into the air. Angrily holding Rem, choking from the floor, the wicked female elf actually grew a long, red, flame-like tail to match her red hair. Her red-orange eyes glowed, and she leaped fifteen feet up, slamming Rem hard against the palace floor. After the terrible deed was done, Sparkle stood before me, saying, "Now, where were we?"

What in the two worlds had she just become? I again found myself beneath the tall elf woman. She peered hungrily at me with her new tail shifting from side to side. Suddenly, I could hear an otherworldly music playing, and Sparkle seemed to be choking. She slowly lifted from me, and I saw Darkdancer enter the room from a small, broken doorway. It was opposite the way we had came in. The tall, brown-haired vampire started to spin gracefully like a ballerina, coming ever closer. The more Darkdancer twirled to the haunting music, the higher Sparkle raised from the palace floor, eventually pressing the female elf hard into the twenty-five feet high ceiling, til it cracked under the pressure. Dailania then simply stopped.

She stared at the helpless elf with her angry, blue, cat-like eyes. Sparkle seemed to be growing stronger with every passing second. Her eyes glowed all the more, and she was starting to fight the tall princess' hold on her. In a single powerful downward arching motion, Darkdancer flung her hands towards the floor, slamming Sparkle into it with such force, that when she landed, the impact created a small, smoke-filled crater, breaking the palace floor around her. The elf laid there unmoving and the music stopped. Darkdancer ended her dance, pulling a sharp, shiny dagger that was at her side. It extended into a five-and-a-half-feet spear. I immediately went over to Vale, pulling the elf's silver charm from Vale's neck, while Darkdancer carefully helped Rem up, proclaiming, "No one hurts my little brother, you crazy elf bitch!"

Understandably pissed, Vale walked over to the fallen, pointy-eared woman. Jacking Sparkle into the air easily with one hand, the Second Princess of Greyveil bit angrily into her neck. After taking a few mighty gulps, Vale threw Sparkle like a sack of wet doorknobs, sliding her cruelly across the floor.

"That is for Adam!" Vale said, wiping her sexy, full lips. Clearly, Sparkle was lucky that the second princess, had eaten that cowardly guard earlier. I immediately used my power, to break Sparkle's mind control spells over Rafe and Cloven, who were still standing nearby like glassy eyed zombies. Once healed, they were both completely out of it. I guess it takes a while for the mind to recover. Vale and I tucked them out of harm's way, much like we did with Aldett. Then we ascended the expansive twin staircases with Rem and Dailania.

Chapter Twenty-Seven

On the second floor, everything was dark. Only the light of the twin moons showed, shining through the somewhat distant seven-feet tall windows. Seeing another staircase near the beautiful windows, I told everyone to follow me. As we slowly crept through the elaborate shadows, in the wide-open space, we passed several fallen vampire guards. It looked as though they had been trampled somehow.

"What happened to them?" I whispered through the sounds of battle coming from outside, below.

"I have no idea," Darkdancer answered, clutching her spear.

Coming closer to the simple staircase, I heard a weird clicking noise. I had heard it once before, deep in Reev's dreadful catacombs. It seemed to click louder and louder, faster and faster. We all looked up and there on the ceiling was a huge, single horned, black beetle. It had glowing orange, round eyes that pierced the darkness. Its horn was like that of a rhino's; only, it was much bigger and longer. The enormous insect was about the size of a freaking minivan.

Dear God, I turned white as a sheet, and the giant bug dropped from the ceiling. When it flipped onto its six colossal insect legs, it busted the floor apart, its great weight sending us all tumbling down, to the dark room beneath us. The room was of course large and spacious, much like many other palace rooms.

But this one was filled with lots of white-sheet-covered furniture. Obviously, it was being used for storage. While we all recovered quickly in the rubble getting to our feet, the great insect screeched and screamed, barreling into Darkdancer. Caught beneath the large bug she dropped her spear, trying to hold back the insect's deadly, black, snapping jaws. Immediately Rem hopped onto the creature's back, stabbing it with his sword. Vale and I rushed in to help as well. But the hard shell of the creature opened up, knocking us away violently to reveal mammoth cicada-like wings. The insect bucked wildly, fluttering its colossal wings, appearing to lose all control, while the little vampire rode its back cowboy style. Amazingly, Dailania managed to get to safety from beneath the creature, retrieving her spear. The six-legged beast sent white-sheet-covered furniture crashing down everywhere. Vale and I were barely able to avoid it, nearly crushed under someone's old, flying love seat. Regrouping as Rem continued to ride the insect's back, we all charged, trying to jump onto the big beetle, using our weapons. Its outer shell closed up again. With a mighty effort, it flung us all from itself like we were rag dolls. Then, moving much faster than you would expect a huge bug to, it snapped and clawed at us all, tossing me clear across the darkened room easily. Dailania speedily blocked its path, attacking with her spear before it charged. The creature was truly terrifying. All the wounds and damage we dealt to the thing, healed in a matter of seconds. Crap! It seemed to be immortal. Having no better ideas, we tried once more. All together as one, we attacked, giving a great battle cry. The big beetle spun in place, knocking us all down as it screeched. When Rem finally hit the floor with a thump, the beast seemed to focus on the little vampire, barreling straight for him. As the powerful insect closed in, Rem yelled "Stop!..."

Amazingly enough, the great black, shiny, immortal beetle obeyed, watching Rem as if waiting for another command. *No freaking way!* I thought, as my mouth gaped wide open. The frightened little vampire looked at us bewildered. We all shrugged our shoulders at him.

"Um, step back!" Rem said. The big bug obeyed.

"Sit!" the little vampire commanded. With a room shaking thud, that, too, was done. I looked up to the staircase we had tried to reach.

"Hey, we can still climb up to the stairs," I told everyone. A large chunk of the second story had fallen, making a slope that led directly to it. Rem slowly tried to creep over to us, passed his happy, new bug friend. The giant beetle actually licked him a few times like a dog, screeching happily.

"Hey, I think he likes me!" Rem said, rubbing its big buggy head.

"You are so not keeping that thing!" Darkdancer breathed.

Rem smiled, continuing to rub its head as if to say, *You want to bet?* "You know, he is really kind of cute," Rem told her.

Instantly, both princesses rolled their beautiful eyes in disbelief.

Rem then added, "When he is not trying to kill you."

"Rem, why don't you stay here? To make sure your new pet doesn't play too rough, with anymore vampire guards," I said.

"Oh, and if you want to trample a few elves, I am not opposed to it!" the little vampire smiled, giving me a little vamp salute.

Vale, Darkdancer, and I then climbed the fallen debris, to ascend the stairs to the next floor. Once on the third level, again, the ceiling was high, about twenty-five feet; the carpet was blue, and everything was eerily quiet. Geez, there was almost nothing at all in the gigantic room. Immediately, we were attacked by three foul, shrunken, flying heads out of the darkness. They screamed and snapped at us furiously, but we skillfully made quick work of the horrific things. Continuing on, Darkdancer, Vale, and I passed a few tall magic crystal-powered lamps. Through their gentle light, we saw that we had at last found the deathreaper.

He was facing one of the many wide, tall, complexly made tinted windows that lined the palace wall. Transfixed, Reev watched the devastation in the courtyard below. At his brown, leather-booted feet laid King Sevorift, immobilized and covered in many silver charms. We tried to slowly sneak up on the reaper. Then his chilling voice broke the silence.

"I knew that you would come, Human. I have been waiting for you," Reev said, as he turned to face us. Oh, crap! I had totally incinerated him before. I destroyed him completely, and now he doesn't even have a scratch! "Did you enjoy my pet death beetle Zageari downstairs, Adam?..."

"No, I didn't care much for it," I told him. "But the young vampire, Prince Rem, thanks you for your kind gift."

The reaper appeared puzzled a moment.

Then the big, black death beetle flew passed the castle windows, with an overjoyed Rem riding its back. I would have giggled, but the reaper had me tense.

"You really are quite the nuisance, aren't you, Boy? You and your pathetic vampire bitches!" Reev declared, while he watched the fantastic sight.

"But I admit freely that you certainly surprised me, back in the catacombs, Adam. Yet, I have the divine power of death itself. The secrets of the abyss are mine to know. You cannot kill me so easily, Boy, though, clearly, you have managed to earn my respect. Death respects death, Adam, and in death, I sense that you are most gifted. Therefore, once Drexelon has finished with you, your gifted soul will live on as a part of me, forever."

Oh wow, if this is how he treats people who earn his respect, I think that I would rather not have it.

"Release my father, Reaper!" commanded Vale.

"I am afraid I can't do that Princess," Reev retorted, kicking the red-bearded vampire king in the face. "This windbag is so full of himself, he didn't think I could possibly beat him. Too stupid to put his guard up, he didn't even notice the elves' leader charming him from behind. How he became king, I will never know. Perhaps, the vampires are not nearly as smart, as I give them credit for. The dumb bastard!" Reev said, stomping the motionless king.

"Stop it, Reev! It's me you really want. Let the king go!" I demanded.

"Oh, you are so right, Adam. You tortured me with magical flames, and buried me alive in my own catacombs! I totally intend to take my time with you, Boy. Let's get the party started!" the deathreaper proclaimed, kicking the green armored king like a football, into his two daughters. When they collapsed onto the blue-carpeted floor, Reev was on me in the blink of an eye, his curved sickle slashing wildly away.

Nearly overwhelming me, he spoke, "The charms around the king's body are made of my own silver reaper's blood. The only way to release them is to defeat me in glorious combat."

Seeing an opening, I kicked the black-robed death figure in the stomach. Once he was stunned, Darkdancer quickly pulled the red, sparkly bow from her long, brown hair, throwing it to strike Reev in the center of his pale, blue-haired face. Wow, it had actually been a weapon the whole time! I wanted to believe that it was all over right there, but we weren't that lucky. Reev plucked the deadly bow from his face, crushing it in his black-fingernailed hand. The silver blood that slowly oozed down the cut, retreated back inside of him, and the wound closed immediately.

"That was pretty good, Princess," he said as he absorbed his bladed weapon into himself. "Here, let me try!"Reev blurted out. The reaper took a deep breath, and sharp silver darts sprang up all over his body. He took another inhale, and they all shot from him, with all the force of a gun firing. The darts flew in every possible direction. I dived by pure instinct, while the princesses did the same. It was a sheer miracle that he missed us all. We managed to get back to our feet, and Reev laughed.

"That was quite amusing!" he said, rematerializing his curved, bladed sickle into his wicked hand. "I underestimated you before, Adam. It won't happen again!" the reaper breathed. He instantly ran screaming towards Dailania, Vale, and me.

We were immediately sucked into a furious, sword-swinging battle. Reev was quick, powerful, and merciless. He held the three of us at bay with no problem at all, showing amazing skill with his blade. The reaper then dealt me a terrible blow to my head, putting me momentarily out of the fight, when I tried unsuccessfully to attack him. Straightaway he turned his attention to the two princesses. They danced around him, slashing and working together with their sword and spear. The girls looked so much alike, with both their long, red and brown hair down. It was a thing of beauty, when they went toe to toe with the reaper, in a dance of death. Ultimately, the two female vampires' eyes both shone a frightening, complete red. As near twin predators, Vale and Dailania caught Reev in truly devastating moves. While Darkdancer held him in place from behind, Vale did a flying, wind-powered, corkscrew-like kick, hitting the reaper in the stomach with tremendous force.

Immediately after execution, Vale followed it up with a backwards flip-kick, striking Reev powerfully in the face, when it was done. Music began and Darkdancer started to ascend high into the air, carrying the deathreaper, whom she was clutching possessively to herself, striking a pose behind him. When she could go no farther, the tall, brown-haired princess spiraled towards the floor with terrifying force, crushing Reev into it, all her weight and might spearing her body, elbows first, into the deathreaper. The music stopped, and the blue-carpeted room vibrated powerfully, under the awesome impact. It even created a sizable crater, that warped the surface of the entire floor. For a moment, I thought we'd all go tumbling down, to the lower levels, just like with Zageari.

Yet Reev appeared to recover quickly, going on the offensive. This guy was really tough, apparently. I rejoined the battle, fighting him furiously with the two vamped out sisters. Eventually, the reaper blocked both myself and Vale with his sickle, hitting Darkdancer super hard across the cheek, with his other hand. She crumbled to the floor, becoming normal again, trying to come to her senses. Then focusing on myself and the remaining princess, Reev kicked Vale so hard, she hit the floor belly first. The redhead also returned to normal, cradling the place where Reev had struck her. It was just him and me now. The reaper stopped his attack, taking me in with his silver eyes. I noticed Spectra, Dailania's long-eared, black stripped, orange familiar. She was circling our dreadful battle in the shadows.

"A part of me regrets this, Human, but I have no choice."

Reev focused his awful power. I could feel a terrifying aura coming from him.

Immediately, I too, focused. The blade of the elven sword that I was holding, began to glow a powerful gold.

"Phantom force!" Reev's voice rang out. A multitude of grim reaper scythe blades sprang from his body. On long threads of liquid silver, they slashed everywhere. Thanks to my magically enhanced speed and reflexes, I was just able to retreat far enough, that the wild and raging blades missed me, by only a hair.

"Aaahh! What is it going to take?" the black-robed death figure yelled.

The two princesses only stared dumfounded from the floor.

Reev and I once again clashed in battle. With every strike of my blade, sparks, and mini explosions filled the open space, of the large room. I kicked the reaper to the floor, he sprang up and hit me, with a mighty uppercut in return. Our blades crossed with awesome force. Then grabbing him, I ran with all my might, plowing Reev hard into the castle wall, which seemed to disintegrate and crumble against my force. The reaper dropped his sickle, punching me with all his strength. I stumbled in retreat, a little amazed, I was still breathing. Dropping my sword as well, I punched him back, with magically charged golden fists of fury. Our fight had degraded into a bloody knuckled man to reaper fistfight. I struck him, knocking a small shower of golden sparks from his face. He retaliated by nearly knocking me senseless. Back and forth, we traded blows, the force and magic of which was destroying the huge, blue-carpeted room we fought in. Finally, we stopped and began staring one another down, panting hard under a thick layer of our own sweat. My ears rang like bells in the totally decimated palace room. Darkdancer then spoke the words "*Sen nu sa lin!*"

Instantly, Spectra was engulfed in powerful, red flames. Without hesitation, the flaming familiar struck a mighty blow, across Reev's face. The deathreaper screamed, clutching his head. He spun in place, abruptly running for the large, tinted windows, where he fearlessly jumped straight though them. They shattered on impact into a gigantic shower of broken glass. Quickly retrieving my sword, I courageously followed behind him. Maybe forty feet up, I had no fear, as I sailed through the air in pursuit of Reev, landing hard upon my feet, on the grassy ground.

"He went that way!" a familiar voice said. Looking behind me to my left, I saw that it was a black-cloaked, lightly armored, magical weapon wand wielding Swicer, fighting against ten horrible undead. The corpses tried desperately to attack me in that moment, but the tall, tattooed vampire was casting impressive spells, while simultaneously sword battling, and backed up by his three bat winged brothers in battle. Swicer had been my tall, winged friend from Aldett's vampire Honor Guard. "Go! We will hold them off, Adam!" he told me.

Swiftly following his instruction, I immediately shot out after the wicked deathreaper. Soon, I saw him staggering away across the battlefield. As I closed in for the kill, he simply stopped. There in the war-torn courtyard, Reev began to laugh. He turned to me with a frightening gaze.

"Now, everyone will see you for what you really are. You are not a savior, Adam! You can't even save yourself!" Reev threw his hands down in a powerful motion.

Suddenly and without warning, we were surrounded by a giant, ninety-feet-across circle of haunted flames. If you looked closely enough, you could even see faces screaming in their light.

"The time for games has ended, Adam. It is time you knew what you are truly up against."

Darkdancer and Vale arrived, but they were unable to go beyond the frightening flames that surrounded us.

"Adam, we can't get in!" Dailania yelled.

Vale tried a strong wind spell, but the evil flames only grew, reaching and threatening to overtake her. Reev took a small, black crystal from his robe, breaking it in his hand. When its dark contents spilled out, he said these words in a terrifying voice: "*Zen nu sha zin,* invincible shadow of Drexelon, I call upon you!"

With a boom and an awesome, smoke-like swirl of blackness, a mighty fifteen feet tall, shadowy figure arose. It had red, fractured eyes that peered through the night like dim lanterns, and a long, spiky mane. Being only a shadow, it's body appeared to shift, and warp unnaturally from moment to moment. Possessing a built, male physic, its arms were huge, as were the bull-like horns on its head. The evil titan stood there radiating power on sharp dragonesque feet, its dangerous tail whipping wickedly. When it spoke, it was even more horrifying than the voice of the deathreaper.

It proclaimed, "Human, you will come to me, now!" As the words came out, it actually created a small sonic boom.

"The hell I will! I am not going anywhere with you, Horn Boy!"

My God, the thing looked like a giant, unwashed Satan. I crouched defensively, getting ready. My blade glowed an even more powerful gold, and the battle began. Reev came at me this time, materializing a long, sharp, silver scythe, but I sensed that he was winded. Knocking his blow aside, I kicked him in the gut, just in time to dodge the shadow's gigantic fist, when it hit the ground with horrifying force. Thinking I was safe for the moment, the huge, dark beast warrior turned his head. The horn closest to me grew out super fast striking me. When it hit the grassy ground, I stumbled a bit and peered through the ghostly flames, seeing that much of the fighting around us had stopped. Many of the elves and vampires were now only watching me, as if the fight I was in right now, would decide the outcome of this war. Reev came at me again, slicing and slashing with his shiny scythe. I blocked the evil death figure, and rolled before the mighty shadow's wicked tail could strike me. Through the dirt and debris kicked up by the shadow's might, Reev again pressed his attack. I was able to hold onto his scythe, punching him multiple times in the face, to the glow of the evil flames. Suddenly, the great beast charged. I was nearly crushed by his incredible weight, while Reev fell by pure chance out of harm's way. Wow, I didn't even think shadows could have weight! In its unstoppable rampage, the evil creature actually passed through the wall of haunted flames. It then horrifyingly turned back to me. Its feet seemed to cave in the ground beneath it. Then terrible, black beams of darkness fired from its great horns. God! This is really starting to suck! I accelerated as fast as I could, but was still singed by the blast. I couldn't see it very well against the dark night sky. The great shadow walked slowly back through the evil fire, reentering our arena. It wasn't even paying attention to the flames. It was then that I knew this thing was hella strong. A super deep sort of purring came from the creature. The grass around its big feet started to die swiftly, and once again, it charged. I tried to dodge, but the deathreaper grabbed me, holding my legs in place, while the horned shadow titan careened towards me. The vicious shadow threw forth a huge, terrible claw. Helpless in the deathreaper's grip, I could only hold up my still glowing blade, and brace. When the beast and I finally collided in an awesome shockwave of power, I was surprised to see, that I was holding off the titan's menacing claw.

"This can't be real!" Reev said in disbelief.

I flung the great beast's hand back, cutting it, then struck the reaper's blue-haired head with the hilt of my sword. He hit the grassy ground, and the monster screamed in pain.

Vale and Darkdancer showed up in that moment. They both flew above us on mighty, winged steeds. Their twin length but different colored hair blowing in the night wind, as they rode Wingrider and Nightheart. The two huge bats flew closer just outside the flames, confronting the gigantic evil shadow. Then as if somehow rehearsed, the two mammoth bats fired simultaneous beams of devastating sound. The beast weathered the fury of the twin blasts, shielded by its great arms, while I retreated to safety. Once the breathtaking attack had ended, the terrible shadow screamed a huge sonic boom. Two synchronized blasts, just like the ones that Darkdancer and Vale had just fired, shot from its horrid mouth, knocking the girls from the sky.

"Nooo!" I shouted as Reev laughed. "The shadow is every bit as inde-structible as the demon king himself, Adam! In all Phantasma, nothing can harm it! Surrender now and the needless deaths will end!"

Extremely pissed, I looked the reaper in his silver eyes. Reading my emo-tions, he shut his mouth, while it was still attached to his face. I punched the weakened reaper a few times for good measure. When he was doubled over in pain, I walked straight for the mighty shadow beast. It saw me coming and broke into a raging rampage. We came closer and closer. When the shadow was about to crush me, under the weight of his great arms, I unleashed an all-con-suming, golden inferno from my very depths. It covered the shadow titan almost completely. The surrounding warriors—vampire and elf alike—watched in astonishment, while the immortal shadow roared, writhing in pain. Even then, the evil beast tried to attack through the power of my inferno. When it kneeled close for its deadly strike, I focused the golden flames into a short, but powerful blade of purest magic, which I used to pierce the head of the beast, stabbing it right between its glowing, fractured, red eyes. The creature slowly seemed to freeze in time. Then, suddenly it was just gone.

"Is that it?" I wondered. Immediately, there was a powerful, magical ex-plosion.

Thunder and lightning came from out of nowhere, as a huge ring of its spectacular force, spread out over everything. The deadly flames that encircled us, were easily blown out. Many from the watching crowd were thrown from their feet, while others barely weathered the dazzling event.

Reev laid flat on the ground, laughing. Had he gone mad?

"The power to kill the invincible demon! Perhaps, there is something about you, Adam Westlin!" he said.

All of his undead throughout the courtyard, were immediately drawn back into the ground. As I got to my feet, everyone who remained simply stared.

"Useless human!" I heard a brass-armored elf say. He pointed his crossbow at me.

"No!" the deathreaper shouted, and with a flick of his wrist, Reev sent a newly materialized silver dagger, into the heart of the elf soldier.

The other surrounding elves all pointed their crossbows. I heard the words, "Phantom force!" cried out by Reev's sinister voice. The reaper ap-peared to transform his entire body into liquid silver, sending twenty or thirty gleaming scythe blades on long, silver strings, to dance across the enemy elves.

Once they were all dead, disarmed, or in retreat, the reaper's liquid silver body just seemed to be absorbed, into the ground.

Wow, what the hell was his problem? I mean, was he my friend or my enemy? I thought as I stared at the empty place, where he once laid. Well, whatever hell he has gone off to, I hope they have really good councilors there.

"Elven forces, stand down! Our new objective is to secure the human boy, Adam Westlin!" came Sparkle's commanding voice. I looked around to find her.

She was standing only about forty feet from me.

"No!" said another fearsome voice into the cool night air, this time coming from the vampire king. Two sets of majestic wings sprang from his back. One was like the dark wings of an angel, the other like huge, leathery bat wings. Sevorift Annadraus Shadowwind stood in the palace window, that Reev had broken.

"Adam belongs to the vampires! Retrieve him at once, my faithful servants!" he commanded.

Before anyone could do anything, Taya suddenly rushed in on the back of an amazingly fast, gigantic grey wolf. The huge sixteen-feet long from snout to tail beast, growled fiercely, having awesome, glowing, amber eyes. The great wolf-mount barked a devastating ball of compressed, deadly sound. It was only a warning shot. All the surrounding soldiers instantly backed off.

From atop the majestic, grey wolf, Taya told me, "They all want to imprison you or worse, Adam! Get on, I can take you to safety!"

"But you work for the vampires!" I said. "I am not going back to that tower, Taya!"

"My name isn't really Taya! I am Luna Luminara, the First Princess of the Lunar Kingdom of Tearra Zan. You saved my life once, Adam. Let me save yours now!"

I took her hand, mounting the mighty, grey wolf. Then we launched quickly into motion, faster than any animal I had ever seen. As we sailed over the impressive, white palace gate, beneath the bright twin moons, I heard both Vale and Darkdancer's voices cry out painfully.

"NOOOOOOOO!" they both screamed. The awful sound rang out, to break my heart.

To be continued